Jonathan Wylie is
Julia Smith, a marri
in Norfolk. Havin
major London publishing house, they sparked
each other into creative life and began writing
as a team a few months after setting up home
together. For the past six years, they have been
writing full-time. *Across the Flame* is their thirteenth novel.

Also by Jonathan Wylie

Across the Flame

Jonathan Wylie

ORBIT

An *Orbit* Book

First published in Great Britain by Orbit 1996
This edition published by Orbit 1997

Copyright © Jonathan Wylie 1996

The moral right of the author has been asserted.

A CIP catalogue record for this book
is available from the British Library.

ISBN 1 85723 468 5

Typeset by Palimpsest Book Production Ltd
Printed and bound in Great Britain by Clays Ltd, St Ives plc

Orbit
A Division of
Little, Brown and Company (UK)
Brettenham House
Lancaster Place
London WC2E 7EN

*This book is dedicated (with necessary apologies)
to the residents and friends of Loggos.*

*Grateful thanks are due to Robert Steemson
for his help and advice.*

Prologue

All about her the desolate, majestic landscape of the open moor stretched as far as the horizon, a rolling panorama of green and brown studded with the steel grey of granite. Grass, heather and new growths of bracken glistened as the setting sun appeared again beneath the fast-moving clouds. The air itself seemed to sparkle in the aftermath of the shower, and the fecund smell of wet earth filled her nostrils.

It was all so familiar, and yet she could not get her bearings. She recognized nothing, and this frightened her. Although she knew that the moor always kept *some* secrets, even from those who had lived there all their lives, she could not understand how she had become lost, could not even remember beginning the walk. The luminous daylight was fading now, dusk only a short time away, and mist was lapping about her feet. She would soon be blind as well as hopelessly lost.

A small movement on the ground caught her eye, only to disappear instantly in the gloom. But in looking down she saw, in amazement, that within or beneath the blanket of grey there was a faint glimmering, lines of light marking pathways through the invisible terrain. Although logic insisted that there must be some natural explanation for this eerie phenomenon, she could not help recalling the legends about moorland pixies, whose efforts could – depending on their notoriously fickle whim – bring stricken travellers either to safety or to a gruesome death.

She pressed ahead, shaking off these fanciful visions, but had gone only a few paces when she caught another glimpse of movement and stopped again. Suddenly, a patch of mist before her cleared, revealing a flat grassy space. In its centre, only three yards away, was a small snake, its green scales luminescent even in the fading light. For a moment the reptile lay quite still, apparently watching her, then weaved its way over to a flat square of damp stone, moving with frightening speed. Once there it stopped, motionless once more, and lay in the shape of a circle as if intent on swallowing its own tail.

Warily, she moved closer, drawn by more than curiosity, and looked down – then gasped, her heart racing. The circle that now lay upon the smooth rock was no longer a snake but an old, rusted iron ring embedded in the granite. Had the snake been an illusion, an hallucination prompted by her own fevered imagination? Or was she dreaming, and none of this real? All she knew was that there was no choice but to act out the next scene in this bizarre play. The slab at her feet was clearly a trap door. The question was, what lay below?

She knelt down and gingerly stretched out a hand to grasp the ring. She half expected it to squirm away, but the cold metal remained inanimate, grating against the stone as she twisted it upright. The weight of the slab would surely be more than she could lift, even if it were not securely embedded in the turf, but she was determined to try. Why else had she been led there?

Bracing herself, knees bent, arms and back kept straight, she pulled hard, only to lose her balance and fall over backwards as the thick slab rose easily and smoothly, revealing only darkness beneath. She scrambled up and found the slab balanced upright on one edge – reminding her of a gravestone – then stepped around it to inspect the opening.

Now what? But she already knew the answer. Staring down into that impenetrable shadow, she recognized the inevitability of all her actions. Everything had led her here. She had no choice but to go on.

Reaching in with her hands, she found a ledge of rock, but beyond that was total darkness. Perhaps it was a vertical drop, an old mine shaft? She picked up a stone and dropped it in, and almost immediately heard it hit solid rock; then there were several more clinks, becoming ever fainter, as it bounced down what she was now convinced was a stairway.

She gingerly lowered herself over the edge, going down backwards, as though she were descending a ladder, searching out each new step with her feet as she held on with her hands. Her boots grated on rough granite, and her fingers ached as they grasped the cold, damp surface. Twice she banged her knee painfully and was grateful for the sturdy material of her jeans. She was soon engulfed by the void, her only reassurance the shrinking square of grey sky seen through the trap door above. Then came a bend in the stairs, and even that was gone. She almost lost her nerve then, but just as she was bracing herself to climb up again, a voice sounded from far below, calling her name.

She froze, chilled and horrified as she realized that there was no way she could refuse this summons; she recognized the shrill young voice and her heart responded to the mixture of despair and hope in the little girl's cry.

'I'm coming!'

The words sounded louder than she had intended or expected, and they boomed and echoed in the darkness. Just as the last reverberations died away, distant lights sprang to life far below, to either side of the steps. It was only a faint glow, like the ghostly illumination of the paths on the moor, but it was more than enough for her to see that she was suspended high in a vast murmuring cavern. She stifled a scream and squeezed her eyes shut, clinging with all her might to the stairs that held her. But she could not rid herself of the memory of that dreadful brief glimpse. The stairway ran on down, crooked and steep, with nothing on either side but thin air, an abyss plunging to rocks unimaginably far below. Vertigo assaulted her, and she was sure that she would lose her grip, her balance, roll one way or the other and plummet over one of these dual cliffs. It was the landscape of nightmare, terrifying and yet absurd – as if she had been transported into a fantastical cartoon world where such constructions were possible.

For a few thunderous heartbeats she could hear nothing

3

except the rush of blood in her ears, but then the achingly familiar voice called again, pleading with her to continue her descent.

So she took a deep breath, slowly winding a cocoon of stillness and calm about herself, quelling the first rush of terror. Opening her eyes became her first goal, and she achieved it after some effort. The spectral lights still burned, but she kept her gaze focused first on the stone immediately below her face and then, by carefully twisting around, on to the way she must go. She avoided the massive emptiness beside her as best she could, and steeled herself to move.

The steps themselves looked solid and secure enough, and she began to crawl backwards again, moving laboriously and with fearful caution.

The awful descent seemed to last an eternity and she felt the short hairs sticking to the back of her neck, beads of sweat forming on her forehead. For a while she appeared to be making no progress at all, her tortured limbs threatening to cramp with every movement, but she gradually realized that the light was growing brighter, the stairs less steep. She risked turning to sit upright and found herself almost at the bottom, the jagged but relatively level floor of the cathedral-sized cavern only a few feet below her. The relief was so great that she did not notice the absence of the calling voice.

Standing up on legs that still felt shaky and weak – but were at least no longer paralysed – she completed her journey. As she reached the bottom of the stairs, she saw a rounded archway cut into the cave wall ahead of her. The light beyond it wavered and swayed, then grew stronger – and the reason for that soon became clear. She heard heavy footsteps and the girl's siren voice, and then a tall figure emerged, carrying a lamp. She glanced down beside the newcomer, expecting to see the child, but he was alone. As she looked up at his face, the man's lips moved and the false voice of the little girl called her name again, but this time with a cruel, derisive tone.

'Please come to me. I need your help. The flames are making me cold.'

His expression echoed his tongue's mockery with a smile that faded into cold stillness as he studied her closely.

She stared back, too shocked and disbelieving to utter a sound. This had to be a dream, and yet she knew it was not. She knew every detail of his thin, arrogant, angular face intimately; the jutting cleft chin, the full sensual lips, the strong nose, the deepset eyes of fathomless black beneath a pale, high forehead. His dark, curling hair was mostly hidden beneath a black, four-cornered hat and he wore a voluminous, soft grey blouse under a black tunic. He was looking at her now just as he had always looked at her, measuring her disdainfully, and yet at the same time with an almost sensual possessiveness.

He stooped to set down the lamp and, when he turned back to face her once more, he was smiling again, though his shadowed eyes remained coolly inquisitive.

'You recognize me.' It was a statement, not a question, and he used his own voice this time, rich and curiously accented.

'I . . .' She was finding it difficult to think, let alone speak. 'Why have you . . . brought me here?'

'It's time,' he answered simply. 'You must surely have expected me to respond eventually?'

'But you're not real!' she burst out.

'Oh, I am very real,' he assured her complacently. 'You, of all people, should know that.'

'Me? I don't even know your name.' She was still totally bewildered.

'Of course you . . .' he began, then hesitated, considering. 'My apologies. There is so much of her in you, it is easy to suppose . . .' He bowed flamboyantly, mocking her. 'I am Allessandro Massimiliano. The world knows me by other names, but you will have to learn them for yourself. I have much to teach you that is of far greater importance.'

'Teach me what?' she cried. 'Why am I here?'

'Because you are my apprentice again.' He smiled. 'For as long as I need you.'

5

None of this made any sense to her, and she shook her head helplessly.

'What would you like me to show you?' he went on blithely. 'It's all here. In the very rocks you live on, stored in memories that are distorted by time but are living still. Shall we begin with a few of the simpler tales, the images you might easily recognize?' He pointed to the vast open space behind her. She turned to look – and was stunned by what she saw.

Afterwards, she could not tell how long the kaleidoscope of visions had lasted. In a very real sense, time itself had ceased to have any meaning. She could only watch and wonder.

First there was a flaming cartwheel, bound with straw and pitch, rolling and bouncing down a hillside, pursued by boisterous children. She cowered, feeling the scorching heat and smelling the acrid smoke before the scene suddenly vanished. It was replaced by an old man encased in clear crystal – his fragmented image repeated endlessly by the refraction of light from torches held by the ghostly figures of men in silver armour. After that came enormous black hounds, beasts with scorching red eyes, their howls fading as they ran into the lichen-covered ancient woodland. Then came a man in a green mask, living twigs and leaves interwoven with his hair and beard; a serpentine river calling out for its annual sacrifice; and a circle of standing stones that stretched and groaned, their brute shapes slowly changing into the likenesses of men whose beards were stiff with moss, their clothes tattered and encrusted after their long imprisonment. Their slow dance under the midsummer moon was the last of the visions. As the spell came to an end she fell to her knees, exhausted and afraid.

'Stop it! Stop it!' she cried. 'Why are you doing this to me?'

'It's time,' he repeated simply, releasing her.

Time for what? she wondered helplessly.

1

'Where were you?'

Anya looked up at him, a dazed expression on her face.

'Miles away.'

Luke had come in to find her sitting alone in their living room, staring into space. Although it was growing dark outside, there were no lights on, making the room seem smaller than it was. He switched on a lamp and looked at her again.

'You look pale. Are you OK?'

'A bit of a headache, that's all.' She smiled briefly, shaking off her preoccupation.

'Want me to get you anything?' he asked.

'No thanks.'

For a few moments Luke stood watching her in silence. She looked so tiny, so self-contained, with her legs tucked beneath her on the sofa, and her delicate face almost porcelain white beneath the short, spiky black hair. He wanted very much to take her in his arms, to crush that small but surprisingly resilient frame against his own solid, stocky body, but he could not allow himself that luxury. If he did, he would be lost. Instead, he walked over, kissed her lightly and sat down beside her, not touching. They were both acutely aware of that narrow separation, and of what it meant.

'Anya . . . ?' Luke glanced at her, but she did not meet his gaze, nor acknowledge her name. He knew it would be unwise to continue, especially if she was suffering from the beginnings of a migraine, but he could not help himself.

There had always been a self-destructive element to their relationship, but now he was plagued by the feeling that time was running out. They had been living together for over five years, in the rambling old house that Anya owned. And although certain aspects of their life together – including their sex life – were as wonderful as ever, he sometimes felt as though he was still a guest in her home. In some ways he knew no more about her than when they had first met. He had been captivated then by her elfin figure, her restless energy, those huge, child-like brown eyes and her habit of wearing clothes that varied from incredibly sexy to aggressively tomboyish, but which were always of one stark colour – black. Five years; they had been both the best and the worst of times.

'Anya?'

'What?' she asked quietly, still not looking at him.

'Why do you have to go?'

'Oh, Luke. How many times must you ask? I need time on my own, away from distractions. You know that.'

'Is that all I am?' he asked, unable to keep a tinge of bitterness from his words. 'A distraction?'

'Of the most delightful kind,' she told him, turning to face him for the first time. Her smile was unconvincing, as if she sensed what was coming next.

'Let me come with you,' Luke pleaded. 'I've got some leave due.'

'No.'

'That's it? Just "no"?'

'I don't have to explain myself to you.'

'Oh, no. God forbid you should compromise your precious independence.' The hurt had intensified, and he lashed out, sarcastic and cruel.

'Don't start, Luke,' she replied wearily.

'*I'm* not the one who disappears for weeks on end every few months,' he protested. 'Don't you ever wonder how that makes me feel?' Unable to sit still any longer, he got to his feet and went over to the window.

'Yes, of course I have,' Anya told him. 'It just can't be helped.'

8

Luke spun round and stared at her.

'Why not?' he demanded angrily.

'I don't see why you resent it so much!' she snapped, getting angry herself now and ignoring his question. 'When it's obviously perfectly all right for you to be out tramping round on the moor at all hours of the day and night.'

'That's my job,' he replied with exasperation, loading every word with bitter emphasis. 'I'm a Dartmoor Ranger.'

'I'm not likely to forget it.'

'What's that supposed to mean?'

'Anything you like,' she retorted dismissively.

The room became very still. Even their expressions froze – Luke's infuriated, Anya's face a brittle mask of false serenity. They both knew that this was the moment to back down, to turn away from the volcano's edge. But they also knew that neither would retreat now. The fire below burned too fiercely.

Luke moved first. He turned round abruptly and closed the curtains with more force than necessary, so that the runners squealed in complaint and the material flapped and billowed. Anya started violently at the sudden motion.

'At least tell me where you're going,' Luke implored quietly, his back still to her.

This was an old argument. He always promised himself that he would not beg, that he would accept her inexplicable need for solitude, but his resolve crumbled every time he faced the prospect of being without her.

'I can't. That would spoil it,' Anya said gently, striving to remain pleasant despite the tension between them, still hoping that they could stop, leave it there.

Luke stared blindly at the curtains only a few inches in front of his nose, his thoughts going round in endless, resentful circles. All she would ever allow him to do was put her on the train to London. He had no idea where she went from there, never knew how long she would be away. He told himself, in vain, that he ought to be used to it by now. It had happened often enough, and each time he was only given a few hours notice – a couple of days at most – before she was gone.

Anya vanished from his life completely, only to reappear, unannounced, weeks or even months later, with no word of explanation. He would come home from work one day and she would be there, acting as if nothing had happened. Those were the times when he knew he should have tackled the problem, prised the truth from her, but he was always too overwhelmed with happiness at her return, and could not bring himself to risk being the cause of friction. Each time he waited for the right moment to broach the subject. It never came, of course, and in the end he always managed to convince himself that this time she was back for good. Until she left again.

In the past he had sometimes been desperate enough to resort to subterfuge – something of which he was always ashamed – surreptitiously searching her handbag for tickets, passport, any clue as to her destination. He had never found anything. The only clues came on her return – and yet were so vague as to be meaningless. She was often suntanned, fitter and more healthy, and always in a much more relaxed state of mind. That in itself rankled – it was as though she had to get away from him in order to purge the darker side of her nature – but, at the same time, it made their reunions all the more joyful, and made him less able to spoil them with unwelcome questions. So the circle turned again, and Luke saw no way of halting its unwelcome progress. And here they were again, back at the beginning.

'Don't you trust me?' he asked, caught between anger and sadness.

'Of course I do.' Anya sighed. 'Some things just have to be private.'

'And that's all the explanation I'm ever going to get, isn't it?'

Anya did not answer. There was nothing she could say.

'Is there someone else?' Luke asked in a low voice, still not looking at her.

'No!' she cried instantly, but then faltered momentarily as her spiteful memory conjured up a vision of the face that had come to haunt her. 'Of course there's no one else.'

The minute hesitation had not gone unnoticed, however,

and when Luke turned round to face her, his gaze would have struck sparks from steel.

'You don't sound very sure.'

'A man in every port, eh?' It was Anya's turn to be sarcastic. Then she softened. 'I don't need anyone else, Luke. I've got you.'

'But only when you want me,' he responded bitterly. 'Well, perhaps it's time you stopped taking me for granted. Maybe one day you'll get back from one of your mysterious jaunts and I won't be here.'

He noted with a kind of malignant satisfaction that this barb had struck home. Let *her* know how it felt to contemplate desertion. And yet, at the same time, her wounded expression made him feel cold and sick, and he wished his words unsaid.

Anya had grown very still again, and looked even smaller, as if she were shrinking deeper into herself. But Luke knew the sometimes frightening passion that slept with her, the coils of emotion that were wound dangerously tight. There was an ominous intensity to her quiet, like the airless minutes before a summer storm.

'I need you,' she said softly. 'I love you.'

'I love you too,' he said automatically, realizing that even those talismanic words could be used as weapons. 'Which makes it all the more galling to know that you won't trust me.'

'Trust isn't always so easy,' she said painfully.

'Really?' he exclaimed in mock disbelief. 'I would never have guessed. Look at me, Anya. *Why* can't you trust me? I'm not your father!'

'Leave my family out of this.'

'I won't run out on you like he did.'

'You just said you might,' she pointed out reproachfully. She could not stop the tears from welling up in her eyes, and that only made her angrier.

'Christ!' Luke glanced up at the ceiling, his fists clenching. '*You're* the one who keeps leaving.'

'But I keep coming back.' She was half shouting now,

matching his vengeful tone. 'Besides, you're a fine one to talk about trust. What about you? Accusing me of having another lover is hardly very *trustful*!'

'What am I supposed to think?' he countered. 'I'm just boring old Luke, content to sit here in Devon all my life. I don't have your artistic temperament. Aren't you Bohemians supposed to have lovers all over the place? To constantly replenish your palette with new oils?'

'Shut up! You don't understand.' Anya had leapt to her feet and was glaring at him fiercely from across the room. 'I can't stand it when you get like this.'

'Like what?' he exclaimed. 'Truthful? I'm sorry I don't understand. Perhaps it's because I don't have your advantages, the money your aunt left you, this house. The time you're able to have for yourself. Some people have to work for a living.' He was flailing wildly now, without logic, wanting only to hurt her.

'That's rich, coming from someone who lives here for free,' she retorted, repaying him in kind.

'Oh, I pay my rent,' he grated. 'You may not deign to take my money – but you get your pound of flesh.'

'What does *that* mean?' she demanded furiously.

'Who is it has to put up with your moods, your tantrums and sulks? Who . . . oh, never mind.' Luke waved his hands in the air in an expansive gesture of hopelessness. 'I need a drink.'

He strode over to the cabinet and poured himself a large whisky. Anya, fuming, watched him as he stood with his broad back to her, tossed back his drink and poured another. She could see the tension and hurt that mirrored her own in every movement.

'If it's so bad here, then perhaps you should go,' she said in a tight, small voice, then wished in the same instant that she had not spoken.

Luke turned round slowly, glass in hand, and this time it was his eyes that were brimming with tears. When he spoke, his voice was steady and resigned. There was a small measure of peace in his face that came from reluctant but inevitable acceptance. It was always he who backed down on these occasions. Anya either would not or could not.

'No,' he said. 'I won't go. You mean far too much to me. You'll go off, and I won't ask any more questions. You'll come back whenever you want to, and I'll be just as glad to see you.'

Anya's relief was palpable. Luke watched as her whole body relaxed slowly, her outline growing visibly softer.

'Do you want a drink?' he asked.

'A few moments ago I'd've thrown it at your head. I might still.' But her tone was light, negating the threat.

'Better not use the good crystal then,' Luke commented gravely, and she smiled for the first time in what seemed like hours.

A few minutes later they sat together on the sofa, Anya's head resting on Luke's solid chest, his arm around her. The emotive aftermath of the row still filled the room, but at least it was over. After all the spite, all the sharp blades they had flung at each other, their reconciliation was all the sweeter. Before long, as they both knew, they would be in bed together, their lovemaking given extra tenderness and urgency by the need to heal their self-inflicted wounds, and by the imminence of separation. Anya's departure still loomed ahead of them, but for now they would bridge even that gulf.

2

Luke began work early the next morning, telling himself that he was lucky to have a full day ahead, one which would keep him busy but still allow him to get home in time to see Anya off in the afternoon. Constant activity would surely dull the edges of his brooding.

He spent some time checking and cleaning his tools – half hoping that Anya would wake up before he left – then climbed into the Landrover and drove to the headquarters of the National Park Authority. There he picked up some management agreement documents he had promised to deliver to an old friend who farmed part of the eastern moor. The papers could easily have been posted, but a personal visit was always appreciated, and this morning it suited Luke's purpose very well. John Cox was a year or so older than Luke, just past thirty, and the two had known each other since childhood. As a Ranger, Luke had a wide circle of friends and acquaintances, but there were few to whom he was willing to talk openly about personal matters, especially about Anya and her idiosyncrasies. John was one of that select group, and there would be time for a much needed chat before Luke's next task, leading a guided walk on the high moor.

John was a bachelor, and the interior of his granite walled house – and especially the kitchen – was always in a shambles, in marked contrast to the immaculate upkeep of his fields and farm buildings.

Luke was greeted cordially and invited in for coffee.

They talked about business for a while, John scanning the documents. Finally he grunted and looked up.

'Well, that all seems straightforward enough, for a change,' he observed, then added, as if sensing that his friend needed more than this, 'you've got a few minutes then?'

Luke nodded.

'So what did you really want to talk about?' John asked.

'What do you think?'

'She's gone again?'

'This afternoon.'

'And you've still no idea where she's going or when she'll be back?'

'No, none. But it's not just that – although it's hard to bear.'

'What else?' John prompted gently.

'I'm worried about her. She's been having nightmares recently, but won't talk about them, and she seems so full of stress. I mean, I know she had a dreadful childhood, but she's a grown woman now . . . and . . .' The words had tumbled out in a rush but now Luke faltered. 'And sometimes I have no idea what's going on in her head. You should see some of her paintings.'

'Weird?'

'Weird doesn't cover it. Some of them are just horrible. And she jumps at shadows, as if she's . . . I don't know.' He shook his head, obviously bewildered.

'Anya's always been the nervous type,' John pointed out.

'Tell me about it,' Luke replied with feeling. 'Don't get me wrong. I still love her to bits. She's usually wonderful to be with, but at other times – especially the last few weeks – it's hopeless. I can't do anything right. Everything annoys her, even the smallest of noises. There are some mornings I have to *suck* my cornflakes.'

The farmer laughed, then steepled his calloused fingers and adopted a pompous, professorial tone.

'In my vast experience with women,' he intoned solemnly, 'I've discovered that they're all like that sooner or later. Raging hormones, don't you know.'

Luke grinned briefly, recognizing the sexism inherent in John's argument. 'No, it's more than that,' he said with a sigh.

'There's nothing else that's happened recently that might make her behave oddly?'

'Not that I can think of.'

John looked thoughtful for a while, then drained the last of his coffee and put the mug down with a decisive clunk.

'You want my opinion?' he asked briskly.

'Of course. That's why I'm here.'

'You two still love each other, right?'

'Yes, but she's got a funny way of showing it. Going away . . .'

'Then that's the most important thing,' John interrupted. 'Hang on to that. You love each other. Anya's temperamental and complicated, even by female standards. She wants someone to look after her but, perversely, needs her independence too. A lot of people are like that. Anya just takes it to extremes, and she's obviously proving something to herself when she goes away.' He paused, looking at his friend. 'As for you, you may sometimes do a good impression of the world's calmest individual, but you're not. Putting the two of you together is like watching over bracken after a dry August. There're bound to be a few fires sooner or later, and it doesn't take much of a spark to start one. On some level Anya knows that, and perhaps her trips are her way of reducing the risks and controlling the course of the flames before they get out of hand. Psychological swaling, in fact.' He grinned, inordinately pleased with the metaphor. Luke was speechless, and smiled in spite of himself. 'Besides,' John went on, 'didn't you once tell me that she was always better when she came back?'

'Yes,' Luke admitted. 'A fact not designed to make *me* feel any better. If leaving me does her so much good, then why doesn't she make it permanent? Or am I just a convenient house-sitter?'

'Maybe coming back to you does her good too,' the farmer suggested. 'And she *does* keep coming back.'

16

'That's what she said last night,' Luke responded gloomily. 'I don't know what it proves, though.'

'That she wants to be with you,' John said simply.

'For a while. The same old merry-go-round.'

'You can get off any time, you know. Do you really want to?'

'No. But it hurts. And I can't see an end to it.'

'But you always knew that you took Anya on her terms or not at all,' John reminded him. 'She's always been honest with you, hasn't she?'

Luke nodded, acknowledging the truth of his friend's words.

'Come on,' the farmer said, getting up. 'Some of us have work to do.'

Luke glanced at his watch and swore softly. He would only just make the starting point of the walk on time. However, as they went out into the yard, he could not help but make one last observation.

'What worries me more than anything,' he said, 'is that Anya might need help. I'm not the one to do it, obviously. It would need a professional. But how the hell am I supposed to suggest that to her?'

When Anya woke up and found herself alone, she was filled with both sadness and relief. From the moment she opened her eyes, she was aware of a strange internal clock ticking away. She did not know when the alarm would go off, but she knew that it would be soon, and that her decision to leave was the right one. What had happened the night before only made her even more certain. Despite this, she suddenly felt as though she were drifting, incapable of doing anything. She half considered catching an earlier train but knew that would hurt Luke even more, and so spent the morning pottering aimlessly about the house, achieving nothing. It was only when it was nearing one o'clock and she was getting hungry that she remembered she had a lunch date, and rushed out to her car.

Unlike Luke, Anya had very few close friends, and Sheila

17

was the only one she saw regularly. Sheila Jourdain – Luke called her 'Sheila-who-must-be-obeyed' – was an accountant, and helped Anya prepare her tax returns and kept an eye on the tangled web of her finances. But she was much more than just a professional adviser; she was also, in a sense, Anya's agent, handling the sale and transportation of her paintings, reminding her of the deadlines for her commissioned work, and encouraging her more personal artistic endeavours. More importantly still, she was also an inexhaustible source of gossip and good humour, as well as a sympathetic listener.

Anya arrived at the pub just in time to squeeze her car into the last space in the granite-walled car park, and she ran across the road to find Sheila zealously guarding one of the outdoor trestle tables.

'God, I'm sorry,' she said breathlessly. 'Have you been waiting long?'

'I have a drink,' Sheila replied, waving her gin and tonic, 'it's a lovely day, there's a beautiful view. What's half an hour between friends?' With a smile she nodded at a glass of cider on the table. 'Drink up. Though how you can stomach that stuff is beyond me.'

Anya sat down and obediently took a sip.

'I really am sorry . . .' she began.

'And I really don't mind,' her agent cut in firmly. 'I've ordered food for both of us. Your usual horrendous concoction of saturated fats, and a salad for me.'

'Good. Thanks.'

'How you stay the shape you are eating the way you do is a miracle,' Sheila added ruefully. 'I only have to *look* at chips and a spare tyre starts threatening to burst my girdle. It's not fair. You don't even get much exercise.'

'You know I can't be bothered traipsing out to the gym,' Anya said, 'and running is so boring.'

'But exercise is good for you mentally too,' her friend persisted. 'I always feel great when I've been out running.'

'Afterwards, yes,' Anya agreed with a grin. 'That's because you've stopped.'

'You're hopeless,' Sheila decreed, then, with one of the

18

abrupt changes of direction that were typical of her conversation, added, 'So, you're off on your travels again?'

'Yes. This afternoon.'

Sheila did not bother to ask for any details. She knew from experience that she would not get any answers.

'OK. Is the "Moonrider" picture finished?' she asked, referring to the artwork for a book cover which had to be delivered to the publishers in London within the next two weeks.

'Yes,' Anya replied. 'You can pick it up any time.'

'Good. I'd like to come over this afternoon but I can't. I have another pressing engagement.'

'Kevin Costner dropping in for tea?' Anya suggested.

'No such luck. Actually, I think Alan Rickman's more my type.' Her smile became dreamy and lascivious. 'Mmm. Anything you say, Sheriff.'

'Down, girl. You shouldn't salivate in public.'

'That's right,' Sheila complained. 'Rob me of my few remaining pleasures.'

'What *are* you doing this afternoon?' Anya asked.

'Going through the books of a sixty-year-old boat builder in Plymouth,' the accountant replied, coming back to earth.

'Perhaps he'll take you away from all this on his yacht.'

'I doubt it,' Sheila said resignedly. 'He's practically bankrupt and hopelessly married. Besides, I don't think I could run off with someone whose teeth have a habit of baling out whenever he sneezes.'

'You certainly know how to pick your clients!' Anya commented, laughing.

'Yes. But I can't imagine how I ended up with you,' her agent retorted. 'Any other works of artistic genius I should see?'

'There's a few I've finished. Luke'll show you. You can do what you like with them.'

'Fine. Leave it to me.'

The food arrived and while Anya ate hungrily, Sheila picked at her salad, occasionally reaching over to stab one of her companion's chips, and regaled her with a tale from her seemingly endless store of gossip.

19

'I know you shouldn't speak ill of the divorced, but this is really too good a story to pass up,' she began, and Anya smiled. It was typical of Sheila, as the survivor of two short-lived marriages, to come out with such a remark.

Sheila went on to explain that a friend of hers, whose husband had moved in with his secretary, was apparently taking her revenge by making a fool of herself with a much younger man.

'And I mean *much* younger,' she went on, between mouthfuls. 'He's half her age and looks as though his mother weaned him on steroids. He's so thick he can hardly string one word together. His lips move when he signs his name.' She waited until Anya stopped giggling long enough to swallow some of her pasty, then carried on. 'He couldn't exactly be called a great romantic, either. Apparently, he was *very* direct about what he wanted from her.'

'It would save time,' Anya pointed out, 'but "Get your knickers off" is hardly the greatest chat-up line, I suppose.'

'Oh, it is if you're with the right man!' Sheila exclaimed, 'but . . .'

'I don't think she's making a fool of herself at all,' Anya cut in. 'She's having a great time – and you're jealous.' Her lips curled mischievously.

'Bitch,' her agent retorted, good-naturedly. 'When did you get to be so insightful? It can't last, anyway,' she added, with a degree of satisfaction. 'She's got children older than him.'

'Did you never want to have children?' Anya asked.

'Goodness, no. That would've complicated things no end.'

'Why?'

'Children are horrible,' Sheila stated. 'They're selfish and cruel and noisy. And, worst of all, they're honest. They're just not civilized.' She looked suddenly suspicious. 'You're not getting broody are you?' she asked accusingly.

'No,' Anya replied sadly. 'I don't think I'd make a very good mother.'

3

Anya's studio was the largest room of her house, occupying
fully half of the upper floor, and it served as both workroom
and haven. Even Luke would not disturb her in the wide,
airy room whose large, uncurtained windows and skylights
made the most of the variable Devon light. The paraphernalia
of her trade littered the bare floor and various benches; easels,
frames, jars and bottles, tubes and brushes. The paintings
themselves were strewn about apparently at random, giving
the room a chaotic appearance.

Anya headed there as soon as she got home but, for once, she
was not in the least interested in her own work. The studio's
one internal wall was almost entirely covered in a huge cork
notice board, on which were pinned a bewildering variety of
prints, postcards, photographs and messages. Among the personal memorabilia were reproductions of several works of art
that, for a variety of reasons, had especially intrigued Anya.

Most noticeable among them were several Mark Rothko
abstracts, their wonderful blocks of pure colour evoking an
astonishing range of moods. Competing for any onlooker's
attention were large prints of Turner's haunting 'Dawn with
a Sea Monster', Monet's unsurpassed epic of contemplation
'Water-Lilies', and Arnold Böcklin's 'The Isle of the Dead',
the grim, moated ruin that had inspired Rachmaninov.

But for Anya, some of the most treasured items were
hidden away amongst the clutter; postcard-sized copies of
such things as Alexandre Calame's 'Rocks near Seelisberg',
a vertigo-inducing, horizonless Alpine panorama of plunging

cliffs, a half-dead tree clinging precariously to the edge of the abyss; Anselm Feuerbach's knowing 'Iphigenia'; and Caspar David Friedrich's mystical 'City at Moonrise', with its twin spires rising over silvered water.

And yet, today, none of these attracted Anya's attention. The postcard she was interested in had been turned over, pinned facing the board so that its subject was invisible. With a look of strange determination in her eyes, Anya took it down and, without even glancing at it, slipped it into her jacket pocket.

Ordinarily, Luke would have taken great pleasure in leading the six-hour guided walk over the high moor. He was in his element amid the bleak grandeur of this ancient landscape, and it was a perfect day for being outdoors. He usually enjoyed sharing his knowledge of the moor, and he was thankful that the majority of today's party were not only properly equipped for the terrain but were also capable of asking intelligent questions – and, at times, appreciating the scenery without the need for constant chatter.

What kept the expedition from being truly enjoyable was, of course, the fact that his thoughts constantly returned to Anya and her imminent departure. The gloom engendered by the prospect of separation coloured his mood, although he obviously kept this from his fellow walkers. He reminded himself that John had been right. Anya's obsessive need for periods of absolute independence could not be broken by force, and he was determined not to make any more fuss. The only way he could hope to keep her was to let her go.

His early start meant that he was able to return home as soon as the walk was over, arriving in plenty of time to take her in to Newton Abbot station. He heard her moving about upstairs as he kicked off his boots.

'Hi!' he called. 'It's me. You ready?'

'Almost,' she replied. 'I'll be down in a few minutes.'

Luke could not bear to watch her packing, so he stayed downstairs. The process would not take long. He always thought that she took remarkably little for her extended absences, but that was just another unsolvable mystery.

'Want some tea?' he shouted.

'No thanks.'

Luke boiled the kettle, took his mug into the sitting room and slumped wearily into a chair, trying to ignore the cold, empty feeling inside his chest. Anger flared briefly – why did she have to go? – but he quickly suppressed it.

His eyes fell upon a small black and white photograph in a silver frame on the sideboard. As the sole reminder of Anya's past it had always fascinated Luke, and he picked it up now to study the picture. It showed two identical little girls, dressed in frilly, brightly coloured frocks, sitting on a lawn and laughing at someone who had obviously been standing next to the photographer. The child on the left had raised a small hand to point at whoever they were looking at – one of their parents, Luke assumed. He turned the frame over and read the familiar label. In neat script someone had written 'Meredith and Anya Caplan, aged 3'. Luke knew – because he had been told – that the one pointing was Meredith, the older of the twins by some fifteen minutes, but he would never have been able to tell them apart himself. He could see the embryonic shape of the Anya he knew in the child's face, her dark eyes and short black hair, but he could see it just as well in Meredith, and he had often wondered whether the two were still identical twenty-five years later.

Luke had never met Meredith, nor any other member of Anya's family. She only rarely talked about them – and then generally under protest. What little Luke knew came from his own insistent promptings – Anya had a politician's skill at not answering questions – and what he had learnt explained her reluctance to talk. She obviously had few happy memories of her early life.

Her father had walked out on them when the twins were still very young – soon after the photograph had been taken, apparently – and had vanished from their lives completely, divorcing their mother and moving away. Then Anya's mother had died and the twins had been brought up

23

by an elderly aunt, who was also dead now, and who had left the girls a considerable fortune in property and shareholdings, thus enabling them to lead independent lives.

Luke had always been both puzzled and surprised that Anya and Meredith never seemed to get in touch. Having no brothers or sisters himself, he imagined that it would be only natural to keep in contact with one's siblings, and surely with twins that bond would be even stronger. And yet there was nothing, unless . . .

Anya came bounding down the stairs then, taking them two at a time, and tossed her black canvas bag down on to the hall floor. Seeing Luke she smiled and came into the sitting room, looking at him warily as she tried to gauge his mood. He grinned to reassure her, and saw her raised eyebrows as he put the photograph back on the sideboard.

'Do you go to see Meredith on your trips?' he asked before she could say anything.

'No. Just forget about her, will you,' she replied, coming to sit on his lap.

'Why have I never met any of your family?' Luke put his arms around her.

'You wouldn't want to, believe me!'

'Why don't you ever see her?' he persisted. 'I thought twins were supposed to be close.'

'I've told you before,' Anya said patiently, 'it's just too painful. Meeting her would bring back too many memories. We'd suffocate each other. Everyone always expects twins to act alike, dress alike, enjoy the same things – and we're not like that. We're different people. Besides, her work means that she travels a lot, and it's impossible to keep up with her.'

Anya had never specified just what her sister did for a living, saying only that she thought it was 'weird', and implying that it had something to do with translating – which would make sense of the constant travelling.

'Don't you miss her, though?' Luke asked. 'Surely it's natural —'

'We're close still, but in a remote way,' Anya cut in. 'We just don't need to see each other to prove it, OK?'

24

'Do you ever know what's going on with her?' he said, his fascination renewed. 'You know, like telepathically?'

'No,' she replied sharply, obviously becoming irritated.

Luke recognized the warning, but could not resist informing her of an item of trivia he had recently discovered. It was as though, having forbidden himself to talk about her departure, he was finding other ways of needling her, of voicing his frustration and annoyance.

'Did you know that there's a town in Ohio called Twinsburg,' he revealed brightly, 'and every August they have a Twinsday weekend, a big gathering with look-most-alike competitions, and so on.'

'So what?' was Anya's only response.

Luke hated Newton Abbot station. He had been through this scene too often, waiting helplessly on the platform, biting his tongue, trying not to let his misery show. He was glad when the train pulled in on time. Any delay would have just prolonged the agony. Anya hugged him and he kissed her, knowing it was expected, trying not to think.

'Bye,' she murmured. 'See you sometime.'

'See you sometime,' he repeated dully.

'I love you,' she whispered and was gone, picking up her bag and stepping lightly on to the train. Moments later it pulled out.

'I love you too,' Luke whispered, as he watched it dwindle into the distance.

By the time he got back to the empty house, his self-imposed numbness was dissolving. He missed her already. He felt like crying, and a masochistic desire to wallow in her absence led him upstairs to the studio. He wandered round aimlessly, looking at but not really seeing her pictures, then told himself he was being stupid and left. Amid all the clutter, he had no reason to notice that one of her postcards was missing.

The guard's voice droned on over the Tannoy, using that special tone of someone who has been trained to sound bright and cheerful but whose repetitious and basically uninteresting

25

task inevitably leads to boredom. Anya paid the announcement no attention and, on impulse, reached inside her jacket pocket and found the postcard.

'. . . hot and cold drinks. A restaurant car is . . .'

As Anya turned the postcard over, a familiar face stared back at her disdainfully.

4

Twin oars dipped silently into the silvered water of the vast lake, propelling the dark boat towards the gateway that was the entrance to the island. The ferryman was dressed in drab brown, but the stooped figure in the bows wore a shimmering white robe, his face invisible beneath its hood. At his feet, the coffin was also draped in white cloth, and garlanded with flowers, their gaudy colours incongruous in the sombre scene.

Anya stood quite still, watching as the funeral barge made its stately progress towards her. At first she was mesmerized by its approach but then, as her racing heart gradually slowed down, she was able to glance at her surroundings. The massive, square stone gateposts were topped with ugly brass statues of strange beasts. Cliffs rose to either side of her, with windows and door frames apparently cut from the rock itself, their blank eyes looking down upon the small courtyard in which she stood. Behind her tall dark cypress trees waited, guarding their secrets in the cold still air; overhead, the sky was a thunderous grey that made her want to run for shelter.

Anya shivered, wondering why she had been abandoned in this alien, pagan landscape. Then, as she suddenly realized where she was, the dreadful cold intensified.

Water lapped softly against stone as the boat drew alongside the shadowed quay and the ghostlike figure stepped lightly ashore. He looked up, threw back his hood and smiled – and Anya once again found herself looking into the mocking eyes of her tormentor. She was afraid, but not surprised.

'Why have you brought me here?' she breathed.

'It is not I who seek out the places where we meet,' Allessandro replied smoothly. 'Do you think of some part of yourself as dead? Is that why you wait for me on this island?' He sounded both curious and amused.

'I did not choose this meeting,' she protested.

'Choice is not the issue,' he told her with exaggerated patience. 'You and I are one; master and servant, teacher and pupil, artist and apprentice. For now, we have need of one another.'

'I don't need you!' Anya exclaimed shrilly. 'I don't *want* you.'

'Everything you know, I know,' he went on, ignoring her outburst. 'Although it will take me a little time to find my way around your world, it has much to interest me. It presents quite a challenge.'

Anya felt a tiny dart of satisfaction at the evident uncertainty that lay beneath his arrogant confidence. The fact that he did not yet completely understand her world must surely give her some advantage. But those hopes were dashed with his next words.

'Do not begin to doubt my capabilities,' he told her evenly. 'Someone must bring order to this chaos, and I have all the time I need.'

His complacency grated on Anya's frayed nerves.

'Who *are* you?' she screamed.

'You already know that,' he answered, with infuriating smugness. 'It was you who found me, after all, you who saw beneath the surface.'

'No,' Anya whispered. 'It's not possible!' She looked at his smiling face, his every feature giving the lie to her words. The impossible *had* happened. 'I . . . I don't understand. How . . . ?'

'It's an old story,' Allessandro said impassively. 'I was not the first – nor will I be the last – to be betrayed by a jealous woman. You already know some of the stories. Merlin, for instance.'

'Merlin! But . . .'

'He was a fool to let Nimue trap him so.'

Anya fought desperately to keep her bewilderment in check. The conversation was becoming more surreal by the moment. How could Allessandro be talking about a character from legend as though he had been real? And yet she could not help but recall the vision in the cave, the old man frozen in crystal.

'He is dead, or sleeping still,' Allessandro went on. 'It amounts to the same thing. But I – I am back in the world.'

No, you're not, Anya thought, with a terrifying rush of insight. *You're in my mind, that's all.*

Allessandro laughed.

'This is but the first step, my sweet Constanza,' he remarked, as if she had spoken aloud. 'When you have learnt more and I am ready, we will go on.'

Anya wanted to ask where they would be going, and to what, but the use of the unfamiliar name had thrown her already disordered thoughts into even deeper confusion.

'My name's not Constanza,' she said quietly.

'It was in that other age,' he replied. 'It was she, my beloved apprentice, who tricked me, almost – I admit – almost defeated me. But it is you who will pay the price for her treachery. It cannot go unpunished. Ah, the faithless Constanza. Never was a woman so ill named.' He sounded wistful now, almost admiring.

Anya did not understand why – or how – she should be punished for another's still unexplained crime, but she had to push aside these new fears as another aspect of Allessandro's earlier words sank in. He had compared himself to Merlin.

'Are you . . . are you a sorcerer?'

'Of course,' he replied, without hesitation. There was no trace of sarcasm or ridicule in his voice. He was simply stating a fact, as though he were admitting to being a plumber or an accountant. 'Surely you recognize the signs of power. You have the potential too, though you try to deny it.' He paused, staring at her with dark-eyed condescension. 'Your strength will never match mine, of course. I am an authentic Artist of Truth. How else can you explain my presence here?'

29

Anya had no answer to that, beyond a hopeless rejection of patent reality. This *was* happening, however bizarre it seemed. To deny it was pointless.

'And . . . Constanza . . . trapped you?' she hazarded.

'Yes.'

'How?'

'That's not important now,' he snapped impatiently. 'More to the point is the fact that, unlike my sometimes illustrious predecessors, I was not so blinded by love or lust that I forgot to prepare a way of escape.' He paused expectantly.

'What was that? The way of escape?' Anya asked, knowing she had no choice.

'Why you, of course,' Allessandro replied happily. 'I would have thought that was obvious by now. All I had to do was wait.'

5

'—situated near the front of the train, between the first class and standard accommodation. A full menu . . .'

The guard's announcement droned on, but Anya paid it no attention. She put the postcard face down on the table, let out a long breath and tried to shake off her disorientation.

'Are you all right, dear?'

'What? Oh, yes. Thank you.' Anya smiled – albeit with difficulty – at the old lady sitting opposite her, who had leant forward and touched her hand lightly.

'Are you sure? You look a bit peaky.'

'I'm fine. Really,' Anya lied, only wanting to be left alone.

'That's good,' the grey-haired woman continued, her concern relentless, 'because for a few seconds there I thought you might be going to faint. Your eyes went all blank, like you were staring right through me. Gave me quite a turn, I can tell you.' She laughed self-consciously.

'I'm sorry,' Anya said. 'I was just daydreaming.'

'You see, I had a cousin once,' the old lady went on confidingly. 'She used to do that. Petty mal, the doctor called it. Epileptic, you know,' she added, lowering her voice as so many people did when discussing other people's ailments. 'She was a pretty girl like you, that's what made me think. But of course you'd know if it was anything like that.'

Anya smiled and nodded without speaking, hoping her companion would take the hint. At the same time, she could not help wondering whether there might be something in

31

what she had said. *Epilepsy – is that what this is? Is it possible that I'm just ill?*

'Listen to me,' the old woman prattled on. 'You'd think I'd have more sense at my age. I'm the one with arthritis and Lord knows how many pills to take. A young thing like you won't have anything wrong. I do hope I haven't worried you.'

Shut up! Anya begged silently. Her gaze had fallen on the postcard again, and all her doubts and fears had returned in full measure. Epilepsy could not possibly explain what was happening to her. *Please, God, I don't want to end up like my mother.* She started to pull the card towards her, wanting to hide the evidence.

'Is that your boyfriend?' the old lady asked eagerly, nodding towards the hidden picture.

'No.' Anya lifted it to show her inquisitor.

'Oh, silly me,' she exclaimed, laughing with embarrassment. 'I thought it was a photo.'

'It's just an old painting,' Anya said, remembering.

The entrance hall to the National Gallery in London had been crowded with tourists, studying floor plans and leaflets as they tried to decide what to see first. Anya wandered through the throng, picking a route at random. An hour later she was in a happy daze, having seen only a tiny portion of the works on view, and was wondering why she had not set foot here for so many years. She was vaguely familiar with several of the paintings, but inspecting the originals deepened her appreciation of them immeasurably – and there were so many that were entirely new to her. Much of what she saw was not to her own taste, but her favourites – both old and new – entranced her so that she stood gazing, hardly thinking or breathing, while those with more crowded timetables hurried by.

She wandered into the next room and stopped, transfixed. As their eyes met across the centuries, all sound vanished. No conversations, no footsteps intruded upon their private communion. Anya stared, and he stared back, as alive now as he had been when the artist first set his miraculous brush in motion.

He was seated in an angular wooden chair, holding an open book, and looking back at the viewer over his left shoulder. The background was dark, a uniform grey broken only by a monogram, which looked like the letter V superimposed on an A. Anya studied the techniques involved, admiring the brilliant rendition of the material of his bulky, silken sleeve, and wondering why the hands and book seemed so inarticulate by comparison – almost as if they had been deliberately left out of focus. She saw how the light had been carefully contrived to emphasize the subject's pale, striking features and to provide contrast in the almost monochrome design. But, most of all, she simply gazed, her attention drawn back time and again to his extraordinary eyes, eyes that saw the world as a hawk sees its prey. They were hypnotic circles of pure black, intelligent, disdainful and utterly self-aware.

Anya forced herself to look aside – and the sounds of the day returned. The caption beside the painting read 'Portrait of a Young Man. Andrea del Sarto, 1486–1530'. Inside the frame, the painting was little more than two feet high, and yet it was one of the greatest masterpieces she had ever seen. Even now that it no longer held her spellbound, now that the rest of the world existed once more, Anya was still held by admiration. She felt as if she knew this anonymous young gentleman, who had been dead for over four hundred years but who lived on because of another man's genius. Anya knew, with an honest sadness but without rancour, that none of her own paintings would stand such a test of time.

At last she tore herself away, and continued her haphazard exploration. Several other pictures held her attention, commanded both her respect and – in some cases – her instant love, but nothing had quite the effect of that one small, shadowed portrait. At the end of the day, footsore but content, Anya went to the shop and bought several postcards to take home with her as inadequate but faithful reminders of her discoveries. One of the postcards which subsequently took its place on her studio wall was, of course, 'Portrait of a Young Man'.

And there it might have ended, the painting only one of

many to catch Anya's eye, the incident when they had first met forgotten in the rush and complexity of her own life. There it might have ended, but of course it did not. Ever since that day, now seven months in the past, Anya had been plagued by intermittent nightmares, vague, meaningless dreams that left her tired and fearful. Gradually, their imagery had grown more coherent and he appeared more and more frequently, a threatening presence who nevertheless continued to attract her. He spoke a language she did not understand, shouted at her, smiled and stared. She woke feeling humiliated for no good reason, afraid of his ominous and ever-growing strength.

Soon his face distracted Anya in her studio, drawing her eyes to his, even from the other side of the room, and she turned the postcard over, setting his face to the wall. And yet she could not bring herself to throw the card away, or to burn it, and so rid herself of its curse. She could confide in no one, least of all Luke, and slept with her own terrors.

After a time there had been a partial respite. The nightmares grew less frequent, and other matters clamoured for her attention. But now, it seemed, a new stage had been reached. The dreams were no longer enough for him. The young man was anonymous no longer. Anya knew his name, had heard it from his own lips. Allessandro Massimiliano. Alexander the Great. Was he mocking her even with his choice of name? *The world knows me by other names, but you will have to learn them for yourself.* How could these visions be explained? Epilepsy? Migrainous hallucinations? She did not take drugs. Her mind shied away from the more obvious possibility. She had contemplated madness all too often.

How could this be happening? How could the scenes she had witnessed and taken part in last so long and yet be over in just a few seconds of her waking life? How could he seem so real, this self-proclaimed sorcerer brought back to life by her unfevered imagination? And if he *was* real, why was he tormenting her? What did he want, with all his talk of apprentices and magic tricks?

As if her life wasn't complicated enough already.

*   *   *

34

'Of course, my granddaughter – the youngest one – she's off to university soon. They grow up so fast. It hardly seems possible.'

The old woman's voice brought Anya back to the present with a sense of resentment mixed with confusion. She had obviously been running on, oblivious to her listener's preoccupation and, right now, Anya did not want to hear about grandchildren, about a safe, normal, everyday life.

'I'm sorry,' she interrupted. 'I have a headache and I'm really tired. Would you mind if we sat quietly for a while?' She tried to smile but could not really find the strength to make much of an effort. If her companion found her rude, that would just be too bad.

'Of course,' the old lady replied with a half-smile, her tone betraying only disappointment, not umbrage. She produced a magazine from her bag, and settled down to read.

Anya slid the postcard into her pocket without looking at it, sat back and closed her eyes, forcing herself to think about her destination. The speeding train was only the first stage of the long journey, which would be tiring. But it would all be worthwhile once she arrived. Once she was there – whatever happened – nothing else would matter.

6

Anya was flying alone, far above a strange land. She looked down upon mountain ranges and dark ravines, jagged cliffs and barren plains, vast forests with a huge variety of ever swaying trees. There were flying creatures everywhere, miraculous in their diversity of shape, size and colour – luminous blues, reds, vivid greens, silver, and every shade of grey. It was a land of occasional monsters too; pendulous, translucent beasts of prey and great, slow-moving invertebrates whose sucking tentacles were the stuff of nightmare. Deep shadows hinted at unknown perils. And it was a land of lost treasures, cast-offs from another world, half buried or impaled upon deadly black spikes. This all lay beneath a swirling, mirror-surfaced sky where Anya floated in safety like some inquisitive, ponderous cloud, casting a giant shadow over the strange world below.

She loved snorkelling. It lit up her artist's imagination, every new movement revealing new vistas, new realms of wonder. The warm water was buoyant and crystal clear, populated by scores of fish that, either singly or in glittering shoals, explored her fanciful land, weaving within the seaweed forests and disappearing into crevasses in the rocks. Anya kept a special watch for the wind-blown jellyfish, knowing from painful experience that a sting, while not serious, would hurt for hours and then itch for days. The much rarer appearance of an octopus or squid represented no threat, even though the sight of them made her shudder. These creatures were far too shy to venture close unless she stumbled on their lairs by mistake – and even then they would flee, more frightened of her than she was of them. Anya always took care not to step on any of the plentiful spiny sea-urchins but, for the most part, she merely lay in the water, letting the gentle swell move her as she watched the 'land' below. It was so fascinating and yet so peaceful and relaxing that her greatest danger was that of getting a sunburnt back.

Eventually she swam back towards the stony beach and waded from the shallows, her plastic shoes easing her progress on the occasionally slippery, shifting rocks. Towelling herself off briefly, Anya looked around, took a deep breath of herb-scented air and felt a great release, filled with pure joy at being back in this beautiful, familiar place. The limestone cliffs that marked the southern end of the bay were topped with greenery, outlined by a clear blue sky. Inland, olive trees in their dry-stone walled terraces crowded down to the beach, providing shade for the hottest hours of the day. Her boat, which – never knowing how long she would need it – she hired by the day from Yiannis, was moored to a rock and floated serenely on the dazzling blue water. Surely, Anya thought, nothing unpleasant could ever intrude upon this idyllic setting.

Ahead of her lay the leisurely journey back to the village, dinner at the Taverna Vassilis and a second blissful night's sleep in her lovely, primitive cottage in the hills above. And after that . . . who knew how many days of similar, lazy, indulgent perfection? Time moved more slowly here. Even her own internal clock seemed to have stopped ticking.

Anya let the late afternoon sun warm her skin and dry her black, one-piece swimming costume, listened to the electric chatter of cicadas and revelled in the luxury of doing nothing. Out beyond the bay a few small boats buzzed past, but no one came closer, and she kept the beach to herself.

When the prospect of food finally became more attractive than continued indolence, Anya stuffed her belongings into a small rucksack, and threw it onto the boat. Clambering aboard, she set the outboard motor roaring into operation and hauled herself away from the shore with the stern rope.

Swinging round out of the bay, she followed the coastline south until she came to the large stone breakwater that marked the entrance to Loggos harbour. Then she slowed the engine and coasted towards the village.

Loggos itself was always a source of great pleasure. It had changed little in all the years that Anya had been coming there, the space for development restricted by the surrounding hills and 'progress' slowed by the temperament of the Greek islanders. Discerning tourists came here for the tranquillity and for the old-fashioned, natural charm of the small fishing port. Here there were none of the high-rise horrors that had despoiled so much of the Mediterranean – although Anya had heard of vague plans to convert the disused soap factory into apartments. She hoped, selfishly, that this would never happen. Loggos was perfect as it was. The houses, with their white or pastel painted walls, brightly coloured shutters and red tile roofs, were grouped around the harbour, where an armada of small boats – ferries, a few yachts, fishing smacks and hire craft – were moored. The inner harbour was ringed with a few tavernas, two general stores, a bakery, a tiny church and the harbour-master's house. Higher up the slopes, houses nestled among trees, as if distancing themselves from the intermittent bustle.

Vassilis was her favourite eating place. It was a long, white, one-storey building with only the width of the village's one road between it and the water. Outside, tables lined the road, which was so narrow that diners' chairs often had to be moved aside when the island's bus came past. Delicious aromas were already wafting from the kitchen but Anya knew that it was too early for Vassili to begin serving, so she sat at one of the tables, ordered a small bottle of ice-cold retsina and watched the world go by.

It was a colourful scene in the last of the sunlight, with the houses and brightly painted boats reflected in the still water of the harbour. Locals and visitors strolled by, fishermen mended their nets, cats prowled expectantly and children roamed freely, peering into the water and pointing excitedly at each new discovery. Occasionally a car, taxi or scooter went past. No one seemed to be in any great hurry to get anywhere. Beyond the bay, the distant mainland was half hidden by haze – and might as well have been as remote as the moon.

The noises that filled the air were equally varied and colourful. Outboard motors purred, the bus hooted a warning as it rounded the sharp bend on the coast road on its way down into the village, dogs barked sporadically and cocks crowed, oblivious to the time of day. Greek conversations ebbed and flowed all around her, many of them sounding like arguments, although clearly they were nothing of the sort. Boats creaked in the gentle swell, and water lapped and gurgled against concrete.

As the evening progressed, the tables began to fill up. Anya ate stifado, savouring its deliciously rich onion gravy and the beef so tender that it must surely have been cooking for days, with perfect chips fried in the local olive oil. Finally, after parting with what seemed an absurdly small amount for such a splendid meal, Anya retired to the nearby café for a tiny cup of strong, sweet coffee and a Metaxa brandy to fortify her for the climb up to Dendiatika.

As the evening was still mild, she decided to ignore the steeper, more direct route and instead walked along the older path via the ruined windmill that stood atop the headland. Only the circular walls were left, but they looked solid enough to last centuries, the secrets of their construction partially revealed by the twisted logs inside the stonework. Bushes now grew inside the mill, covered with small red berries, but it was still possible to go in and climb onto the top of the walls. From there the views were among Anya's favourites. Loggos and its harbour nestled below, looking like something from a child's toy box, while to the north and south the island's twisting coastline receded in tranquil, sunset beauty. To the east, the lights of the mainland were just becoming visible.

Reluctantly, Anya turned inland and headed through the trees for the tiny, straggling village that she thought of as her second home. The house in Dendiatika consisted only of one large, stone-built room. From outside, apart from the solid, green painted door and shutters, the place looked as if it was falling into disrepair, but although the dusty walls were finished roughly and the roof tiles were uneven, they were solid enough. Inside it was cool and dark, with basic furnishings kept to a minimum. A large bed stood in one corner. At the other end of the room was a stove and a seldom-used heater, a plain wooden table, two chairs and a few cupboards. Two large chests provided further storage space. The central area of the tiled floor was often cluttered with paintings and equipment, but it was relatively clear at the moment as Anya had not yet begun any serious work. Almost all her painting on the island was done outside, with everything only brought back inside overnight.

Water had to be fetched from an outdoor tap, which was connected to a nearby sterna, and there was a very basic latrine in a tiny outbuilding – itself half hidden by the branches of an unruly tree. Electricity provided a single socket and two lights, but the circuit was temperamental and boiling a kettle would often be enough to plunge Anya into darkness.

Her landlord, Nikoluzos Arvonitakis – known as Niko – lived in a fully modernized apartment in Loggos, and could not comprehend her attachment to this inconvenient, antiquated shell of a house, but he was happy to keep it habitable for her. She paid a minimal rent annually in advance, on the understanding that she was free to use the place at any time without having to give advance notice. Anya knew that he sometimes let the house out to others, although he denied this cheerfully. On one occasion she had found paintings stored there which were not her own, and someone else's clothes were kept more or less permanently in one of the chests – but some sixth sense obviously helped Niko keep it free for her arrival. As long as that was the case, the infrequent intrusions were never resented.

Anya went to bed that night full of contentment and, for the first time in months, unafraid of what her dreams might bring.

7

The flickering began five days later.

During that time Anya had swum, sunbathed, read two novels, gone for long walks and begun two paintings based on an amalgam of images seen while snorkelling. She had spoiled herself with good food and drink, and had slept soundly and serenely. The nightmares and other more recent horrors had begun to recede as she fell naturally into an altogether simpler mode of existence. Here, in spite of her passing acquaintance with several people, she was essentially a stranger. Here she owed explanations to no one, least of all for the things she did not understand herself. Artists were supposed to be eccentric, after all.

Her self-sufficiency amazed her. On some days she spoke to no one at all until she ordered her evening meal, and finding that her vocal cords still worked often came as something of a surprise. This quiet solitude filled her with pleasure. She began to feel safe. But then, suddenly and in unexpected ways, her anxieties returned.

The first time it happened, Anya assumed it was the after-effects of too much brandy. She was walking home after dinner, skirting the roofless limestone walls of the derelict factory, when she saw something move out of the corner of her eye. She looked up at the incongruous statue of a Greek god, glowing softly in the evening light. She had always found the continued existence of such a statue on the ruins of the otherwise undistinguished building rather endearing, but now it filled her with disquiet. Had it really moved? Of course

41

not, she chided herself. It had probably just been a bat flying past. Certainly there was nothing to be seen now. She walked on, trying to convince herself that it had been nothing, while her memory played tricks on her. *Had* there been a fleeting glimpse of someone – or something – on the parapet?

The track became a steep path which turned sharply to the left beneath the towering form of the factory's long-dormant chimney. It had always looked precarious, shored up in various ways and with wide, ominous cracks in the brickwork, but now it seemed to be actually creaking in the wind. Anya looked up, suddenly fearful, just as a wavering, impossible light from inside, shining out through the cracks, went out. She stared, wanting to run, but her legs refused to move. The light did not reappear, and the creaking stopped. A few moments later, feeling rather silly, she turned and went on.

All the way along the path that zigzagged up the hill between the olive groves and the scattering of villas, Anya kept jumping at shadows, startled by every small noise. She found herself climbing faster than normal, her heart thumping as she rushed up the new spiral steps that covered the steepest part of the ascent. By the time she reached her house, she was perspiring freely in spite of the fact that she was wearing only her swimming costume and a cotton wrap, and she splashed her face with water before going inside. There, in familiar and comfortingly private surroundings, she recovered quickly and began to feel very foolish. Nevertheless, she took longer than usual to fall asleep that night.

Anya's misgivings began to seem even more ridiculous in the morning sunlight, and she donned black shorts, singlet and hiking boots to set off for a walk, determined to make the most of the relatively cool air. The island's flowers had always delighted her, and wandering in the shade of the plentiful trees – cypresses and firs as well as the omnipresent olives – was one of her favourite pastimes. There were almost always flowers in every season, and Anya studied them all anew with an enjoyment that made her wonder, for the umpteenth time, why it was that such beauties of nature did not inspire her to paint them. *Not weird enough for you?* she thought, and smiled.

It was an innocent gecko that spoiled her mood. She was passing one of the whitewashed villas on the outskirts of Dendiatika when the small lizard shot out from almost under her feet, and seemed to fly up the wall until it came to rest under the eaves. The sudden movement startled Anya more than it should have done, and she cried out involuntarily. From then on, fleeting images of half-seen movement, whispers of activity, plagued her constantly. She was forever glancing round just too late, never able to see what had attracted her grasshopper attention. As her imagination naturally began to fill the void, each rustle came to mean not just a harmless, timid gecko but a poisonous snake. She pictured scorpions following her every step, monsters around every corner.

Passing the local church, with its characteristic separate bell tower, she looked over the wall into the graveyard. Several of the tombs had fading photographs set in glass-covered recesses. Anya had always found this commemorative practice either touching or macabre, depending on her mood, but this time – when she perceived yet another unexplained and instantly stilled movement among the faces of the dead – the effect was too much for her already strained nerves. She broke into a run and pounded back down the track to her house.

Once there she hurriedly gathered up her swimming things, meaning to set out on foot for the nearest beach, intent on soothing away all thoughts of ghosts or hidden presences in the welcoming waters of the sea. But just as she was turning to go, another dark flicker came from the corner of the room and Anya swore shakily under her breath, imagining a huge, loathsome spider. Was she to be safe nowhere?

She set off at breakneck speed, ignoring the danger of a twisted ankle in her haste on the rugged track. All she wanted was a return to her earlier carefree good humour, and she craved the soft embrace of the sea. Only once on the way down was she distracted. The gnarled root of an ancient olive tree writhed across her path, like a long dead snake, and – for one horrible instant – seemed to come back to life, to squirm and rear up at her. Anya stamped down hard, proving to herself that it *was* only wood, then regretted her impulsiveness as her foot was bruised even through the thick sole of her boot.

Angry now as well as distressed, she reached the shore at last. Ignoring the group of holidaymakers at the far end of the beach, she threw off all her clothes, pulled on her costume, grabbed her snorkel and mask, and waded eagerly into the water. She was soon floating on the placid surface, gazing down at the sea bed far below. Her peace of mind returned, as she deliberately slowed her breathing and let her muscles relax. She felt calm and weightless. Anya was a strong swimmer, confident of her abilities even in much rougher conditions than these. At least here all the movement she could see was in the open; nothing was hidden or evaded her gaze. There was no malice or guile in the fish below her. She watched, fascinated, as an octopus edged its way out of hiding.

And the whole world turned white. Two grotesque albino eyes gazed back at her and a gaping brown maw came sucking up out of the primeval mud. Anya's mind balked at the sight, repulsed and terrified, yet also moved to something like pity. What *was* this massive apparition? Where was she? The ocean and sky had become one, an amorphous grey mass only half illuminated by the rising sun, and she was alone with this alien sea monster.

Then she realized where she was, though the knowledge did nothing to alleviate her terror. *This is not real!* she cried silently. *I do not live in a painting!*

'It is as real as you make it,' Allessandro replied, emerging from the murk and placing a gentle hand on the creature's terrible head. 'Down!' he commanded, and laughed as the monster began to sink back into the mire.

'Leave me alone!' Anya screamed.

'You might as well ask me to leave myself alone,' he replied dismissively, his smile fading. 'Did you really think I'd forgotten you? I am learning all the time. You can *see* me when I touch your world now, can't you? Soon everyone will see, and we can go on to the next stage.'

'No!' The denial was instinctive. Anya did not know what he meant, but knew that she was threatened somehow. She was terrified.

'The Greeks believed that there was – is – a force more powerful than all the gods of men,' the self-proclaimed sorcerer remarked, ignoring her cry. 'They called it "Ananke" – what has to be – but what is the point of the existence of such a power? Unless it is to be *used*?'

But not by you, she protested silently.

'Why not?' he asked, smiling as he read her thoughts. 'Are you one of the Fates, one of the daughters of Ananke? Do you spin the thread of every life on earth?'

'You're insane,' she hissed.

'The Fates were all innocent young girls like you,' Allessandro went on, still ignoring her. 'Apollo once got them all drunk, to delay the death of his beloved Admetus. That must have been the wildest party ever, don't you think?'

Anya no longer had the strength or inclination to speak. She just wanted this to be over. She wanted to run away and hide.

Her tormentor went on regardless, continuing the one-sided conversation. He still looked vaguely amused, and watched her condescendingly.

'Of course, according to legend, it was Poseidon, not Apollo, who created this island,' he said. 'Lopped it off with his trident. He wanted a private haven for himself and the Nereid Amphitrite. Naturally, the myth is supposed by scholars to have grown from the folk memory of an earthquake, but they forget that such things were also the province of Poseidon the Earthshaker.' He paused before adding, 'Perhaps we could try to emulate him. It should soon be within my capabilities. Just think of it, a brand new island paradise all to ourselves.'

'I am not your lover!' Anya protested, anger and disgust momentarily overriding her fear.

'But you could be,' he remarked, and was gone.

She found herself thrashing about in the churning seawater, the bubbles that burst in her ears sounding like the fading tick of a clock. Below her the octopus retreated again, but she did not even see it. Her mouth hurt from biting down on the rubber, and she was suddenly terrified by the thought of drowning. What had possessed her to swim out into such deep water? For a few moments she could not even remember where she was, but instinct drove her floundering towards the shore.

8

'Hi, Luke.'

'Sheila, come on in. I'd expected you before this.'

'You know me. I always like to cut things fine.'

'Want a drink?' he asked amiably. 'Coffee?'

Sheila could smell the whisky on his breath, though he was clearly still sober.

'No thanks. You're not the easiest person to get hold of, you know. I've tried phoning several times, and I came round last Tuesday night. There was no one in.'

'I was working,' Luke explained, wandering back into the sitting room.

'At nine o'clock?' Sheila sounded surprised. 'You're keen.'

'Not much else to do at the moment,' he answered resentfully. 'You sure you don't want a drink?' he added, refilling his own tumbler.

'OK. Thanks. Got any gin?' she asked, recognizing his desire for companionship.

'Yes, but the tonic's probably flat. I'll see if there's any in the fridge.' He left the room, and while Sheila waited for him she looked around. The sitting room was almost too tidy and clean. If Luke was brooding, at least he was not going to pieces. Most men she knew would have reduced their homes to a complete shambles if their wives or girl-friends had gone away for an unspecified length of time. She wondered if he was as controlled in his thoughts as he was in his actions. Luke returned with a bottle and a tray of ice.

'Success,' he announced, waving her to a chair. He mixed her drink, then sat down next to her. 'Cheers.'

Sheila raised her glass, then sipped appreciatively. When Luke did not speak, she broke the silence herself.

'How long's Anya been gone now?'

'Eight days,' he replied dully, looking at his watch.

And how many hours? Sheila wondered. *Most people would've just said a week, but he's counting the minutes. Poor man.*

'You don't know . . .?' Luke began, then faltered, knowing his question was pointless.

'I've told you before,' she said gently. 'Anya doesn't confide in me about her trips. I've tried to ask her, but it's useless. I've given up. Not something I do lightly, as you know. Anyway, why would she tell me and not you?'

'Because it's me she's trying to get away from.'

'Oh, Luke, it's not as simple as that.'

'Isn't it?'

'You know it isn't. Besides, she always comes back.'

'So everyone keeps telling me,' Luke complained, 'as if that excuses her disappearances. I just hope it does her some good. I'd hate to think I was feeling this small for nothing.'

Sheila leant over and patted his knee, looking at his broad shoulders and wide, boyish face.

'Small is one thing you'll never be,' she said, wishing there was someone who would be as devastated as this if *she* left temporarily. Except, of course, that if there was, she would have the sense never to leave at all. Damn Anya and her secrets.

Luke grinned feebly.

'It's all right to be angry, you know,' she told him softly.

'What would be the point?' He paused, shrugging. 'I just hope she gets better.'

'Better? What do you mean?'

'Come and have a look at her paintings,' Luke said, draining his glass. 'And you'll see.'

As Sheila followed him upstairs, she wondered whether his own melancholy was making him melodramatic, or whether there really was something to worry about. The studio was in darkness when Luke opened the door but, as he flipped switches, light and colour swept over her and the familiar scent of the room filled her nostrils. She did not see any of the new paintings immediately.

'Anya left a list of the ones that are ready,' Luke muttered, as he shuffled through the mess on top of the desk.

'There's only one I must take now,' Sheila reminded him.

'"Moonrider", I know. That's on the easel, over there.' He had found the list and was scanning it as she folded back the protective covering from the artwork. What she saw came as a relief.

'This is perfect. Just what they wanted.'

Luke said nothing.

The painting depicted a knight in silver armour riding a beautiful white horse. Glittering mist rolled around the animal's galloping feet and the whole scene was lit by a full moon that hung in a black, starless sky. It was a thoroughly professional piece of work – as well as being suitably fantastical.

'You think I'm overreacting, don't you?' Luke said unexpectedly. While Sheila had been examining 'Moonrider', he had been sorting through the other paintings on the list.

'I don't see anything to worry about here,' she admitted.

'Then come and see what Anya's own, undirected imagination produces,' he said, and placed a second frame on an empty easel.

Sheila did as she was told, then recoiled in horror. 'My God! Where did this come from?' she breathed, suddenly understanding Luke's alarm.

Most of the canvas was a smoky grey colour. In the centre, dwarfed by her surroundings, was the figure of a small child, apparently sitting in an invisible chair. Her rigid body was only half seen and her arms were held tightly by her sides as if constrained, her hands held out of sight. Only her face was clearly visible, the skin stark white, eyes wide in terror. Her mouth was hidden from view by a wide black strip of shiny tape wrapped tightly over her lips, gagging her and bottling up the inevitable scream. The reason for her fear was not within the little girl's field of vision, but she could obviously sense what the onlooker could see all too clearly. Two huge black hands of smoke, each crooked finger large enough to dwarf the child's body, were reaching out from the darkness behind her like monstrous shadows. Soon, it was implied, they would engulf their victim, crush her out of existence. And she could not even cry out for help.

'It's called "Cold",' Luke informed Sheila quietly.

She was speechless. Although the power of the imagery and its execution were undeniable, the painting was horrible beyond words.

'Anya often says that she paints what she remembers from her dreams,' Luke went on. 'Doing that somehow exorcizes them, robs the images of their power, and so she's able to forget them. That's why she's always happy for you to take them away once they're finished. Selling them is like the final stage of the therapy.'

'Selling *this* could be difficult,' she said, finding her voice at last. 'It would make a great cover for a horror novel, but the galleries won't touch it.' She had no need to voice her own horror at the thought that the scene might have come from one of Anya's nightmares.

'That's the worst,' Luke stated confidently, 'but some of the others are just as weird.'

'Show me,' she said weakly.

The next canvas was vastly more attractive and colourful but, as Luke had pointed out, was distinctly odd. It was almost twice as wide as it was high, and the top third of the painting consisted of meticulously reproduced, raging dark flames and billowing black smoke above a thin wavering line that separated this conflagration from the rest of the picture. The lower part consisted of a stylized, beautiful pattern of jewelled blues and greens, the subtle variations of colour suggesting peace and serenity. It was entirely abstract in nature, with nothing recognizable for the eye to fix upon – in marked contrast to the ultrarealistic flames above.

Sheila found the whole effect rather unsettling, though the painting was attractive. It seemed to suggest the sea, covered with burning oil – she recalled the horrifying aerial television pictures of Kuwait during the Gulf War – but with the waters below apparently unaffected by the appalling blaze. And yet the almost jewelled water had the peacefulness of sterility. Nothing moved there; nothing lived.

'We should send this to Greenpeace,' she suggested, in a half-hearted attempt to lighten the mood.

Luke merely nodded.

'It's called "Beneath the Flames",' he said.

'That's literal, for Anya,' Sheila mused, taking a last look at the inferno. 'What's next?'

Without saying a word, Luke replaced the painting with one showing a detailed moorland landscape, tors and valleys rolling away into the distance beneath a mottled sky. It was entirely naturalistic – which was very unusual for Anya – and Sheila found herself searching for hidden clues as to her friend's real purpose. But nothing was revealed and she frowned, finding the apparently innocent picture rather disturbing.

'Creepy, isn't it?' Luke observed, echoing her thoughts.

'Yes, but why? It . . .' She paused, at a loss to explain their joint reaction. 'It's Dartmoor, I presume.'

'Nowhere I've ever seen,' Luke told her.

'And you've seen most of it.'

'I'd've thought so.'

'Why imagine something like this when the real thing's all around her?' Sheila wondered aloud. 'Does it have a title?'

'No. The list refers to it simply as "the landscape".'

'Very helpful,' she commented dryly. 'Anything else?'

'Oh yes. You're going to love these.' He led her across to where three small frames were propped against a wall. 'These are known collectively as "The Mansions of Eternity",' he announced. 'Anya's not usually so pretentious.'

Sheila crouched down to get a better look. Each part of the triptych showed a stage in the impossible journey of what she took to be an elevator. In the first one, the lift was ascending through a hole in the roof of the building, and beginning to fly. Although the doors were closed, silhouettes of the passengers were visible through glass panels. The top of the lift was covered with a square pyramid, rather like a roof. In the second picture this was the only part visible, poking out from the top of a cloud that floated in an otherwise clear blue sky. The final part of the trilogy reversed the perspective. Instead of looking at the airborne lift from a distance, the point of view was from inside, with clouds and sky and the land far below seen through the glass panels. It was eerie enough to induce a feeling of vertigo, with a further unnerving element provided by half-seen reflections in the glass, sinister shapes and faces – none of them clear, but prompting uncomfortable thoughts about who was sharing the lift. It seemed to be quite a crowd.

'I'm beginning to think I'd need a degree in psychiatry to try and understand this lot,' Sheila said, only half joking.

'My thoughts exactly,' Luke replied, quite serious. 'I think she needs help.' He was hoping for confirmation, something to make the idea sit more easily in his own mind, but his companion did not oblige.

'That's too big a jump for me,' she said, straightening up. 'These may be strange, but she's done odd stuff before.' Anya had always varied her styles, although this bunch was unusually eclectic, even for her. 'Besides, you said yourself that painting this stuff is like therapy for her. I don't think . . .'

'But she still needs to run away,' Luke interrupted. 'Maybe it's from herself, not from me,' he added quietly, as if the thought had just occurred to him.

'Maybe,' Sheila agreed. 'And each time she comes back, the pictures are gone, cleared away from her life, her mind. Seems like a good system to me.' She smiled, trying to put a positive slant on the discussion, but Luke remained silent, unconvinced. 'Is that the lot?' she added. 'Or are there any more?'

'Just one.' Luke picked up another large canvas and turned it round to the light. It was a bleak portrait, showing a half-dead tree, bent almost double by a relentless wind, beneath a lowering sky. It had been executed with a minimum of brush strokes, yet the impression of tortured, yet stubborn and resilient strength was immediate and striking. It was clearly the best of all her recent work.

'"The Breath of Twins",' Luke informed her. 'At least I know what *that* means.'

Sheila looked at him expectantly.

'The wind,' he explained. 'Some primitive tribes believed that twins could control the weather.' It was another strange fact unearthed by his curiosity.

Later, while Luke was helping her to load the paintings into her car, Sheila's thoughts turned to Meredith.

'You've never met Anya's sister, have you?' she asked.

'No,' he replied with a shrug. 'It's as though Anya's ashamed of her, or something. Does she talk about her to you?'

'No.'

'It's not as if Meredith could be any weirder than her sister,' Luke remarked with a rueful smile.

53

9

Meredith Caplan began the last and least favourite stage of her long journey home by stepping aboard the launch that would carry her from Hugh Town on the island of St Mary's to St Agnes. Although the day-trippers crowded round the sides of the boat, she sat in the centre, putting as much space as possible between her and the waves. The seas around the Isles of Scilly could be rough at any time of year and even now, on a pleasant summer's day, the wind-built swell of the Atlantic was likely to make crossing St Mary's Sound something of an adventure. A simple brass plaque on the launch's bulkhead read 'Dunkirk 1940', and Meredith thought that the brave little boat was capable of a much longer and far more dangerous journey than the one ahead of her.

Her life, she mused, seemed to consist of one journey after another, an episodic voyage of discovery. The path she had chosen was an ever-turning circle which, every once in a while, felt like a treadmill. Even so, she would never complain. That was not in her nature, and would have been a betrayal of her special talents. She was driven to help people; it was her whole *raison d'être*, but she knew that to do so effectively she needed some time for herself. And her time was always so limited! It would be impossible for a clairvoyant even far more adept than she was to see how all the demands on her could be fitted in.

Meredith smiled to herself as the launch left the sheltered harbour and headed into open water. The future was usually as much of a closed book for her as for anyone else. She was only granted an occasional glimpse at a necessary page every so often. Her guides were patient. They understood her limitations, and did not try to force her to go beyond them. By the same token, they only told her what she needed to know. That was more than enough for Meredith, who thought it was a fair exchange.

Her almost constant travelling and the lack of continuity in the way she lived were tiring, and eventually she always came to the conclusion that she had to go home. Her stays on St Agnes were the only times when she was able to recoup her energy, refuel her systems. The population of the island was no more than eighty or so, and she knew almost everyone by sight, but even her close friends made no demands upon her. What help she gave to the small community was that which she chose to volunteer.

The fact that she had bought a house there, even though it stood empty for much of the time, gave her a status somewhat above that of most visitors, and her easy-going charm had soon blunted what little resentment there had been towards another absentee owner. Most of the resident islanders were aware of her strange abilities but, after some initial curiosity and unease – now years in the past – this too had been accepted and was now unquestioned. The days when a small boy, greatly daring, had confronted her with the words, 'My dad says you're a witch,' were long gone. St Agnes was now, simply and emphatically, home.

That too was only appropriate, because it had been on St Agnes – or rather on the adjoining island of Gugh – that she had first glimpsed her future. She had been ten years old at the time and, in retrospect, the whole episode should have been both shocking and frightening to a child, but in fact it had been neither. It had been wonderful, literally eye-opening, and her only disappointment had been that her aunt, who had been close by, had not been able to share the experience. Her foster mother had treated the whole thing as yet another childish piece of imaginative play-acting, and had soon grown tired of Meredith's insistence that it was all true. That was the first evidence Meredith ever had that her talents would not be welcomed or even recognized by everyone. She was too young and too naive to realize it at the time but, as her understanding grew, that first lesson would remain with her, saving her from many potential embarrassments.

The exact events of that fateful day were hazy now – so much had happened since – but some details and, above all, the marvellous feeling it had engendered were indelibly imprinted on her mind. A holiday away from her aunt's large and rather gloomy house in the Midlands had been a rare and exciting event in itself. This was not because her aunt lacked the necessary funds, but because she disliked travel more and more as she grew older, and so the voyage to somewhere as exotic as the Scillies had been an enormous adventure.

When they arrived, Meredith was immediately enchanted by the islands, but it was only when their party reached St Agnes that the little girl decided she had found paradise. She instantly made a promise to herself that one day she would live on this wild yet peaceful island, where the sea and granite fought their daily battles, where flowers bloomed by the thousand and all manner of seabirds filled the air with their soulful cries. Unlike most similarly wishful ten-year-old vows, this one was destined to be kept – after a fashion.

Meredith had roamed happily all over the small island, exploring every cove and pathway and, inevitably, had crossed over the Bar to Gugh at low tide and found the standing stone known as 'The Old Man of Gugh'. It leant over at a drunken angle, its unworked, lichen-mottled surface looking rough and very old. The stone was surrounded by a circle of grass, where the heather had been worn away by the onslaught of the feet of many visitors, and that only marked it out as even more special. Meredith approached the monolith carefully, watching to make sure it would not topple over, and stretched out a hand to touch the grey stone.

Immediately, the sky became darker, and the shape of the island seemed to change, with the sea appearing much further away. Even the seagulls were quiet. Meredith noted curiously that The Old Man was now standing upright and that there were marks painted on its surface, near where her fingers still rested. She wondered whether she had been responsible for these changes, but could not remember anything happening. It was only then that she saw the people. They were standing as if frozen, staring at the stone. They all seemed very hairy, and were dressed in what looked like sacks. Although the group looked very funny, Meredith knew that it would be rude to laugh. She turned to say hello, but they vanished as she took her hand from the rock. The sky brightened once more, the sea was back where it had been, and the only other person in sight was her aunt, who was walking slowly along the path towards her, leaning on her stick.

Meredith turned back to the stone and quickly put her hand on it again but, to her disappointment, nothing unusual happened. Later she learnt that The Old Man was indeed very old, dating from the Bronze Age, but it was some years before she accepted that she had been sent back into the past, had seen memories stored in the rock long, long ago. By then she also knew that no less than fourteen ley lines passed through the spot where The Old Man stood. At the time, however, she had merely been elated – and also very confused.

Now, eighteen years later, Meredith always made a pilgrimage to the standing stone whenever she returned to St Agnes. She had never again seen a glimpse of the past, and never really understood why she had been granted the first, but she felt, with some justification, that this was indeed her spiritual as well as temporal home.

That childhood vision had been the start of a long road, one that Meredith was travelling still. For a long time she had been constrained by circumstances, but as soon as she was old enough and sufficiently independent to choose her own course in life, the confirmation of all her vague beliefs and hopes had been quick in coming. Her psychic abilities were very real, and she felt strongly that she had been given them for a reason. Although she did not know why she had been chosen by the guides, she understood that she had no choice but to use these precious gifts. To do otherwise would have been to damage her own mental, spiritual and physical health. In fact, after her initial confusion, Meredith was never in any doubt, and willingly learnt all she could, putting her knowledge into practice whenever she could.

Defining her capabilities was difficult; her fields of study all tended to overlap, but her expertise was greatest in three specific areas. The first of these was psychometry, the 'reading' of objects. The Old Man had provided her with the first intriguing taste of this skill, but she could now relay information about the history of almost any object, about the events it had 'witnessed' and the people it had come into contact with, merely by holding it in her hands or touching its surface. Of course it was necessary to restrict her readings to specific targets. If she were to experience the entire history of everything she touched her senses would be completely overwhelmed, and she would either go mad or be unable to register anything coherent. Only very infrequently were the 'memories' of an object so strong that they were revealed without a conscious effort on her part.

Her second psychic career was as a medium. The 'guides' who had enabled her to overcome her early misgivings and helped her choose her own direction, were disembodied voices with whom she could converse either silently or aloud, without awkwardness, and in spite of the fact that they were invisible and, to everyone else, inaudible. They had become her new family, and it was difficult not to think of them as real people – although, in a conventional sense, they were what could only be called spirits. It was they who allowed Meredith to contact other spirits, the voices of the dead. She had accepted the mysterious guides easily enough, but this development had caused her a great deal of heart-searching and doubt, until eventually it too had become part of her normal routine. She used this skill rarely and only for very good reasons; it was a privilege she did not wish to abuse – and besides, the process was exhausting.

These two talents were controversial, of course. If people chose not to believe in her abilities, she could only accept their lack of faith with sadness but understanding. The whole psychic field had been made vastly more complex and dangerous by the inevitable charlatans who preyed

58

upon the gullible and those searching desperately for some reassurance. Scepticism was a healthy trait when kept in fair measure, but the antagonism her work sometimes provoked was horrifying. Through it all, however, Meredith remained convinced in herself. Her visions, her guides and their wisdom were genuine, but she was still glad that her third and main vocation was as a healer. In this field she could produce incontrovertible evidence of her powers, could witness the benefits of her work directly and see it affect the lives of others for the good.

Meredith had no formal medical training and scarcely knew what she did when she touched the hands or forehead of a patient, but her successes, especially in cases where conventional medical science had failed, were all the proof she needed. Here too it was her guides who actually did the work. She merely acted as a conduit for their healing energies, but naturally it was she who saw the end results. Although she garnered the praise and gratitude from both the sick person and their families, she was always quick to credit those who had helped her.

Of course, she did not always succeed. Some diseases had progressed to a stage where even the guides' power could not help, but where Meredith could not heal she could at least alleviate unnecessary suffering and try to make the acceptance of the inevitable easier. Her quiet confidence and gentle sense of humour were important, if less spectacular, tools of her trade.

And it all began here, Meredith thought, as the launch pulled into the sheltered waters of Porth Conger and chugged towards the New Quay. The crossing had been mercifully calm, but she was still glad to have reached solid ground. She was home.

10

'Hello, Mum, it's Meredith. Can you hear me?'

There was no response, though Meredith could sense the other's presence, waiting and listening. She smiled to herself, thinking how ironic it was that this was the one communication her guides could not help her with.

'I just wanted to check that you're all right, Mum. Are you happy?'

The only reply was an inaudible mumbling and a weary sigh.

'Can you hear me?' she repeated. 'Or should I talk to someone else?'

'Is Anya there?' The frail voice sounded old and confused.

'No, she's not here,' Meredith answered patiently. 'I haven't seen her for a long time.'

More silence followed, and she realized that it was hopeless. Even trying to make contact had been a mistake. It did her mother no good and weakened her own resolve.

'I'll say goodbye now, Mum. I'll try again another time. Perhaps you'll feel more like talking then.'

She waited, but there was no answer.

'Bye, Mum.'

Meredith had long since accepted that her life was not her own to organize just as she wished. Stronger forces were at work. *Ananke*, she thought. *That which must be*, then wondered where the knowledge of that strange word had come from. She had no objection to the destiny the Fates had spun for her but, with so many calls upon her time, she was always determined to make the most of the hours she had for herself. In the five days since she had arrived on the Scillies, she had slipped into the slow pace of island life with immense pleasure. Her small house, on the far side of Middle Town from the quay, was a snug haven, filled with things she loved. During her long absences it was cared for by a neighbour, Alice, who kept the tiny garden trim, cleaned occasionally, and made sure that all was secure from the ravages of the weather. She also collected the post and transcribed messages from Meredith's answering machine so that the tape did not run out. The telephone number was known only to a select few, and because her friends were all aware of her almost constant travelling only important messages were left. On this visit there had been nothing that could not wait a few days, though Meredith knew she would have to turn her attention to them soon. In the meantime, she gave herself up to the joys of St Agnes.

The daylight hours were spent walking, reacquainting herself with every inch of her beloved island, from Horse Point in the south to the rocky shoreline near Browarth in the north. She crossed the causeway to Burnt Island and watched the awe-inspiring Atlantic breakers, looked out to the west past the gull colony of Annet and the Western Rocks, whose treacherous waters had wrecked countless vessels, to the distant, lonely Bishop Rock lighthouse. The whole character of the westward view changed with the state of the tide. When it was full, there were only a few isolated rocks to be seen to the south of Annet, but as the ocean receded vast numbers of jagged rocks appeared, like a fleet of dangerous, dark submarines. It was a panorama Meredith never tired of.

She crisscrossed Wingletang Down, with its strange, natural granite sculptures and visited Beady Pool to hunt for treasure. The fact that she had never found any of the beads, from the 300-year-old wreck that had given the cove its name, did not stop her trying again. She visited the maze at Troy Town, walking carefully to the centre and back out again – another oft-repeated ritual, and one which was supposed to bring good luck. She circled Gugh, including her habitual visit to The Old Man, and even paddled from the Bar, the strand of beach between the two islands. The water was cold even in warm weather, and Meredith had no intention of following the example of some younger, hardier visitors who swam in the sheltered bay. She preferred to walk, and she did so every day with an energy that belied her small frame. On her various travels she always tried to keep fit through aerobics or jogging, knowing she worked better when she felt physically strong, but here all she needed was her constant wandering and the elixir of the sea air.

Meredith occasionally stood still long enough to do a little painting. She did not have the talent of her sister, and thought of herself as a copyist rather than an artist. Her favourite subjects were birds, animals and flowers, the natural life of the islands – with an occasional seascape if she was feeling ambitious.

In the evenings, when the day-trippers had left and the island was quiet again, she was welcomed into island society. She renewed many friendships either at home or visiting her neighbours, or spending a convivial evening at the Turk's Head, the quayside pub. Conversation came easily to Meredith, who was equally comfortable with either old or young. Her companions often found themselves talking openly about quite private matters, as if she were one of the family, rather than an occasional, if regular, visitor.

Her appearance made her easy to recognize, even from a distance. She favoured mildly eccentric, occasionally impractical clothes, most of which were in a variety of primal colours – reds, blues or yellows – or a mixture of swirling pastel shades. Closer to, her delicate features, short-cropped dark hair and large, wise brown eyes were equally distinctive. An easy-going temperament, soft voice, and abundant patience and generosity all made her popular with the islanders and visitors alike, and yet her unmarried state and physical attractiveness caused no friction. Over the years Meredith had had several admirers, but they had been kept firmly at a distance – sometimes at great cost to her own feelings –

because she knew that a long-term relationship was impossible for her.

Returning alone from the inn one evening, she walked along the concrete road – the only one on the island – passed through Higher Town and on up towards the disused lighthouse. This structure could be seen from every part of the island, and was still painted white for use as a daymark for shipping. Before reaching the top of the hill she passed the shop whose enterprising owners stocked an incredible variety of goods for both the locals and tourists. Their ancient labrador was on guard outside as usual. He was half asleep, but roused himself when Meredith approached and allowed his ears to be ruffled in passing. Most animals, and not just those as docile as this one, trusted Meredith instinctively.

She continued westward, between the high hedges that protected the flower growers' fields in the central part of the island, and found herself thinking about legends from the Scillies' past. Archaeology had established that they had been inhabited for millennia, and that the present islands were much smaller than those of earlier times. It was possible that they had once been connected to Land's End in Cornwall some twenty-eight miles to the east, but the mythology went much further. The Scillies, or so the legends said, were the last remnants of the lost land of Lyonesse – which itself might have been part of the fabled continent of Atlantis. One hundred and forty villages and their churches were supposed to lie beneath the sea between the islands and the mainland, and in certain places walls, buildings and even forests could be seen underwater. Conventional historians attributed such myth-making to the accumulated folk memory of several floods and the gradual rise in sea level over many centuries, but Meredith liked to believe in some of the fanciful tales. She loved the idea that the Scillies were the last resting place of King Arthur and his surviving knights, saved from Mordred's deadly pursuit by Merlin's calling upon the ocean to rise against the true king's enemies. She also wanted to believe that the Scillies were the Hesperides of ancient Greek mythology, the Isles of the Blest, where dead heroes rested in immortal peace and the

63

abundance of perpetual summer. These ideas were, of course, completely unprovable, and held as ridiculous by modern theorists – but Meredith knew that the granite memories of the islands held more than anyone could ever substantiate. Her feelings, her special sensitivities, enabled her to accept a world where science and mythology could coexist in perfect harmony. But of course, not all legends are pleasant.

That night she dreamt of earthquakes, tidal waves and volcanoes, and awoke with an uncomfortable sense of foreboding. She knew it was time to leave.

The messages and invitations had piled up and, with some reluctance, Meredith went through them, made several phone calls and set her life in motion again. Her idyll was over, and she felt a quickening of her spirit as she anticipated returning to her neglected vocation. She would leave tomorrow, getting the launch back to St Mary's and then taking the light aircraft to the mainland. Today would be spent saying farewell to her island. In the course of an afternoon it was easy enough to walk the entire coastline of St Agnes and Gugh, and Meredith did just that, revisiting all her favourite haunts and savouring the glorious views and the untainted, salty air.

It was an exhilarating day, the sky clear but with a strong, biting westerly wind and, after her time on the island, Meredith felt buoyed up and ready to work again. Only one incident kept that final day from being perfect. She was on Gugh in mid afternoon, its bleak landscape made more welcoming by the warm sunlight, when she spotted a small tree, almost bent double by the prevailing winds. She could not recall ever noticing it before – trees were a rarity here – and yet she found herself staring at its twisted shape, half thinking that she recognized it from somewhere. Then, without seeing the connection or even registering the odd jump in her thought processes, she began to worry about Anya. Something was happening to her sister. Something bad. But how could she help?

And then the feeling evaporated as fast as it had come, and Meredith told herself not to be silly. Her twin was quite capable of looking after herself.

11

Luke could sense the difference in the house even as he turned the key in the front door, but the apparition that greeted him inside nonetheless took him by surprise. He hardly had time to shut the door behind him when a giant black bat erupted from the sitting room and flew down the hall towards him. It could have been a scene from a low-budget horror movie but for Anya's beautiful, joyous face at the centre of the dark whirlwind. Her oversize tunic flapping, she leapt into his arms and he caught her, laughing. She was back.

Luke held her as she hugged him fiercely, her arms and legs wrapped around his neck and waist. Her small body shook gently and he smiled, thinking she was laughing, but when he finally set her down and pulled back so that he could see her face, he was surprised to see it wet with tears.

'What is it? What's the matter?'

'I was so afraid you wouldn't be here,' she replied, wiping her eyes and sniffing. 'I couldn't even go upstairs to see if your clothes were still there.'

'They're still there,' he told her gently. 'I'm still here.' She had always been glad to see him on her return, but had never before shown this intensity of emotion. Luke kissed her, wondering what the outburst meant.

'I need you,' Anya whispered. 'You're the only stable thing or strength in my entire life. I couldn't bear it if . . .' She held him even tighter, burying her face in his chest.

'I'm here,' he repeated, torn between concern and happiness. 'And I'm filthy. I've been wading in a swamp with twenty overkeen volunteers for most of the day. You're going to get covered in mud.'

'Don't care,' she mumbled defiantly, then looked up and smiled as Luke fished out a handkerchief. She took it gladly. 'I'm sorry,' she said as she dried her face. 'It's just that . . .'

'There's no need to explain. I know how it feels.'

Anya looked at him, then nodded, lowered her gaze and blew her nose loudly. Luke stared at her, knowing that he did not understand her – perhaps he never would – but knowing too that he loved her beyond measure. She inspired in him feelings that would have seemed contradictory before they met – possessiveness and protectiveness, lust and tenderness – but which seemed perfectly complementary now. Even in her current dishevelled state, she was so beautiful, so alive, so full of mystery. She had been gone just over a month, less than on many previous occasions, but to Luke it had seemed like a lifetime. And yet, now that the waiting was over, now that she was here again, he had already forgiven her. He was simply happy, even though he was sufficiently self-aware to know that by such a reaction he was once again fitting into *her* pattern, the cycle she dictated. It was his turn not to care.

'I love you,' he said softly, and was rewarded as she turned her huge, shining brown eyes up to look at him.

'I love you too.'

Luke saw for the first time that her face was tanned, but bit down the inevitable questions.

'It's wonderful to have you back,' he told her, then grinned. 'But I really do have to take a shower.'

Anya let go reluctantly and Luke kicked off his boots, shed his jacket and ran upstairs to the bathroom. Throwing the rest of his clothes on to the floor, he stepped into the shower and began to wash away the layers of sweat and grime. A couple of minutes later, the shower's frosted glass door opened, and Anya slipped in beside him. It was quite crowded in there, but neither of them seemed to mind.

Just before they fell asleep that night, Luke gently kissed Anya's forehead, nose, neck and lips, and then released her from his embrace.

'I'm glad you're home,' he said in a voice full of weary contentment.

Home? Anya thought. *Is that where I am?* This, she supposed, was as close as she would ever get, but the word 'home' had not had any real meaning for her since she was a very small child. It was a sad thought, but she refused to let it spoil the comfort of this night.

Unusually, it was Anya who woke first the next morning. She left Luke asleep, watching him as she dressed quietly, and feeling an immense tenderness and gratitude towards her lover. He had asked no questions, done nothing to remind her that their reunion, however sweet, was only necessary because of the separation that had preceded it, a separation of her making. As luck would have it, today was Luke's day off, so he was able to have a lie-in. In spite of their tiredness – Luke's from long days filled with hard work and little else, Anya's from travelling – they had spent most of the night celebrating their renewed devotion, satisfying all their immediate physical and emotional needs. For now, she was happy to leave him to rest, knowing they had the whole day ahead of them, and many more beyond that.

She crept out of the bedroom and began to renew her acquaintance with the house. Her studio was the first room she visited, and it struck her as unnaturally empty, altogether too tidy. She was glad that the last batch of pictures were gone, and wondered briefly what Sheila had made of them, but knew she would have to begin filling the space again soon. She regretted the fact that she had had to leave her latest creations in Greece.

Outside the windows the resident house martins were performing their swirling aerial ballet and their rapid, swooping movement was almost hypnotically graceful. Anya watched them for a while, but knew that she would never try to capture such wild elegance on canvas. Her work came from her inner world, not the one around her. That this should sometimes make her paintings uncomfortable or even frightening seemed only natural to her. It had always been like that.

67

As Anya turned to leave, she was brought up short by the sight of the posters and cards on her notice board. She froze, her eyes darting back and forth between two in particular, not wanting to remember but unable to suppress the memories. She tore her gaze away at last, and left the room, closing the door firmly behind her.

She wandered aimlessly downstairs, through the kitchen, utility room and pantry, the seldom-used dining room, then walked the length of the hall twice before settling in the sitting room. There she noticed something that had escaped her attention the previous evening. A half-completed game of Scrabble was laid out on a small corner table. As she glanced at it, one word seemed to jump out at her. MALADY. That too prompted an unwelcome memory, that of the ramblings of a talkative old woman, but this time Anya was determined to do something about it. There could be no harm in checking.

A quick search among the bookshelves soon produced the *Concise Medical Dictionary*. *Every hypochondriac should have one*, she thought, trying to deflect her unease as she skipped through the pages, found the entry and began to read.

'Petit mal; brief spells of unconsciousness, lasting 5–15 seconds, in which posture and balance are maintained, the eyes stare, the mouth twitches and the head nods slightly.'

What, no drooling or foaming at the mouth? Anya wondered, making an effort to convince herself that she was not taking this seriously.

'The electroencephalogram, in attacks only, shows spike/wave complexes (three per second).'

Whatever that means.

'Attacks are easily evoked by voluntary overbreathing (a useful diagnostic test) or after sudden emotion or fright. As the stream of thought is completely interrupted, children with frequent petit mal may have learning difficulties. The attacks begin at any age after 5 years (seldom before).

'Drug treatment (often with *ethosuximide or *diazepam) is usually very effective. Petit mal subjects are potentially epileptic; unless given a prophylactic *anticonvulsant they will have a *grand mal seizure sooner or later.'

There the entry finished. There was no mention of hallucinations or visions, of associated delusions or mental illness, nothing about perceived distortions of time. What was described was frightening enough, especially the part about the inevitable progression to full-blown epilepsy, but surely it could not explain what had been happening to her. Anya had no idea what she looked like during the attacks – she only had the old woman's word for that – but some of the symptoms seemed to correspond. The external time scale was about right; her stream of thought was certainly interrupted – *more* than interrupted – and the onset was clearly linked to sudden emotion or fright. And yet surely it could not be that simple.

'Well, there's an easy way to find out,' she said aloud, wondering how to 'voluntarily overbreathe' with Luke nearby to help if necessary but without alarming him.

She pushed the thought to the back of her mind and, in a mood of fatalistic masochism, looked up the indicated cross-references. Diazepam, she discovered, was more commonly known as Valium, and the side effects of ethosuximide sounded even less attractive. The description of a 'grand mal', a major epileptic fit, was horrifying, but bore no relation to what she had experienced. The whole exercise left her feeling vaguely nauseated, and had done nothing to reassure her. The spectre of her mother still hung over her like a poisonous genetic curse. She had not been an epileptic. She had been mad.

A small sound behind her made Anya jump, and she quickly shoved the book back on the shelf before turning round to see Luke, in a dressing gown, standing in the doorway. He yawned massively, then grinned.

'Why aren't you worn out too?' he asked accusingly. 'I feel as if I could sleep for a week.'

'Women have more stamina than men,' she replied, smiling in spite of her wildly thumping heart. 'It's a proven medical fact.'

'Really? We'll have to put that to the test later. What are you doing?'

'Just checking up on you,' Anya replied archly, pointing at the Scrabble board. 'Who've you been playing with?'

'What's it worth?' he asked mischievously.

'It? Two points, unless it's on a double word score.'

'Very clever,' he remarked. 'As it happens, I've been playing with myself. No comments please. It's just like do-it-yourself crosswords, really.'

'So, no intimate evenings with your lady friends then?' Anya teased. She was playing with fire and she knew it, but she had been so rattled by what she had read and by his unexpected interruption that she was grasping at anything that might distract him.

'Serve you right if I had, you little witch,' he said as he approached her. 'But it's your spell I'm under, no one else's.'

He took her in his arms and kissed her, but she could not respond as she would have liked. The word 'witch' had chilled her, summoning up even earlier memories, unbidden and unwanted. However, Luke did not seem to notice her preoccupation.

'Have you had breakfast?' he asked.

Anya shook her head, clinging to him, her thoughts elsewhere.

'Want some coffee?' he added.

But Anya was not listening.

12

Anya was clinging on for dear life. Her feet scrabbled help-lessly against sheer rock, and she knew she must not look down. Both her arms were hooked round the bare branch of a half-dead tree, which itself leaned out precariously over the edge of the cliff. Far below, the blue sea was a distant echoing whisper.

The tree roots shifted and a few pebbles rattled away and plunged into the abyss. Anya could hardly breathe. She was too frightened to scream, and hunted desperately for some purchase, some way of reaching the safety of the cliff top that was only a few tantalizing feet away. But there was nothing to help her, and every movement threatened disaster. She knew with a horrible certainty that, sooner or later, she was going to fall. Either the strength in her arms would give out or the frail tree would be uprooted.

Help me!

Allessandro appeared on top of the cliff, looking down at her impassively, and Anya was so terrified that she was glad to see even his dreaded face.

'You see how it is when you anger me?' he said.

Anya was too surprised to respond, her intended plea for help cut short by his words. How had she angered him?

'The irony of it did not escape my notice,' the sorcerer went on coldly, ignoring her wide-eyed bewilderment. 'You turned your weakness into strength, barred my way by locking the very door that had allowed me to enter in the first place. You made me start again, wasting my time, but I hold all the keys, Constanza. You cannot shut me out for long, and I have all the time I need.'

'Help me,' she gasped. His words had made no sense, and her immediate peril overrode any attempt at understanding. She was dizzy with fear, and could feel her grip on the branch slipping.

'So now you want my help,' he observed sarcastically. 'How touching.'

'I'd be no use to you dead,' she sobbed, prompted by an inexplicable flash of insight.

His black eyes narrowed dangerously.

'There is more than one form of death,' he stated. 'Don't think to bargain with me. I can choose your path. I can pull you to safety or let you fall.' By way of illustrating the point he kicked the bole of the tree, which shifted and creaked. Anya screamed as more fragments of earth cascaded past her face and were swallowed by the void.

'Please,' she begged hoarsely.

'Such aid must be earned,' he went on, impervious to her terror. 'You must learn to trust me, to welcome me. I am your true lover now, not that poor beast you were coupling with.' His angular face crumpled with evident distaste. 'You should have no time for such primitive sensations now that I am with you, don't you agree?'

Anya recalled her earlier cry – *I am not your lover!* – but in her present predicament was willing to say anything, deny nothing.

'Yes,' she whispered. 'Yes, yes.'

'Speak up, mia cara. Tell me who your true lover is.'

'You are,' she grated, while trying unsuccessfully to suppress her vitriolic thoughts.

Allessandro laughed. 'Such invective from one so sweet,' he exclaimed, mocking her. 'But you have shown willing at least. Take my hand.'

He reached forward, but only so far. To grasp the proffered hand Anya would have to release her grip on the branch and lunge sideways, leaving her totally at his mercy. There would be no way back, no second chance. Her fearful hesitation made him laugh again.

'You must learn to trust me,' he repeated, and did not move any closer.

Anya tensed herself and then, using the last of her failing strength, flung herself towards him. He did not betray her. He caught her hand in a firm grip, waited for an endless moment, then drew her slowly, carefully, up on to solid ground. For some reason Anya had expected the touch of his hand to burn like ice or acid, but it was warm, dry and strong – and she found herself surprisingly reluctant to let go. As he released her, her legs gave way and she sat down with a bump, then edged backwards, away from the precipice. When she felt safe, she closed her eyes and listened to the sound of her heart thumping. Everything else was so quiet for so long that she wondered if he had gone, but when she at last opened her eyes he was standing with his back to her, gazing out over the vertiginous panorama. For a brief instant it occurred to Anya that she could rid herself of her tormentor. One push and . . . But she realized immediately that this was impossible. Her head was still reeling and her body so weak with relief that she doubted whether she could stand up, let alone commit murder.

'The Vierwaldstatter See,' he said unexpectedly. 'Beautiful, isn't it? It's good to see the Alps again.' For a few moments he sounded almost human, but then he turned to face her and the rapacious glint was back in his dark eyes.

'I had not realized you were familiar with the Aradia,' he remarked. 'You hide some of your secrets well, but they will all be mine sooner or later.'

'I don't know what you're talking about,' Anya replied, genuinely puzzled, but stung by his complacency.

'La vecchia religione,' he explained, rolling his tongue around the words with evident pleasure. 'The old religion.' When she still showed no signs of comprehension, he added, 'Witchcraft. Aradia is the Gospel of the Witches.'

'I want nothing to do with witchcraft,' Anya cried, the denial an automatic reflex.

'Don't you?' he asked curiously. 'It must hold some fascination for you, surely. After all, your mother —'

'Leave her out of this!' she shouted.

'My, my, aren't we touchy,' he remarked scornfully. 'Very well, we shall leave the topic for another time. It always seemed so limited to me anyway. All that emphasis on reproduction and fertility is so unnecessary. Common humanity has bred like rabbits without any outside help, and magic can – and should – be used for so much more.'

Anya was feeling distinctly uncomfortable at this turn of the conversation. And she hated the fact that she could obviously hide little from him. Not even her thoughts were private, it seemed, and the enforced intimacy made her feel very uneasy. She was almost glad when Allessandro continued talking, giving her the benefit of one of his self-satisfied lectures. Relieved of the need to speak or even think, she merely listened at first but then, as the subject matter became clearer, she found herself paying rapt attention.

'I've been wondering what it was like for you to see me again,' he began, 'to be present at my rebirth. After countless dull stares and witless gawpers, here at last was one capable of seeing, of understanding. I doubt whether you know how truly remarkable you are, mia carina.'

The compliment and the endearment made Anya want to cringe, but she held herself aloof as best she could. He was obviously talking about the painting.

'Andrea wanted so much to be a peacock,' he went on, smiling with a mixture of derision and nostalgia, 'but he was too graceless for that. And could there ever be a more pointless creature than a dowdy peacock?'

'Andrea del Sarto?' Anya asked, as curiosity overcame her resolve to remain silent.

'Andrea d'Agnolo,' he corrected her. 'He was called del Sarto because his father was a tailor, a common tradesman. I don't think Andrea ever forgave him for that, although his garments were among the finest in Florence. The son of a tailor dresses well, they say, although on Andrea even the finest robes hung like rags. But he played the part as best

74

he could, was seen with the right people, worked hard at his schooling, his apprenticeships. He even went to France for a year or so, but the competition at François' court was too fierce, so he came running home like a whipped dog. Lucky for him, really. War was coming between France and Rome. Perhaps even Andrea had been able to foresee that. By then, of course, he was like all the rest, painting religious nonsense to salve the pious consciences of rich men, prostituting his talent with endless Madonnas and a few portraits whose vain subjects could find no one better.'

'But his portrait of you was brilliant,' Anya protested.

'Yes, but that was done for love, not money,' he replied promptly. 'Constanza beguiled him into it, and once the bargain was struck he had no way out. I saw to that. And his was not the only hand at work.' He paused significantly, clearly waiting for her to prompt him further, but Anya bit her tongue and remained silent. Allessandro would have to sing his own praises alone.

'Andrea painted the portrait,' he went on eventually, 'but I was the one who imbued his work with my power, my spirit. Oh, he was pretty with his brushes, could see the shift of light, the nuances of form and texture, but so did many an artisan. Do you really believe that his two-dimensional likeness would have lasted so, would have been prized all these long centuries if *I* had not infused it with substance, with *life*? Without me it would have been the mere scrapings of oil on linen.'

Anya had neither the strength nor the inclination to argue. To the best of her knowledge she had never seen any other work by Andrea d'Agnolo – whose double-A monogram now made sense – but if she had, it had certainly not had the same immediate effect. But if what Allessandro was saying was true, it only made the whole thing more mysterious. Questions filled her brain. How – and why – had he done such a thing? What did this have to do with his having been trapped by Constanza, whose mantle she had apparently inherited? And why had *she* been the only one to be able to see that special quality in the painting nearly five hundred years later? However, the sorcerer obviously had no intention

75

of providing her with any answers just yet. His oration was in full flow, his gaze focused on some distant point in space and time.

'Andrea was weak. To this day I don't know whether he left the pages of my book blank through fear or ignorance. Did he sense some hidden danger in the alchemical text? Did he fear being burned as a heretic if he even copied the words from afar? Or could he make neither head nor tail of it all and was merely ashamed of his illiteracy? Either way, it was evidence of a small mind, limited and dull.

'Constanza laughed at him when he put his mark on the painting, and she joked with me about how we could improve upon his artifice by means of our own. Andrea had enough pride to be angered by that – which only made the joke funnier of course. He grew abusive then, so much so that I felt obliged to prove our point. Oh, Constanza was *very* clever. She even made me think it was my own idea.

'I was used to travelling without the need for movement, of course. Everyone with any talent then was.' He paused, thinking. 'Your prosaic time calls the process an out-of-the-body experience, I believe. The mind is not meant to be tied to our physical reality. It is only the pitiful narrowness of most men's vision that leads them to assume so. I simply placed myself *within* the painting, made it live from inside. Nothing could have been easier, and the look on poor Andrea's face when he saw the difference it made to his commonplace handiwork was worth a hundred times the effort.'

'But something went wrong,' Anya put in. 'Constanza trapped you.'

The black eyes snapped back into focus, and he glared at her as if he had forgotten the existence of his audience and resented the interruption. But then he smiled.

'Yes. I can admit that now. She bound me, entwined me in a spell of my own invention, preventing me from returning to my own body.'

'Why did she do it?'

'Power, of course. What else? She thought that my trapped spirit would be hers to command, my talent added to hers. It

76

was never so – I am too clever for that, at least – and it annoyed her greatly. I expected her to release me when she realized her error, but she chose not to, whether through fear of retribution or from pique I do not know. I would have forgiven her, but she never gave me the chance – and that is itself unforgivable. My body died, as flesh must eventually, and Constanza made Andrea forget that I was still alive in the portrait. She kept the picture, and I watched her grow old and hateful, until she died a wretched and embittered hag. Even then I was not free, however. For that I needed someone else.'

'Me?' Anya said in a small voice.

'You, my dear,' he confirmed. 'Everything else is beside the point now. Andrea and Constanza are long gone. You are here. I waited for your coming for so many, many stale years. Can you believe that some imbeciles even once thought the painting was Andrea's self-portrait? The man had a face like a bulbous ape! I have had to tolerate so much idiocy, as well as the dreadful tedium, but all the time I was looking for that one elusive, unquenchable spark. And I found it in you. It was like walking through an unlocked door after thinking it had been barred for ever. You were the key, the perfect key, and my long wait was over. How fitting it is that you are also an artist.' He stretched out both slim hands as if offering to help her to her feet. 'Come, Anya,' he said softly. 'I will carry all your burdens now.'

Slowly, and without fully realizing what she was doing, Anya raised her arms in response and let him take her hands in his own.

13

'What?'

'I asked if you wanted some coffee,' Luke repeated patiently.
Something in her tone made him feel uneasy. He loosened her
grip, which had become almost painfully tight, and moved
back to look at her, holding her shoulders gently. 'Are you
OK? You're a bit pale,' he said, his concern growing. All her
recently acquired colour seemed to have drained from her
face. 'Are you ill?'

'No.' Her attempt at a smile was patently unconvincing.

'Are you sure?'

Anya did not answer, her thoughts in disarray. She did not
understand what was happening to her, but was terribly afraid
she knew *why*. Her mother's legacy still haunted her. All her
life Anya had fought against becoming her own mother, had
been willing to do anything to dissociate herself from that
malign influence. And yet, of all the phobias induced by her
childhood, the greatest of all was the one it seemed she could
not fight. There was no way to defend herself from the enemy
within.

'Tell me what's wrong,' Luke pleaded.

Anya was still shocked by what had happened, but as she
looked into his worried face, her mind was beginning to
recover. Why had it happened now, here? This was where
she was supposed to be safe, in control – as much as she ever
was. And surely what she had just learnt was a vindication, an
alternative to what she had always feared. Yet how could she
tell anyone that she was *possessed*? It was ridiculous, absurd.

Mad. She did not live in sixteenth-century Italy or the Spain of Torquemada, but in England in the 1990s. Such a theory would explain so much, but could not be voiced aloud. Even if it were true, it was bound to be misinterpreted – and she would be back with the other explanation. No one would believe her – and in the eyes of the world she would have become as mad as her mother. Even Luke, poor, long-suffering Luke, could not fight this battle for her.

'Anya, talk to me,' he begged, unnerved by her continued silence. 'What's wrong?'

'Do you think I'm ill?' she whispered eventually.

'I don't know,' he groaned. 'You hurt sometimes, that's obvious. You haven't ever come to terms with your past, and you keep having to go away . . .'

'So you *do* think I'm ill?'

'Sometimes I think you might need help,' he admitted nervously. 'Your paintings —'

'Are just paintings,' Anya snapped. As she stared at him, her fear and bewilderment turned to anger. It was a familiar process and one she took no pleasure in, but she was unable to halt its progress. She needed Luke to reassure her that she was sane, that everything would be all right. She did not need this.

'Poor little Anya is sick!' she exclaimed. 'Oh, that would be convenient, wouldn't it? Such a facile way of explaining away all my faults, my eccentricities.' She felt their newly regained harmony evaporating as she lashed out blindly, and hated herself. But she couldn't stop. 'Well, it's not that easy.'

'Whoever said it was easy?' Luke muttered, stunned and hurt by her sudden fury when he had only been trying to help.

'God. Sometimes I wish I *was* just ill,' she sighed, ignoring his comment.

'What?'

'Don't you ever feel like that?' she asked, suddenly weary. 'Wouldn't it be nice just to go to your bed, submit to some creeping malaise, a virus or infection sucking all the needs

79

out of you, all the wants – all the things that make life so unbearably heavy? Just to lie there, warm and helpless . . .'

'Abdicating responsibility,' Luke cut in, thinking with some resentment that this would be typical of her.

'Exactly!' Anya cried triumphantly. 'What could be more blissful?'

'This is ridiculous,' he said, exasperated. 'You're always miserable when you're ill, you know you are.'

'Oh, so I'm *not* ill now?' Anya raised her eyebrows questioningly, baiting him.

As the pause stretched, she watched the changing emotions on his open face.

'No,' he admitted finally, with a tentative smile. 'You're just being you.'

Anya grinned back. She had won a Pyrrhic victory, deflected his well-meaning concern with shameful ease. He did not deserve to be treated so, but she had no choice.

'Well, are you going to make that coffee?' she enquired tartly. 'Or do I have to do everything around here?'

'Do I really have to do this?' Anya asked plaintively.

'Yes. Why ever not?' Sheila replied. 'There's plenty of time. The deadline isn't for four months.'

'That's not the point.'

'What is, then? You're very good at this sort of thing. Paul was delighted with "Moonrider". It's only natural that he'd want you to do the sequel.'

'I can do it, but commissions like this are so restrictive,' Anya complained. 'I can't do myself justice. It's like asking Linford Christie to run the hundred metres in Wellington boots.'

Sheila laughed as she pictured the scene.

'Well, if you won't do it to satisfy your artistic ambitions, how about for the money? I can probably get them to pay a bit more.'

'I don't need the money. You know that.'

'Well, I do!' her agent responded. 'Ten per cent of nothing won't even feed the cat.'

'You paint it then,' Anya suggested truculently.

'Now you're being silly, dear,' Sheila remarked, adopting the tones of a long-suffering schoolmistress. 'Look, I may be a worthless parasite and an interfering old bag to boot . . .'

'You're not that old,' Anya said, grinning.

'. . . but my knowledge of elementary psychology tells me,' the agent went on, pointedly ignoring the interruption, 'that your self-esteem will suffer if you don't earn any quantifiable rewards from your work. And your last few paintings . . .'

'Don't you start. I paint what I want. If you or Luke or anyone else doesn't like the results, that's no concern of mine.'

'I'm not asking you to stop following your muse, but what's wrong with doing a little commercial work as well? It's not as though you're tied to a strict brief. You can read the typescript and come up with your own ideas.'

'Oh, all right.' Anya glanced at the thick folder that lay between them on the kitchen table. 'Is the book any good?'

'How would I know?' Sheila replied. 'I'm only a money-minded Philistine. You're the one with the soul of an artist. Besides, I haven't read it.'

'Great,' Anya muttered.

'All I know is that it's another fantasy. Right up your street, as I said to Paul.'

'You've already told him I'd do it, haven't you?'

The accusation rolled off the older woman like water off a duck's back.

'How could you even think such a thing?' she asked, all offended innocence. 'If I weren't such a resilient character I'd be mortally hurt.'

They grinned at each other in mutual understanding.

'Want some more tea?'

'No thanks.' Sheila glanced at her watch. 'I should be going.'

They got up, and Anya followed her agent into the hall.

'Give my love to that gorgeous man of yours.'

'He's not mine, any more than I'm his,' Anya retorted. 'People don't possess each other, you know.'

81

'Ah, the idealism of youth,' Sheila said wistfully. 'If he's not yours, could I borrow him for a bit?'

'No.'

'Worth a try,' the agent said with a shrug.

'Sheila?'

'Yes.'

'Do you know any witches?'

'Several,' she replied promptly.

'I'm serious. Real witches.'

'What?' Sheila hesitated. 'Charm warts, cure snakebite, that sort of thing? You can't want a love potion, surely. Luke's already daft about you.' She grinned. 'There's no accounting for taste.'

'Actually, I'm looking for someone to put a curse on you,' Anya said, 'but you're not supposed to know about it.'

'Oh well, in that case . . .' Her agent paused to think. 'My mother used to swear by one old dear, but she may be dead by now. I'll make enquiries, if you're really serious . . .'

'I am.'

'Am I allowed to ask why?'

'Just curiosity. I've been doing some reading on the subject, and it made me want to know more.'

'OK.' Sheila recognized the signs, and knew that she would get nothing more out of Anya.

'Don't mention this to Luke. He thinks I'm weird enough already.'

After Sheila had left, Anya went back up to her studio to look at the two paintings begun since her return to Devon. She had been back a week now and, on the surface at least, life was normal again – at least as normal as it could ever be in their household. She and Luke had resumed their volatile but generally loving relationship; they had both gone back to work; and Sheila was reassuringly the same as ever. Best of all, there had been no further sign of Allessandro, no excursions into unreal landscapes. Anya had even tried voluntary overbreathing, but that had only produced a spell of dizziness and momentary nausea.

As the days passed, she tried to convince herself that the

horrors were all over, that there would be no more of the illusory attacks now that she supposedly knew their origin. But she tried in vain. Hope as she might, she could not accept the idea that the sorcerer had left her for good. She was left waiting, trying to work out some way of counteracting his insidious infiltration of her life.

The idea of witchcraft had been suggested by Allessandro himself. Anya had overcome her instinctive revulsion and, as she had told Sheila, had done a little research. What she had discovered was enough to sustain her curiosity. The book the sorcerer had mentioned, *Aradia*, had been translated from the Italian by an anthropologist named Charles Leland and published in 1899, but she had no idea how to get hold of a copy, even supposing she wanted to. She very much doubted that it would be stocked by her local library.

The sources she did have at her disposal informed her that witchcraft had been tolerated and even respected everywhere until the thirteenth century, when the 'witch craze' had started at the same time as the Black Death. Over the next four hundred years, hundreds of thousands of women had been tortured and burnt all over Europe. Witchcraft had carried the death penalty in England until 1736, and the practice of throwing suspects into ponds to see whether they would float – and were thus guilty – continued almost into the following century. It was only in 1951 that the law forbidding witchcraft had finally been repealed.

Some of the less orthodox scholars equated witchcraft with an ancient fertility religion and the worship of Diana and Mother Earth, others with the horned god Pan, who later metamorphosed into the Christian Devil – but whatever its origins, there was evidence to suggest that some sort of primitive magic did indeed work. Apart from curing warts, ringworm, bleeding and the like, witches were reputed to be able to cause storms and shipwrecks and, of course, to put people under malign curses. This last was called 'overlooking' someone, and was apparently done with the use of witches' bottles. These were usually of green glass, corked and buried upside down at a significant site – under a house, below a crossing point of paths, and so on. Handmade pins were often found driven through the cork and inside the bottle, together with blackthorns and evil-smelling liquids. This obscure set of images had inspired one of Anya's new paintings, although her interpretation was, as usual, imaginative rather than literal. Looking at it now, she wondered whether such a malignant container lay beneath her own house. The idea seemed ridiculous, but perhaps no more ludicrous than several she had contemplated recently. And if a witch could place a curse on someone, wasn't it reasonable to suppose that she could also remove one, whatever its source? But how could any country wise woman even hope to match Allessandro's powers? He was so strong, so . . .

Anya caught herself up and tried to push all such thoughts from her mind, deliberately turning her attention to the other half-completed picture. This was a variation on 'Beneath the Flames', with the proportions altered and the design more complex. But the imagery could not hold her. The past was calling again, insisting on being heard.

About a month before their fourth birthday, the twins had been sitting on Meredith's bed, dressed only in identical pink panties and conversing in whispers. They spoke in their own secret language, the one they used when they either did not want anyone else to understand or, as now, just for the pleasure of it. The sounds of impatient movement came from an adjoining room, as cupboard doors slammed and drawers were wrenched open and shut. Obeying their mother's strict instructions the girls kept quite still, waiting for her to return with their clothes. This was a daily ritual, but one which acquired greater significance on Sundays when the whole family went to church and they all had to look their best.

Eventually their mother returned, and the twins fell silent. The clothes she chose for them were always in pretty flower colours – rose pink, primrose or lilac – which she declared to be 'feminine'. Their Sunday outfits were decorated with frills and bows, and always seemed to consist of several layers, even on the hottest days. As they allowed themselves to be dressed, they thought of the singing in church and giggled together. Grown-ups were so silly when they sang, and they all appeared to take it so seriously.

'Are we going in the car?' Meredith asked. The car was a recent acquisition, and was thus still a novelty for the girls. It was old and very big, with a back seat wide and deep enough for them to roll around and fight if they wanted to. They wouldn't do that today, of course, because it was Sunday, but they still looked forward to the drive and to emerging from their impressive carriage in front of the other children at church.

'No. We're walking. It's a lovely day and it's not far.'

'It's miles,' Meredith objected.

'We're walking,' their mother said firmly. 'That's why we have to hurry.'

'Can we call in at Mrs Wellie on the way?' Meredith asked.

'Her name is Mrs Wellington,' her mother rebuked her sternly, 'and no, we can't. I'm sure she doesn't want to be bothered with silly little girls.'

'She's a witch,' Meredith announced, as always the more forthright of the twins.

'No she isn't! That's a wicked thing to say. There are no such things as witches.'

'She has a black cat,' Anya offered as evidence.

'And she charms warty things,' Meredith added. 'Yuck!' The girls giggled together, but were silenced when they saw their mother's expression.

'Witchcraft is a sin,' she told them angrily. 'It says so in the Bible. And you know what the wages of sin are, don't you?'

The twins nodded solemnly, eyes wide.

'And the Bible also says "Thou shalt not suffer a witch to live",' their mother went on, 'so Mrs Wellington can't be one, can she?'

'Otherwise we'd have to kill her,' Meredith concluded brightly.

'Of course not.'

'But—'

'Be quiet, Meredith! Witches will burn in the fires of hell, like all sinners – and I don't want to hear any more on the subject. You are *not* to talk to Mrs Wellington, do you understand?'

The girls nodded in unison. Their mother looked them over, then glanced at her watch.

'You'll have to do. Come on, quickly.'

They trooped downstairs, a pretty, delicate procession, where they were met by their father. He was waiting, silent and impatient as always, in his uncomfortable new suit and tie. He looked pale, tired and irritable and smiled only briefly when Meredith did a twirl to show off her petticoats.

Two months later he would leave them for good, and their mother's world – which, unknown to the twins, was already falling apart – would disintegrate completely.

For a brief, uncomfortable moment Anya actually felt a pang of pity for her mother. The woman had been a monster, but no one could say how much of that had been her own nature and how much the result of circumstances. Already saddled with a cold, increasingly alienated husband, the arrival and infancy of two intelligent, lively and rebellious girls was too much for her. In those faraway days the twins had been close, their relationship bordering on the telepathic, although Meredith had always been the undisputed leader. But in spite of their closeness, they often fought each other with blind ferocity. It was only when they were threatened by a common enemy that they worked together as a formidable team. They had driven their mother to distraction, both by their almost constant quarrelling and by their equally irritating unity at other times. Although it could never excuse the way she had treated them – nothing could do that – it might go a little way towards explaining it.

Anya shook her head as if to clear away the cobwebs of memory, took one last glance at her paintings and went downstairs again. Another Biblical quotation, this time from the Book of Samuel, popped into her mind. *Behold, to obey is better than sacrifice, and to hearken than the fat of rams. For rebellion is as the sin of witchcraft, and stubbornness is as iniquity and idolatry*. As always, the daunting words were spoken in her mind by her mother's voice, but at least now their message could be considered and rejected if necessary. As a child this, and all the other religious dogma constantly rammed down their throats, had been merely incomprehensible and frightening.

In the kitchen, Anya picked up the typescript, deciding to fight words with words. Taking it into the sitting room, she noticed that Luke had left her another message on the Scrabble board. This was the latest of a series that had begun soon after her homecoming. The game had been left out, and one morning she had spotted the first of what was to become an extended conversation. Luke had laid out I AM UNDER YOUR SPELL, and when Anya had replied with MY SPELL IS BETTER THAN MY SPELING, the process was underway.

Neither of them spoke about what they were doing, as a matter of honour, making sure that they moved the letters when the other was not around. This did not happen on a regular basis, but only when they felt like it. Luke's next effort had been STAMINA TESTING TONIGHT, to which Anya had responded IF YOURE SURE YOURE UP TO IT. After that there had been a long wait before Luke set up FILL IN THE ——, using one of the blank squares to complete the instruction. Below was ANYA WOULD LIKE ☐☐☐ FOR HER BIRTDAY. Unable to resist the temptation she replaced this with WHAT IS A BIRTDAY QUESTION MARK. His rejoinder had been in two parts; BIRTHDAY SMARTASS and ONLY TWO HS AVAILABLE. Anya's birthday was then only a few days away and she answered his original request with her next message; SURPRISE ME EXCLAMATION POINT. Three days had passed since then, and the latest missive now lay before her, again in two parts; SURPRISE ARRANGED and WHY PUNCTUATION FETISH.

Anya was intrigued by the thought of a surprise, but was happy to wait for that without further comment. Instead she replied to the second half with JUST TELL ME WHAT FETISH YOU WOULD PREFER. When she had finished she cleared the unused letters to the side of the table and, smiling, went to the sofa and began to read.

14

The following day, Luke came home in the middle of the afternoon to find Anya watching a documentary on TV. He slumped down wearily beside her, and she kissed him absent-mindedly.

'You're home early.'

'Six hours repairing dry-stone walls is enough for one day,' he replied, looking at the television. 'What are you watching this for?'

'Anything's better than working on "Moonrider Two".'

'Book no good?'

'It's very good,' she admitted. 'I'm just not in the mood. I've done several sketches and thrown them all away. I keep getting sidetracked by my own stuff, but I can't concentrate on them either.'

Luke watched the documentary for a while, thinking how nice it would be to be able to forget his job when it was cold and raining and he wasn't 'in the mood'. On the TV screen a very old, very English professor in a tweed jacket and bow tie was expounding a peculiar theory linking the Pyramids and stone circles to astronomical calculations and fertility cycles. His condescending tone and archaic appearance soon got on Luke's nerves.

'What a sad old duffer,' he commented.

'I think he's rather sweet,' Anya said indulgently.

'What a waste of life, though, stuck in his ivory tower . . .'

'At least he's happy – and harmless,' she replied. 'These days most old men with strange ideas are judges.'

Luke laughed and left her to it, going into the kitchen to make tea. The phone rang as he was on his way out to his tool store, and he stopped to answer it.

'Luke Tasker.'

'Hi, Luke. It's Sheila. Is Anya there?'

'Yes. Hang on.' He covered the mouthpiece and called to Anya, then waited for her to pick up the extension before replacing his own and going about his business.

That evening, over dinner, he asked what Sheila had wanted.

'Nothing much. Nothing important,' Anya replied, a little hesitantly. 'Just to tell me that the deadline on "Moonrider Two" has been brought forward, worse luck. And to tell me about a new gallery opening. The owner lives just to the north of the moor. I might go and visit her tomorrow.'

Luke nodded, thinking that this was unusually keen of her, but that a little encouragement might help her over her current impasse. Work had always been important to Anya, and it would be nice if she could feel in a better frame of mind about it before he sprang her birthday surprise. He was looking forward to it himself. Because of the school holidays August was always the busiest month of the year for the team of rangers but, thanks to the cooperation of his colleagues, he would not be missed for a few days.

The next morning, long after Luke had left for work, Anya came downstairs to find that he had responded to her enquiry about fetishes. His message began WHAT ABOUT and went on at some length, but the letters of the following words were all placed face down on the board. Smiling, she turned them over one by one and almost blushed, understanding now why Luke had been so coy. *There's no answer to that*, she thought, laughing to herself. *At least not one I can think of at the moment*. Then her smile faded, and she went to fetch her car keys.

An hour later, after some searching in the winding, high-sided Devon lanes, she stopped the car outside a cottage and checked the name and address Sheila had given her.

Her heart was racing, and she felt hot and cold at the same time. She closed her eyes and heard the all-too familiar voice admonishing her, threatening her with the torments of eternity if she did not turn back. She knew her mother was wrong, that it was all just dangerous nonsense, yet she could not stop the voice. It made her feel small and afraid and alone. Abruptly she turned the key in the ignition, slammed the engine into gear and drove off again with a squeal of tires on asphalt.

For the rest of that day Anya worked almost obsessively, producing several alternative rough designs for the cover of 'Moonrider Two' and then doing some of her own painting. Entirely absorbed, she forgot to eat any lunch and jumped when the front doorbell rang and the outside world intruded upon her own. It was Sheila.

'Hello. What are you doing here again so soon?'

'Is that the way you greet all your guests?'

'I'm sorry. Come in.'

'I just wanted to see how you were getting on,' her agent said, following Anya down the hallway.

'I'm fine.'

'Did you go and see Megan?'

'No. I've been too busy,' Anya replied, brushing aside the memory of her abortive trip that morning. 'I've done some roughs for Paul.'

'Great.'

'I'll go and fetch them. Help yourself to a drink if you want one.'

Anya went upstairs as Sheila entered the sitting room. When she returned with the sketches she found her agent looking at the Scrabble board. When Sheila turned round, the expression on her face was a mixture of surprise and amusement.

'What flavour ice cream?' she asked curiously.

'You shouldn't read other people's private correspondence,' Anya replied. Her voice was stern, but she felt the colour rise in her cheeks.

'Chocolate?' Sheila suggested merrily. 'Pistachio? And you'd better adjust the central heating, otherwise —'

'Shut up,' Anya ordered, laughing with embarrassment. 'Come and look at these.'

Her agent relented and did as she was told, taking each of the roughs in turn and reading the notes that Anya had attached to them on overlays.

'These are good,' she declared. 'Inspiration obviously came after all.'

'Desperation, rather. I panic when people change deadlines.'

'There's still plenty of time,' Sheila reminded her soothingly. 'I'll get these off to Paul tomorrow.'

'Thanks.'

'Now, are you going to tell me what you really wanted to see a witch about?'

'I've already told you. Just curiosity.'

Sheila was obviously unconvinced.

'Research, really,' Anya added. 'One of the paintings I'm doing . . .'

'OK, OK. It's none of my business, I know.' She smiled. 'Mind you, if either of my ex-husbands ever find out about all the enquiries I made, they'll be quaking in their boots.'

'Why do I get the feeling you don't find that idea too unpleasant?'

'I'd ask this Megan woman to transform them both into toads, but I don't suppose anyone would notice the change.'

Anya laughed. 'Were they really that bad?'

'Let's just say I've seen more attractive creatures crawl out from under stones. Anyway, how can you ask such a question? They didn't appreciate me, so how *could* they be anything other than wormlike imbeciles?'

'You have a point there,' Anya conceded.

'There aren't many like Luke, you know. He's worth hanging on to.'

'You're right,' she said. 'I wouldn't put up with me. I don't know why he does.'

'Don't you? I'd've thought it was pretty obvious.'

Anya nodded solemnly.

'He's arranged a surprise for my birthday,' she said.

'Apart from the ice cream?' Sheila asked, with a mischievous glint in her eyes.

'That's just a joke.'

'Well, what's the surprise then?'

'If I knew, it wouldn't be a surprise, would it?'

'You have a lot to learn, young lady,' her friend informed her. 'Men can only keep secrets if you let them. Are you going away?'

'I don't know,' Anya explained patiently. 'It's a *surprise*.'

'Well, if you are, I hope he tells you soon. You know what they say. Romance is taking you to Paris for the weekend. Love is telling you the day before so you can iron your best dress.'

'I'll remember that,' Anya said with a grin.

'And just in case you're flying off to exotic places,' Sheila added, rummaging in her handbag, 'you'd better have this now.' She handed over a small package, wrapped in red and gold paper, with a label attached stating that the parcel was not to be opened until 15 August.

'You shouldn't have,' Anya said quietly, touched by the gesture.

'It's a bribe,' her agent explained. 'To make sure you feel guilty enough to get some work done and earn me my ten per cent. I needn't have bothered, really,' she added, brandishing the sketches. 'I'd obviously already convinced you.'

Anya ignored the facetious explanation, and weighed the package in her hand.

'Thank you.' It was the first birthday present, apart from those from Luke, that she could remember receiving for several years. Having lost contact with all her family, she had thought that there was no one else who even knew the date. So Sheila's gesture meant a lot, whatever the contents of the box. On this occasion it truly was the thought that counted.

When her friend had left, Anya found that her impulse to work was also gone. She was longing for Luke to come home, but knew from his schedule that this would not be for another two hours or more, so she decided to cook him a special meal. Ordinarily, her cooking was haphazard and last minute by nature, and she did not share Luke's patience for complicated dishes. But now she wanted to show him – in the most traditional manner possible – just how much she valued him. An inventory of the pantry revealed the necessary ingredients for a wonderful-sounding mushroom and Madeira sauce which, according to the recipe, was supposed to be used with roast fillet of beef but which, Anya reckoned, would go just as well with the steaks she had found in the refrigerator. She set to enthusiastically, but her efforts were doomed almost from the start.

Beginning with the simple tasks, she spiked two large potatoes ready for baking in the oven, then prepared some Brussels sprouts so that they could be cooked at the same time as the meat, once Luke was home. As she finished, one of the sprouts skipped off the chopping board, rolled across the floor and disappeared under the cooker. Cursing, Anya went down on her knees and tried to retrieve it with a wooden spoon. The dust and grime she discovered revolted her, and there was no sign of the renegade vegetable. She was about to give up when, as she peered into the dark crevice, her head resting on the floor, her eye caught a small movement. It was only a shadow within shadows but it repelled her, as she imagined a vile spider or worse. And then she saw, quite distinctly, two tiny glistening eyes looking back at her. The image only lasted for an instant, but Anya half screamed and scrambled to her feet, feeling quite sick. As she did so she banged her elbow on the table and rattled the implements upon it. The bottle of Madeira rocked, seemed to become steady and then, perversely, toppled over. Despite Anya's despairing efforts, it fell to the floor, smashing violently upon the tiles and spreading a deep red puddle set with glittering shards of glass. Anya jumped back from the explosion, swore and rubbed her elbow.

After a minute or two she calmed down enough to clear up the mess, all the time trying to remember if spiders had eyes in the normal sense. The unwelcome presence under

94

the cooker haunted her thoughts, although she tried to convince herself that she had imagined the whole thing. But she was determined not to give in. Sheer stubbornness and anger at her own clumsiness made her resolve to defy the capricious fates.

There was no more Madeira but she found a half-full bottle of port which, she decided, would make an adequate replacement. Chopping onions produced the inevitable tears and, with her vision impaired, she began to see tiny movements everywhere. Every mark on paintwork took on a life of its own and every reflective surface mirrored hidden creepings. She was forever turning, thinking the kitchen was infested but never actually catching sight of any of the revolting interlopers. Eventually this distraction made her cut her thumb, staining some of the onion a delicate shade of pink. Although it was only a small injury, it stung dreadfully and she could not get a plaster to stick properly. However, she was at last able to get the untainted onions simmering in the port, and turned her attention to the rest of the sauce. This became lumpy as soon as she tried to stir in the flour, and by now her sensitized eyes were crying with frustration. She made the best of it and mixed the two parts together, then took a small taste. It was vile, and burnt her tongue, adding injury to insult. Anya threw the spoon across the room, where it hit the wall and clattered onto the floor.

She stormed out of the kitchen and slammed the door behind her, then flung herself onto the sofa in the sitting room and tried to compose her thoughts. She was angry with herself, with the uncooperative food, with the inexplicable distractions – and she still could not stop her eyes from watering. After half an hour of self-pity and a large glass of whisky – something she never normally drank – she returned to the kitchen to find that she had left the gas on and the sauce was beginning to caramelize. She had also forgotten to put the potatoes in, so they would not be ready for at least another hour. In the event that did not matter, because Luke was late getting in from work, by which time Anya had abandoned her culinary efforts and was picking dismally at a small, wilting salad.

'Phew. What's that disgusting smell?' he asked as he came into the kitchen.

'Madeira and mushroom sauce,' she snapped, adding illogically, 'or it would have been if you'd been home on time.'

'Sorry. You know I can't always—'

'It's dark already,' she cut in. 'What have you been doing?'

'A scoutmaster – of all people – broke his ankle on Yes Tor,' Luke explained. 'We had to help him down.'

Anya found herself resenting the fact that he had a cast-iron excuse for being late – and hated herself for it. None of what had happened had been his fault, but she had no one else on whom to vent her spleen. Another small flicker in the corner of the room caught her eye and she glanced round quickly, only for it to disappear.

'This place is driving me mad,' she muttered.

'Why?' Luke asked, immediately concerned.

'There's spiders or bugs or something crawling around everywhere. I keep seeing them.' When she told him the whole sorry tale, Luke made the mistake of treating it lightly.

'Any port in a sauce, eh?' he remarked with a grin when told of the Madeira's demise. But Anya was in no mood for humour, and Luke eventually felt compelled to take over the cooking and to search the kitchen for insects. He found none.

'Maybe it was a poltergeist,' he suggested. 'That would explain the runaway sprout and the smashed bottle too.' He meant it as a joke but was disconcerted by Anya's response.

'You think that's funny, do you?' she cried angrily. *You can see me when I touch your world now, can't you?* The remembered words only made her more frightened. 'Well, I *don't*. Why can't you ever see things from my point of view?'

'I try –' he began, taken aback by her vehemence.

'No, you don't,' she retorted. 'You run about on your precious moor practically twenty-four hours a day, playing the hero, while I'm stuck here going crazy.' She stopped abruptly, gasped for air, then stormed out of the room. Crockery rattled in the cupboards as she slammed the door behind her a second time.

Luke looked after her, dumbfounded, and fighting to control his own temper. Shouting back would only make matters worse, but it was hard not to retaliate in the face of such blatant injustice. His fears about Anya resurfaced and, pausing only to make sure no more food would be spoiled, he followed her slowly.

He found her on their bed, crying into the pillow. Sitting beside her, he gently kissed the back of her neck, and waited. Gradually her sobs decreased to a miserable snuffling, and he pulled her up and put his arms around her shoulders. Anya clung to him, hiding her tear-stained face.

'You know you mean more to me than anything,' he began hesitantly. 'I'm sorry I was late, but it really couldn't be helped.'

'I know,' she said in a muffled voice.

'It was so sweet of you to think of cooking us a special meal,' he went on. 'I'm sorry it went wrong. We'll make up for it another time. Forgive me?'

'There's nothing to forgive,' Anya replied quietly, facing him now and wiping her eyes. 'I'm sorry I was so nasty . . . You're the last person I should —'

'Shh,' he cut in. 'It's over and done with. Let's forget it.'

'You're so much nicer to me than I am to you,' she persisted, then added with a weak smile, 'but you're satisfied with less.'

Luke grinned ruefully.

'What you need is a couple of day's holiday,' he said.

Anya's damp eyes suddenly sparkled into life.

'My birthday surprise?'

'We leave tomorrow at noon. We'll be away three nights. Pack a couple of smart dresses as well as the usual stuff.'

That's love, Anya thought, suddenly overcome with emotion. Sheila had been right.

'Where are we going?'

'That's the surprise,' he replied, and could not be coaxed into revealing anything else.

Sheila, Anya reflected happily, had not been right about everything.

15

The taxi arrived promptly at midday and took them to Newton Abbot station – which for once was a place of excited happiness rather than desolation. From there, rather than setting out for London as Anya had guessed, they took the train in the opposite direction, arriving in Penzance in the late afternoon. By then Anya had a good idea where they were heading, but there were still surprises in store. She had never been in a helicopter before and the twenty-minute journey was noisy but smooth and exhilarating, especially when the Isles of Scilly came into view, like jewels in the endless sea. They landed on a grass field near the Abbey on the island of Tresco, amid the lush greenery that covered the southern end of the isle. Then, much to Anya's delight, they were ensconced on a small tram-like trailer which looked as though it belonged on a fairground. It was pulled by a small tractor, and conveyed them and their luggage directly to the luxurious Island Hotel.

Anya was enchanted by the views of white beaches and blue seas, by the granite cottages, the vast array of flowers and the avenues lined with palm trees. The hotel itself proved equally welcoming. Their room overlooked the sound between Tresco and St Martin's, which was strewn with tiny islets with wonderful names like Rascal's Ledge, Crump Island and Little Cheese Rock. To the north, the white tower of Round Island lighthouse shone white against the sky. And, as if all this were not enough, there was a huge arrangement of flowers awaiting her on the dressing table, with a card that read simply 'All my love, Luke'.

'You arranged all this without me knowing?' she exclaimed happily, throwing her arms around his neck.

'Like it?' he asked, smiling at her excitement.

'It's wonderful. Everything's absolutely bloody wonderful!'

'I hope you don't mind the surprise not actually being on your birthday. I thought you'd rather wake up tomorrow and be here already.'

'Oh, yes! What bliss.'

They ate dinner that night in the hotel's spacious, airy restaurant, with its colourful mural by Marcus May depicting the island in full bloom. The delicious food was the perfect way to forget about the previous night's fiasco. As they lingered over coffee, the maître d' came to their table to check that everything had been satisfactory.

'Perfect, thank you,' Luke confirmed.

The maître d' turned to Anya with a smile.

'Welcome back, Miss Caplan. It's been a long time since your last visit.'

Puzzled, Anya glanced at Luke, but he seemed equally confused.

'I've never been here before,' she said. 'I've only ever been to the Scillies once and that was years ago, when I was ten.'

It was the maître d's turn to look surprised.

'My apologies, madam. I must be confusing you with someone else.' He began to turn away but Luke called him back.

'Anya, Miss Caplan, has a twin sister. Is it possible she's been here?'

'Ah, that must be it,' the man replied with evident relief. 'Miss Caplan, the other Miss Caplan, comes here for lunch every so often but she rarely stays overnight. I am sorry for my mistake.'

After he had gone, Luke glanced at Anya who appeared lost in thought.

'What a coincidence.'

She nodded, a puzzled expression on her face.

'Do you think Meredith might live on the Scillies now?'

'I've no idea,' Anya replied, wondering why her sister, an

infrequent visitor, should have been remembered from among so many thousands of the hotel's guests.

They sat in silence for a while, each with their own thoughts.

'You don't seem very curious,' Luke said eventually. 'Don't you want to find out more?'

'No. It's too late.'

'It's only just occurred to me,' he went on. 'Tomorrow is Meredith's birthday too. Don't you even want to send her a card?'

'I've told you before,' Anya said with a shrug. 'I wouldn't know where to send it. Let's not talk about her, Luke. I want this time to be just for us.'

The next morning, Anya awoke to find that the weather, like Luke's arrangements, was perfect. A champagne breakfast arrived via room service, and they ate together and toasted the day. Luke then produced several parcels which she opened ceremoniously one by one, revealing a bottle of her favourite perfume, a biography of Monet, two new paintbrushes, a packet of balloons with 'I am 28' printed on them and a floppy black velvet hat. Her delight increased with each discovery – and there was the added bonus of the present from Sheila, which turned out to be a pair of beautiful earrings, black jet studs in a plain silver setting. The note inside read 'I hope you've got an outfit to match these'.

Once the unwrapping was completed, Anya was told that, as this was her day, she must choose how it was to be spent. She was feeling particularly cosy and much loved by then, and she half thought of suggesting that they spend the whole day in bed. But the prospect of exploring the island was too enticing. The bedroom would still be there that evening.

They walked the rugged northern end of the island first, visiting both castles; Cromwell's solid round fortress on the shore, and King Charles' more romantic but infinitely less practical ruin on the hill above. They clambered down into Piper's Hole, feeling like children playing at smugglers, discovered prehistoric cairns amidst the heather and watched the other islands rise from the sea as the tide receded. A lunchtime drink at the New Inn was followed by an afternoon spent discovering the many pleasures of the greener, gentler southern half of the island; the long white strands, the tropical Abbey gardens with its fabulous flora, sculptures and collection of ships' figureheads; the heron-stalked lakes and rocky coves. And all about them the sea was like glass, and bluer than the Atlantic had any right to be.

Then, pleasantly weary, they returned to the hotel, luxuriated in a long, scented bath and watched dusk descend on the island.

'Have you had a good birthday?' Luke asked.

'Oh, yes! It's been magical.'

'And it's not over yet. There's still dinner to come.'

'And bed,' she added, sliding her arms around him. 'Don't forget that.'

'I hadn't,' he replied, smiling.

Anya was happier than she had been in months. She felt that the shadows could not touch her here.

Over breakfast in the restaurant the next morning, they made plans for the day. Luke was keen to hire a boat and explore by sea, perhaps visit Bryher. Anya wanted to get hold of some snorkelling equipment and brave the cool water, but they couldn't bring themselves to do anything in a hurry. When they finally finished their meal, they got up and strolled back towards their room.

16

The sun-dappled path stretched out before her, sloping gently downhill between almost symmetrical pairs of date palms. On either side was a profusion of plant life that had come from all over the world. Cacti, tree ferns, aloes, camellias and lilies flourished here, their colours and scents mingling to form one exquisite living collage. In the distance, Anya could see the Great Pool and the grey stone of the Abbey, and beyond that the placid ocean beneath a few wispy clouds in an otherwise blue sky. As she walked on, a large, exotic bird moved out of her way slowly, its gaudy red and blue plumage redolent of tropical jungles.

On a day like this it was easy to believe the travel brochure's boast that Tresco was indeed a paradise on Earth. She turned to say as much to Luke, but he was nowhere in sight and she felt a first slight tremor of unease. Had he already set off in search of a boat? Anya could not remember what had been arranged. In fact she could not remember leaving their room or beginning their walk. Where was Luke? Where was everybody? The sun was high in the sky and the daily launches from St Mary's would have arrived by now, bringing their loads of day trippers. And yet the island was completely deserted. Even a place as tranquil as this should not be so deserted in midsummer.

Fighting panic, she looked around at the landscape that was almost too perfect – and suddenly knew, with a horrible yawning certainty, that what she saw was not real. She was inside the paint-thin world of the mural – and that could only mean one thing.

'It's so much better this way, don't you think?' an all too familiar voice remarked. 'We can have the whole island to ourselves.'

Anya spun round to find Allessandro only a few paces away, his silent approach confirming her fears. Dread, loathing and something else, something almost approaching excitement, fought for precedence in her mind. And yet a very small part of her welcomed his arrival. His being there meant that she was not alone in this perfect land, which had become alien and empty. He seemed quite at ease, stooping to enjoy the scent of a radiant bloom as if this were his natural habitat.

'I thought it was time we talked again,' he said carelessly, straightening up and looking at her with fathomless dark eyes. 'Another island paradise, another conversation. What could be more fitting? Shall we walk?'

He set off without waiting for an answer, strolling down the path at a leisurely pace. After a moment's hesitation, Anya gave in to the inevitable and hurried to catch up.

'These islands have a remarkably rich history,' the sorcerer commented as she reluctantly fell into step beside him. 'They have been home to holy men, pirates and princes, exiles, magicians and prisoners. These rocks have seen a thousand ships founder, been pounded by innumerable storms, and yet they survive, their granite tops the last remnants of a greater land. It's as if your Dartmoor had sunk halfway into the sea. Is that why you feel so at home here?'

The question startled Anya. She had been lost in her own thoughts, the sound of his voice a distant rumble, as meaningless as the whispering of the sea. She was happy to let him talk, wanting only to remain silent. She wanted to do as little as possible, to simply endure this visitation – and then flee.

'I . . . I never thought about it,' she mumbled, but Allessandro was not taking any notice of her, happy to continue his apparently pointless monologue.

'The Scillies have had many names over the centuries,' he told her. 'Small islands are uniquely powerless in times of war. They are never worth the trouble it takes to defend them, and are thus swept back and forth by the tides of history. Is that why they fascinate us so?'

Anya made no attempt to answer his rhetorical question.

'Or is it their self-contained nature, their comprehensible human scale that attracts us?' he went on thoughtfully. 'A false sense of security, wrapped around by the protective, bountiful sea? In peacetime they certainly have advantages for trade. They were dealing in Cornish tin here long after their own supplies ran out. Trading with Phoenicians, Greeks, Romans, adventurous merchants from the other side of the Pillars of Hercules. Who knows? Perhaps Poseidon came here too. Was he the jealous god who returned Lyonesse to his underwater realm? Think, Anya, what an adventure it would be to reverse his misdeeds, to play god and raise an earthquake that would reshape the world.'

He seemed carried away by his own eloquence, his eyes shining with an unholy excitement. Anya averted her gaze with some difficulty. Allessandro was dangerous, insane, but there was a paradoxical attraction in such powerful madness, such lofty dreams. She understood clearly for the first time just why that long ago Constanza had been his consort, before she had turned betrayer.

'We could do it, Anya!'

'We?' she said, her voice barely more than a whisper.

'Together we could shake the sky itself,' he replied fervently. 'It is your only choice, your only way to live. You can be a witness of my glory.'

'How?'

'You must submit to me,' he told her, then looked skyward. 'Oh, Constanza, my little one, if only you had seen, if only you had trusted me, what marvels we could have created together!'

He took Anya's hands in his own, and she found that she had neither the strength nor even the desire to resist. He stared at her with molten intensity.

'You have been given another chance. Think of it! Think of our powers combining to produce such wonders as the world has never seen.'

'And if I choose not to submit?'

The rapture left Allessandro's face in an instant, and his expression grew stern. She watched him fighting to suppress his anger.

'You can slow me down,' he stated flatly, 'but you cannot stop me. You do not have my capacity.' He did not sound complacent, as he had often done before, but emanated total confidence.

'Then why do you want me to surrender?' she asked. 'If your victory is assured?'

'Oh, Anya, why choose rape when so much more pleasure, so many *mutual* benefits would come from your willing and graceful submission?'

His fingers were hot against her own now, and Anya felt her body's warmth increase in response to his words. Abruptly she withdrew her hands.

'But you would rape me if you had to?' she said quietly.

Allessandro did not answer immediately. His expression had grown cold.

'I know all your fears, Anya,' he responded eventually. 'If I had to, I could make what time remains to you a constant torment. Do you want that?'

Anya shivered at his ominous words. *What time remains to you.*

'And if I still resisted?' she whispered.

'I would destroy you,' he replied with chilling conviction. 'Utterly. It need not be so. It is your choice.'

He turned away and walked on, leaving Anya to the contemplation of her own death – and his. *There is more than one form of death.* Staring at his retreating back, she imagined plunging a knife into it, imagined gaining her freedom through his murder. But the thought of violence appalled her. The very idea of it was like another betrayal.

Allessandro turned back to face her. 'You cannot kill me,' he told her contemptuously. 'You might just as well try to kill yourself.'

Anya got the impression that he had been fighting to control his temper, but now his expression grew warmer, his voice milder.

'Come. We should talk of happier things. Let me demonstrate a little of what your life could encompass.'

He set off again, striding purposefully now so that, after a moment's indecision, Anya had to run to catch up with him. As she did so, she discovered that the geography of this false island no longer corresponded to that of the real Tresco. Or perhaps some sorcerous magic was at work, transporting them from place to place. But she had no time to wonder at such things.

Before them lay the quay at New Grimsby. It was deserted. The sheltered harbour now only contained one boat, which was moored to the pier. Allessandro led her towards it. The only sounds were the gentle whispering of the breeze, the lapping water and the cries of seagulls.

The sorcerer helped Anya into the small boat, then untied the bow rope and stepped down himself. He set the outboard motor in operation by the simple expedient of telling it to start – something that did not surprise Anya – and guided the craft out into the bay.

'Where are we going?'

'Hell Bay.'

This, Anya knew, was a famous part of the coastline of Bryher, named for the ferocity of the Atlantic waves which could turn the water into a cauldron of white foam and spray. It was completely exposed to westerly gales, and was reputedly an especially spectacular sight in a storm. There seemed little danger of that on such a calm day, however, and she knew better than to question Allessandro's plans.

The boat skimmed northwards in the narrow channel between the two islands, then headed out into the open sea, riding the swell as she rounded Shipman Head and came south again, following the west coast of Bryher. Even in such peaceful conditions, Hell Bay was breathtaking when seen from sea level. Dark cliffs towered above the slow-moving sea, which itself was studded with treacherous boulders. It took little imagination to understand how wild a scene it could be in bad weather, and Anya shivered involuntarily.

'Use it,' Allessandro said unexpectedly.

'What?'

'Your imagination. Use it to conjure up a storm, like the witches of old were supposed to do,' he replied, smiling.

Without thinking, she glanced at the open sea to the west, picturing mountainous waves and dark purple storm clouds veined with lightning. And then, to her absolute and instantaneous terror, they became real. The first enormous, white-capped breakers surged towards them and Anya screamed and cowered low, knowing that the tiny boat would be smashed to fragments within moments. Hell Bay growled in anticipation.

'Now I will keep my part of the bargain!' Allessandro cried. 'You will come to no harm, little one.'

Anya did not believe him, *could* not believe him, and knew with utter certainty that she was about to die. The wave was almost upon them, but when it swirled around their boat the craft rose majestically, crested the top and was not carried along by the surge. The monstrous rush of water smashed into the cliff only fifty yards away with a roar that eclipsed the thunder, bursting in a vast white explosion. The wind howled like a banshee, competing with the noise of the sea, and more gigantic waves swept into the bay, detonating on the rocks and filling the air with swirling, snarling water-devils as the ocean below boiled and seethed in sudden torment. And yet, amidst all this roaring, deadly violence, their small craft rode serenely up and down in its own invisible, protective bubble.

'You see!' the sorcerer yelled above the howling of the storm. 'What can we not do together?'

At last Anya believed. The storm could not touch them. None of this was real.

'Oh, but it is,' Allessandro cried, laughing with exhilaration as he released his hold for a moment. They were the longest, most terrifying two seconds of Anya's life as the boat, suddenly unprotected, slid down a vertiginous wall of water as though on a diabolical roller coaster, and careered towards the teeth in Hell Bay's granite jaws. She was thrown down into the bottom of the boat, feeling as if she had left her stomach far above, too terrified even to scream as spray lashed at her face and soaked her clothes. Then, just as abruptly, Allessandro resumed his guardianship and the boat rode quietly once more.

Anya recovered slowly, amazed to find that she could still breathe, and became hypnotized by the maelstrom. To see the relentless power of such a storm from the inside was truly awe-inspiring. It was impossible – and yet that was what she was doing.

'Now you begin to understand,' the sorcerer exclaimed triumphantly, and she could not help but share in his elation.

Anya could not say how long the storm lasted, nor whether it died away naturally or because she and Allessandro prompted it to do so, but eventually the wind abated, the skies cleared and the ocean grew slowly calm. By then the sun was low in the western sky and when they made landfall on a deserted beach somewhere on the southern end of Bryher, she knew that sunset could only be an hour or so away. A whole day had passed, and still there was no end in sight to her ordeal. What could Luke be thinking? What would he do if she was not back by nightfall?

'Where are we going?' she asked as she followed the sorcerer ashore. 'Why aren't we going back to Tresco?'

Allessandro did not answer, but just walked on purposefully as if he knew where he was headed. Anya had no choice but to follow. She knew that there was a hotel on the island and that it was easy enough to get a boat to Tresco, but . . . it wasn't that simple. This was not the real Bryher, and even if she managed to get back to Tresco it might well still be deserted, a ghost island. Everything around her was some incomprehensible extension of a painting. She could not return to Luke until Allessandro released her.

The cottage stood alone among fields of flowers, half hidden by tall, protective hedges. He led her inside and they found a meal laid out on the kitchen table; lobsters, crab meat, bread, salads and fruit, cheese and tiny almond cakes. Anya discovered that she was ravenous and, when she had persuaded herself that the food was real, and not a false banquet from a fairy tale, she ate her fill. Allessandro watched her, amusement in his dark eyes, and kept her wine glass and his own well filled.

By the time they had finished their meal it was dark outside and, whether because of the after-effects of the day or the influence of the wine, Anya felt utterly weary. Her limbs seemed unbearably heavy, and she could hardly keep her eyes open. When Allessandro came and picked her up in his arms, lifting her from the chair as though she weighed no more than a feather, she did not resist. It seemed to Anya that it was almost as if Allessandro was trying to be kind. And she had spent most of her life longing for kindness. It was only after he had carried her upstairs and laid her on the bed that her instincts for self-protection awoke. Even so, she could do nothing to prevent him from leaning over to kiss her lightly.

'No,' she mumbled, trying to turn away.

'You must learn to trust me, mia cara,' he whispered, and touched her lips gently with his fingertips. Darkness swallowed her.

In the next moment, or so it seemed, it was morning, and sunlight streamed in through the uncurtained window. There was no sign of Allessandro, no sound from below. Anya felt stiff and sore, but remembered nothing of the night. She was naked beneath the sheets, her clothes piled neatly on a chair, and she knew he must have undressed her. But what else had he done? Mentally she checked her body. Although there was nothing that could not be accounted for by the exertions of the previous day, she was still troubled. Her sleep had been too deep to be natural.

She thought of Luke and her heart sank. He must be frantic by now. Filled with a new, fragile determination she got up, dressed and went downstairs. Breakfast was laid out, but she ignored that. The house was quiet and there was still no sign of Allessandro. Outside it was another glorious day and, acting on instinct, Anya made her way to Town Quay.

He was waiting for her there, in the boat. She got in without a word and they set out, completing the short trip across the channel in just a few minutes. They landed on a still unpopulated Tresco.

'When is this going to end?' Anya wailed.
'When do you want it to end?' he asked complacently.
'Now. Please.'
'Very well.'
The world about her dissolved.

17

When Anya came to, she found herself lying on the restaurant floor. Luke and another man – one of the waiters – were kneeling beside her and, hovering above them, other anxious faces looked down.

'Is she all right?' someone asked.

Between the onlookers Anya could see the mural, beautiful but still and lifeless. Then she returned her unsteady gaze to Luke's face. He was smiling bravely now, trying to hide his own worries and to reassure her. Like all Rangers, he had been given extensive training in first aid, but he was still glad to see Anya open her eyes. He had no idea why she had fainted so suddenly, but it was good to see the colour returning to her cheeks after her brief spell of unconsciousness.

'Should I call for the doctor?' the waiter asked.

'No. I'm OK,' she replied automatically, surprised to hear her voice sounding strong and sure.

'You fainted —' Luke began.

'What day is it?' she interrupted, and he laughed, thinking she was joking. When he saw the expression on her face, he became uncertain.

'August sixteenth,' he told her. 'The day after your birthday.'

'And we've just had breakfast?'

'Yes. Are you sure you're OK?' It was only two minutes since Anya had fainted, but the experience had obviously disorientated her completely.

'I'm fine,' she confirmed, and sat up with Luke's help.

The waiter had brought a glass of water, and he offered

111

this to her now. She sipped gratefully, and struggled to understand what had happened to her. An entire day had been compressed into just a few seconds. She need not have worried about Luke missing her; her body at least had been with him all the time. Only her mind had wandered. Bryher, Hell Bay, and the cottage began to drift away, like the memory of a dream.

'Thank you,' she said, handing the glass back.

'Is there anything we can do?' the waiter asked. The other onlookers had drifted away now, although hotel staff waited nearby, ready to be of assistance if required. The sounds of breakfast being served and eaten had resumed quietly.

'No, thank you. I'm all right now.'

'Shall we go back to our room?' Luke suggested. 'You can rest for a bit.'

Anya nodded, and he helped her to her feet. With Luke reassuring the concerned staff that all was well, they returned to their room arm in arm. Although she felt steady enough on her feet, her mind was still reeling. In the room she sat obediently, propped up on the bed, while Luke made her a cup of tea she didn't really want, and tried to make some sense of it all.

The apparent distortion of time had been a feature of all her previous experiences but none of them, however bizarre, had been as extreme as this. Nearly twenty-four hours of her subjective time had passed in the blink of an eye. She had walked, sailed, eaten and slept. Looking down at her stomach she wondered what an examination of its contents would reveal; just breakfast, or the meal from the cottage, the tastes of which she could remember clearly? It was a grotesque, macabre thought, and her mind shied away from it – only to dwell on equally unpalatable memories. She recalled Allessandro invoking Poseidon, crazy talk about earthquakes and raising Lyonesse. And she remembered his demands for her submission and the threats that had accompanied her mention of refusal. *What time remains to you.*

And then there was the literally incredible storm. Had she been part of its creation? Had it really been created at all?

112

Or had it existed, like everything else, only in her mind? The weather outside the hotel room was as placid as before and clearly, if the violent storm she had witnessed had been genuine, then it had occurred in some other reality, not this one. Her intellect rebelled, bemused by such a concept, and she turned to what was perhaps the most important question of all; what had happened to her overnight? There were no answers. She had fallen fast asleep at the mere touch of Allessandro's fingertips – perhaps at the same time as her own body had become unconscious in the 'real' world. The fainting, Anya realized, was the first ever physical effect of her visions in the real world, apart from a momentary loss of attention. What did that mean? Were the attacks becoming more powerful, more damaging, as well as lasting longer? Had she fainted before her 'day' with the sorcerer or – as she was inclined to believe – afterwards, as reaction had set in?

Anya took another sip of tea and glanced at Luke who was sitting watching her, his expression a mixture of concern, hopeful encouragement and loving tenderness. She smiled, wishing with all her heart that her life could be simple, so that loving and being loved would be easy, not hemmed around with mysteries and nameless fears. Luke deserved better.

'What happened?' she asked quietly.

'I was going to ask you the same thing.'

'I've no idea. Tell me what you saw.'

'Well . . . You were walking out of the restaurant a little ahead of me. I saw you hesitate in mid-stride as though you must have forgotten something, perhaps left your handbag at the table, but then you just crumpled up and keeled over. I was able to break your fall a bit, but you still landed heavily. There's a bump on the back of your head,' he concluded apologetically. 'I was so worried about you.'

'I'm sorry.' Anya remembered banging her head on the boat seat as she was thrown down, and reached round to feel for the lump.

'Don't be sorry,' Luke told her seriously. 'Just be OK.'

'How long was I unconscious?' she asked.

'A few seconds, that's all, but it seemed much longer.' He

grinned unexpectedly. 'Did we overdo it last night? Has your renowned stamina run out on me?'

Anya was about to say that he had not even been with her last night, but stopped herself in time and smiled back.

'It's never had that effect before,' she replied.

Suddenly, Anya wanted to tell him everything, and to hell with the risk of him thinking she was mad. She even opened her mouth to try, but found herself instantly and helplessly tongue-tied. Then, to her own surprise and even more so to Luke's, she heard herself begin to talk about her childhood. It was as if, of all the secrets she had kept from him, the stories of her early years were now the least disturbing – and she needed to share at least *some* of those secrets.

'I remember, when I was little, there was a tree at the bottom of our garden. It used to fascinate me, but I never knew why. Now I think I do.'

'Why?' Luke asked, confused by this bizarre change of subject.

'It was dead,' Anya went on. 'All that was left was an increasingly brittle skeleton, a bleached wooden climbing frame for the ivy that had smothered it. I used to dream about that ivy, and wake up terrified that it had grown over the bedroom window and door so that there was no way out. Meredith thought I was stupid, wouldn't let me tell our parents about it. She said the tree was just old dead rubbish, and that the ivy hadn't killed it but was reshaping it into something different. But I knew better. In a sense, *we* were the ivy.'

Luke could make neither head nor tail of this so when she paused, staring into space, he waited and said nothing.

'Do you think, even at the age of four, that I was able to subconsciously recognize a visual metaphor?' she asked earnestly.

'Eh?' He was now quite out of his depth.

'Was I an artist even then?' Anya went on. 'When I was too young to know what I was doing? Painting in my head?'

'What metaphor?' Luke asked, trying to keep up with her ramblings.

114

'The tree represented our parents, their marriage – and it was dead,' she explained. 'All that was left was the empty shell, the structure without the life, a mere shape. The real tree was gone.'

'And you and Meredith were the ivy?' he ventured uncertainly.

'We killed it, yes. Squeezed what sap was left out of their marriage.'

'Christ, Anya!' Luke exclaimed. 'Don't be so morbid. You weren't responsible for what happened between your parents. You were only kids, for God's sake.' He was horrified that such bitter self-recriminations had lain hidden and festering for so long.

'Even a child is known by her doings,' Anya intoned.

This sounded like a quotation, and her next words confirmed Luke's suspicion.

'That's from the Bible. My mother was always quoting the Bible. You know, stuff like, "For the imagination of a man's heart is evil from his youth," and "Can a man take fire to his bosom, and his clothes not be burned?"'

'Cheerful words for children's ears,' Luke commented, feeling utterly sickened. He almost wished Anya's mother was still alive, so that he could tell her just what he thought of her.

'Then there was the old favourite, used if we ever questioned anything she said,' Anya continued. '"Honour thy father and thy mother." Although that one fell out of favour somewhat after Daddy left.' She smiled weakly.

Luke remained silent, wishing she would stop, but unable to make himself tell her so. Instinct told him that she needed to unburden herself – and it was what he had often wanted her to do, after all – but he had no idea why it was all coming out now.

'She never recovered from his leaving,' Anya went on. 'The irony of it was that she knew, as a woman and a wife, that she should be subservient to him. The Bible told her so. He was her lord and master, her breadwinner and protector, and he could do no wrong. She never complained, even when he grew silent and cruel, because "it is better to dwell in a corner of the housetop, than with a brawling woman in a wide house." But when he abandoned us, she was lost, cast adrift. When she finally accepted that he was gone for good, her life was over, literally.'

'I'm sorry,' Luke said softly. Inside him, anger was boiling now. He could not bear to think of Anya, as a little girl, being mistreated in any way. He wanted, impotently, to step back in time and protect her from any evil.

'I am not my mother,' Anya stated. The sadness was gone from her voice now, and had been replaced by a vehemence that surprised him. 'I will never be like her.'

'Of course not,' Luke agreed and then, prompted by the memory of her recent outburst – *I was so afraid you wouldn't be here* – he added, 'And I'll never be like your father.'

Anya looked at him.

'You don't want to be my lord and master?' she asked with a half-smile.

'Chance would be a fine thing,' he replied, grinning, then added seriously, 'It's gone, Anya. The past doesn't matter any more. It's only the present that's relevant.'

She appeared to be struggling to believe him, her face still but her eyes lost in thought. Finally she nodded.

'You're right. And we're wasting a perfect day talking about old rubbish.' She practically jumped off the bed and Luke stood up too.

'Are you sure you're OK?

'Yes. Absolutely,' she replied determinedly.

'What do you want to do then?'

'Hire a boat and go to Bryher.'

An hour later they stood on the hill above Hell Bay and watched the slow, powerful surge of the slumbering ocean. Even though Anya had never been there before, every detail of the place was exactly as she remembered.

'Wow!' Luke breathed. 'It doesn't take much imagination to see how wild this place would be in a storm.'

'No,' Anya said. 'It doesn't.'

116

18

'I wish we could've stayed longer,' Luke said as they arrived home late the next day. 'But you know what it's like round here in the season.'

'Of course,' Anya replied. 'And it was the best birthday treat I've ever had.' She meant every word, but was also aware that it wasn't just the pressure of work that had brought them home. Luke had arranged what must have been an expensive trip, and paid for it all himself. She knew that his resources were limited, but that he liked to retain some degree of financial independence. 'I'll never forget it.'

The next morning Anya lay in bed for some time after Luke had left for work. The trip had indeed been unforgettable, but for reasons she could never explain to him. Thinking back, there were only two possible explanations for what had happened. Either she was insane and the whole thing was the latest, most expansive stage of her self-imposed delusion, or Allessandro was real and what he had told her was true. Both alternatives were equally terrifying.

Could she be mad yet still be able to question her sanity? She did not want to believe that, dared not believe it. As far as she knew, her mother – who had been genuinely deranged – had never questioned her visions, her voices, her messages from saints and angels. But if Anya was sane, as she so desperately wanted to believe, then it meant that the sorcerer was who he said he was, and that the threat he posed was genuine. Yet what could she *do*? Her experiences had always seemed authentic to her, but they did not affect the real world – apart

117

from that one brief fainting spell. They had all taken place in her mind. As long as they stayed there, what, ultimately, was the danger? How could Allessandro carry out his threat to destroy her?

Anya recalled her heart-stopping fear as she hung precariously over an Alpine cliff or as their small boat plummetted down the side of the storm-driven wave. She knew that even if she was not mad now, she soon would be if forced to endure such moments with any regularity. Was that to be her inevitable fate? Instinctively she denied it. Better to die . . .

'I have to assume that I'm not mad,' she said aloud to the empty room. 'In which case I'm possessed in some way. So what am I going to do about it?'

She thought of the National Gallery, of the first time she had seen Allessandro's portrait, and she imagined returning armed with a sharp blade, or with petrol and matches, perhaps a large bottle of nail varnish remover. But she was sickened by the idea of deliberately destroying such a priceless work of art, even if it was the lair of her tormentor. And in any case, she knew it would be pointless. Allessandro was no longer trapped there. She had set him free somehow, and to attack him via the painting would be futile.

So how else could she oppose him? She could not approach the church for an exorcism; the very idea was repellent. Her tormented childhood had robbed her of any faith in that quarter. Perhaps she should try witchcraft. Could Megan charm Allessandro out of existence in the same way as she removed warts? This prospect seemed so unlikely that Anya actually smiled. Even so, she had reached the stage where some action was necessary, and so she decided to go and see the wise woman. After all, what harm could it do? If she *had* inherited some ancient curse, then this might be a solution. She got out of bed and dressed slowly, realizing that she was now taking seriously ideas that a short time ago she would have considered preposterous.

It was then that a treacherous, seductive thought entered her mind. Perhaps there was another alternative after all. She could accede to Allessandro's demands, submit her will to his – or at least pretend to. Anya could not deny the paradox which made the sorcerer attractive as well as frightening. Evidently, power could act as an aphrodisiac, and to be included in his grand adventures – even in a subordinate role – would be to share in untold exhilaration. *Think of it, our powers combined to produce wonders.*

Our powers, Anya thought. Could she really play the part of Constanza, even down to her final, bitter victory? It would be a perilous course. She was no sorceress to match wits and skill with Allessandro. Even to pretend to yield might be all he needed to crush her entirely and make the surrender real. And yet, the same small, traitorous voice insisted, would that necessarily be so bad? After all, she had enjoyed . . .

'Don't be so stupid!' she exclaimed out loud, thinking of Luke and disgusted with herself for even considering being unfaithful to him.

She went downstairs and discovered that the Scrabble interchange had begun again. Luke had laid out a new message. CAW SAID THE CROW. Anya was almost sure that this was a quotation from something she had read, but could not place it at first. She thought about it for a while, glad to have something trivial with which to occupy her mind, then smiled. Picking out the letters she needed, she set out the expected response. BALLS SAID MILLIGAN. *Puckoon* was a novel that both she and Luke adored. Anya was still grinning at the thought of Spike Milligan's comic genius when she left the house.

The journey to Megan's cottage took less time now that she knew the way, but Anya waited several minutes in the parked car as she psyched herself up for the meeting. It was not so much the remembered warnings of her mother that made her hesitate, more the sheer effrontery of what she was about to do. Marching in on a complete stranger and announcing that you were in thrall to a sixteenth-century Italian sorcerer was not something you did every day – and, even if the witch accepted Anya's outrageous statement, what was she supposed to do about it? It was much more likely that Megan, like everybody else, would advise her to seek psychiatric help.

She was a modern witch after all, not a wart-encrusted hag with a pointed hat, a flying broomstick and a black cat for a familiar.

At that precise moment, as Anya was tormenting herself with these internal arguments, a black cat emerged from a hole in the hedge, gave her one long, meaningful stare, then trotted purposefully across the lane into the field opposite. It all seemed so blatant, so deliberately stage-managed, that Anya could only laugh nervously. She got out of the car, her mind made up at last, and walked up to the gate, a wrought-iron frame between two mundane concrete posts. The garden and cottage beyond were quiet and still, and she hoped that, after all this, Megan would not be out.

Stretching out her hand to release the catch, Anya felt a sudden tingle in her wrist and fingers, something like static electricity. Then the gate burst into flames.

She jumped back, crying out in shock and alarm. Her heart racing, she forced herself to watch for a few moments, noting without understanding that the flames, while enveloping the gate, did not blister the paint on the metal. Nor were the nearby leaves of the hedge affected. But for her the flames were worse than real.

Anya turned and fled. In the field opposite a cat miaowed loudly. To her panicked ears, the sound was like demoniacal laughter.

Anya's reaction to her latest traumatic experience was to pretend that it had never happened. The implications were both too bewildering and too horrendous to contemplate, so she shut them away, denied everything and forced herself to keep busy. That meant painting, the one occupation that made time meaningless and could focus her entire attention. Even the fact that her two current works in progress concerned witchcraft and fire respectively neither deterred nor distracted her. Losing herself in her art meant that she could step outside the rest of her life, view it from a distant standpoint, divorced from the mundane nature of genuine experience. Her paintings might act as therapy, as Luke and Sheila had surmised, but if so the process was entirely unconscious.

Under her deft brushstrokes the bottle took shape, its dark green glass glinting enigmatically; the blackthorn foliage grew and twisted, bearing its round black fruit; and tarnished pins impaled the cork. Anya worked for hours, forgetting everything else, then stood back, nodded and cleaned her brushes before moving on to the other painting, her sequel to 'Beneath the Flames'. Minute details in the jewelled sea occupied her for a long time, but eventually she turned her attention to the oily flames and billowing black smoke. Her concentration was intense, producing images almost photographic in their realism, and when, finally, she relented and allowed herself a few moments' rest, her thoughts turned not to recent events but to those of her long-suppressed past.

The church was much more crowded than usual. It must have been a special occasion, although Anya – seated on a hard pew, her legs dangling – had not known what it was. She was on one side of the erect figure of her mother, Meredith on the other. The twins were dressed identically in yellow frills. Their father was not with them, and in fact the girls had not seen him for some time now, something which made them sadder and more subdued as the days passed. Their mother had told them that he had had to go away and when asked about his return would only reply, 'Soon.'

The vicar stood in his wooden pulpit, the one with the carved eagle on the front, which Meredith liked but which Anya thought was too scary for a church. He was talking endlessly about something the girls did not understand. Words like repentance, suffering, kindness and tolerance washed over them in meaningless waves while they tried to fidget without their mother noticing. Every so often she would whisper something under her breath in response to what the preacher was saying, and as the sermon rolled on, her comments became louder. A boy in the row in front glanced round once, only to be silently admonished by his father. Another child giggled and someone behind them made shushing noises, but Anya's mother was oblivious to the disturbance she was causing. The twins were not so lucky. Young as they were, they were not immune to the agonies of embarrassment, and when their mother finally spoke out in a strident voice which carried easily to all corners of the church, they were mortified.

'Won't listen to this! What does he know, silly old goat? All men are stupid goats.' She stood up abruptly, gathered her coat and pulled the girls down off the seat. She was either unaware of the strange looks and outraged whispers that followed their exit or cared nothing about them. Even the vicar faltered momentarily in his turgid oration, adding to the general air of embarrassment.

'Meredith, you really musn't talk in church,' their mother scolded in a loud voice, as they trooped down the aisle. 'And Anya, if you can't be more careful, I'll have to put you back in nappies.'

The twins' small faces were burning with shame now, and they practically had to run to keep up, each led firmly by a tightly held hand. Anya felt tears sting her eyes. And worse still, as if to justify her mother's fraudulent insinuations, something hot and wet was running down the inside of her leg.

One of the wardens met them at the door, his kindly face betraying unease and concern. When he asked in a whisper if they were all right, if they needed any help, the only response was a loud, contemptuous command to get out of their way.

That night the twins lay in bed, staring at the ceiling and unable to sleep. Meredith eventually voiced the fear that Anya had been unable to consider.

'Daddy's never coming home.'

'He is, he is!' Anya cried. 'Soon.'

'No, he isn't. His toothbrush's gone.'

Faced with this unanswerable evidence, Anya could only repeat her hopeless assertion.

'He's coming home soon. Mummy said so.'

'He took almost all his clothes too, and Mummy burnt the rest. That's what made the nasty smoke in the garden yesterday,' Meredith claimed.

'Shut up,' Anya mumbled, beginning to cry again. 'Shut up. I hate you.'

The bedroom door creaked open at this point and the girls froze, thinking they were about to be told off for talking when they should be asleep. But when their mother turned the light on, making the twins blink in surprise, there was no sign of anger in her face. Indeed, as Anya hastily wiped her eyes, she thought that she had never seen her parent looking more beautiful, more serenely happy.

'I've got something to show you. Come and see.'

She led them down to the sitting room, where all the lights had been turned off and the only illumination came from the wavering flames of an open log fire.

'Look.'

'What?' Meredith asked, looking around while Anya could only stare in bewilderment at her mother's rapturous face.

'In the fire,' she explained. 'The Angel Gabriel is there in the flames.'

The twins looked.

'Say hello to our visitor.'

'Hello,' the girls parroted obediently.

'He's going to look after us now that . . . until your father comes home,' their mother told them.

Anya looked at Meredith to see whether she was going to respond to this, but her sister remained silent. Anya wondered if she could see the angel too. He must be there if Mummy said he was, but she could not see anything, no matter how hard she tried.

The fire crackled and spat as the logs shifted, and their mother laughed softly.

'You're quite right,' she said. 'They should be in bed. Come on, girls, back upstairs.'

It was the first of many conversations between their mother and the archangel that the twins were to overhear.

*   *   *

Anya started as the door behind her opened and she came back to the present with a rush.

'Hi. Am I disturbing you?' Luke asked, peering round the door.

As she turned to face him, his expression grew concerned and he came in.

'What's the matter?' he asked, taking her in his arms. 'Why are you crying?'

It was the first time Anya had been aware of her tears. They were being shed for a frightened and unhappy four-year-old girl, who now seemed like a stranger from a distant land.

'Memories,' she muttered indistinctly.

'Do you want to talk about them?'

'No. They're not important now.'

Luke could not help feeling relieved by her answer. His practical nature had not equipped him to deal with complicated emotional matters, though he was guiltily aware that perhaps he ought to try. If Anya's memories had made her cry, then maybe they were important enough for him to insist on her talking about them, getting them out into the open.

But, as so often before, he took the easy option and let her keep her secrets.

19

Two days later, while Luke was enjoying the rare privilege of a well-earned lunchtime drink at the Warren House Inn near the centre of the moor, a familiar voice assailed him from the end of the bar.

'Slacking on the job again, eh, Tasker?'

He got up, smiling, and moved to join his accuser. She sat at the old wooden table between the door and the fire which, by tradition, was kept alight all year round.

'Hello, Sheila. What are you doing here?'

'The same as you,' she replied with a grin. 'Skiving off between jobs.'

'I'll have you know that this is my part of the moor,' Luke informed her. 'I wouldn't think *you* had many clients up here.'

'Just passing through. How's Anya?'

'Moody, as usual,' he replied wearily. 'Did you know she fainted while we were in the Scillies?'

'No. Is she OK?'

'She says so, but . . . I don't know.' Luke shook his head. 'She wouldn't see a doctor, and her new paintings are just as peculiar as the last lot. Have you had any luck with them?'

'Not yet,' the agent admitted.

'How about the new gallery?'

'What new gallery?'

'The one you told her about a few days ago. She said she was going to visit the owner.'

'Oh. Oh, yes,' Sheila said, catching on but unable to hide her initial confusion.

Luke gazed at her intently.

'You didn't tell her about a new gallery?' he asked quietly.

'Yes . . . no.'

'Do you know where she was planning to go?'

'I think you'd better ask Anya,' she replied akwardly. 'She . . .'

'Asked you not to mention it to me?' he completed for her. Sheila nodded. She felt awful.

'Damn,' Luke breathed softly. 'What else has she been lying to me about?'

Anya was standing over the Scrabble board when Luke arrived home that evening. The latest message read WHAT WAS PURPLE AND RULED MACEDONIA. She had been puzzling over the riddle for some time, but only thought of the answer as Luke's key sounded in the front door. She smiled. When she got the chance she would set out the letters: ALEXANDER THE GRAPE. Her instincts for childish humour had obviously survived another birthday. But there was no time for that now and, in keeping with their convention, she moved away from the board before he came in.

She sensed the tension in Luke as he kissed her briefly, and wondered at its cause, the Scrabble joke forgotten. He went to the drinks table, picked up a bottle, then put it down unopened and turned to face her.

'I saw Sheila today,' he remarked.

'Did she say anything about "Moonrider Two"? I'm waiting for Paul's reaction to the roughs before I go any further.'

'She didn't mention it,' Luke said stiffly. 'She did, however, tell me there was no new gallery opening locally, which means you couldn't have been going to visit the owner last week.'

Anya said nothing, and the silence stretched.

'So who were you going to see?' he asked eventually.

'None of your business,' she snapped without thinking, lashing out as always when she felt defensive.

'Nothing about you could possibly be my business, could it? It's not as though we actually live together or love each other, after all.'

126

'Don't!' Anya cried, hurt not so much by his vicious sarcasm as by the knowledge of the pain that had produced it.

'Haven't you got enough secrets?' he went on, torn between anger and sadness. 'Give me some credit. I may not be terribly bright, but I can see that something's wrong and it's getting worse. How can I help when you won't even tell me what's bothering you?'

'I can't,' she said helplessly. 'You've no idea —'

'Of course I haven't!' he exclaimed bitterly. 'How could I? You won't tell me. Am I supposed to be a mind-reader?'

'It was a witch,' Anya blurted out.

'What?'

'That's who I went to see. A witch. But she was out, so I didn't.'

Luke was dumbfounded.

'I didn't see any point in telling you because it all came to nothing,' she added. 'You think I'm strange enough as it is.'

'A witch?' he repeated, as if he was still trying to accept her story. 'What on earth for?'

'Research. One of the paintings I'm doing is based on old tales of local witches, and I wanted to meet one for myself.' She was feeling slightly calmer now, her resolution bolstered by the familiarity of the alibi she had already used with Sheila.

'You don't believe in that stuff, do you?'

'I don't know. I was curious, that's all.'

'And I'm not allowed to share in your curiosity?' he said quietly, returning to his initial grievance.

'Of course you are. I'm sorry, it was stupid of me. Forgive me?'

Luke gazed into her soulful brown eyes and tried to tell himself not to back down. There was still something wrong, so many things she was not telling him, but he could not bear to hurt her any more. The present moment always weighed most heavily in his thoughts. Anya would tell him what the matter was if she wanted to, in her own good time. If not . . .

'I forgive you,' he said. 'I'm sorry I got cross.'

* * *

Anya had stopped thinking, and was now merely waiting. Five days had passed since her second abortive visit to Megan's cottage, and in that time she had decided that she alone would control her fate. If she chose to fight Allessandro, there would be no one to help her; no one could make her decisions for her. The sorcerer had been silent for almost a week, but Anya knew it was only a matter of time before he appeared again, and almost found herself wishing for his next assault. She needed resolution, one way or another.

Why was he delaying? Did it mean that he was unsure of himself, that his boasts of unstoppable power were false? Was there an invisible chink in his armour? Or was his caution merely the result of having to catch up with nearly five hundred years of the world's history? There was only one way she was going to be able to answer these questions, and for that she was dependent on Allessandro himself.

And so she painted, filling in both time and canvasses with an obsessive zeal that led her to miss meals and ignore the telephone. In the evenings, when Luke was home, she tried to relax and succeeded to some degree. Luke recognized her new-found calm and rejoiced in it, without being wholly convinced that their problems were over. He welcomed her sudden burst of creative energy, but wondered whether such concentrated effort was an attempt to divert her mind from whatever was troubling her. She had even taken to getting up in the mornings as early as he did and going straight to her studio when he left for work.

The morning of 23 August began that way. Outside, the weather was still and mild, a thick white mist lying over the moor. That would soon evaporate, leaving the promise of a fine day. For both Anya and Luke, however, this was to be the day when the long-anticipated storm finally broke.

Anya stared at the second version of 'Beneath the Flames'. It bothered her. Unlike several recent compositions, this painting just refused to come together. Every time she looked at it she found reasons for new dissatisfaction and made the necessary adjustments, but it still came no nearer to completion. A tiny hand had appeared near the bottom of the abstract, jewelled sea, and she could not remember putting it there. Her own work often surprised her, especially when she was in full flow, but the hand seemed out of place, a sign of life where there should be none. The flames – which covered almost half the canvas – were still as violent as ever, but now, above the previously all-conquering smoke, there was a thin line of pale blue. The sky was not entirely blotted out, and the childlike fingers seemed to be straining towards this remote and vague promise of freedom. But the weight of water and the fiery barrier made the fulfilment of such yearning seem impossible. Although it seemed to Anya that the symbolism was somehow important, understanding eluded her.

Lost in speculation, she did not realize at first that her studio had vanished, that the glittering sea now stretched endlessly all about her and that the shifting patterns of light and dark above were the flames and smoke of her own creation. Even so, when she saw the image of Allessandro swimming towards her through the silvery blue kaleidoscope, she was not greatly surprised. In fact she felt a measure of relief, as well as a tremor of fear.

'Interesting,' he remarked, looking about him as he drew near.

'Where've you been?'

The sorcerer glanced at her curiously, taken aback by her forthright greeting.

'Exploring,' he replied, deciding to take the question at face value. 'Do you have any idea how many connections there are in a human brain, how much information is stored, how complicated the levels of consciousness are? It's been fascinating.'

He smiled, and Anya felt vaguely nauseous. It was *her* brain he was talking about. Was it really possible that he could explore inside her mind, while she remained unaware of the intrusion? Pushing this horrible thought aside, she put another question to him, one of several she was waiting to ask.

'Did you set the flames on Megan's gate and make the cat —?'

'You did that yourself,' he cut in. 'I enjoyed the show

129

immensely. You obviously have an unsuspected talent for comedy as well as magic.' He laughed at her bewildered expression, then looked up at the raging inferno. 'Poor Anya. You never will be able to reach across the flame, will you?'

'Wh . . . what do you mean?' she stammered.

'You'll understand eventually,' he replied, with a vague wave of his hand. 'Shall we dispense with this artifice?'

He made another casual gesture, and Anya's studio re-established itself around her. The painting of sea and fire was just that once more; a painting. She was still trying to work out what had happened, why the vision had ended so soon, when a ghostly figure stepped out from behind the easel.

'This is so much more convenient, don't you think?' Allessandro said, and smiled.

20

Anya took an instinctive step back, then felt all her muscles petrify as she stared at the transparent figure. That Allessandro was there, now, in her own studio, was undeniable. All her painstakingly formulated theories flew out of the window. This could not be happening inside her mind; he might appear ghostlike but he was as real as Anya herself, and beyond even her fondly imagined hope of control. His initial method of resuming life was no longer relevant. The only thing that mattered was that he was now capable of creating himself as a separate, independent entity – and was thus more dangerous than ever.

Anya glanced at her watch. The second hand ticked on, confirming her fears. Time had not stopped, or even slowed. Allessandro had reentered the common flow of all humanity. The sorcerer spread his hands and raised his eyebrows, mocking her astonishment.

'Why so surprised, little one? I told you we would move on to the next stage soon enough. Now that I am truly back in the world we can make real progress.'

'We?' she asked faintly.

'Of course. We are partners, are we not?' he replied blithely. 'This is a learning process for both of us – surely you understand that by now?'

Anya was too astounded to try and make sense of this. She was still coming to terms with the idea of conversing with a man who moved and talked normally, yet who was translucent. She could see the details of his skin, hair and clothes clearly, but at the same time she could see everything in the room on the far side of him with almost equal clarity.

'What *are* you?' she breathed.

Allessandro laughed.

'A good question. Language can be so inadequate. "Ghost" is probably the best word available, but even that hardly tells the whole story, as you must realize. The path I have travelled may well be unique. Perhaps we will have to invent a new word, just for me.'

'Can you . . . touch things?' she asked nervously.

'I'm still having a little trouble with that,' he replied, smiling at his own candour.

He put out a hand, placed it flat upon the back of the easel and pushed. Anya moved instinctively to catch the painting but stopped when she saw the spectral hand pass slowly through the wood and canvas and emerge on the other side. The frame of the painting shivered slightly, as though it had been caught in a sudden draught, but was otherwise unaffected.

'You see,' the sorcerer remarked with mock disappointment, 'I am not yet ready to lift such weighty things, but that will come. I have been practising already, as you may have noticed.' He grinned mischievously. 'I think I would enjoy being a poltergeist for a while.'

Anya thought back to her disastrous attempt to cook Luke a special meal, and remembered how the kitchen had seemed to be infested by invisible bugs.

'Other things are much easier, of course,' he added. 'Air, for instance.' He puffed out his cheeks and blew, and she shivered as she felt the faintest touch of breath on her face. 'Or the fire that burns in metal,' he went on, 'that you call electricity.' He looked up and Anya followed his gaze as the overhead lights came on of their own accord. 'In my old lifetime such lamps would have been called a miracle, the work of sorcerers,' he said respectfully. 'Now they are commonplace. This world has much to offer – and I intend to sample it all, when I am ready.'

His final words gave Anya a tiny glimmer of hope. There was time yet. Perhaps.

Allessandro glanced at her strangely and the lights went out again.

'Surely you are not still contemplating trying to oppose me?' he said in a tightly controlled voice. 'You could not be that stupid.'

The fact that he was obviously fighting to control his temper gave Anya another glimpse of hope. If the possibility of her opposition still angered him, then all was not lost.

'Don't be absurd, my dear,' he said with exaggerated patience. 'My victory is assured, and is only a matter of time. Your only choice is whether to join me or be crushed. You would enjoy the former much more, I assure you.'

'Constanza beat you,' Anya claimed. There was obviously no point in trying to conceal her thoughts. 'Why can't I?'

'She did not,' he replied wearily. 'At best what she achieved was a dishonourable stalemate. It gained her nothing and cost her more than she ever knew. Besides, do you think I would be fool enough to fall for the same trick twice?'

'Then I have no choice but to submit?' she said, a hint of doubt in her voice.

'True enough, although you obviously don't believe it yet. You will soon. Take my hand.'

He reached out his right hand, palm upwards, fingers outstretched. Anya hesitated, then gingerly placed her own hand on top of his. Although it was like brushing against the lightest of feathers, the warmth of his touch was undeniable.

'The human body is a remarkable thing,' the sorcerer remarked, as she held her breath, wondering what was coming next. 'It is capable of so much. Pleasure, for instance.'

A wave of sensual euphoria, so strong that it was almost a physical force, swept through Anya's body. She closed her eyes, and gave a small, half-strangled cry.

'Think, Anya. You experience all this from a simple touch of hands. Imagine what it would be like to kiss me, to make love.'

Anya tried to imagine, but failed. She opened her eyes and

found him gazing at her intently, like an ardent lover. Her breath was coming in short gasps.

'Of course, every action has its opposite,' he said, his dark eyes turning malevolent.

A second surge ran through her, but this time her nerve ends vibrated with excruciating pain. She cried out, and stumbled as she pulled her hand away.

'Does that make your choice easier?' he asked mildly.

Anya was angry now, angry and confused. She felt somehow defiled.

'Leave me alone.'

But the sorcerer only laughed. Furious, she picked up an empty glass jar from the table and hurled it at her tormentor. Although her aim was good, the jar passed straight through him and shattered against the wall on the other side of the room. Allessandro did not even flinch, and laughed even more loudly, but there was a weariness in his eyes now. Anya knew intuitively that his stay in the real world was costing him considerable effort.

'Go away,' she begged.

'Your wish is my command,' he said and bowed low, mocking her. As he straightened up, his ghostly shape dissolved into flames and he was gone in an instant.

Anya stared at the empty space he had left behind. She felt utterly drained, but knew that this was only the beginning. He would be back. He would grow more solid, more powerful, until eventually he would be real. She could only guess at what would happen to her then, but the idea filled her with terror.

21

That evening, as Anya waited for Luke to come home, she was filled with a truly desperate longing. She had decided to confide in him. In spite of her fears and her long experience of automatically hoarding the awkward secrets of her life, she was now at the end of her tether, and had no one else to turn to. Even so, each minute that passed tested her resolve and she had to keep reminding herself why her decision had been inevitable.

After Allessandro's spectacular exit, Anya's mind had been in turmoil. She was overflowing with wild emotions, constantly on the verge of tears and quite unable to concentrate. Nothing, neither action nor thought, could hold her attention for more than a few seconds and, as time passed, the disorientation grew worse. The physical strain was awful too. She felt exhausted and yet restless, veering between nervous, reflexive fidgeting and absolute lethargy. Eventually she curled up on the sitting room sofa, in an almost foetal position, and in spite of her agitation, had fallen deeply asleep. When she woke it was dusk and she was stiff and sore, but at least she found that she was able to start getting her thoughts in order.

Allessandro's appearance in the real world had changed everything. The rules of the game had been altered to suit him and it was now, as he had said, a new stage of the process. What came next could only be even more threatening. Anya knew that projecting himself into her space and time had cost the sorcerer dearly, but it had also usurped her own energy.

She still felt drained. The next time he came back he would be stronger still – and she would be weaker. And so it would go on until he had taken all her strength. What would she be then? A frail ghost, completely under his spell? Helplessly insane? Dead? Each of the alternatives was appalling, but she had no idea how to halt his seemingly inexorable progress.

Even in his present feeble state, the sorcerer's powers were remarkable, and she trembled at the memory of that ecstatic pleasure and equally intense pain. The temptation he had set before her was frighteningly persuasive. How could anyone choose torture over gratification like that? And yet, could he be trusted? Even if she submitted to him, what guarantees did she have? What was to stop him using her, then leaving her dead, insane, or in constant torment? In one of their earlier encounters, he had compared her to Constanza. *It is you who will pay the price of her treachery.* That did not sound like someone who now claimed that the two of them were 'partners'. The only logical conclusion was that her surrender would help him – at the very least, speed up his progress – and that her continued resistance would prove unpleasant for him, as well as her. Even if it were true that she could not win in the end – not even a Pyrrhic victory such as Constanza's – then she still had to try. And she knew now that she could not carry on the fight alone.

Having made the decision to tell Luke, she tried to rehearse the words she would use, but everything sounded either nonsensical or paranoid. In the end she knew that she would just have to trust to her instincts and hope, against all the odds, that he would understand.

The only scrap of comfort she gained from all this intro-spection was the realization that she was very different from her mother in one specific way. Her parent's insanity had manifested itself most obviously in public. She had displayed a complete lack of any sense of social embarrassment. Anya was the reverse, almost obsessively so. That did not prove that she was sane, of course, but it made her feel better. She was having to force herself to talk even to the one person who was closest to her, whom she knew loved her dearly and who had been trying to offer his help for some time. The thought of speaking to anyone else – even to Sheila – about her predicament was horrifying. And her attempts to contact the witch had been fraught with doubts and possibly self-imposed barriers. *You did that yourself.* Somehow, Anya had to find a way to open the gate between Luke and herself, the gate she had until now kept closed and locked.

When he came in at last, she smiled as best she could, mixed him a drink and sat beside him on the settee. After a few initial, meaningless pleasantries, she summoned up all her courage and found her heart hammering against her rib cage.

'Luke?'

'Mmm?'

'You know I've seemed a bit strange lately?'

He looked at her and nodded slowly, his glass frozen half way to his lips.

'Well, I . . .' Anya hesitated, wondering if it was too late to step back from the brink – and knowing the effect her own worried expression must be having on Luke. Blindly, she plunged onward. 'There's a man . . .'

'Oh, Christ,' he groaned, his dismay immediately obvious.

'No!' she cried, instantly regretting her clumsy words as he jumped to the entirely natural but erroneous conclusion. 'I didn't mean it like that. I'm not having an affair. I love you. There's no one else.'

Even as she spoke, treacherous thoughts whispered that there *was* someone else, someone who had invaded her being as intimately as any lover. And she was shocked and ashamed to see the effect her words had had on Luke. He had stiffened until his body seemed rigid, and the colour had drained from his face. His eyes were moist, and he looked utterly miserable. Her hurried explanation had only partially restored his equilibrium.

'What did you mean then?' he asked in a whisper.

'I mean . . .' Anya paused, wondering how on earth she was going to do this. 'There's a man . . . who's been following me. He just appears . . .'

'A prowler?' Luke was concerned now. 'Have you called the police?'

'No, no,' she said helplessly. 'He's not real. More like a ghost.'

Luke stared at her in open disbelief while she cursed her own ineptitude and searched frantically for the words to go on. Her hands were shaking now.

'Are you telling me,' he said eventually, 'that you think this house is haunted?'

'No,' she replied. '*I* am.'

Luke took some time to consider this statement, while Anya, tongue-tied, begged him silently to ask another question so that she could explain further.

'What does that mean?' he asked finally. 'How can you be haunted?'

'He comes with me wherever I go. He started off just inside my head and we met in paintings, but now he's coming out into the real world. He . . .'

Luke held up a hand to halt the flow of words.

'Wait a minute,' he said. 'This doesn't make any sense.' His face had become an unreadable mask, and that frightened her. 'How can anyone be in your head, except as something imaginary?'

'I know what you're thinking,' Anya replied, almost eager now that they were addressing the central issue, 'but he *does* exist. He's a separate person, a sorcerer, and I was his way back into the world.'

'A sorcerer?' Luke was unable to conceal his incredulity.

'Yes.' Having no choice, she ploughed on, though she knew how absurd she must sound. 'He lived in Italy in the sixteenth century, but his spirit got trapped and he was only able to escape again a few months ago.'

'Into you?'

'Yes.'

'So, in a sense, this spirit has possessed you?'

'Yes, but he's only taken over part of my mind. I can still fight him and make sure that he doesn't get the rest. But I can't do it alone any more. That's why I'm telling you.'

Now that she had begun, she was keen to explain more, to tell the whole story, so that he would have to understand. But Luke's next question took her by surprise; his thoughts were obviously taking a different direction.

'Does this have anything to do with your going away?'

'No. That's something else altogether,' she answered without thinking, then began to wonder if that really was the case. She had no time to reach any conclusions, however, because Luke was asking another question.

'Do you know what this man looks like?'

'Yes. I can show you.' She fetched the rather battered postcard and passed it to him.

Luke stared at the miniature portrait as if he could extract its secrets by sheer willpower, but his expression remained noncommittal. Eventually he turned it over and read the description on the back.

'"Portrait of a Young Man. Andrea del Sarto 1486–1530. The National Gallery."'

'His spirit was trapped in the original painting,' Anya hurried to explain. 'Until he saw me.'

'You went to the National Gallery on one of your trips?'

'Yes.'

Luke was silent for a long time, and Anya had to bite her tongue to prevent herself from asking him what he was thinking.

'Do you see him all the time? Is he here now?'

'Of course not!' She almost laughed. 'I've only seen him a few times.'

'How many?'

'Five . . .' After a moment's thought she corrected herself. 'No, six. Until today it was always in paintings.'

'I have no idea what you're talking about,' Luke said helplessly.

'You remember that time at the hotel, when I fainted?'

He nodded.

'Allessandro was there then. I spent a whole day and night with him in —'

'Allessandro? He has a name?'

139

'Yes. He told me. Allessandro Massimiliano.'

'Go on,' Luke said quietly.

'We were inside the restaurant mural at first, but it expanded . . .'

'You were only unconscious for a few seconds,' he objected suddenly. 'Are you saying a whole day passed for you in that time?'

'Yes. It's always like that, though that was by far the longest. Time is different, somehow.'

'Like in dreams?'

'They're more than dreams,' she stated with certainty.

'What happened?'

As succinctly as she could, Anya told him of her adventure on the otherworldly islands and then, at his prompting, described her earlier experiences – in the underground cavern, on the 'Isle of the Dead', with the sea monster, and on top of the Alpine cliff. He listened quietly, only interrupting when he was totally confused. When she went on to expound her theories about the sorcerer's growing strength, Luke seemed to be taking it all in quite calmly, but she had no idea whether he was convinced.

'But it's different now?' Luke asked. 'He's no longer just in the paintings?'

'He doesn't need them any more,' Anya replied, and described the ghost-like apparition in her studio that morning. 'He's *here* now, and he's going to get even more powerful each time he appears. We have to stop him before it's too late.'

Luke knocked back the last of his long-forgotten drink, then stared down at the empty glass in his hands. The silence stretched until Anya could not bear it any longer – and then she realized, with absolute certainty, that he did not believe a word she had said. The sad expression of concern on his face when he finally looked up was confirmation enough. She could not blame him. Her story had sounded far-fetched, even to her – and she knew it to be the truth. Even so, she could not suppress a tiny spark of anger.

'You think I'm mad, don't you?' It was half accusation, half plea.

140

'No,' he said firmly. 'But I do think you need help.'

'Oh, come on, Luke! That's just hiding behind words.'

'Psychiatry has helped millions of people who aren't mad.'

'That's not what I need.'

'What *do* you need then?'

'I don't know. An exorcist, maybe.'

'Oh, please!' Luke exclaimed, showing a touch of exasperation for the first time.

Anya felt that the whole conversation was sliding out of control, and knew that her attempt to make him understand was doomed. But she could not stop now.

'That's why I wanted to see the witch. To see if she could remove —'

'Stop it, Anya, please,' Luke cut in firmly.

'I can't. I need you to believe me. What chance do I have unless you do?'

'I love you,' Luke said simply, in a voice full of agonized bewilderment. 'I would do anything to keep you safe, to make everything all right for you, but you can't ask me to do the impossible.'

His sincerity was breathtakingly clear, but his reaction was everything that Anya had feared. He thought she was mad.

'You'll do anything except trust me,' she said, with the bitterness of failure in her weary tone.

'That's not fair!' he cried in self-defence. 'I've listened to all you've had to say, but it's . . .'

'Crazy?'

'Frankly, yes. How can you expect me to believe that a five-hundred-year old ghost just leapt out of a painting in the National Gallery and possessed you? Even if he was ever really in there, why pick *you* out of millions? Why has it happened now, after so long?'

'I don't know!' Anya wailed. 'He said I was special.'

'And you are, my love. Very special. But not because of this.'

'What will it take to make you believe me?' She was desperate now.

Luke just shook his head.

'Stay with me tomorrow,' she suggested earnestly. 'Maybe he'll come back and then you'll see him too.' Luke was a practical man. He needed proof.

'I'll stay with you tomorrow,' he promised, 'but not to look for ghosts. We'll ring Dr Morgan and get some advice.'

'No! You can't do that. You've no right.'

'Please, Anya. I'm only trying to help,' he pleaded, and held out a hand to her.

'Get away from me.' She leapt up and ran from the room.

That night, in spite of Luke's conciliatory efforts, they slept in separate rooms.

22

Anya woke very early, after a restless night full of vaguely threatening dreams. But they vanished from her mind as soon as she realized where she was and remembered what had happened the evening before. Remorse overcame her feelings of anger and she went out on to the landing, meaning to try and make her peace with Luke. However, all was quiet beyond their bedroom door and she decided to let him sleep on. He got little enough rest as it was and, if she was honest, Anya was a little afraid of how he might react to her this morning.

She went downstairs quietly and made herself some coffee. She wondered about making a special breakfast as a peace-offering but recalled her last, catastrophic attempt to produce a culinary masterpiece and decided against it. Outside, the early morning sky was overcast and grey, and the trees were swaying in the strong wind. There had been rain overnight, and the fast-moving clouds promised more to come. The long spell of fine weather had come to an abrupt end, but Anya was too preoccupied to see anything symbolic in that. She sat looking out of the window for a while, sipping her coffee and wishing Luke would wake up. Eventually, unable to keep still any longer, she got up, refilled her mug and wandered aimlessly into the sitting room.

She saw the new message on the Scrabble board immediately and went over to read it. I AM SORRY WE WILL GET RID OF HIM was spread over three lines. Anya's spirits leapt. Luke had believed her after all! If only he had had the courage

143

to tell her of his change of heart in person, instead of leaving it for her to find like this, she would have been saved a night of misery. But that did not matter now. She was no longer alone.

It was only then that she took in the final part of the message, which was set neatly in the bottom right hand corner of the board and well separated from the rest. CHICCO D UVA. What did that mean? Like all lovers, Anya and Luke had private terms of endearment but this was entirely new to her. There was a small but precise gap between the D and the U of the second word, which might imply the presence of an apostrophe. *Chicco d'uva*? If that was the case, it was even more likely that this was in a foreign language – not one of Luke's strong points.

There was something odd about the first word, but for a few moments Anya could not see what it was. Then she had it. There were only two C's in a Scrabble set. Where had the third come from? She picked up the first letter and looked at it closely. It seemed genuine enough, but when she ran a finger over the surface, to see whether Luke had used black ink, it was completely smooth. Although this tablet was one of the blanks, she was somehow seeing the indented letter C with a miniature number three beside it.

The truth hit her with the force of a blow, and the morning grew suddenly colder. She knew now what the enigmatic words meant. Chicco d'uva was Italian for grape. Alexander the Grape. *Allessandro*.

The message was not from Luke at all, but from the sorcerer – with the implication that Luke was to be 'got rid of'. Allessandro had evidently become more adept at moving objects in the real world and, moreover, was able to operate independently of Anya, haunting her home even while she slept. With a sinking feeling in her stomach, she realized that the sorcerer had already reached his 'next stage'. He was indeed moving much faster now.

Resisting the impulse to sweep the suddenly horrible message aside, Anya replaced the letter carefully. She ran upstairs and as she burst into the bedroom, Luke glanced up, bleary-eyed. He looked at her warily as she sat on the edge of the bed.

'Will you get up and come downstairs?' she begged him. 'I've got something to show you.'

She waited as patiently as she could while he slid out of bed and put on his dressing gown. Luke followed her to the sitting room without saying a word and was obviously nonplussed – as she had known he would be – when she pointed to the Scrabble board.

'Did you leave this message?'

'No. Of course not,' he replied, looking up at her.

'Neither did I,' she told him eagerly. 'It was him. Allessandro.'

'Don't, Anya, please,' Luke groaned.

'It's true,' she persisted. 'Chicco d'uva means grape, like in the joke. Alexander the Grape. Allessandro.' The words tumbled out, their meaning obvious to her, with no thought given as to how they would sound to Luke. 'It's him, really it is.'

'He's awfully neat for a poltergeist,' Luke commented, with the hint of a smile.

'Don't patronize me,' she snapped.

'Look, Anya. I don't know what you're trying to prove with this . . . this charade, but if you really believe your ghost did this, then you're in more trouble than I thought.' Although his expression was one of concern and bemused fondness, he could not help betraying his rising irritation. 'If you didn't do this, how do you know the first letter there is a C?'

'I can see it is,' she replied, her hopes sinking.

'But it's a *blank*,' he explained patiently.

'You can't see it?' Anya whispered.

Luke did not reply, merely gazing at her with a look of such tender sadness that she was soon on the brink of tears. Then he took her in his arms and she held him tight, knowing it was an empty gesture – and also knowing that she had nowhere else to turn.

'You *have* to get help, Anya,' he told her softly. 'You must see that now.'

She could not respond. There was a lump in her throat that made speech impossible, and her eyes were brimming with tears of frustration, anger, and self-pity.

'He'll never understand. Let's get rid of him. He's just a burden to you.'

The voice came from behind her, out of the blue. Anya stiffened, then extricated herself from Luke's embrace and turned round slowly, hardly daring to breathe. Allessandro was standing, arms folded, next to the still-drawn curtains of the front window. Although he was transparent, he seemed, to Anya's frightened eyes, to have gained a little solidity since the previous day.

'What is it?' Luke asked anxiously.

'He's here,' she breathed, pointing, then glancing back at Luke.

'Where?'

'By the curtains.'

'He can't see me,' the sorcerer remarked contemptuously. 'He hasn't got the imagination for it.'

'Don't you see him?' Anya pleaded, ignoring the interruption. 'You *have* to.'

'There's nothing there, Anya.'

'There is!' she insisted despairingly.

Allessandro laughed, but only she heard him. He put out a spectral hand and pushed through several folds of the curtain, making it sway gently.

'There!' Anya exclaimed. 'He made the curtain move.'

'That's just a draught from the window.'

'No, no, no. It's him!'

'I've had enough of this.' Luke's patience was exhausted. 'You're just scaring yourself with this nonsense. Come on.' He took her arm and led her firmly from the room. In the kitchen he sat her down, then pulled up a chair in front of her. 'Listen, my love, I don't know what's going on here and I'm not qualified to guess. If we ring Dr Morgan, he'll be able to suggest someone who is, someone who can help you, make these visions go away.'

'No mere sawbones will be able to do that,' Allessandro

remarked as he sauntered, unconcerned, through the kitchen door. Anya glanced at him, then looked back at Luke quickly.

'There's nothing there,' he reassured her. 'He can't follow you.'

Allessandro snorted and went to lean nonchalantly on the draining board behind Luke. Anya racked her brain for a way to demonstrate his invisible presence but, given that he was unlikely to cooperate with her and knock something over on cue, she could not see how it could be done.

'Shall I phone the doctor?' Luke asked gently.

Anya could only shake her head dejectedly. She was alone again.

'Why do you put up with this dullard?' Allessandro enquired caustically. 'You're worth a dozen of him. I've seen cockroaches with sharper wits.'

'Shut up!' Anya half shouted. 'Shut up.'

'What? I'm only trying—' Luke said stiffly.

'Not you,' she interrupted, then felt all her resolve crumble. She put her head in her hands and wept. Luke reached out a tentative hand, wanting to comfort her.

'I'll get rid of him for you,' the sorcerer said.

Just then the telephone rang, making both Anya and Luke jump. He swore under his breath and went to answer it.

'Luke Tasker.'

'This should be interesting,' Allessandro remarked. 'Now you'll see where his real loyalties lie.'

Luke listened for a few moments, then swore again.

'This really isn't a good time,' he said. 'Can't anyone else do it?' There was another pause while he listened impatiently. 'All right, all right.' He hung up.

'Don't leave me,' Anya begged before he had a chance to speak.

'I have to. Two kids just got into Postbridge after walking in circles for most of the night. One of their companions has broken his ankle up on the high moor. Stupid little bastards.'

'It's not true. It's a trick,' she said, glancing at Allessandro's smiling countenance.

147

'Don't be ridiculous,' Luke replied shortly. 'I have to get dressed. The helicopter's on the way to pick me up.'

'Then let me come with you,' Anya pleaded.

'You can't, you know that. Listen, ring Sheila and ask her to come over. Tell her it's an emergency. I'll be back as soon as I can.' He started towards the door, then hesitated and looked back. 'You will be OK, won't you?'

'No,' she said miserably.

'See how easy he is to fool?' Allessandro pointed out smugly. 'How quickly he abandons you?' He waved a hand and the scene froze. All sounds of the outside world vanished, and Luke stood like a statue. Anya glanced at the clock on the wall and saw the second hand click once, then become still.

'What are you doing?'

'This is your chance to be rid of him for good,' the sorcerer replied. 'He's as helpless as a babe. All you have to do is pick up one of those knives there and stab him. What could be easier?'

Anya was too horrified to respond. How could he even *think* that she would harm Luke?

'This is growing tedious,' Allessandro stated with a touch of irritation.

Suddenly, Anya got up and grabbed one of the long kitchen knives from the rack he had indicated, but instead of approaching Luke she lunged at the sorcerer, intent on murder.

'Oh, please,' he said disgustedly and made a casual gesture. In that instant, Anya's arm became numb and the knife slipped from nerveless fingers. As it left her hand it floated in midair, then dropped very gradually towards the floor.

'You have much to learn, my dear,' Allessandro told her indulgently, and released the spell.

The blade clattered to the floor and Luke came back to life, a look of astonishment on his face.

'How . . .?' he began, glancing back and forth between Anya and the chair where, for him, she had been sitting only a moment before.

'You see, he'll rationalize even this,' the sorcerer prophesied.

148

Luke shook his head, as if to clear it, then walked over to pick up the knife and put it away.

'Be careful, Anya. You could hurt yourself dashing about like that.'

Anya was too dumbfounded to reply.

'I have to go,' he added apologetically, then left the room and ran up the stairs. Anya turned back to Allessandro, whose face was now etched with tiredness. His exhibition had not been without its cost.

'Alone at last,' he said with mock satisfaction. 'Sadly, however, I must also leave you now. How about a kiss to speed me on my way?'

Anya's obscene reply made him laugh.

'Such self-denial, and in one so young. Remarkable,' he commented dryly. 'Farewell, Constanza. Until next time.' He disappeared, blinking out of existence in an instant.

Anya stared at the now empty space, listening to the sounds of her heart beating, of the wind buffeting the house and of Luke's hurried preparations upstairs. But hidden among these mundane noises was an ominous ticking. And, for the first time ever, Anya knew that she had wound the clock herself.

When Luke returned home less than an hour later, he was frantic with worry and very angry. The whole thing had indeed proved to be a wild goose chase, a cruel but plausible hoax, and he could not rid himself of the memory of Anya's prophetic words. *It's not true. It's a trick.* After waiting for the helicopter at the pick-up site for some time, he had radioed in and met with flat denials and a ribald comment about his drinking so early in the day. When he had finally convinced himself that he was alone in responding to the supposed emergency, he drove back to the house like a madman. What he found when he arrived made him more frightened than he had ever been in his life.

The front door had been left open, and the house was in a shambles. Luke dashed from room to room, calling Anya's name. The kitchen looked as though it had been visited by a tornado; chairs and table overturned, broken glass and rubbish from the bin strewn over the floor. A quick glance at the sitting room revealed similar signs of disturbance; books had been pulled from shelves, Scrabble letters swept onto the carpet, and one set of curtains was hanging askew. Upstairs there was less disruption and the studio appeared untouched, but there was no sign of Anya anywhere. Luke flew back downstairs, three steps at a time, meaning to phone the police. As far as he could see, nothing had been stolen but a break-in seemed the most likely explanation. All he wanted was to find Anya safe, to know that she was all right. Visions of lurid kidnapping stories leapt into his mind, and he cursed himself viciously for having left her alone.

It was only when he reached the hallway that he saw the note, pinned to the inside of the front door. He pulled it off and anxiously read Anya's hurried scrawl.

I'm sorry, Luke. I have to go. Don't blame yourself, no one can help me. I'll be back when this is sorted out, one way or another. I love you. Anya.

Underneath was a brief postscript.

I'm sorry about the mess. Allessandro was angry.

Luke crumpled up the paper in his fist, shut his eyes tight and took a deep, painful breath. Perhaps there was no longer any need to ring the police. Anya herself, not a would-be burglar or kidnapper, was responsible for the violence. But he had to find her, had to get help for her. She was obviously seriously disturbed, and he dreaded to think what peril her delusions might lead her into. At least he had a good idea where she might have gone first – and she could not be that much ahead of him.

Luke went out, slamming the door behind him, and checked to see that Anya's car had indeed gone. Then he ran to the Landrover and set off in pursuit.

Luke found Anya's car outside Newton Abbot station, as he had expected. He only glanced at it as he ran past, but that was enough to see that it was badly parked, the door unlocked and the keys still in the ignition. This evidence of her haste made him feel even worse. Hurried enquiries brought the unwelcome news that the London train had left some twenty minutes earlier, but no one on the platform staff or in the ticket office could recall seeing anyone of Anya's description. Even so, Luke's best guess was that she was heading for Paddington, and he wondered desperately whether there was any way he could get there before her. The only airport in the Southwest of England with regular flights to London was Plymouth. Luke glanced at his watch. By the time he got there, even if he was lucky enough to catch a plane immediately, he could never get from Heathrow to Paddington in time. And he had no idea where she might be headed from there, so getting the next train was equally pointless. It was hopeless.

Luke searched the station as best he could, just in case Anya was still there, receiving several odd looks from staff and passengers, but was soon convinced he was wasting his time. He walked back to the car park, considering the options left open to him. Could he get the train stopped? No, that was absurd. He wasn't even sure she was on it, and British Rail's transport police were very unlikely to agree to such drastic measures. Was there anyone in London who could meet her off the train? Luke had lived in Devon all his life, and knew no one in the capital. Alerting the station authorities would be fraught with difficulties and he doubted that they would take him seriously. Anya could be on another train altogether, or have got off at any of the stations before Paddington. Anyway, what was he supposed to say to them? That his girlfriend was in danger because she believed she was possessed by an ancient sorcerer from a painting in the National Gallery?

Bowing unhappily to the inevitable, Luke gave up any idea of immediate pursuit. He needed time to think. Without any real expectation of finding anything useful, he searched Anya's car for clues, but found nothing. He then radioed one of his colleagues to arrange cover for his appointments, explaining that he would not be able to get to work that morning, and asked for someone to come in to Newton and pick up his Landrover. That done, he climbed back into Anya's car and drove home slowly, his mood veering between misery and self-directed rage.

Back at the house, he telephoned Sheila. Anya had not called her agent that morning – that had been a forlorn hope at best – and Sheila had no idea where she might have gone.

'This is sudden,' she commented, 'even for Anya. She's only been back for three weeks. Didn't she give you any warning?'

'None at all. But that's not the half of it.'

'What's going on, Luke? Do you want to talk about it?'

He did not reply, thinking that although he would be glad to share the burden – and, surely, there could be no objection to his talking to Anya's closest friend – actually doing it was another matter.

'Are you OK?' Sheila asked, finding his silence unsettling. 'Is there anything I can do to help?'

'Maybe. Is there anyone you know who could meet the train in London?'

'My sister works somewhere near Paddington. I could try calling her. She's never met Anya, but she isn't too hard to recognize.'

'Would you?' Luke said gratefully. 'It gets in at ten to twelve.'

'That doesn't give us much time. I'd better phone now. What is she supposed to say to Anya?'

152

'Tell her to phone me and, if possible, ask your sister to stay with her until I can join them. I know it's a lot to ask . . .'

'I'll try. I'll call you back when I have any news.'

'Thanks, Sheila.'

Luke broke the connection and immediately dialled another number. A woman's voice answered.

'Hello, Lillian. It's Luke Tasker. Is David on duty today?'

'No, he's here. I'll get him for you.'

After a short pause, David Yelling – a local police sergeant whom Luke had known since he was a boy – came on the line.

'Hello, Luke. How's tricks?'

'Not too good at the moment.'

'Is this by way of an official call then?' The policeman's voice had become grave.

'Semi-official,' Luke replied. 'Anya's disappeared again.'

'Hardly the first time is it, though?' David said sympathetically.

'This is different.' Without explaining the exact nature of Anya's disturbed state of mind, Luke described the situation and asked for David's advice.

'Well, you can hardly file a missing person report when she's only been gone a couple of hours,' the sergeant replied sagely. 'In fact, given that you'd have to admit she goes off on her own quite often, it'd be hard to get her disappearance taken seriously. She's always come back all right before.'

'But —'

'Is she likely to be a danger to anyone?'

'I don't know. Would it help if I said she was?'

The policeman considered this for a few moments.

'It might,' he conceded, 'but you'd get caught up in a terrible lot of red tape. It'd make things pretty sticky for Anya too, if and when the police caught up with her. The London boys have got too much on their plate to have much time or sympathy for a case like this,' he added. 'I wouldn't advise it.'

Luke had already reached the same conclusion.

'I'm not even sure she's heading for London,' he admitted.

153

'And I don't really think she's a danger to anyone, except herself maybe.'

'I'm sorry, son,' David concluded. 'I'll keep an ear open, but I don't really see how we can help right now.'

'Thanks anyway. Bye.'

'Good luck. She'll be OK, I'm sure.'

Luke put the phone down and it rang again almost immediately. He snatched it up.

'Hello.'

'It's me,' Sheila began. 'Just to let you know, my sister's on her way to the station. I won't phone again until later in case Anya tries to get through to you.'

'Thanks, Sheila. You're an angel.'

'Just a friend,' the agent replied, matter of fact. 'Talk to you later.'

Luke sat by the telephone for some time, watching the clock and praying. Although the minutes seemed to crawl by, midday eventually came and went, and his anxiety increased by degrees. He stayed where he was, willing the phone to ring. Nothing happened and in the end, unable to stand the waiting any longer, he decided to see whether he could discover any clues in the house. Anya had left in a great hurry, so it was possible she might have overlooked something for once. He began his search downstairs, tidying up the mess as he went, then headed upstairs to continue his apparently fruitless task.

As always, Anya appeared to have taken very little – her black bag and a few clothes were the only items he could identify positively as missing – and his only discovery of any note, while astonishing, did nothing to suggest any possible destination. Tucked in the corner of a drawer, which had been left open after being obviously ransacked, was a thick wallet full of unsigned £100 traveller's cheques. Luke counted them slowly; there were thirty-five. He was just trying to work out the significance of his find when the telephone rang.

'Hello,' he said breathlessly, after bounding downstairs.

'Luke, it's Sheila. Bad news, I'm afraid. Emily got to Paddington just after the train pulled in. She saw most of

154

the passengers come out, but there was no one who looked like Anya, so either she was one of the first off or she wasn't on the train at all. I'm sorry.'

Luke groaned inwardly. His last hope of following her trail was gone.

'Thanks for trying,' he said, doing his best to hide his disappointment. 'I appreciate it.'

'No problem. I just wish we'd been able to help. Is there anything . . .?'

'No, really. You've done enough already.'

'Want to talk? I can come over if you like,' she offered.

'No, not now. I ought to call work. I might ring you this evening, if that's OK.'

'Of course,' Sheila agreed. She was really worried now – and wondered what Anya was up to.

Luke checked in with the National Park's headquarters, and arranged to stay at home for the rest of the day. Not for the first time, he felt lucky to be part of a team whose members supported each other so well. Then, realizing that he had eaten nothing all day, he made himself some toast and forced himself to chew and swallow, even though he was not really hungry. He was still on edge, hoping vainly that Anya would get in touch.

It was only when he had finished this desultory meal that he recalled seeing mail on the front doormat. Although it could not be important, he went to fetch it, needing something to do. Most of the correspondence was addressed to him and was wholly uninteresting, but there was one letter for Anya with a Bristol postmark. Luke stared at the anonymous, typed envelope, wondering what it contained. It wouldn't have any bearing on Anya's disappearance, having been posted before she left, but he could not rid himself of the urge to look inside. He had never before opened any of Anya's mail, although he had been sorely tempted to do so during earlier trips. But now he felt justified in taking liberties. He was worried sick, but he was also angry with her for putting him in this predicament, and invading her privacy in this trivial way was the only means he had of punishing her.

155

He slit the envelope with a knife and took out a single sheet. The letter was typed on the headed notepaper of a private hospital near Bristol and, as Luke scanned the contents, he felt even more of the bedrock of his life turn to quicksand. Nothing about Anya was simple, not even her secrets. How many more lies would he discover before they were through? He went back to the beginning and read the entire letter again.

Dear Miss Caplan,

I apologize in advance for contacting you about a matter which you may find painful. I am also sorry to be the bearer of bad news. A short time ago your mother, who has been a patient here for the last twelve years, suffered a stroke. At first it was thought that this latest illness would prove fatal and, although happily this has not been the case, it became necessary to get in touch with Mrs Caplan's next of kin. Our contact name was Miss Meredith Caplan who is, I believe, your sister. However, her telephone is permanently connected to an answering machine and to date we have had no response to any of our messages, nor to the letter we sent her.

In the meantime, your mother began to ask for you and continues to do so now that her recovery is nearly complete. It is my understanding that you have had no contact with your mother for several years (and it has taken me some time to track down your address), but I hope you will now consider coming to visit her. Failing that, if you know where your sister might be contacted, I would be grateful for the information.

Yours sincerely,
Dr Elizabeth Burrows

Luke gazed at the signature which, in defiance of the traditions of her vocation, was clearly legible. The 'bearer of bad news', she had called herself, but her letter revealed more than she could have envisaged. At least now Luke had something to do.

He picked up the telephone again.

24

Two hours later, Luke turned off the M5 and followed the directions he had been given. At the entrance to what looked like a country estate, he was met by a gatekeeper who checked his name against the list on his clipboard before raising the barrier to let him through. Luke drove down the long avenue and parked outside a large Victorian building which had obviously once been rather grand but now looked somewhat dirty and run down. Several of the windows, he noted with some trepidation, were barred.

Inside the main entrance, he introduced himself to the receptionist who conveyed the news of his arrival to Dr Burrows. Luke sat in an uncomfortable chair and waited, wondering what he was doing there. He was already finding the atmosphere oppressive.

Matters took a turn for the better when the doctor arrived, a few minutes later. She was younger than he had envisaged, an attractive woman with shoulder-length blond hair, and dressed in a knitted cream tunic and knee-length skirt rather than the expected white coat. Her smile was genuinely welcoming.

'Mr Tasker, I'm Elizabeth Burrows. Thank you for coming.'

'Thank you for letting me,' he replied as they shook hands.

'No problem. You're about the nearest we can get to Mary's next of kin, even if you're not officially part of the family. Besides, it sounded as though you have reasons enough of your own for coming. Let's go and have a chat in my office before we see Mary.'

They set off down the bare but warmly lit corridor.

'I didn't even know what her name was until today,' Luke confessed. 'Anya told me her mother was dead.'

'Family members often find it easier to deny the existence of someone who is mentally ill, especially when traumatic events occurred during their childhood, as they undoubtedly did with Anya,' the doctor replied.

She led the way into a large, cluttered room and waved Luke to an armchair before seating herself behind the desk.

'My letter must have come as quite a shock to you.'

'Yes,' he admitted simply and refrained from adding that it had been only the latest of several recent surprises.

'OK. Let me fill you in on a few details. Mrs Caplan, Mary, is a paranoid schizophrenic. It's an extremely serious condition, and she's been more or less confined in various psychiatric hospitals for the last twenty-four years, the last twelve here as you know. She suffers from frequent hallucinations and has what, in layman's terms, is known as a persecution complex. She can be suspicious, hostile and excessively sensitive and, like most schizophrenics, has become increasingly withdrawn over the years. You'll need to bear all that in mind when you meet her.'

Luke nodded, already feeling intimidated by the prospect.

'As if that's not enough,' the doctor went on, with an apologetic smile, 'Mary has one other problem which has ruled out any hope of social rehabiliation, but I'll come to that in a moment. What concerns me most right now is the change in her behaviour since her stroke. That was almost exactly a month ago, and her recovery has been remarkable, all the more so for someone of her overall mental condition. It was only after this episode that she started asking to see Anya. It was the first time she had shown any interest in anything not connected to her delusions for a long time, and I was intrigued. That was why I was keen for you to come, so that I might get another side of the story.' She paused, collecting her thoughts. 'As you know, we tried to contact Meredith first. I left several messages on her answering machine and wrote to her, but we've had no response. In the meantime, my colleagues at the DSS managed to track Anya down, but even then they could only give me an address, not a telephone number.'

'Mine is the only name listed,' Luke explained. 'Anya prefers to be ex-directory.'

'Which brings us up to date,' Elizabeth concluded. 'There's more to tell and I'm sure you have some questions, but I'd like to hear about Anya now, if I may, and how you come to be here.'

Luke hesitated, then decided to ignore her request, at least for the moment, and ask the question that was uppermost in his mind.

'Is schizophrenia a hereditary condition? Could it be passed from mother to daughter?'

'There are often strong genetic factors in the causation,' the doctor replied carefully, 'but they're by no means the only ones. Others, such as environmental stress, can be just as important.'

Luke became very still, and lowered his eyes, although he remained aware of the doctor regarding him closely.

'Tell me about Anya,' she prompted.

And so Luke told the story as quickly as he could, describing Anya's secrecy concerning her past, her need to go away at frequent intervals and her strange non-relationship with her twin. Then, reluctantly, he gave an account of her recent revelations. Elizabeth seldom interrupted, asking only an occasional question, and Luke concluded with Anya's latest and most worrying disappearing trick.

'I had hoped coming here might help me find her,' he went on. 'For all I know she might have been visiting her mother when she was away on her trips. But . . .' and he paused, noting the expression on the doctor's face, 'I don't suppose that's the case.'

'No. I'm sorry,' Elizabeth Burrows said. 'You're the first visitor Mary's had in over two years. I've been checking the records.' She tapped a file on her desk.

'Who was that?'

'Meredith.'

'Could you give me Meredith's address and telephone number?'

'I don't see why not.' She wrote them out and handed the piece of paper over. 'She doesn't seem to be there much, though. I hope you have better luck than I did.'

'Thanks,' Luke said, pocketing the folded sheet. 'Do you . . . do you think Anya's ill, like her mother?'

'That's difficult to say from the little you've told me, but her hallucinations would certainly bear further investigation. Whatever their cause, it's obviously not a straightforward case.'

Luke could not help smiling ruefully.

'I know, I know,' Elizabeth said. 'You could have told me that.' She smiled and Luke felt enormously grateful to her for her calm and professional manner. He had not known how much he had needed to talk to someone who would understand.

'Do you know why Mary wanted to see Anya?' he asked.

'I was hoping you might be able to shed some light on that,' she admitted frankly. 'Mary won't be drawn, at least not by me.'

'You think I . . .?'

'Who knows?'

'But we've never met,' he objected. 'I never even knew of her existence until today, and she almost certainly doesn't know of mine.'

'Maybe, but you're from Anya. That might count for something. I hope so, anyway.'

'I'll do my best,' Luke promised.

'Before we go, I need to know if you smoke?'

'No. Why?'

'So you don't have a lighter or matches on you?'

Luke shook his head.

'Mary can be very devious at times,' the doctor said. 'I may want to leave the two of you alone and it's quite possible that she'd try to trick you into giving them to her, or even steal them – and that could have serious consequences.'

'Her little problem?'

'Not so little. Pyromania is a very unusual side-effect of her illness. A great number of her delusions are concerned with fire, especially in a religious context, and the obsession spills over into physical reality. We caught her once, in the days when she was more mobile, trying to siphon petrol from one of the doctor's cars. And that was after she had had to be moved from two of her previous hospitals because part of them burned down. Three people died in one of the fires, but Mary survived, much to her disappointment.'

'They were suicide attempts?' Luke was appalled.

'It's the only way she's willing to die, and we keep saving her,' the doctor told him. 'I often wonder if it wouldn't have been better for her if she'd succeeded that first time. That's a terrible thing for a doctor to say, I know, but . . .' She shrugged.

'The first time was twenty-four years ago?' Luke guessed, knowing he was right. Anya and Meredith had been four years old then.

'Yes. Her husband had left her, and she couldn't cope. She set fire to the house while she was still inside. She told me that when the firemen pulled her out, they were amazed that she'd survived.'

'So that was why the twins were sent to their aunt?'

'I suppose it must have been. It was a long time ago, and records aren't always what they should be, but there's no question that she was unfit to care for young children.'

'Christ,' Luke breathed. 'No wonder Anya never wants to talk about her childhood.'

'I've no idea whether there was any physical abuse,' Elizabeth said gravely, 'but at that age a child's mind is even easier to hurt. Seeing your home burnt to the ground can't be easy at any age.'

Luke found himself filled with a growing hatred for the sick woman, and wondered whether he really wanted to meet her after all. Elizabeth evidently understood his dilemma.

'You've had a lot to take in,' she said gently. 'Are you ready to see Mary, or would you like to wait a while?'

'I'm ready,' he replied heavily.

The room in which Mary Caplan lived was on the first floor of the hospital, with a window overlooking fields and trees. It had an old-fashioned feel, and the furniture was worn and faded.

'Mary, I've brought a visitor for you,' Elizabeth said as they entered.

The wheelchair positioned next to the window swung round jerkily and Mary looked at the newcomers. Her face was a coarse version of Anya's, but the hair was grey and her body had turned to fat. When he looked more closely, Luke could see a vague slackness about her left side, the only reminder of her recent stroke. She stared at him intently, then turned away again.

'I'm not talking to him,' she declared shortly. 'He's a man.'

'He's Anya's boyfriend,' Elizabeth explained.

'No, he isn't,' Mary replied flatly. 'He's not the one she's with. I've seen him in the flames.'

'Who have you seen?' Luke asked softly.

There was no reply. Mary was evidently keeping her promise not to talk to him.

'Who have you seen?' Elizabeth tried.

'The one she's with. The angel from the picture.'

After that, try as they might, neither Luke nor Elizabeth could coax another word out of her.

25

Luke drove home, lost in helpless speculation. Could Mary possibly know about Allessandro, 'the angel from the picture'? It seemed ridiculous, yet the coincidence was hard to accept. Elizabeth had all but discounted the episode, saying that her patient's rare speeches were full of obscure references to angels, demons and the like, but she had no ready explanation for the mention of a painting. Even so, she had promised to obtain a copy of the portrait that Anya had shown Luke and present it to Mary to see if there was any reaction. The doctor's opinion was that this would be extremely unlikely, but she was happy enough to try. Other than that, all she could do was promise to get in touch with Luke if either of the twins contacted their mother.

Luke felt as if his whole world had crumbled about him in a single day; first there had been Anya's incredible confession and subsequent flight, which in itself had been like something from a horror movie, and now this. How was he supposed to sift the truth from the clutter of lies he had been told in the past, and from the sometimes even stranger evidence he was discovering for himself? What he had learnt about Anya's childhood had made him dreadfully angry – and all the more frustrated by his current impotence. The old woman's stubborn silence after that first enigmatic statement had infuriated him to the point where he had had to leave the room, fearing his own potential for violence. Mired in his own distress, he would cheerfully have strangled Mary if by doing so he could have helped make Anya safe. Her mother's current frailty could not excuse past cruelties to the little girl who had grown into the woman he loved.

Luke now understood Anya's previously inexplicable dislike of any open fire; she had converted her house to central heating before moving in, and had insisted on fitting smoke alarms. In this respect at least, she was obviously quite different from her mother. On the other hand, it was beginning to seem possible that she had inherited her parent's schizophrenia, even though it manifested itself in markedly different ways. If this *was* the case, might she also be potentially suicidal? The idea made Luke feel quite sick. And could it also explain Anya's single most obvious eccentricity, her need for those secret trips? What was she running away from?

It was late when Luke finally got home, and he was exhausted both physically and emotionally. All the rooms were dark and empty and he knew, without looking, that Anya had not returned. He thought of going straight to bed with a hot drink, but knew that there was one last thing he must do first.

As the kettle heated up, he picked up the telephone and dialled Meredith's number in the Scillies. After four rings there was a click as the answering machine went into action. The recorded voice that spoke in his ear disconcerted him slightly, and he realized that, subconsciously, he had been expecting Meredith to sound like Anya. The shape of her vowels was the same but, even on tape, the tone was softer, more mellifluous, without the sharp edges so often present in Anya's voice. The message also contained an element of self-deprecating humour that Luke did not fully understand, but which was unlike Anya's habitually edgy contact with technology.

'Hi, this is the all-seeing Meredith Caplan. Unfortunately, I'm not here right now so I can't see who you are. If it's important, leave a message after the thing that goes beep. Please speak clearly because some mediums are clearer than others. Over to you.'

The tone sounded and, although Luke had mentally rehearsed

what he intended to say, the unconventional introduction made him stumble awkwardly to begin with.

'Hello ... My name is Luke Tasker. I'm ... your sister Anya's partner ... friend. She's missing ... and I'm worried that she might be in danger. Please, if you hear from her or if you know anything of her whereabouts, contact me at once.' He gave his own telephone number, then concluded, 'Thank you ... Bye,' before putting the phone down.

Luke had little hope that his call would bring any results, but there seemed nothing else he could do. Everything he'd tried so far had come to a dead end. The confirmation that Meredith lived on St Agnes explained her regular visits to Tresco and, in other circumstances, he would have been pleased by the discovery. Now it was just one more piece in a complicated jigsaw that he seemed to have no chance of ever completing. He went to bed feeling wretched and lonely, alternately cursing Anya and longing for her. He had suspected for a long time that love was not subject to reason, and this day had given him all the proof he would ever need.

Luke returned to work the next day. He avoided the well-meaning enquiries from his colleagues and immersed himself in the job as best he could. Even so, Anya was never far from his thoughts and he made clumsy mistakes all day; he was glad to be engaged in nothing more hazardous than organizing volunteers in litter clearance and leading a guided walk.

Sheila rang that evening and, when she realized how complicated the situation had become, insisted on coming to see him. They spent a long time discussing Anya, her recent behaviour and the news about her mother, but neither of them had any positive ideas about how to find her. Sheila called Megan, the self-styled witch, just in case Anya had been to see her after all, but she obviously had not.

In fact the only real benefit from the evening was Luke's marginal feeling of relief at sharing his troubles a second time, and this time with someone who was not a stranger.

It was a small comfort, but a tangible one. Over the next few days Sheila kept in touch regularly. Every time the phone rang Luke could not suppress a surge of disappointment that it was not Anya's voice on the line, but he was grateful for her concern nonetheless.

When, five long days after Anya's disappearance, the telephone rang in the early evening, Luke prayed that it would be Anya but expected to hear Sheila. It turned out to be neither.

'Mr Tasker?' The enquiry was tentative, and Luke did not recognize the voice.

'Yes.'

'My name's Alice Tennant. You don't know me, but I'm a neighbour of Meredith Caplan.'

'Oh,' Luke said, wondering where this was leading. 'On St Agnes?'

'That's right. She's away a lot, with her work, and so I check her answering machine every week or so. That's how I got your number.'

'Have you any news for me?' he asked, more eagerly now. 'Do you think Meredith might know where her twin is?'

'No, Meredith hasn't been home for over a month, but I may be able to help anyway. I met Anya the day before yesterday.'

'What?' Luke exclaimed, hardly daring to believe his ears. 'Where?'

'In Hugh Town. That's on St Mary's, here in the Scillies.'

'I know. Is she staying there?'

'I don't know, I'm afraid. At first I thought it was Meredith, they look so alike, but she had no idea who I was. And all her clothes were black. Meredith would never wear anything like that.' Alice paused. 'She did seem to be acting very strangely.'

'How?'

'Very nervous, almost frightened. She was always glancing over her shoulder, even while we were talking, as if she thought someone was following her.'

Luke's fears rose up again, competing with his elation at this fortunate encounter.

166

'It was only when I listened to your message this evening,' Alice went on, 'that I realized she might be in trouble. I only wish I'd checked the machine sooner. I do hope you don't mind me meddling in things that are none of my business, but I thought —'

'No, no. Of course not,' Luke cut in. 'You've done me the most enormous favour. Have you any idea where she might be now?'

'I'm afraid not. If I'd known it was important I'd have asked but, to be honest, we didn't talk much. She seemed anxious to get away. I don't know if she's left the Islands, but a lot of visitors have been scared away by these ridiculous earthquake stories. Stuff and nonsense, of course, but you know what people are like.'

This surprising information rang a bell in the back of Luke's mind, but he ignored it for the moment.

'Is there anything you can think of, anything Anya said, that might help me find her?'

Alice thought for a few moments.

'I'm sorry, no.'

'If you *do* remember anything, please let me know. I think I'll come down to the Scillies myself to see if I can pick up her trail,' he said, making a sudden decision. 'May I take your number? In case you see her again or if Meredith gets in touch?'

'Of course.' She gave him the number. 'But unless Anya comes to St Agnes I won't be seeing her for the next few days at least. I don't get off the island much. I wish I could be of more help.'

'You've been the most enormous help already. I'm very grateful. Thank you.'

'You're welcome,' she replied softly. 'I hope you find her.'

They said goodbye and Luke immediately rang to book himself on the eleven o'clock flight from Exeter the next morning. He also called his boss and explained that he needed a few days' emergency holiday, and was relieved to have this accepted with a minimum of fuss and without him having to give precise reasons. Then he phoned Sheila to

167

tell her the latest developments, and went upstairs to pack a few things into his trusty rucksack. He had no idea how long he would be away, but he kept the clothes to a minimum. He also pocketed the traveller's cheques. They would help pay his way if extended travel became necessary, and might also make it more difficult for Anya to leave again if – God forbid! – she should return home while he was away. Just in case that happened he left a note for her, prominently displayed on the kitchen door, explaining where he had gone and begging her to stay.

When he had done all he could in the way of preparation, Luke felt too restless to sleep, even though it was getting late and decided, out of idle curiosity, to investigate Alice's comment about earthquakes. He remembered having seen something about them in the *Western Daily News* but had thought nothing of it at the time. The article, when he eventually unearthed it, was written in a light-hearted manner and was mostly anecdotal. A few facts emerged, however. There had apparently been several small tremors in the Scilly region, some of which had been strong enough to rattle windows and frighten both people and animals. Little structural damage had been caused, but the harm to the tourist trade had been rather more serious. Scientists confessed to being baffled by the seismic disturbances in what was usually a very stable part of the Earth's crust, and they emphasized that there was no reason for panic; it was very unlikely that there would be further tremors.

The reporter had then included some rather less serious comments from various other sources. These ranged from local boatmen who had noted odd effects on the islands' tides to the self-styled Druid who proclaimed that the tremors signalled the return of King Arthur, and who predicted a whole series of catastrophes which would lead to the end of the world unless humanity mended its ways. There were also eye-witness accounts of dolphins, seals and schools of fish acting in peculiar ways, and of strange lights under the sea.

The piece gave the overall impression that the whole episode had been something of a joke, which only the gullible or owners of expensive china had taken seriously. However, a more sombre footnote recorded a serious, unexplained fire at a hotel in Hugh Town. It was not yet known whether its cause had anything to do with the tremors. The guests had been evacuated, and several had received medical treatment for shock, minor burns and the effects of inhaling smoke, although none had been seriously injured. The possibility that Anya might have been staying in this hotel was not lost on Luke and the description of the mysterious blaze worried him, coming so soon after the revelations about her mother's pyromania. He tried to convince himself that he was fretting over nothing, that this was just a coincidence, that there were dozens of hotels and guest houses in Hugh Town and the chances of Anya having stayed in this particular establishment were extremely slim. Yet he could not rid himself of a sense of foreboding, and eventually went to bed feeling very apprehensive.

After setting the alarm, Luke lay awake for several hours, unable to suppress the morbid imaginings of his overexcited brain. When he had had no idea where Anya was his fears had been vague and ever-changing; now that he could picture her in a specific context, they had come into focus and were all the more unsettling. He finally fell asleep, desperately wishing for morning so that he could be on his way.

26

Luke woke a few minutes before the alarm was due to go off, and got up immediately. He went downstairs and made himself some coffee, wondering for the first time why Anya had chosen to go to the Scillies. Had she been looking for her sister? Or was there some other, more obscure reason? He had no way of knowing, but was itching for action now. Pouring the coffee down the sink and rinsing out his mug, he collected his rucksack and was about to leave – even though he knew he would get to the airport far too early – when the post came tumbling through the letter box. He flicked through it quickly, and his heart seemed to miss a beat when he saw a postcard showing the Island Hotel on Tresco.

Discarding the rest of the mail, Luke turned the card over and glanced at the signature at the bottom. His utter dismay when he saw an unfamiliar name there was mitigated almost immediately when he noticed Anya's name in the text of the very short message – which was written in a cultured, neat hand, quite unlike Anya's untidy scrawl.

Dear Luke,
I think you should know that Anya's here. She needs your help.
    Yours in haste,
    Verity Nyman.

Luke had no idea who Verity Nyman was, nor why she was taking an interest in Anya's welfare, but at least it was confirmation of her whereabouts, and made him all the more certain that he was right in going there. The postmark was 27 August, three days ago, the same day Alice had met Anya in Hugh Town.

Luke glanced at his watch. There was still plenty of time before he needed to set off. It took him a few minutes to find the number, but then he phoned the Island Hotel and waited breathlessly for them to answer. *Please God, let her still be there.* He had no idea what had drawn Anya back to the hotel, but he could only hope it had been enough to keep her there.

'Island Hotel, Tresco. How can I help you?'

'I'm enquiring about a guest at the hotel. Do you have an Anya Caplan staying with you?'

'I don't believe so, sir. Let me check.'

There was a pause, while Luke's hopes plummeted. The receptionist came back on the line.

'Did you say Anya Caplan, sir?' she asked, enunciating the syllables of the name with unnecessary care.

'Yes. Is she there?'

'I'll just transfer you to our duty manager, sir. Please hold the line.'

There was a click, and Luke swore under his breath as he wondered what was going on.

'May I ask who's calling?' said a man's voice.

'Luke Tasker. I'm Anya Caplan's partner. I stayed at your hotel with her earlier this month. It's vitally important that I contact her,' he replied impatiently. 'Is she there?'

'She *was* here, Mr Tasker, but she checked out on the morning of August twenty-seventh,' the manager replied coolly.

'Damn! Where did she go? Do you know?'

'No, sir. I don't. I wish I did. Miss Caplan stayed for two nights only and left in a great hurry. She apparently took the launch to St Mary's, but we haven't heard from her since.'

'So she could be on one of the other islands or have left the Scillies altogether?'

'That's correct,' the manager replied formally. 'In view of the unfortunate circumstances surrounding her departure, it seems unlikely that she will be returning here.'

Luke began to feel sick.

'What circumstances?' he asked apprehensively.

'As I mentioned, Miss Caplan left in some haste. It was only after her departure that we discovered the condition of her room. It was, to put it mildly, in a state of considerable disrepair. Fortunately the breakages were minor, but it involved our staff in considerable extra work.'

'Oh, no,' Luke breathed, realizing why the man's tone had been so cool.

'We later received complaints from the guests in the adjoining rooms,' the manager went on, 'about disturbances during the night, raised voices and the sounds of a scuffle in the early hours – although the room had been booked for single occupancy.'

'Could the argument have been with an intruder?' Luke asked, rising automatically to Anya's defence, even though he knew he was clutching at straws. The damage sounded too much like what had happened to his own home.

'I think that's most unlikely, especially given Miss Caplan's subsequent actions. Frankly, this is not the kind of behaviour we expect from our guests.'

'I'm sorry. Anya may well be very ill. If you'll send me the bill, I'll pay for the breakages.'

'That won't be necessary, sir,' the manager replied stiffly, then, his voice softening, added, 'I'm sorry to hear of the young lady's illness. She appeared quite well while she was here, you understand. In fact, until this unpleasant incident, she had been a most charming guest.' He paused briefly. 'I recall your earlier visit now. She fainted in the restaurant one morning. Is her illness connected with that?' There was concern and sympathy in his voice now.

'It may be,' Luke answered dourly.

'Well, this is most unfortunate,' the manager concluded. 'I hope you manage to find her soon.'

'Thank you. There's one last thing you may be able to help me with. Have you had anyone called Verity Nyman staying at the hotel recently, or is anyone of that name on the staff?'

172

'No one of that name works anywhere on Tresco,' he replied with certainty. 'Let me check the guest lists.'

Luke heard the faint clicking of keys on a computer console, then there was a pause.

'No. No one of that name has registered here this month. But there are other places on the island where she could be staying.'

Luke's spirits fell even lower.

'Thank you for looking,' he said resignedly. 'And I'm sorry about the problems.'

'These things happen, sir.'

Luke sat staring at the telephone for some minutes after he had replaced it. He was sunk in sudden gloom, convinced now that Anya was out of reach again – just when she had seemed to be within his grasp – but knowing that he would still have to go and see for himself. That her delusions were becoming violent was now beyond doubt, and he dreaded what might happen to her if she did not receive help. Then again, was the alternative much better? When – if – he caught up with her, it was plain that their life would never be the same again. Everything – recent events, her ancestry, her secrets – pointed to some kind of serious mental illness, and Luke was beginning to doubt his own ability to cope with what that would entail.

Overcoming his self-imposed lethargy, he collected his rucksack, put the postcard and a recent photograph of Anya in his pocket and went out to the car. Driving up the A38, he began to ponder yet another baffling question. Why go from Devon to the Scillies via London? That made no sense. He knew from his earlier study of railway timetables that there was no train from Newton Abbot to Plymouth until after 10 a.m. – and even later for Penzance – so Anya could not have gone that way. Her only alternative that fateful morning would have been local services – and that was not logical either. Not that anything had seemed logical recently, he thought dismally. Of course, Anya could have got off the London train at Exeter and flown from there, as he was about to do. That at least made sense. He had assumed she was

173

going all the way to Paddington because on all her other trips she had bought a ticket for London. The duty manager at the Tresco hotel had said that she stayed two nights and left on the 27th. Only two nights. So where had she slept the night of the 24th, the day she had left home? If she had flown from Exeter on the same day, she could have stayed on St Mary's, but surely she would have had time to get to Tresco if that was where she had been headed. The useless speculation was beginning to make his head hurt, so he gave it up and concentrated on driving.

At Exeter airport he left the car in the long-term car park and checked in. Then, finding that he still had well over an hour before the flight was due to take off, he sat in the airport café and watched the activity on the runways outside. The minutes dragged by as he tried to think of anything else he could have done, imagining clues he had missed, but at last he was called to the tiny departure lounge, given his seat allocation and then led out to the small, twin-engine plane. His seat was in the row immediately behind the pilot, and so he got the best of the spectacular views on the journey. The route took them directly over his beloved Dartmoor and for a while he lost himself in picking out the tors, roads and other landmarks. Then came the less familiar landscapes of Cornwall, its ports, rivers and coves followed by the beauty of St Michael's Mount and the awe-inspiring cliffs of Land's End. Finally, after less than an hour, the islands themselves floated into view, white strands outlining the green and brown patchwork of land amid the vivid Atlantic blue. After a seemingly casual, curving approach over Hugh Town, the pilot made a perfect landing on the humpbacked runway and Luke was in the Scilly Isles again.

Now that he was actually there, he felt acutely embarrassed about his self-imposed task. He was no private investigator. How was he meant to go about finding Anya, even supposing she was still there? The obvious place to start was Hugh Town itself, where she had last been seen, so he took the airport bus with the rest of the passengers. The driver asked them all where they were staying, and when Luke admitted that he had nothing booked, he was advised to try the Tourist Information Centre. It seemed as good a place as any to begin his search.

After a short drive they reached the town, which was crowded on to a narrow strip of land between the main part of the island of St Mary's and the much smaller offshoot known as The Garrison. The friendly staff in the Information Centre were able to suggest several alternatives for his accommodation, but could not tell him anything useful when he showed them Anya's photograph. Following their advice Luke made his way to the Police Station, threading his way through the lanes and alleyways of the town with the help of the map he had been given.

The officer on duty listened attentively while Luke explained his purpose in being there and told him all he knew of Anya's movements. Once again her picture produced no sign of recognition, but at least the policeman seemed to be taking the matter seriously, in spite of Luke's deliberately vague description of Anya's 'illness'.

'Can I keep this, sir?' he asked, indicating the photograph.

'I'd rather hang on to it.'

'I'll just take a photocopy then, if I may. It won't be perfect, but better than nothing. Won't keep you long.' The young man disappeared into a rear office and then returned a few moments later with a copy. He wrote a few details on the blank part of the sheet.

'Are you staying in town tonight?'

'Yes, but I don't know where yet.'

'Get in touch again tomorrow, then. I'll check with my colleagues and see if we can dig anything up for you.'

'Thank you.' Luke left, thinking how splendid it must be to live in an island community where the police could carry out their business in such a friendly and informal manner. He found himself a room in a guest house overlooking the harbour and the town's northern beach. He dumped his rucksack, then went out again, cashed a traveller's cheque at the bank on Hugh Street, and bought himself a sandwich for lunch. He ate it while wandering the streets, half expecting to see Anya's small, dark figure among the groups of locals and tourists. But that, he knew, would be the luckiest of chances, even in a place as small as this, and he was engulfed by a fresh wave of despair. What was he doing here? The whole thing was hopeless, just a wild goose chase. He sat on a bench, watching the tide creep in over the smooth, rope-lined sands of Town Beach, and wondered despondently where Anya was now.

Eventually, however, his practical nature reasserted itself and he castigated himself for giving in to self-pity. He had come this far; the least he could do was try everything in his power to pick up her trail. For the rest of the day he tramped around the town, asking in every shop, café, hotel and place of business, showing Anya's photograph. Everyone he encountered listened to him courteously, recognizing his sincerity, but although some were more curious than others, no one could give him any definite information. A few looked at the picture intently and said they might have seen her, and several confused her with Meredith. No one had heard of Verity Nyman. It was a frustrating and ultimately futile exercise, but Luke felt a little better for having done something.

In the evening, feeling weary and dejected, he used one of the public telephones outside the Town Hall to ring Alice, Sheila and the Tresco hotel. None of them had any news for him. He also rang his home number, just in case, but there was no answer there. He ate a solitary dinner, then went on a final walk around the town, peering without much hope into various bars, before returning to the guest house and going early to bed.

27

The flight attendant finished serving the couple in the seats nearest the aisle and then looked across to Anya, who was gazing out of the window at sunlit clouds.

'Would you like a drink from the bar?'

Anya shook her head.

'No, thank you.'

The stewardess moved on and Anya's fellow passengers donned headsets to watch the in-flight movie, leaving her alone with her thoughts. Moving had almost become an end in itself and although she wanted to stop, to find a safe place to rest, she knew deep down that no such place existed. But the knowledge did not prevent her from making the attempt. At least this way she would be far away from Luke, would not suck him into the dark whirlpool that was slowly dragging her down.

She turned to stare out of the window again, thinking how deceptive the world could be. From 35,000 feet the clouds below looked perfectly innocent, white and pure. Yet from below they might be dark, ominous, full of rain or hailstones, thunder and lightning. It took a special talent, or perhaps an unwanted awareness, to see beneath the bright surfaces. Anya closed her eyes and listened to the sounds about her; the constant hum of the jet engines, the synchronized laughter of the passengers watching the film, a baby crying a few rows back, snatches of conversation. It all seemed so mundane, yet so remote.

She was shaken out of her reverie by an exclamation of annoyance.

'Chris, you clumsy oaf! Look at me.' The woman in the seat next to Anya was wiping ineffectually at her dress, where her drink had fallen from the seat-back tray into her lap.

'I didn't . . .' her husband objected, but his denial was overridden.

'Get up,' she snapped. 'I'll have to go to the loo and get cleaned up.'

They manoeuvred into the aisle and the woman strode off while her partner gave Anya a sheepish grin and shrugged before sitting down again. Anya smiled sympathetically and closed her eyes again, only to open them once more a few moments later when she noticed a peculiar knocking sound. Glancing at the window, she had to stifle the scream that rose in her throat. Outside the plane, Allessandro was grinning at her, rapping on the glass with his knuckles.

'That, of course, is only an illusion,' said a smug voice beside her. 'The real me is in here.'

Anya's head snapped round and she found herself trembling from the shock. The sorcerer, still transparent but with more substance than before, was resting in the seat next to her. It was obvious now who had been responsible for the spilt drink, but the man on the other side of Allessandro seemed quite unaware of his presence.

'There really is no point in trying to get away from me. You could never run far enough,' the sorcerer remarked evenly. 'Before long you will have chosen your own fate, to live with me or be crushed alone – but whichever you choose, I will soon be free of you, free to travel where I will. I may return to the Scillies and complete my experiment there. It would be amusing to see how many legends we could fulfil, don't you think? The odd earthquake here, a tidal wave there . . .' He laughed, waving an expressive hand.

'Why are you doing this?' Anya breathed. She was afraid of being overheard, but the holidaymakers around her were either wearing headphones or were engrossed in their own conversations.

'Because I can,' the sorcerer replied simply.

Anya wanted to ask him why he did not care that his

'experiment' might cause untold suffering, but she knew she would not get an answer, and so stayed quiet.

'This contraption really is most impressive, in a lumbering sort of way,' he remarked, looking around. 'Icarus wasn't so stupid, after all. Who would've thought it would get colder as you flew closer to the sun? In any case, I couldn't see any wax to melt on these wings.' He chuckled at his own wit. 'Even so, it's still incredibly vulnerable. All this science without magic is such a waste.' He sounded genuinely regretful. 'Do you realize how easy it would be for one of my talent to cause a tiny fault in one or two crucial mechanisms? The pilots would then be helpless to prevent a crash, for all their supposed expertise.'

'Killing me would hardly suit your purpose now, would it?' Anya whispered. 'You still need me.'

'For the moment,' he admitted grudgingly. 'Still it would have been an interesting thing to observe. Another time, perhaps.'

'Interesting?' she hissed, appalled by his callous attitude. 'Haven't you already done enough? Smashing up furniture was just childish, but the fire at the hotel could have killed someone.'

'You know what happens when you annoy me,' he answered, unrepentant. 'I'm glad to see you've abandoned your more foolish attempts to avoid me.'

Try as she might, Anya could not suppress her instinctive denial of this statement. Her attempts had been delayed, not abandoned, and in any case were not something over which she had complete control. She waited for Allessandro to react to these treacherous thoughts, but he did not appear to have noticed. He was either too preoccupied with his own self-centred ideas, or was perhaps becoming less adept at reading her mind as he grew more independent in the real world. Anya hoped it was the latter, and decided to test the theory as best she could. First she formulated a question in vague terms. The sorcerer did not respond, so she deliberately set the query into words and directed it at him silently. *What would Leonardo da Vinci have thought of this aeroplane?*

179

'He'd have been gratified,' Allessandro replied promptly, as if she had spoken aloud. 'No one in Florence admired his talent more than I, but even I did not realize what a visionary he was. He would have made an excellent sorcerer if he'd only put his mind to it.'

Encouraged by her success, Anya was about to continue her test of the limits of their telepathy, but he forestalled her, turning to smile mischievously.

'Magic can make things so much more interesting,' he commented. 'This craft is very functional, but wouldn't you prefer something a little more . . . unusual?'

The plane vanished, and Anya found herself standing in a square steel box, looking out of glass panels set in its double doors. Beyond the windows were cloud and sky, and the land was far below. She was now flying in the lift from her tryptych, 'The Mansions of Eternity', which had been inspired by images from a dream.

She only had a moment to glimpse the faint reflections in the glass, the shapes and faces of unknown people who had haunted that dream, when, to her horror, the doors slid open and the abyss yawned before her. Trying to throw herself back away from the vertiginous edge, Anya only had time to hear someone laughing before she blacked out.

'Are you all right?'

The woman whose seat Allessandro still occupied had returned and was looking at Anya from the aisle with some concern.

'This should be interesting,' the sorcerer remarked, but only Anya heard him.

'I feel a little faint,' she said.

'Shall I call a stewardess?'

'No,' Anya decided, recovering quickly now that she was back in the real world, and not wanting an embarrassing scene. 'Let me get out before you sit down.'

The woman's husband rose to let her out and Anya tried to push Allessandro as she went. She failed, her hand meeting resistance but passing through his shoulder in a way that

180

made her shiver. However, he took the hint and got up reluctantly and moved into the aisle.

Anya headed for the toilet, which was engaged, and waited outside with the sorcerer beside her. She had to fight back a sudden hysterical impulse to laugh. A flight attendant approached and Anya stepped aside to let her pass, but Allessandro stood his ground, smiling impassively. As the stewardess walked through him, she frowned, shuddered and then laughed a little nervously.

'I think someone just walked over my grave,' she remarked to Anya with a smile.

Why are you real for me but not for them? Anya asked, deliberately directing her thoughts.

'I will be,' he replied complacently, watching the retreating form of the stewardess. 'Soon enough. They're just not willing to see me at the moment. They're not attuned to me as you are, for obvious reasons.'

The washroom became free and Anya stepped inside, half expecting Allessandro to follow her, but he stayed where he was, a thoughtful expression on his face. When she came out he was gone and, even though she watched for his reappearance with some trepidation, Anya was convinced that he would not bother her again on the flight. She returned to her seat and, as she settled in again, her neighbour glanced at her solicitously.

'Feeling better?'

'Yes, thanks,' Anya replied, surprised to find that she was telling the truth. 'Much better.'

The ticking had started again – and Allessandro had not even noticed.

28

Luke was the first down to breakfast the next morning but, as he was finishing his toast and wondering for the hundredth time what to do that day, two elderly couples came into the dining room, deep in conversation. They took the window table next to his, and Luke could not help overhearing. One of the couples had apparently been staying at the Churchill Hotel when the fire had necessitated their evacuation, and were relating the details of their dreadful experience with the relish of hindsight. Acting on impulse – and reckoning he had nothing to lose – Luke stood up and interrupted.

'Excuse me, I'm sorry to bother you but I'm looking for someone who might have been staying at the hotel where the fire broke out,' he began, showing them Anya's photograph. 'I don't suppose . . .'

The group's surprise at the intrusion turned to curiosity when the female evacuee nodded.

'Why, yes. She was there.'

'Really?' Luke exclaimed, hardly daring to believe his luck.

'Wouldn't forget a pretty face like that,' the husband commented with a wolfish grin.

'George!' his wife said reprovingly, but without heat. 'That's the young lady the fireman said was very lucky. Apparently the fire started near her room.'

Luke was torn between excitement at this unexpected intelligence and fear for Anya's safety. He hardly knew what to ask next.

'Was she injured? Do you know what happened to her? Where did she go?'

'No one was badly hurt,' the woman replied. 'A few of us went to the hospital for check-ups, but I don't remember seeing her there. We haven't seen her since, have we, George?'

'No, not that I recall,' her husband said, serious now.

'When exactly was the fire?'

'Let's see. We've been here since . . . it was four nights ago.'

That meant the fire would have been the night following Anya's encounter with Alice. Everything came to a dead end after that, and Luke was suddenly convinced that she had left the islands. His fellow guests clearly had nothing more to tell him, and he politely avoided satisfying their evident curiosity about his search. He thanked them for their help and left them to their meal, then went out and walked through the town to Garrison Lane. The same officer was on duty in the police station.

'No luck yet, I'm afraid, sir. No one remembers seeing her, but I've shown the picture around and we'll let you know if anyone spots her.'

'Apparently she was staying at the Churchill when the fire broke out. Do you know what caused it yet?'

'No, sir. It's a bit of a mystery, by all accounts. The investigation will take some time, but I expect it'll all prove innocent enough. We're still taking statements from witnesses.'

'No suspicion of arson, then?'

'We can't rule it out,' the policeman replied, his young face now wearing a calculating expression. 'Do you have any reason to believe Miss Caplan might have had anything to do with it?'

'No, no. Of course not,' Luke said quickly, floundering his way past deep water. 'It's just that no one seems to have seen her since, and I wondered if the shock . . .'

'Nasty business,' the policeman agreed. 'It was lucky no one was seriously hurt. Did you check with the hospital?'

'No. I'll do that,' Luke said. 'If Anya left the islands in the last few days, how could I go about finding out where she'd gone?'

'Well, *The Scillonian* sails every day for Penzance, and there are the planes and helicopters, of course. The booking office at the Steamship Company might be able to help.'

'I've already tried there. They couldn't tell me anything.'

'If she travelled by air, your best bet would be to have a word with the drivers of the airport minibus,' the officer advised. 'The chances are she would have been a passenger of theirs.'

'Thanks. I'll try that,' Luke said, cursing himself for not having thought of this himself. *A fine detective you'd make*, he complained silently as he went to find the nearest boarding point for the bus.

The driver was a large, friendly individual who, between loading suitcases and shepherding his passengers aboard, proved to have an excellent memory for faces.

'Oh, yes. Couldn't forget her. I never knew Meredith had a twin. These women can be secretive, can't they?'

You don't know the half of it, Luke thought. Aloud, he asked, 'When did you see her last?'

'I took her to the airport, let me see, three days ago, in the afternoon. Poor lass had been caught up in that dreadful fire at the Churchill. I guess she'd had enough and wanted to go home.'

If only it were that simple! 'Do you know where she was headed?'

'Must have been Land's End. Getting the train from Penzance, no doubt.'

'Thank you.' Even though the news was disappointing, at least it was definite. 'You've been a great help.'

All he could do now was follow her trail, although Luke was sure it would be cold by now. He went to the travel office and changed his return flight to Land's End, taking the first available seat that afternoon. Having some time to kill, he walked along the beach front and then up the footpath to Buzza, the strangely named location of the hospital. There was no record there of Anya having received any treatment, which was a relief but left him no further forward.

Luke went to collect his luggage and pay his bill, then

waited, brooding, until it was time to go to the airport. If only he had reached the Scillies two days earlier! If only Alice had checked Meredith's answering machine sooner, or the mysterious Verity had written before she had . . . Luke had wasted time and effort, and his few discoveries had only made the whole situation more disquieting. Had Anya belatedly acquired her mother's taste for pyrotechnics? At the very least, it seemed that violent events were now following her around, and it was surely only a matter of time before she suffered for it herself.

Under other circumstances he would have found the short flight to the tip of Cornwall exhilarating, especially the feeling as the tiny plane swooped down to the grass-covered runway. But now Luke's thoughts were concentrated on following in Anya's footsteps. As they disembarked he went into his now familiar routine of asking whether anyone had seen the woman in the photograph. He began with his own pilot, then progressed to other members of the airport staff. Eventually, he was directed to a bus driver who ferried passengers to Penzance station and there, as on the islands, he found his answer. Anya had been booked on the overnight sleeper to London three days earlier. The train had left soon after 10 p.m. Luke was back where he had started. Anya had taken a train to London and from there she could have gone anywhere. He was going round in circles, and he felt like screaming.

After a few despairing, fruitless phone calls, he caught a train to Exeter, took a taxi to the airport, reclaimed the car and drove home. He arrived in the small hours of the morning and immediately fell into a deep, bitter sleep.

He went to work the next day, promising himself that he would concentrate on the job and forget about those aspects of his life over which he had no control. He failed miserably on both counts, which led to some friction with his sympathetic but understandably mystified colleagues. Luke apologized to everyone but did not explain his circumstances, saying only that he was having problems at home. The strain was beginning to get to him, and by the time he got home that evening he was bone-weary and had to stop himself from

185

going straight to the whisky bottle. The ring of the telephone came as a welcome distraction and, as always, brought with it the faintest spark of hope.

'Hello?'

'Luke? It's Elizabeth Burrows. I hope you don't mind me calling.'

'Not at all,' he told her dully.

'Any luck finding Anya?'

'No. I've been chasing my own tail. Have you seen anything of her?'

'No. I think this is the last place she's likely to come,' the doctor said. 'But I do have a rather odd piece of news. You remember the painting you told me about, the one Anya was obsessed with?'

'The del Sarto, yes.'

'I managed to track down a copy in a book on the sixteenth-century Italian Schools, and decided to show it to Mary. However, if I'd pointed the picture out to her myself, her reaction would've meant nothing. She's quite capable of making up stories if it suits her. So I just gave her the book and asked if she'd like to browse through it. She wasn't very interested until she realized that a lot of the paintings were religious, Madonnas and so on, but then she grew quite enthusiastic. I watched her, without being too obvious I hope, and her response when she came upon "Portrait of a Young Man" was remarkable. She cried out and pointed, then turned to me and said, "That's him! That's the one my Anya's with."'

Luke felt himself grow cold. This was insane.

'I told her that it was impossible,' Elizabeth went on, 'that the man in the picture had lived over four hundred years ago, but she was insistent.'

'Did she say where Anya and this man were?'

'This is a delusion, Luke. It's difficult to work out how they're sharing it when they've been apart for so long, but I could've sworn Mary's reaction was genuine.'

'Ask her,' he insisted. 'Ask her where they are.'

'Luke . . .' The doctor began uncertainly.

'Look, if this goes on much longer, I may be the one in need of your professional services,' he said. 'Please, humour me.'

There was a long pause.

'Please.'

'All right. I'll try,' she agreed flatly. 'I'll ring you back.'

Luke sat by the phone and waited, trying to work out what was going on. Could a fantasy about a painting be passed on in one's genes, or through childhood memories? The idea was laughable, yet what other explanation could there be? Even if he took Anya's story of possession at face value, how could her mother be aware of it? Were they linked telepathically? He was lost in the conundrum, and jumped when the telephone rang.

'Me again,' Elizabeth said. 'I've asked her and she didn't know. In fact she became rather abusive and suspicious, accusing me of spying for "that other man, the one who isn't an angel."'

'Meaning me?'

'I suspect so.'

'Well, thanks for trying.'

'I'd very much like to meet Anya when you find her,' the doctor said. 'This is a most fascinating case.'

The overloaded fuse in Luke's brain finally blew, extinguishing the light of reason.

'Fascinating?' he yelled. 'I'm in the middle of a nightmare and you call it *fascinating*?' He began to swear incoherently, unaware of her attempts to placate him, and then slammed the receiver down. For a few moments he stood gripping the innocent telephone, fighting back the desire to hurl it across the room. Instead he headed for the whisky bottle.

An hour later, when he had finally stopped shaking, Luke made himself pick up the phone and dial the hospital. Elizabeth was still there and he apologized sincerely, if somewhat drunkenly.

'I'm sorry too,' she told him calmly. 'It was a thoughtless thing to say. Do you want to talk?'

'Not now. I'm in no fit state. Sorry.'

'Call me tomorrow then, if you want to.'

'I will,' he promised.

But it was a promise he was destined to break. The next morning brought another message, which was to renew his hope and set him off on Anya's trail once more.

29

Luke almost ignored it at first. He was suffering from an unpleasant hangover and finding even simple tasks like switching on the kettle a strain. The post brought only Anya's monthly credit card bill, which seemed insignificant, so Luke put it aside and returned to the kitchen to try and face breakfast. After a while, as his brain began to function properly, he decided to look at it again. In spite of all that had happened he still had reservations about opening Anya's private correspondence. Besides, he had often seen her statements before – she had never made any attempt to conceal them – and they had never contained any obvious clues to her whereabouts during her times away. Why should it be any different now? In the end, however, the temptation proved too great and he was immediately rewarded for setting aside his scruples.

Two entries jumped out at him at once. On 25 August she had spent a considerable sum at Galaxy Plus Travel in London NW1. That was the day after she had left home, so she *had* gone to London, as Luke had initially believed. This had presumably been payment for her train fare and flight to the Scillies, as she had been on Tresco by the next night. She had certainly taken a roundabout route, but what else could it have been? However, the last entry on the statement was even more intriguing. It was with the same travel agent and was dated 29 August, the day after Anya had left the Scillies and caught the sleeper to Paddington. It was a much larger sum, and was surely the cost of her travel to her next destination.

Luke rang directory enquiries to obtain the telephone number of Galaxy Plus Travel and was about to call them when it occurred to him that they were unlikely to be open before 8 a.m. In any case, if he was to follow Anya, then he would have to go via London himself – and would probably have more luck persuading them to give him the information he needed if he was there in person. *What the hell*, he thought, and called his boss instead.

'Don't tell me. You need some more time off.'

'Yes. I know I've been messing you around . . .'

'Don't bother to explain. Take the rest of this week and all of next. Will that be enough?'

'Yes. Thank you,' Luke agreed humbly.

'At least this way the rest of us will know where we are.'

'I'm sorry,' Luke began. 'I just don't know . . .'

'Save it, OK? You wouldn't ask if it weren't important, and you're owed more than enough holiday to cover this. We'll cope.'

'Thank you,' he repeated. 'I'm very grateful.'

'Good luck.'

Luke's next call was to Sheila, to let her know what was going on. The agent insisted on coming over and driving him to the station, and he was glad of her help. While he waited for her to arrive, he packed his rucksack again with fresh clothes and wrote a new message in case Anya came home before him. He was ready when Sheila arrived, with Anya's photograph, her note, her credit card statement and the traveller's cheques safely stowed in his jacket pocket.

'Hi. Know where you're going yet?' she asked as he got into the car.

'No. I'm hoping the travel agents will tell me.'

'Got your passport?'

Luke gave her a horrified look and ran back into the house to fetch it, wondering how he could have been so stupid.

'If it weren't in such bad taste, I'd say you were missing a woman's touch,' Sheila remarked as they set off.

Despite himself, Luke grinned.

'In a sick kind of way I envy you,' the agent went on. 'This could be quite an adventure. The white knight galloping off to rescue his fair maiden.' She was trying to lighten his mood, and Luke knew it.

'My last expedition wasn't exactly covered in glory,' he said. 'All I did was ride round in circles.'

'Perseverance, Sir Luke,' Sheila advised solemnly.

'I'm named after an apostle, not a knight,' he replied. 'Who are you in this fairy tale, anyway?'

'The Queen, of course,' she answered, 'who loves all her subjects regally, but who reserves a royal soft spot for a certain questing knight and his lady.' Then, aware that she had said rather more than she intended, she added quickly, 'Are you OK for money?'

'Yes, I've plenty. I found a load of unsigned traveller's cheques among Anya's stuff. I reckon she left in such a rush this time she forgot to take them. That's obviously why she had to use her credit card at the travel agent's.'

'Dashed clever deduction, Holmes,' Sheila commented, then waited. 'Come on. I've fed you your cue. Don't let me down.'

'Elementary, my dear Watson,' Luke said obediently.

As always, Luke found the sheer size and constant bustle of London quite bewildering, but he phoned Galaxy Plus Travel and then located them with the help of an *A-Z*, arriving mid-afternoon. The window was packed with cards offering holiday bargains and inside, ranged behind a long counter, were five assistants. The nearest looked up and smiled as Luke came in.

'Can I help you?'

'I have a rather unusual request,' he began awkwardly as he sat down. 'I'm looking for someone, a friend of mine, who's gone missing. I believe she was in here recently.' He showed her Anya's photograph and the woman's doubtful expression was replaced by a flash of recognition before becoming carefully neutral again. Luke had expected that he would have to convince them to help him, but now at least he knew he was on the right track.

191

'Just a moment, sir.' She got up and walked along to her colleague at the end of the row. After a quiet conversation, the older woman came over and took the assistant's place.

'Hello. I'm Grace Marshall, the manager. I gather you're trying to trace a customer of ours.'

'That's right. Her name's Anya Caplan.' Luke showed the photo again, but the manageress only glanced at it briefly. 'Have you seen her?'

'May I ask why you're looking for her?' she asked, ignoring his question.

Luke had been ready for this. 'I think she may be ill,' he replied promptly. 'I don't want to go into too many details, you understand, but she's not been herself recently. She travels alone quite frequently, but this time she left in a great rush and in some distress. I'm worried and I'd like to know where she went, find her if I can.'

Grace nodded, looking thoughtful.

'And you are?' she prompted.

'Luke Tasker. I'm her boyfriend. We live together in Devon. Look, I can prove it.' He took out Anya's bill and his own driving licence. 'You see, the addresses are the same. And this is how I knew she'd come here,' he added, pointing at the entries on the statement.

The manageress nodded but still seemed to harbour some doubts. 'Why didn't she tell you where she was going?'

'She never does. For reasons I don't fully understand, she needs to be alone and completely independent every so often. I don't like it much, to be honest, but I've accepted it. But this time it's different.'

'Because of her illness?'

'Yes. Will you help me?' Luke was uncomfortably aware that the other assistants were listening to the conversation and was glad that he was the only customer in the shop. 'Please.'

'Well, Mr Tasker,' she said at last. 'Ordinarily I would be very reluctant to betray the privacy of our clients, but I'm going to make an exception in this case. We'll tell you what we can.'

'Thank you.' Luke's sense of relief was overwhelming.

'I just hope I'm doing the right thing.'

'You are, I promise you,' he said eagerly. 'So Anya was in here on the twenty-ninth?'

'Yes. Miss Caplan and her sister are both quite regular customers here.'

For a moment, Luke was dumbfounded.

'Her sister? Meredith?'

'Yes. We only ever see them every few months, but being twins they're easy to remember – and they share a method of payment which is a little eccentric. Not that we mind, of course,' she added hurriedly.

'Let me guess,' Luke put in, producing the wad of traveller's cheques. 'With these.'

'Yes, that's right,' Grace agreed, surprised. 'Or cash occasionally. That's why it struck me as unusual when Anya paid by credit card last time.'

'Lucky for me,' Luke said. 'I'd never have found you otherwise.' Then something else occurred to him. Had he discovered another lie? 'Do they ever travel together? Anya said they'd lost touch with each other.'

'Never, as far as I can recall. Their requirements are generally quite different. Meredith does a lot of business travelling, rushing between cities, whereas Anya tends to book flights to holiday destinations.'

'Where did she go this time?' Luke asked, returning to his original quest.

'Corfu. Hang on a minute and I'll get the details.' Grace turned to the computer console and typed rapidly, then waited.

'I've never been to Greece,' Luke confessed. 'Whereabouts is Corfu?'

'It's the most popular of the Ionian islands, to the west of the mainland.'

'Does she often go there?'

'Several times, from memory. Ah, here we are,' she said, glancing back at the screen. 'She flew out on the first of September, two days ago. She'd booked a week's holiday, half board, at the Corfu Palace Hotel. Normally she only wants the flight, but this was a last-minute availability and very good value. In any case the charter flight was the first direct connection to Corfu that had a free seat – which is what she was most concerned about.'

'So she'll be at the Corfu Palace until September the eighth?' For the first time, Luke was beginning to think that he might actually catch up with her.

'That's right, but the return flight is quite early in the morning, so you'd have to get there the day before to be sure of catching her.'

'How soon can I get to Corfu?'

'The only way to fly direct is by charter, and they're all pretty booked up at this time of year. We'll do some checking. Ellen, as you've been earwigging, will you get on to that?'

One of the assistants nodded, blushing slightly, and started tapping away at her own keyboard.

'What about scheduled flights?' Luke asked.

'You'd have to go via Athens, then get the local connecting flight on Olympic,' Grace replied. 'That's more expensive and takes a bit longer, but you're less likely to suffer any delays. And I'm pretty sure we can get you there tomorrow.'

'That'll be fine. At the moment expense is not an issue,' Luke stated, tapping the pile of cheques.

'You're sure?'

Luke nodded, but Grace turned to her colleague anyway.

'Anything, Ellen?'

'Nothing before Monday so far.'

'That's cutting it too fine,' Luke decided. 'Book me a scheduled flight.'

'OK,' the manageress said, watching her console. 'Ten-fifteen tomorrow morning on Olympic from Heathrow. Due at Athens four o'clock local time. You'll have about half an hour's wait there, then the flight to Corfu takes about forty minutes.'

'Sounds perfect. Go ahead.'

Grace completed the electronic transaction then issued the ticket with an open return date, while Luke signed and countersigned enough traveller's cheques to cover the cost. When it was done, he felt a renewed sense of relief, combined with a sort of queasy anticipation. He would be flying, quite literally, into the unknown, and the prospect was unnerving.

'Some knight you'd make,' he muttered to himself.

'Pardon?'

'Nothing. Just thinking aloud.'

Grace watched him carefully for a few moments, then evidently made up her mind about something.

'There's one last thing I ought to tell you,' she said as she handed over the documents. 'Anya did seem to be behaving rather oddly when she was here.'

'How oddly?' Luke asked quickly.

'Well . . .' Grace was obviously embarrassed now. 'She seemed very nervous, and made some remarks that made no sense. And she was always looking over her shoulder, as if she expected someone to be creeping up on her. That's partly why I accepted your story about her being ill, but if it was you she was afraid of, then I've made a terrible mistake telling you all this.'

'No. It wasn't me,' Luke stated with conviction. 'I promise. All I want is Anya's safety.'

And I only hope I'm not too late.

30

After the crowded but ordered efficiency of Heathrow, Athens airport had seemed like bedlam to Luke, but compared to Corfu was a model of businesslike calm. Unsurprisingly, the flight from Athens had been populated almost exclusively by Greeks, and few concessions were made to foreigners. Luke's half-hearted perusal of his phrase book had done little to prepare him for the onslaught of this strange language, in which every conversation sounded like an argument.

From the air Corfu – or Kerkyra as it was known in Greece – looked surprisingly mountainous and very green compared to the uncomfortably barren coastline of Albania a few miles to the east. Their landing approach had been over calm, dazzlingly blue water, and they had touched down smoothly. But once they had taxied to a halt and the cabin doors had been opened, all semblance of serenity vanished. The heat was tremendous, even though it was now late afternoon, and Luke felt perspiration pricking his skin before he got to the bottom of the aircraft steps. There were several other planes on the shimmering tarmac, with lines of passengers snaking to and fro, and luggage carts, fuel lorries and other service vehicles scurried about their business. The terminal building, some two hundred yards away, seemed to be swarming with people, crowded into the lounges and balconies, watching the activity of the luckier ones who were actually on the move. As Luke approached the arrivals lounge the heat and noise grew more intense, but his fellow passengers seemed to know where they were going, and he followed hopefully.

Inside, there were few formalities, but Luke had to wait a long time for his luggage. He was eager to get going and could only trust that his rucksack had been correctly transferred in Athens. It appeared at last and he was able to escape from the chaotic, noisy bustle of the terminal to the even more chaotic, noisy bustle of the car park outside. Coaches, taxis, cars and lorries were parked at all angles, apparently at random, over the various approach roads. A constant crawl of traffic weaved its way around parked vehicles and the endless stream of people that flowed to and fro. Horns blared, voices were raised in protest and drivers gesticulated wildly. The heat was like a physical force, rising from the concrete in waves, and there was no escape, even in the shade. The scent of eucalyptus from nearby trees gave the sultry air an exotic tang, but had to compete with the acrid fumes from a hundred engines.

Eventually, after several false starts, Luke found a free taxi and asked to be taken to the Corfu Palace Hotel. The driver looked at him and his less than impressive luggage doubtfully, then shrugged and they set off, accelerating and braking violently as they extricated themselves from the throng. Once on the open road – a somewhat euphemistic term when applied to the narrow and overpopulated streets of Corfu Town – he drove fast. On at least three occasions Luke shut his eyes and braced himself as a collision seemed inevitable but, miraculously, they survived intact, aided by almost deafening blasts from the Mercedes' powerful horn. The trip took less than a quarter of an hour, but seemed like half a lifetime.

The hotel was a modern, four-storey block, surrounded by lush green gardens and myriad fragrant flowers in every shade of red, pink and white. As Luke shouldered his rucksack and made his way inside, he could hear the sounds of holiday-makers splashing in the swimming pool, and caught the enticing aroma of meals being prepared in an open-air restaurant, but paid little attention. Now that he was so close to catching up with Anya, he was excited and nervous at the same time. In all his endeavours he had never once considered exactly what he was going to say to her when

197

he turned up out of the blue. Luke knew that his reasons for trailing her were fully justified, but Anya might not see it that way. And her temper, even when she was in the best of health, was something to be reckoned with. As he entered the cool, marbled interior of the reception area, Luke decided to cross that bridge when he came to it. He had not come this far to turn away now. Anya would just have to accept that his concern and love for her were his only motivation.

The smartly dressed man behind the counter greeted him courteously and Luke was greatly relieved to discover that he spoke almost perfect English. He explained that he was looking for a friend of his, and showed Anya's photograph.

'Caplan, Caplan . . .' the concierge recited as he riffled through some cards. 'Ah, yes,' he added, looking at one doubtfully. 'Mmm. Yes.'

'Is she here?' Luke asked eagerly.

'She *was* here,' the man replied. 'But Miss Caplan is no longer with us.'

Dismay hit Luke like a physical blow. *Not again!* he thought helplessly. *Not again*.

'She arrived last Wednesday, with a group.'

'A group? Was she with anyone?'

'No. She was paying a single occupancy supplement. I meant she was with a holiday tour group booked to stay one week. But she left the next morning,' the concierge added with a shrug which implied that it was not for him to understand the ways of tourists.

Luke swore under his breath. 'Do you know where she went?'

'No, I do not. It is common for our guests to travel, to explore our beautiful island for a few days, but they usually return. Miss Caplan told us she would not be coming back. She made no arrangements to hire a car, and took all her luggage with her. The room has not been occupied since. One moment, sir.'

He turned away, and Luke stared blankly at his hands resting on the desk, feeling doubly lost. Where had she gone? What was he supposed to do now? Her flight back was on

Wednesday, in four days time, and he could wait for that, but there was no guarantee that she would be on it. It was looking more and more as if she had only booked the week's holiday for the convenience of the flight out. Now that Luke thought about it, this plush hotel hardly seemed like Anya's sort of place. The whole expedition was getting ridiculous. He had been quite proud of his detective work, but at this rate he was hardly going to be a threat to Scotland Yard. His progress so far had been of the three-steps-forward, two-steps-back variety, but now he seemed to have come to a complete halt prior to sliding ignominiously back to the beginning.

While Luke was brooding, the concierge had been having a rapid conversation in Greek with a female receptionist, and turned back to him now.

'Apparently, Miss Caplan took a taxi to the Old Port, where the ferries sail from.'

'Ferries? Where to?'

'The mainland, other islands, Italy.' He turned away again and there was another incomprehensible exchange, accompanied by several expressive gestures from the woman.

A little of Luke's determination reasserted itself as he watched. This problem was not insoluble. Anya would surely not have flown to Corfu only to go on by boat to Italy or the Greek mainland. In either case it would have made much more sense to take a direct flight. *Unless*, Luke thought, with a temporary resurgence of pessimism, *she was deliberately trying to cover her tracks*. After all, she had gone from Devon to the Scillies via London, which was equally absurd. If she was working on the same principle on this journey, then his search was hopeless. If not . . . *I have to assume she isn't*, he told himself. *In which case, she's gone to one of the other Ionian islands*.

'My colleague believes that Miss Caplan asked about times of departure for Paxos,' the concierge said.

'Where's that?'

'Paxos is a small island to the south of Corfu. It is popular with tourists who require a less sophisticated, quieter holiday.'

That sounded much more like Anya's type of place to Luke.

'Can I get a ferry there today?' he asked eagerly.

'No. The earliest would be tomorrow morning.'

Luke's plan of action was clear now. He would spend the evening making enquiries at the port, to see whether anyone remembered Anya but, if he got no better leads, he would go to Paxos in the morning. If he drew a blank there he could still return to Corfu in time to check Anya's return flight.

Having made that decision, a disquieting thought occurred to him.

'Was the room here . . . damaged at all?' he asked awkwardly.

The concierge gave him a questioning, vaguely worried look.

'No. Not at all.'

'Was Anya all right? Did she appear ill?'

'I cannot say,' the man replied, glancing at the receptionist who shrugged eloquently. 'I saw nothing wrong.'

Luke felt a measure of relief. The violent incidents were not trailing Anya everywhere, it seemed. He had run out of questions now and, for the first time, began to consider his own immediate prospects.

'Do you have a room for the night?' he asked.

'I'm afraid not. We are fully booked.'

'Have you re-let Miss Caplan's room?'

'No, but . . .'

'Could I have it? I'd be happy to pay in advance.' Luke took out a thick wad of drachmas that he had changed at a bank in Athens airport.

'We are obliged to honour her booking . . .' the concierge began.

'Even if she told you herself that she wasn't coming back?'

The man paused, considering.

'I think perhaps it will be OK. But if Miss Caplan returns you will have to move out immediately.'

'Believe me, if she returns, I'll gladly do anything you ask,' Luke replied.

*　　*　　*

Luke returned to his hotel room – which he insisted on thinking of as Anya's room – late that evening, footsore and wearily anticipating a shower and a comfortable bed. His investigations in the port had been largely unproductive. There were several ticket agencies on or near the docks, but no one had remembered Anya or could confirm that she had sailed for Paxos. Luke had discovered that – if she *had* gone that way – it would almost certainly have been on a high-speed launch called *Pegasus*, which he would be catching himself the next morning at nine o'clock. He was hoping that one of the crew might recognize her photograph and thus reaffirm his own decision to head south.

Once it had become clear that he would learn nothing more that night, Luke had found an open-air taverna overlooking the harbour and eaten a much-needed meal. Then he had wandered the streets of Corfu Town for a while, watching the crowds of tourists intent on enjoying their Saturday night, before retracing his footsteps to the Corfu Palace.

It was an odd sensation going into Anya's room. Although she had been there only three nights earlier, had slept in the same bed, no trace of her presence remained. The room was neat, pristine, anonymous, an exact duplicate of hundreds of others all around. Luke took a long shower, then got ready for bed. He laid out a fresh set of clothes for the next day, then repacked the rest of his belongings back into the rucksack.

He set the alarm on his digital watch, then, as he was reaching over to turn out the light, accidentally knocked the watch to the floor. Leaning out of bed to pick it up, he noticed something small glittering under the bed. Luke reached in and retrieved it, almost falling out of bed as he did so. Righting himself, he stared at his prize.

The room *had* retained a trace of Anya after all. He had found one of the pair of earrings that Sheila had given her on her birthday. Luke gazed at the black stone in its silver setting, trying to analyse his feelings. Although he had needed no confirmation that he had been on the right track thus far, he was still shaken by his discovery. It was as though he had been playing a game until now, a deadly serious game with high stakes, but a game nonetheless. Now it had suddenly become all too real.

Had the clue been left for him deliberately? Or was it just another fortuitous coincidence? Luke told himself that finding the earring was a sign, a favourable omen. He was, after all, in the land of oracles and Olympian gods. Tomorrow, he knew, would bring further discoveries, perhaps even an end to this long-distance version of hide-and-seek.

He laid the earring on the bedside table, next to his watch, and went to sleep filled with a renewed sense of excitement and optimism.

31

Luke awoke not knowing where he was. And even more disconcertingly, he didn't know *who* he was.

The dream that had created his confusion had been like none he could ever remember. Its progression had been remarkably linear, without the nonsensical jumps in time and perspective that marked the passage of most dreams. It had also been vividly complete – not just visually but in every sense – and the residue of its scents, sounds, tastes and textures still clung to his thoughts. Luke generally paid little attention to dreams, but this one was different. As his own identity and situation slowly reestablished themselves, he went over it in his mind.

He – or rather she, because Luke had been aware of occupying a different, undeniably female body – had been walking down a roughly paved, narrow street, flanked by whitewashed and shuttered houses. The olive trees that surrounded the village buzzed with the call of cicadas, and a pink-flowered tree, whose white-painted trunk jutted out into the road, was full of the raucous chatter of sparrows. The tiny birds flew away in a noisy swirl as he passed underneath. Further on, greenery flourished in cracks between the roughhewn, white stones of an old wall. Ahead lay a small harbour, boats bobbing on the gentle waves caused by the wake of a colourfully painted fishing craft.

He turned right to walk along the quayside, and was greeted by a puppy that rose from its sleeping place under a taverna table and padded over on feet that were far too big for its body. Luke squatted down to fondle the soft fur of the dog's ears. As he went on, an old man spoke to him in a language he did not understand, but he replied in the same tongue, in a soft-toned high-pitched voice that was not his own. Passing an alleyway, a general store and a pink walled café-bar, he came into a small open space. There were more tavernas ranged around the three sides of the square, as well as a tiny church. Everywhere he looked there were flowers and vines, trailing over canopies or climbing walls. The warm, early morning air was enriched by the enticing smell of freshly baked bread that overlaid the salty odours of the sea. For a few long moments he stood quite still, not through indecision, but just to savour the pleasures of the place and time. Through another's eyes he saw the bright, wavering reflections in the water, the orange-tiled roofs and white houses which leaned together cosily. He watched the local inhabitants complete their first tasks of the day and prepare for the inevitable influx of holiday-makers, who would rise from their beds later. He felt at home, albeit at second-hand.

Sitting down at a table outside the café, he had a tiny cup of thick, sweet coffee, accompanied by a glass of water. The drink added to his sense of contentment, but when he came to pay, the small blue purse opened with a snap and coins rolled off the table onto the floor. Sharp eyes caught sight of something else too, and he leant down to pick it up with a hand far more delicate than his own. The coins were forgotten for the moment as Luke stared at the small fist with a growing sense of unease. It was clenched round something tiny and hard that pressed into the soft flesh of the palm. Slowly, just as the dream came to an end, fingers opened to reveal a black and silver object, glinting in the sunlight.

Back in his own body, in the hotel room, Luke reached out and picked up its twin from the bedside table. Looking at the earring again, he wondered what, if anything, the dream had meant. He assumed that he had been projecting his own subconscious hopes and fears about finding Anya into an imaginary dramatic scene. But why had it taken such a strange form? And why had it seemed so real? He knew he had been a woman in the dream, but it had not been Anya, of that he was sure. Was this unknown female an unsuspected facet of his own psyche? Or had the dream been another omen, a message? No, that was absurd. The earring had obviously set off the peculiar sequence of meaningless images. It would be stupid to read anything more significant into a shadow play.

His watch alarm went off – he had woken early – reminding him of the need to be on his way, and Luke dressed quickly, checked out and set off for the port. He arrived with plenty of time to spare and, curbing his impatience, browsed in a harbourside shop. Among the eclectic selection of books on display was a slim volume entitled 'Landscapes of Paxos', which looked interesting and featured a pull-out map. Luke bought a copy and slipped it into a pocket in his ruck-sack before boarding *Pegasus*. The modern vessel was quite crowded by the time they set out to sea, with a mixture of holiday-makers, day-trippers and Greeks travelling to and from their native islands. The ride was noisy but smooth as they sped down the east coast of Corfu, then became like a gentle roller-coaster as they reached the swell of the open sea to the south.

As far as Luke could tell from his necessarily limited conver-sations with the crew, none of them remembered seeing Anya, and he gave up being a detective to become – temporarily at least – another tourist. He sat and ate a chocolate-filled croissant and watched the coast slide by until, alerted by the delight of other travellers, he noticed several dolphins leaping energetically into the air before sliding gracefully into the blue water. Like everyone else, he was enchanted by their apparent playfulness. Later they also saw a whole school of flying fish skimming over the waves, glittering like living jewellery. Even the Greek passengers seemed astonished at this sight, and some of the conversations between them and members of the crew became quite animated. Around the same time Luke fancied he could hear a deep rumbling sound, although the roar of the engines made it difficult to be certain. It was like distant thunder, though the sky was quite clear. Shortly after that *Pegasus* ran into several waves that were considerably larger than before, which the captain turned into, so as not to be hit broadside. No one seemed concerned.

Luke watched intently as Paxos came into view, first as a grey smudge on the horizon, then as a silhouette that slowly took on form and character. As they drew slowly nearer, he took out the guidebook, intending to look at the map. But the pages fell open at the preface – and there, in full colour, was a photograph of the village from Luke's dream.

He stared at it in disbelief. He would have sworn that he had never seen the place before, even in a picture, yet everything was exactly as he remembered, down to the last detail, each flower, vine and green-painted shutter. So where had his brain got the information to construct the dream?

The caption read 'Loggos – as perfect as a picture-postcard' and Luke turned quickly to the map. He found that Loggos was the third largest of the island's ports after the capital Gaios, where his ferry was headed, and Lakka in the north. Further investigation revealed another photograph of the village, which only served to confirm it as the location of his dream. Reading the accompanying text informed him, among other things, that the Café-Bar Europa, where his female form had drunk coffee was 'the perfect place to put your feet up'.

What price omens now? he thought, as he watched the rocky inlets and tree-covered hills of Paxos slip by. He knew now that he had no choice but to head for Loggos, whether his dream had anything to do with Anya's whereabouts or not. His own curiosity would not be denied now, even if it was tinged with fear. Luke had no idea what this latest mystery meant, but it was clear that someone, or something – even if it was only his own subconscious – was leading him to the little fishing village. And he certainly had no better ideas about where to start looking for Anya.

The ninety-minute journey from Corfu ended with the slow navigation of the narrow straits between the main port of Paxos and the tiny islands of Panagia, with its nunnery and lighthouse, and St Nicholas, now covered with pines, where a Venetian fortress had once stood. These sheltered waters provided Gaios with an ideal anchorage, and the harbour was full of craft of all kinds, from modest rowing boats to vast, luxurious yachts. The town itself was a larger version of Loggos, white walls and orange roofs, with the ever-present greenery beyond.

Luke shouldered his pack, disembarked and headed for the bustling main square. As it was Sunday, there were no buses running, so he found a taxi and asked to be taken to Loggos. The driver, who looked awfully young to be in charge of the venerable old Mercedes, set off immediately, one arm draped nonchalantly out of the open window as he manoeuvred expertly through the town's narrow streets and headed inland.

Luke watched the landscape as the car climbed into the hills. Olive trees gave way to cypress, and views opened out to the west and south of the shining sea and the smaller sister island of Anti-Paxos. They passed through a couple of villages, their houses strung out along the road, but there was virtually no traffic. The driver eventually took a right turn on to a smaller side road. Several black-faced sheep looked up from their grazing to regard the taxi placidly. Elsewhere, goats were tethered among the trees. Luke identified the next village from the map as Fontana, which seemed to consist almost entirely of small cafés and churches. A derelict olive press stood by the side of the road, which now began to wind downhill in a series of increasingly sharp bends. They were heading for the east coast again, and Loggos.

Finally, they swept round one last bend, with an imperious blast on the horn to warn anyone coming the other way. And there, nestling in the curve of a horseshoe-shaped bay, was the village of Luke's dream.

He was almost overwhelmed by a sense of *déjà vu*. Seeing it in a photograph was one thing; actually being there in person was quite another. He practically held his breath as they turned past two waterfront buildings, slowing down as they drove along the quayside, stopping in the tiny main square outside the Café-Bar Europa. It was a mesmerizing and unnerving experience to arrive in a strange, new place and yet feel that he knew it quite intimately.

Luke managed to shake free of his reverie for long enough to pay the fare, then looked about him once more, wondering what to do now. He was still undecided when, with a jolt that made him gasp and set his heart hammering, he recognized a crop of black hair as it bobbed along behind the café tables and disappeared into an alleyway.

'Anya!' he cried, but it came out as a half-strangled yelp that she could not have heard. Several people nearby turned to look at him, but Luke did not notice. He began to run.

His rucksack hampered him as he skirted the tables and chairs of the café and lurched into the alley beyond. There was another small taverna here, its tables set out ready for the lunchtime trade, but empty now. The alley looked like a cul-de-sac and was only about thirty yards long, but there was no sign of Anya.

Luke called her name again, finding his voice this time, but drew no response. He pounded on, glancing into every doorway, up each set of stairs, but seeing no one, then found that it was not a dead end after all, but turned at right angles back towards the harbour. Luke skidded round the corner and saw her standing outside a small shop only a few paces away.

'Anya!' He ran on, breathless now with more than mere exertion.

She turned and looked at him as he drew near. Her smile echoed his own but there was an odd lack of surprise, or even recognition, in her face.

'Thank God I've found you,' Luke gasped.

She looked puzzled now, and his stomach turned somersaults.

'I'm sorry,' she said. 'I think you've got me mixed up with my sister. I'm Meredith.'

32

Luke felt as if he had been struck by lightning. He stared wordlessly, his numbed mind stuck in a helpless round of denial. It was impossible, ridiculous.

And yet other facts, unnoticed during his hectic pursuit, were slowly registering. Although this woman had Anya's slender build and overall appearance, the other details were all wrong. For a start, she was dressed in bright yellow shorts, a thin white blouse and transparent pink plastic sandals. Her clothes were so far removed from any of Anya's sombre outfits that it seemed almost too obvious a statement. Anyone could change their habitual mode of dress when on holiday, after all. But there were other, more subtle distinctions. Her voice had been mellifluous, gentle and unruffled by his precipitous arrival – just as he remembered it from her answering machine. Anya would have reacted much more strongly to such an unexpected meeting. Meredith's face was calm, and her features were softer than her sister's, her skin tone smooth and fresh in spite of the day's heat. Even her hair, while identical in colour and much the same length as Anya's, seemed less spiky, less agressive in style. She radiated a quiet kind of confidence that was certainly unlike Anya's recent temperamental state. In short, her whole presence was quite different, and Luke was reluctantly forced to the unwelcome conclusion that this was indeed Meredith.

He was too stunned even to begin considering the ramifications of this freakish turn of events. In the face of his bewildered silence Meredith spoke again.

'And you are?' she prompted gently.

'Luke. Luke Tasker.' He still couldn't quite bring himself to accept that she did not know who he was.

'You're a friend of my sister's?'

'Yes. We . . . live together. Do you know where she is?'

'I haven't the faintest idea,' Meredith replied. 'We haven't seen each other since we were kids. What makes you think she's here? Or is this just a chance encounter?'

'I . . . I've been following her . . . from England,' Luke said, feeling very awkward. 'It's important that I find her. Are you sure she's not here?'

Meredith smiled.

'Loggos is a pretty small place. I'd certainly know if she was around. She could be somewhere else on Paxos, I suppose, but even that would be quite a coincidence, don't you think – us being on the same small island after all these years?'

Luke could only agree silently, still wrestling with this latest development and unable to suppress his own internal suspicions. Was it possible that Anya was there too, but that the twins were unaware of each other? That did indeed seem much too far-fetched a coincidence. Could there be some sort of inexplicable conspiracy between the sisters? Judging from first impressions, Meredith seemed open and honest enough. Luke had taken to her immediately, in spite of his confusion, and yet he had no idea whether she was genuinely trustworthy. She was still looking at him sympathetically, apparently aware of his disorientation.

'The sun isn't exactly over the yardarm yet,' she said. In fact it was almost overhead, blazing in a clear sky. 'But we'll just have to be un-British and defy convention. You look as though you need a drink. Come on, I'll buy you an ouzo.'

She touched his arm lightly with a hesitant but friendly gesture, and then set off along the quay back towards the café. Luke followed automatically, not knowing what else to do.

'Talking of the sun,' Meredith remarked casually, 'have you got any suntan lotion? The sun can be pretty fierce out here.

You look as though your skin's seen quite a bit already, but you shouldn't take chances.'

'I'll get some,' Luke promised, thinking what a bizarre conversation this was in the circumstances. 'I only got to Corfu yesterday, but I work outside a lot at home.'

'Where's home?'

'Devon. Dartmoor. I'm a Ranger in the National Park.'

They sat at an empty table in the shade of one of the trees. Meredith waved to the young waiter, who came across and smiled.

'Do you like ouzo? Or would you rather have a beer?'

Luke, who had never tasted ouzo, decided to stick with something familiar.

'A beer, please.'

Meredith ordered and then turned back to Luke.

'How long have you and Anya been together?'

'Five years, more or less.' His mind was still reeling and dozens of questions were whirling in his head but he was unable to formulate them as yet, leaving Meredith to decide the course of their conversation.

'Do you love her?'

The question was asked in a simple, matter-of-fact tone, but Luke still hesitated, unused to such forthrightness from a stranger.

'Yes,' he replied eventually. 'Very much.'

'Good. She deserves that at least.' Then, seeing his bashful expression, Meredith added, 'I'm sorry. I hope you don't think I'm being too nosy.'

Luke shook his head.

'It's my one incurable vice,' she confessed with a grin. 'And you turning up out of the blue like this . . . well, it's made me curious, to say the least. It's been several years since I had any news of my sister.'

'Why don't you ever see each other?' he asked.

'It would be difficult. Our family fell apart a long time ago.' For the first time she looked less than perfectly relaxed. 'I expect Anya's told you about it.'

'Not much.'

'She always was one for letting sleeping dogs lie, even as a little girl,' Meredith said. 'I was the one who opened my big mouth and got us both into trouble.'

The drinks arrived and she added a little water to her ouzo then sipped the resulting cloudy mixture while Luke poured pale beer from his frosted bottle. He drank deeply, thankfully.

'This is strange,' Meredith said reflectively, gazing out over the still waters of the tiny harbour. 'Being mistaken for Anya again after so long. We must still look alike then?'

Luke nodded. 'Very much.' He took out the photograph of Anya and handed it over. Meredith stared at it intensely for a few seconds, then sighed and gave it back. She returned to her contemplation of the sea and, presumably, her memories.

As Luke watched her, studying her profile, he became fascinated by her earring. It was made of yellow plastic with a dyed feather dangling from it, and was swaying gently in the breeze. Anya would never have worn anything like it and, if she had, the tickling of her neck would have driven her to distraction within moments. Luke was also uncomfortably aware of having noted that beneath her translucent blouse Meredith was wearing a flimsy, pale bikini top, but she seemed unaware of or unconcerned by his scrutiny. She was apparently quite at ease. He was suddenly engulfed by a new wave of doubt.

It made no sense! This was *not* Anya. She might look almost the same, but she acted, talked and dressed quite differently. So had he been following the wrong twin the whole time? No, that was absurd. Anya's credit card had been used to buy the ticket for Corfu. And it had been Anya's earring that he had found in the hotel on Corfu. She must be here – or somewhere near – unless . . .

He was left with three possibilities. The first was that the twins had been thinking and acting alike, sharing the same retreat without even knowing it – an outrageous coincidence, which he had instinctively rejected earlier. The second was some sort of collusion between the supposedly estranged sisters. The opportunities for identical twins to confuse various authorities must be endless. They could use each other's passports, for instance. No doubt they could get away with all sorts of things if they wanted to. But why would they want to? What would be the purpose of such an elaborate game? It occurred to him suddenly that Anya could have swapped places with Meredith in the Scillies. That might have been her reason for going there. But he still had no inkling what their motives might have been and, if that *was* the case, why Meredith was lying to him now. Why should she want or need to do that? What was more, if his new theory was correct, Anya might still be in the Scillies – and the thought of that was unbearable.

The final possibility was even more sinister. Could Meredith have stolen Anya's credit card – and perhaps other documents – and passed herself off as her twin? It would only need a change of clothes to fool anyone other than their respective close friends. If so, what had become of Anya? Wouldn't she have phoned him at least, to ask for help? However, even on such a short acquaintance Luke found it hard to believe that Meredith was capable of harming anyone, let alone her own sister. And anyway, why would she have wanted to do such a thing? From the little Anya had told him, their aunt had left both girls well provided for financially and, unless Meredith was a dissolute spendthrift, she could not have needed to resort to stealing.

'What are you thinking?'

Her question startled him out of his puzzlement. They had both been silent for a while, lost in their separate thoughts, but Meredith was obviously ready to resume their conversation now.

'I'm sorry,' Luke said. 'Coming all this way . . . finding you here . . . I don't know what I'm thinking.'

'You're confused and I'm intrigued,' she concluded, taking another sip of her drink. 'Anya and I always kept our lives separate, for good reasons, or so we thought. But meeting you . . . Do you mind if I ask you some questions?'

'Not at all.' His own could wait until his thoughts were

213

better organized and he had had time to assess Meredith more fully.

'Why didn't you come with Anya? Or am I being too nosy? I don't want to pry into personal matters between you two. That's none of my business.'

'She wouldn't let me. This time she left without warning, but she often travelled on her own – I have no idea where she went – insisting that she needed time alone. I didn't like it, but I had no choice in the matter. It was a condition of our staying together, so I accepted it.'

Meredith nodded, apparently seeing nothing untoward about such an arrangement.

'What changed your mind?' she asked. 'You still haven't told me why you felt it necessary to follow her this time.'

Luke did not answer at once, wondering whether he was ready to tell the whole tale yet. He felt at ease with Meredith, in spite of his suspicions, but it was a complicated story and to do it justice he would have to go back to the beginning – a daunting prospect. On the other hand, if Meredith was honest, who better to help him in his search? If she wasn't, he might catch her out along the way.

'I'm worried about her,' he said eventually. 'Otherwise I'd never have tried to catch up with her. As it is, I've made a real mess of it. I've been several steps behind all the way, just missing her at every turn. And then, just when I think I've actually done something right . . .'

'You find me, not her,' Meredith completed for him.

'Exactly.'

'Why are you worried?'

'She's . . . she's been suffering from some . . . er, delusions recently,' Luke answered reluctantly. 'And they were getting worse.'

'About the sorcerer, you mean?' Meredith said softly.

Luke gaped in astonishment once more.

'You *have* been talking to her!' he exclaimed accusingly.

'No. I haven't.' Her calm attitude did not falter.

'Then how do you know about him?' he demanded.

'I've dreamt about him a few times. I did last night,

as a matter of fact. I guessed the images came from my sister.'

Luke took a few moments to digest this new idea. It sounded highly implausible but, other than calling Meredith an outright liar and demanding to know where Anya was, he had no alternative but to accept it at face value.

'You two are telepathic?' he guessed awkwardly. He had heard about twins who were able to share each other's thoughts.

'Oh, no. It's not as simple as that,' Meredith replied with another smile. 'But I've always had dreams about Anya.'

Looking at her, Luke almost laughed. That smile was so familiar, but it came more easily to Meredith's face and stayed longer. And here there were no acid, sarcastic remarks to accompany it, as was so often the case with her sister. Meredith's demeanour, her easy way with words, her mild self-deprecating humour, all invited confidences in a way that Anya could never have done – especially with a stranger.

'I never thought of telepathy as simple,' Luke remarked.

'It isn't,' she replied. 'No one really understands how our minds work, least of all an "expert" like me. We just have to make use of what talents we have.'

Luke was not quite sure what to make of that statement, but he wanted to know more about the dreams.

'You said you "guessed" the images came from Anya. You're not certain?'

'The sorcerer first appeared in a painting,' she told him. 'Naturally I assumed it was one of Anya's own.'

Luke was taken aback yet again. This was downright spooky – unless she was lying and had actually spoken to her sister.

'He did come from a painting, but not one of hers.' He went on to tell her about the portrait in the National Gallery. Meredith claimed never to have seen or heard of it but, without prompting, described the face of the man depicted, his clothes and surroundings. As far as Luke could recall from the postcard, she was perfectly accurate.

215

'You *have* talked to her, haven't you?' he said, but his accusation lacked any real conviction.

'No, I haven't,' she replied, without any sign of anger or resentment. 'I'm sorry if you find it hard to believe, Luke, but I really did see it all in dreams.'

He watched her, half hoping for some telltale sign of dishonesty, but she met his gaze steadfastly and without any indication of discomfort. Eventually it was Luke who gave in and looked away.

'Either you're the best actress I've ever seen or you're as weird as Anya,' he conceded at last.

'It runs in the family,' Meredith told him, grinning.

Luke found himself smiling back at her, despite the uncomfortable truth he knew lay behind her words.

'What else have you seen in your dreams? Anything useful, like where Anya might be now?'

'I'm afraid not,' she said with what sounded like genuine regret. 'The last time I was home – on St Agnes – I had the feeling that something unpleasant was happening to her, but I dismissed the idea as silly. We're grown up now. We're supposed to be able to look after ourselves.' Large brown eyes looked at him. 'But you're not sure Anya can, right?'

'No. As I said, I'm worried about her. I think she needs help, and when she ran off . . .'

'Hang on. This is obviously going to be a long story, and I want to hear it, but I was up early today and I need to eat. Are you hungry?'

Luke nodded.

'Just a minute then . . .' She bent to rummage in her shoulder bag which she had put on the floor beside her chair. She produced a bottle of suntan lotion and a small carton of painkillers. 'Put some of that on,' she instructed, tossing him the bottle, 'while I take these. Then we'll go and eat.'

She swallowed two tablets with the remains of her water while he rubbed his face and arms.

'Headache,' Meredith explained. 'Daft really. If you can't relax here, then you can't relax anywhere, but I haven't been

216

able to shift this one for days. I don't normally resort to these, but needs must.'

'Too much sun?' Luke suggested mildly as they got up.

Meredith laughed. 'It better not be, after my lecture to you,' she said. 'And before you say it, it's not too much ouzo either. Come on.' She left some money on the table and led the way back along the water's edge, past the far entrance to the alley, to a taverna with a single line of tables outside.

'It's Sunday today, so it's safe to sit outside,' she remarked as they chose their places.

'Why is Sunday safe?'

'No buses.'

Luke noted the narrow width of concrete between them and the harbour, and imagined the scene.

'Actually it's pefectly safe when they drive past,' Meredith conceded, 'but it can be quite exciting if you're not used to it. Do you like Greek food?'

'Apart from moussaka, I don't really know anything about it,' he admitted.

'It's pretty basic, but I love it,' she told him. 'I'll order us a selection of things so you can try them, but if you want meat or fish, you'll need to go inside and choose from the cabinet. The fish is especially good, I'm told. Really fresh.'

'You don't eat it yourself?'

'No. I'm a milksop vegetarian.' She grinned. 'But, please, don't let my hang-ups stop you.'

Luke hesitated.

'Are you sure?'

'Of course. Go and choose. I'll sort out the rest.'

By the time Luke returned, the ordering had been completed and already there were a small bottle of wine, some bread and a plate of wrinkled olives on the table. Meredith poured and signalled for him to drink.

'Retsina,' she informed him. 'Complete with resin from pine needles. This is the best wine for a hot day – but it's got to be really cold, otherwise it tastes like the stuff they run outboard motors on.'

Luke sipped gingerly and found the taste strange but oddly refreshing.

'Now,' Meredith said. 'Start from the beginning and tell me everything.'

33

Luke did as he was told. Between mouthfuls, he explained that Anya believed she was haunted, partially possessed by the spirit of a sixteenth-century sorcerer named Allessandro Massimiliano, who was now reemerging into the world. He told her about the visions, which were more than dreams, and which lasted hours or even days for Anya but took only a few seconds of normal time. He described the traumatic evening on which he had learnt all this – now almost a fortnight ago – and Anya's claim that Allessandro's appearance in her studio, in the real world, had prompted her to share her secret with him. This naturally led to the events of the following morning: the Scrabble message, 'Allessandro' moving the curtains, Anya's refusal to accept that she needed help, the phone call which she warned him was a hoax, the curious episode with the knife – and, finally, her disappearance while he was out waiting for the nonexistent helicopter.

'When I got back, the house was in a mess and I found this pinned to the door.' Luke took out the crumpled note and gave it to Meredith, who put down her fork and read the short message. She had been listening to his story in silence for the most part, only interrupting occasionally when she needed a particular point clarifying. Luke was grateful for her calm acceptance of such an unlikely tale.

'And that was when you started following her?' she asked, looking up from the note.

'Or trying to,' he agreed. 'But I kept losing her trail and

having to go home. Then each time something else would come up and I'd be off again.'

'Go on.'

'The first thing happened the same day she left, and was only connected to any of this indirectly,' Luke went on. 'A letter arrived from a doctor in Bristol about your mother.'

'Ah, so you know about one of the skeletons in our family closet, then.'

'I do now, but up until then I'd thought Mary was dead. That was what Anya had told me.'

'Oh.'

'Do you know why she lied about it?'

'I can guess,' Meredith replied quietly. 'Anya may genuinely think of our mother as dead. And I can sympathize with that. It would certainly be easier than having a constant reminder of some of the things that happened to us as children.'

'So I gather,' Luke said heavily. 'But *you* still visited her.'

'Not very often. It was always painful and didn't serve much purpose. I haven't been for over two years. Did you go?'

'Yes, but she wouldn't talk to me. She refused to believe I was Anya's boyfriend.'

'My mother has a problem dealing with men. Among other things.'

'That's not all,' Luke went on. 'She claimed to have seen the man Anya was with, as she put it, "in the flames".'

Meredith nodded, unsurprised.

'Her visions.'

'When we asked who he was she said "the angel from the picture",' Luke went on. 'And a few days later, when the doctor showed her a print of the del Sarto painting Mary identified him without any prompting as the man who was with Anya.'

'Curiouser and curiouser.'

'Exactly. None of this makes much sense to me, but it seems quite possible that Anya's illness is hereditary, in part at least, and that somehow their delusions are linked. I'm no psychologist, but it seems obvious that most of Anya's problems must stem from her childhood – a childhood you shared.' He paused, waiting to see how Meredith would react to his none too subtle probing. For a time she was silent, looking very thoughtful, but when she finally spoke she surprised him once again.

'So now you want to know how I've managed to become a perfectly balanced, socially charming human being in spite of all my obvious disadvantages?' Although the words were lightly spoken, her smile, for once, looked false. 'Or perhaps you think I'm crazy too?'

'I don't even know you,' he protested, with some heat. 'And I don't think Anya's crazy, just that she needs help.'

'I'm sorry,' Meredith said quietly. 'It's . . . it's just that my past doesn't often catch up with me like this. You can't forget, however much you'd like to, but I've got used to keeping it at arm's length.'

'I'm sorry,' Luke echoed. 'I know this must be hard for you, but I'm only trying to help Anya. You understand that, don't you?' When she did not reply, he went on reluctantly, 'I mean, I know about your father leaving and the fire and your mother's illness, but is there anything else I should know?'

'Isn't that enough?' After another awkward pause, she went on, 'I'd like to help Anya too, but the past won't help us find her now. And just so you know, I've never had any mental problems – at least not in the usual sense.'

Luke was frustrated, thinking her statement ambiguous at the very least, but he said nothing.

'A lot of people might think I'm somewhat strange by conventional standards,' Meredith continued, 'but that's neither here nor there. What happened after you'd been to see our mother?'

'Nothing much for a few days. The hospital gave me your telephone number and I left a message on the machine, but it was some time before Alice heard it and rang me up.'

'Alice is a good friend and neighbour,' Meredith stated. 'I'm away so much it's nice to have someone to keep an eye on the place. What did she have to tell you?'

'This is where we come to another coincidence,' Luke

221

replied. 'Alice told me that she'd seen Anya on St Mary's a couple of days earlier. She'd thought it was you at first.'

'Anya was on the Scillies?'

'Yes. Do you think she might have gone there to look for you?'

'I doubt it. As far as I'm aware, she never even knew I had a home there.'

'She did,' Luke told her. 'We went to Tresco together for her birthday and someone at the hotel mistook her for you. But she didn't seem very keen on trying to find you then.' He had been watching Meredith closely during this exchange, but her bemused expression gave nothing away.

'This is all news to me. I haven't been home since the middle of July, and haven't spoken to Alice since then either.' She seemed genuinely surprised. 'So you've no idea why Anya went to the islands?'

'None. Nor why she left, but at least at the time I thought I'd picked up her trail. I arranged to fly out there the next morning, but before I left a postcard arrived from the Island Hotel on Tresco, telling me that Anya was there and that she needed my help.'

'Anya sent you a postcard?' Meredith queried. 'Why didn't she telephone?'

'The postcard wasn't from Anya. It was from someone called Verity Nyman. I've never heard of her. Do you know who she is?'

Meredith shook her head. Her expression had betrayed nothing at his mention of the mysterious correspondent.

'Neither had anyone at the hotel,' Luke went on. 'I rang them straight away, but Anya had already left. And not only that, but her room had been smashed up, as if there'd been a fight.'

'Was she hurt?' Meredith looked shocked.

'Not as far as I know, but that was only the first of several oddities and unpleasant incidents that dogged her trip. Alice had already told me that Anya had been behaving very nervously, but there was worse to come. When I got down there I found that there'd been a fire in the Hugh Town hotel where Anya had stayed after leaving Tresco. It apparently started in or near her room.'

'And so you wondered whether she'd inherited our mother's pyromania?'

'It did cross my mind,' Luke admitted. 'No one was badly hurt – which was a relief.'

'To put it mildly,' Meredith agreed with feeling. 'Anything else?'

'Well, this is going to sound ridiculous, but there were a few minor earthquakes in the area while she was there. Nothing serious, but . . .' He broke off at the sight of his companion's astonished expression.

'Apparently there have been several small tremors around here in the last few days,' Meredith told him. 'I hadn't even noticed, but some of the locals got quite alarmed. But then the Greeks can make a drama out of anything, it's part of their charm.'

Their food and wine had run out long before this and they contemplated their empty glasses in silence for a while, both considering this latest and strangest coincidence. Neither of them felt it necessary to point out that, whatever Anya's personal problems, it was unlikely that weaknesses in the planet's crust were among them.

'More retsina, I think,' Meredith decided eventually, and disappeared into the taverna, reemerging moments later with an open bottle. After the glasses were filled, they resumed their conversation.

'Anya had left before you got to the Scillies, I presume.'

'Yes. I just missed her. I found out she'd gone on to London but there was no way of telling where she'd gone from there, so I had no choice but to go home again. Then, a few days later, Anya's credit card statement arrived, showing that she'd paid over quite a large sum to a travel agent in London.'

'So off you went again.'

'The questing knight,' Luke agreed with a rueful smile. 'The travel agents told me she was quite a regular customer – and, apparently, so are you.' He was watching her reactions carefully again.

223

Meredith's eyes widened abruptly.

'Galaxy Plus?' she exclaimed, looking completely astounded. Luke nodded.

'How extraordinary! I have a small flat near there, for stopovers. They arrange nearly all my travel, but I never knew . . . These coincidences are getting a bit much, aren't they?' she added with a shake of her head. 'I'm beginning to think Anya might be following *me*!' She laughed uneasily.

Luke felt completely out of his depth. As far as he could tell, her reaction had been genuine, her surprise real, but she was right. The coincidences were mounting up alarmingly. Could she really be intent on fooling him for some unknown reason? Was she really that good a dissembler? Or perhaps Meredith's theory was right and Anya *had* been attempting to follow her, for reasons only she could know.

'That's nearly the end of the story,' Luke said quietly. 'The lady in Galaxy Travel said Anya had been behaving oddly. She told me that she'd flown to Corfu but – guess what? – I missed her there too. She only stayed one night, even though she'd booked the hotel room for a week. The receptionist there remembered her making enquiries about ferries to Paxos.'

'So here you are.'

'So here I am . . . but is she? When I saw you . . .' He shrugged, lost for words, and took a gulp of wine.

'What an incredible story,' Meredith concluded. 'We have to find her.'

'And soon,' Luke concurred. 'The fact that she thinks this so-called sorcerer is getting more powerful each time he appears would seem to indicate that her illness is progressive. We've got to find her before it goes too far.'

'Or we have to stop *him*,' Meredith said.

'Oh, come on!' he exclaimed. 'Surely *you* don't believe in ghosts and possession?'

'Have you ever considered that her visions might not be delusions?' she asked mildly. 'That they might be real?'

'A sixteenth-century magician? From a *painting*?'

'Is it easier to believe she's insane?'

That stopped Luke in his tracks. He did not *want* to believe that – he did not like Meredith's choice of words – but what alternative did he have?

'I don't like the idea any more than you do, but given her history, surely it's more likely that she needs psychiatric help,' he reasoned, feeling embarrassed about even having such an argument. 'She was talking about needing to use a witch, or an exorcist, for heaven's sake.'

'They're professions that have been around for centuries,' Meredith countered. 'Are they necessarily so ridiculous?'

'This is all beyond me,' Luke confessed, exasperated now in the face of Meredith's calm reasoning. 'I don't know anything about spirits or visions. I need things I can see and touch, real things I can understand. Perhaps if Anya could give me a reason for all this then it would be easier to accept her story. Why did this Allessandro choose her out of the millions who must have seen the painting? Why has he come back to life now, after four hundred years? Anya herself admitted she had no answers to questions like that.'

'Just because we don't understand something doesn't mean it's impossible,' she stated evenly, unruffled by his vehemence.

'It's just too far-fetched for words!'

'More far-fetched than all these things you've been describing to me?' she asked innocently. 'Even my mother seems to believe in Allessandro.'

'She's hardly the world's most reliable witness!' Luke retorted, but then reminded himself that he had no explanation for Mary's knowledge of the man in the painting. He fell silent, remembering the wavering of a curtain, a knife clattering to the kitchen floor for no apparent reason.

'Spirits do exist,' Meredith stated quietly.

'Don't tell me you talk to them as well,' Luke groaned.

'Frequently,' she replied. 'Although in my case it's by choice.'

Was the whole family as loopy as cable-stitch? Luke wondered. Was this the reason Anya had wanted to keep her mother *and Meredith* a secret?

'I'm a psychic,' she explained simply. 'Healing mostly, a

medium sometimes. That's how I earn my living.' Noting his discomfort, she smiled and added, 'Don't worry. I'm quite normal really. I just try to help people when and where I can.'

Her sincerity was self-evident, but Luke found himself tongue-tied. He felt as if he were swimming into ever deeper and more dangerous waters – but, like the shark, he would die if he stopped moving forwards. All his instincts had made him warm to Meredith; he had liked her from the beginning, as soon as he had recovered from the shock of her not being Anya. And nothing that had been revealed since, none of the suspicious coincidences, had altered that original impression. He knew their fates were linked now, for better or worse, whether he liked it or not. The fact that she was psychic put her remarks concerning her dreams about Anya into an altogether different and disturbing light, but Luke was too befuddled to work out the exact consequences of her revelation. He sipped more restsina, suddenly feeling very tired.

'How long have you been on Paxos?' Meredith asked. 'Where else have you looked?'

'I only got here this morning,' he confessed. 'And I got a taxi straight to Loggos.'

'Why start here?' she asked curiously.

Luke hesitated, reluctant to admit his own reliance on an inexplicable experience after all the sceptical things he had said.

'Tell me,' Meredith prompted. 'I'm a good listener.'

That's true enough, Luke reflected, and gave in to the inevitable.

'You're not the only one to have prophetic dreams,' he said bashfully. 'Last night, in Corfu, just before I woke up, I dreamt about walking into this village. I didn't know at the time that it was Loggos, but then I saw a photo in a guidebook. It seemed like a sign.'

'There's hope for you yet,' she told him approvingly, and they grinned at each other. 'What happened in the dream?'

'Nothing very spectacular.' He shut his eyes, trying to re-create the images in his mind's eye. 'I remember looking

226

at all the houses, the sparrows in the tree, all the flowers. And fondling a puppy's ears. There was the smell of baking bread and I had a drink at the café . . .' He opened his eyes to find Meredith staring at him again. 'What? What have I said?'

'You weren't yourself in the dream, were you?' she said.

'No. I was . . .' Luke stopped, remembering the unheeded sensation of being tickled by feathers below each ear.

'You've just described my start to the day,' Meredith went on. 'I often have the sensation of someone else looking through my eyes, but I never dreamt it might be you. Recognize this?' She produced her purse and laid it on the table. It was the same one Luke had seen. 'Maybe I'm not the only one who's psychic around here.'

Luke was dumbfounded. This was all too much. How could this be happening to him? Then, abruptly, he began to search among the coins in his trouser pocket. When he found what he wanted he laid it on the table between them.

'I found this in the hotel room in Corfu,' he said. 'It's Anya's. In the dream . . .'

Before he could finish the sentence, Meredith snapped open her purse and took out an identical earring.

'I found this under my table at the café this morning,' she said as she laid it next to its partner. 'It looks as though Anya's been in Loggos after all.'

34

Luke stared at the earrings which represented his final vindication, the proof that he had indeed been on the right track, that Anya was nearby. And yet the proof came enmeshed in further mysteries. It had been Meredith, not Anya, whose sensations had invaded his dream and drawn him to Loggos – and he was still no nearer to uncovering the link between the twins, if any existed. Meredith seemed as astonished as he was at yet another unsettling coincidence.

'You found it?' he asked eventually.

'Yes. I wonder what drew me to it,' Meredith said thoughtfully. She picked up both earrings and held them in her closed fist, then shut her eyes and grew very still.

'What are you doing?' Luke ventured after a few moments.

'Trying to see whether they can tell me anything. There's no point in having my prodigious talents if I can't use them for something like this. Shhh, now.'

The faint self-mocking tone in her voice was back, but as she fell silent again her expression became serious and her eyes remained closed.

'These were a birthday present . . . but not from you. An older woman, a friend.' She paused, inviting confirmation.

'They were from Sheila, Anya's agent.'

'Anya obviously didn't have them long enough to leave much impression,' Meredith added, frowning with concentration. 'Just flashes . . . a lot of strong emotions, but nothing coherent. She . . . she was wearing them the day she left home . . . but there's nothing after that.' She opened her eyes and shrugged. 'So much for me playing psychometric detective.'

Luke did not know what to say. He was not sure whether he believed that Meredith had actually learnt anything from the earrings and, in a sense, it did not matter. She hadn't told him anything he did not already know. And, in any case, he needed to find out where Anya was *now*, after she had lost or discarded the earrings. Psychometry would not help him there.

'It was never going to help us find her now,' Meredith said, echoing his thoughts. 'I just hoped there might be some clue. You've been playing detective longer than me. What now?'

'We'll ask around,' Luke replied. 'Show people her photo, see if we can get some idea where she's staying or where she might have gone.'

'We're going to confuse a lot of people,' Meredith commented.

Her prediction proved horribly accurate. They started with the local residents, the shop and taverna owners who might have served Anya. Most of them, naturally enough, mistook the woman in the photograph for Meredith, and the explanations that followed sometimes only puzzled them even more. Almost all of them had a working knowledge of English, more than enough to deal with the normal needs of tourists, but this was hardly a normal enquiry. Even the waiter and the owner of the café, where Anya must have been, could only respond with shrugs and eloquent gestures.

The local holiday reps, to whom the problem could be explained more fully, were equally unforthcoming. Anya was not booked into any holiday accommodation in the village but, other than that, Luke learnt nothing of use. One of the guides commented that even if she had seen Anya she would have assumed it to be Meredith. None of their attempts to tie down times when Meredith knew she had been elsewhere, nor Luke's questions about the colour of her clothing, produced any results.

By that point, Meredith had become convinced that they were getting nowhere. As she pointed out, Loggos was a small place and if Anya had been there for any length of time then she would almost certainly have been aware of it herself. However, Luke refused to give up until he had approached yet more people, especially English holiday-makers with whom he could converse easily, but he learnt nothing and received many strange and dubious looks for his pains. Eventually, feeling wretched and very disappointed, he had to admit failure. They ended up, back where they had begun, at the café.

'Now what?' Luke muttered.

'Tomorrow we can try further afield,' Meredith replied promptly. 'The buses'll be running, so we can check with the drivers – and the taxis – to see if they remember taking Anya anywhere. If we don't have any luck, we can go to Lakka or Gaios ourselves and start again. They're both much bigger places, but we should be able to cover them between us.'

The reps had already promised to check with their colleagues in the other resorts to see whether Anya was registered there, and Luke had been given various telephone numbers – a car hire firm, the island's only hotel, doctor's surgeries and so on – so that they could make further enquiries. Even so, their absolute lack of progress when he had seemed so close to success made it difficult for him not to feel depressed and pessimistic. He was grateful for Meredith's plans, which allowed him to avoid a little of the responsibility for making decisions.

'Right now,' she went on, 'you look all in. There's nothing much more we can do here. Why don't we go for a swim?'

It was an appealing idea. The anxiety, surprises and ultimate disappointment of the day had taken their toll, and Luke was also physically exhausted. His clothes were caked with sweat – especially his back, from lugging his rucksack about – and the effects of the heat and his lunchtime drinking had caught up with him. The calm blue sea looked enormously inviting.

'I haven't got any trunks.'

'Then buy some,' she told him practically.

Luke did so, then walked with Meredith along the road,

round the promontory and down the path to the local stone beach. There were few people left this late in the afternoon, and the ice-cream vendor at the edge of the olive groves had already gone home for the day. As Luke struggled to change, wrapped around with his small towel, Meredith stripped off her shorts and blouse and sat on a rock. He could not help noticing that her pale blue bikini seemed to cover very little of her lightly tanned body.

'You know, if you come at the right time of year and walk through the olive groves here in the evening, the air is full of fireflies,' Meredith told him. 'It's magical, straight out of a fairy tale.'

'You've been to Paxos before, then?'

'Several times. I love it here. It's a very special place, but I never get the chance to stay for more than a few days.'

'Why not?'

'Guilty conscience,' she replied. 'I have to go home, catch up on my messages. Get my life and work going again.'

'How long have you been here this time?'

'Oh, a few days. I ought to be going soon.'

The idea filled Luke with sudden panic, and an unexpected sense of loss.

'You will stay and help me find Anya, won't you?' he asked quickly.

'Of course.' She seemed about to say more but evidently thought better of it.

'Could your . . . healing abilities help her?' Luke wondered hesitantly. 'I mean, are they . . . applicable?'

'I don't know. I'd like to try. If she'll let me.'

Again Luke sensed that she was not saying all that was on her mind, but he could not blame her for having reservations. The sisters had not seen each other for many years.

By now, Luke was ready and they walked down to the water's edge together.

'Watch out for sea urchins,' Meredith warned. 'If you get any of their spines in your foot it can be nasty.'

Luke was careful as he waded in. The water was perfectly clear, so the black urchins were easy to spot and avoid. He dived in and swam out into deeper water, revelling in the refreshing caress of the sea. Treading water, he looked back to see Meredith still in the shallows.

'Aren't you coming in?' he called.

'I'm fine here,' she replied. 'You go on.'

By the time Luke got back, the day's perspiration and dust washed clean away, Meredith had been out of the water for some time. She was lying on the beach, letting the last of the day's sun dry her. She looked extraordinarily relaxed and beautiful.

'Feel better?'

'Much better,' he said. 'You don't know what you're missing.'

'I'm not a very good swimmer,' she told him, 'and I'm frightened to get out of my depth. I don't even like boats much.'

'And yet you live on the Scillies and choose another small island for your holiday?'

'It's not gentlemanly to point out a lady's perversity,' she informed him, and they grinned at each other. 'I prefer walking. Paxos is great for that. If we weren't otherwise occupied, I'd've liked to show you around.'

'I'd have liked that,' he sighed, 'but . . .'

'Have you arranged somewhere to stay?' she asked, as if it had only just occurred to her.

'Not yet.'

'Better come with me then,' she decided. 'I've got a small hovel in the hills on the other side of the village. It's pretty basic and it'll be a bit cramped with the two of us, but it's better than nothing.'

'Sure you don't mind?' Luke asked, realizing that he had been hoping for just such an invitation, assuming that he and Meredith were now allies and would stick together.

'Of course not. It'll be good to have some company for once.'

Her comment made Luke realize that he had been blithely taking it for granted that Meredith was alone. It was only now that he had any confirmation of the fact. For all he knew she might have been there with her husband – though surely she would have mentioned any companion before now. He glanced at her hands, but she wore no rings.

Meredith consulted her watch.

'The shops'll be open again now,' she said. 'I'll buy a few things and we'll eat supper at the house. OK with you?'

'Fine. But I'd like to come down to the village again in the evening, to see whether Anya's returned.'

Meredith's 'hovel' was reached by a steep, sometimes winding path that threaded its way between the olive terraces and lemon-scented gardens of villas on the slope to the north of Loggos. Laden down with groceries as well as Luke's pack, they were glad of the abundant shade. Near the top they passed a tiny white-walled chapel, complete with its own shrine and miniature bell tower, and decorated with blue painted versions of the Greek flag. From there the path joined the network of various tracks linking the less ostentatious dwellings scattered among the trees.

The cottage was one of the smallest and apparently most dilapidated of all the buildings. As they approached, Meredith pointed out a nearby shed.

'That's the loo,' she informed him. 'Take a torch if you go at night, or I won't be held responsible for the consequences.'

She unlatched the door and switched on the light, then opened the shutters. Inside, belying its outer appearance, the house was solid and homely. Meredith dumped the shopping on the table as Luke looked round curiously.

'Only one bed, I'm afraid,' she said, indicating the large divan in the far corner. 'There's room enough for two, but I don't know you well enough for that.' She grinned. 'We'll set you up over here.'

'Fine,' Luke said, a little too quickly.

'This must be weird for you,' Meredith observed thoughtfully. 'Poor Luke. Don't worry. We'll find her.'

He nodded, feeling rather like an awkward adolescent. His gaze fell upon a half-finished painting, propped up on a shelf.

'You paint too, then?'

'I dabble, but I don't have Anya's gift. Even as a girl she had a wonderful eye for shape and colour. I'm strictly an amateur, more of a copyist really.'

The subject of the incomplete painting was a selection of brightly coloured flowers, realistically portrayed but with none of the verve or idiosyncrasies that made Anya's work special.

'It's good,' Luke lied, peering closer.

'You should know better than to lie to a psychic,' she responded. 'It doesn't work. My talents are in other areas. How emotional do you get over vegetables?'

The abrupt shift in topic disconcerted Luke for a moment. Meredith held up a purple onion by way of explanation.

'I love eating them,' she said, 'but I dissolve into floods of tears when I chop them up.'

Together they prepared the meal; cheeses, salad, onions, olives from a huge plastic tub, bread, fruit and halva, all washed down with bottled water.

'That was great,' Luke said when they had finished eating.

'But much too healthy,' Meredith commented. 'We can remedy that right now.' She produced a half-full bottle of Metaxa and poured measures into two small glasses. 'Here's to absent friends.'

Abruptly Luke felt guilty about being so comfortable, about enjoying his time with Meredith. Anya was out there somewhere, going through heaven knows what private torments, and he was wasting time drinking brandy.

'Don't be too hard on yourself, Luke,' Meredith said, catching his change of mood. 'You're doing all you can. Most people would have given up long before this.'

'Are you reading my mind now?'

'Just your face. It's not hard.'

Luke said nothing.

'Don't forget, it's Anya who's led you on this merry dance,' she added. 'She can hardly blame you for not finding her straight away.'

'She doesn't want to be found,' he replied gloomily. 'She'll only be angry with me if I *do* find her. But I have to try. For my sake, as well as hers.'

'My sister has good taste in men,' Meredith said.

Luke felt the colour rise in his cheeks and was grateful for the dim lighting.

'I make a singularly ineffective questing knight, though,' he said, trying to make light of her words.

'Give it time,' she advised. 'It took Gawain a while to find the Holy Grail. How long are you planning to stay on Paxos?'

'Another day at least. Then if we don't have any luck I can go back to Corfu on Tuesday and see if Anya's on the flight home the next morning.' His tone made it clear that he thought the possibility very remote. 'If she isn't, I don't know what I'll do.'

'Come back here,' Meredith said promptly. 'We know she came to Paxos. She's probably still on the island and even if she isn't, this is still the best chance of picking up her trail again.'

'Speaking of which,' Luke said, draining his glass, 'I'd like to go down and spy out the town. Just in case.'

'OK. But before we do, I want to try something.'

'What?'

'I've never asked my spirit guides for help finding someone who's still alive,' she answered, 'but given the circumstances, I'm sure they won't mind.'

35

Meredith stood up and walked over to the bed before Luke had a chance to respond. She lay down and put her hands behind her head.

'I'm just going to relax,' she told him. 'It'll probably look like I'm going to sleep at first – but don't poke me unless I begin to snore, OK?'

'What do I do?' He felt nervous, though she was obviously quite at ease.

'Nothing. I'm going to be talking in here.' She tapped her forehead. 'But it's possible one of the guides might decide to speak out loud. Don't be surprised if my voice changes. If it seems appropriate, you can ask questions, talk to them. If not, just listen. In any case, I'll tell you all about it afterwards, all right?'

Luke nodded.

Meredith closed her eyes and lay still, her hands now folded across her stomach. For some minutes the only movement in the room was the rise and fall of her chest as her breathing became slow and deep. Luke kept as still as he could but, as the seconds ticked away and nothing happened, he began to find the whole thing absurd and rather embarrassing.

At last, just when he felt he could bear it no longer, Meredith sighed deeply and cleared her throat before beginning to speak. The voice that emerged from her lips was unrecognizable, a hoarse, masculine whisper that was almost painful to listen to. Luke's growing scepticism vanished. If this was play-acting, then Meredith was indeed the most amazing actress he had ever seen.

'Does the seeker have a name?'

'I . . . My name is Luke,' he said, hoping he was meant to answer.

There was another long pause, then the same grating voice sounded again.

'Stay where you are, Luke. She will come to you.'

'Anya will come here?' he asked eagerly. 'Back to Loggos?'

The answer, when it came, was not the specific confirmation he had hoped for.

'Stay close to the water. She is in danger. The renegade is beyond our reach now. His corruption spreads. We can only protect those who wish for protection – and even there our power is limited.'

'What do you mean?' Luke demanded. 'Who is this renegade?'

But there was no answer, only another long silence. After a while Meredith opened her eyes and sat up.

'What did all that mean?' Luke asked, now thoroughly unnerved.

'I don't know. The guides seemed reluctant to get involved. It was very odd. They're often almost as obscure as oracles, but it usually becomes clear in the end.'

Only one piece of advice seemed to make any sense to Luke.

'Do you think I should stay here, in Loggos?'

'That's what it sounded like,' Meredith replied, but she was obviously puzzled. 'Close to the water?'

'The harbour?' he guessed. 'Perhaps she's at the café now.'

'There's only one way to find out,' she said, getting up and grabbing a sweater.

'Do you know who this renegade is? Could it be Allessandro?'

'I'm not sure. I tried to explain the situation to them, but it all got very confused. Anyway, I thought you didn't believe in him.' There was a slight note of challenge in her tone.

'He might be a figment of Anya's imagination, just as your guides might be figments of yours,' he pointed out.

'They might be,' Meredith agreed placidly, 'but I don't think you believe that any more than I do.'

'Are you always so reasonable?' he wondered aloud.

'Only when I'm right,' she answered. 'Which is most of the time.'

Their search of Loggos proved unsuccessful, and in the process Luke became aware that several of the taverna owners were regarding him as a bit of a joke. Only an eccentric Englishman, their expressions seemed to say, could possibly want a second woman exactly like the one he was already with. Dispirited and self-conscious, Luke agreed to give up soon after eleven o'clock and they made the long climb back to Meredith's house with the aid of torches.

They were both tired now, and set about making up Luke's bed as soon as they got in. It consisted of a mismatched collection of pillows, cushions, folded towels and blankets for a mattress, with a sleeping bag on top.

'Hardly the Corfu Palace . . .' Meredith said.

'But it's home,' Luke completed. 'It'll be fine. I'm very grateful . . . for all your help.'

'Thank me when we've found Anya. Let's get some sleep now. I tend to get up early in the mornings.'

She had draped a spare sheet over an easel and the back of a chair, to give them both an element of privacy, but Luke still felt awkward as he undressed. Meredith obviously did not share his sensibilities and, although he told himself he was trying not to look, Luke caught glimpses of her as she moved about, getting ready for bed and then switching off the light.

'If you're going to dream about me again,' she said, her voice floating out of the darkness, 'let's do something a bit more interesting than just drink coffee, OK?' She laughed softly.

'I'll do my best.'

'Goodnight, Luke.'

'Goodnight.'

He lay on the makeshift bed and listened to the small sounds of the night. Almost immediately Meredith's breathing changed to the gentle rhythm of sleep, and he envied her ability to put aside all concerns and simply rest. His mind was far too busy to find such desirable peace and for some time he dozed fitfully. When he did fall asleep it was only to wake again some two hours later, in the small hours of the morning.

For the second time in twenty-four hours he did not know where he was, but the moonlight filtering through the open shutters showed him the house in silver outlines and deeper shadows. On the far side of the room Meredith made tiny whimpering noises in her sleep, like those of a small animal, then grew silent again. Hearing her like that emphasized her vulnerability and Luke was suddenly wide awake, aware of contradictory feelings within himself.

He was basically an honest person, and admitting that he was attracted to Meredith was easy enough, but the emotional complications that accompanied such an admission were hard to reconcile. Guilt at his perceived disloyalty to Anya was the least of it. Even thinking about Meredith in such terms seemed vaguely incestuous, although logically he knew it was nothing of the kind. Nevertheless, he found himself wondering how others, twins who married twins for instance, coped with the inevitable dual affinities and possible confusions.

In a strange way, Meredith had all Anya's advantages, especially her wonderful physical appearance and intelligence, but without her twin's increasingly acid and possibly unbalanced temperament. That Meredith was open and trusting, that she was likable and humorous, had already been amply demonstrated in the short time he had known her. Luke was equally convinced that her charming, seemingly uncomplicated exterior hid a character that was far more complex, a personality that could quite possibly prove to be extremely devious. It was also undeniably true that her world encompassed many things that were alien to Luke's. She was obviously a little weird, but that was part of her allure. Luke remembered her golden skin, on the beach, or reaching over to turn out the light . . .

His sleeping bag had suddenly become too hot and constricting, and Luke knew he had to get out. His eyes had adjusted to the light now, and he unzipped the bag as quietly as he could, found some trousers and a sweatshirt and pulled them on. He crept stealthily to the door and let himself out into the night, then, taking several deep breaths, he picked his way carefully over the flagstones and sat down, leaning against the end of a dry-stone wall. The air was wonderfully cool and a zephyr breeze rustled the leaves all around him, making them whisper, and revealing patches of dancing moonlight.

Luke's thoughts returned to Anya, and he finally under-stood that his yearning for her was as much for his own sake as for hers. He wanted to help her, but he also needed to be *with* her. For all her idiosyncrasies, it was Anya that he loved. His almost instant attraction to Meredith was just a side-effect of that longing, a substitute he knew now would prove illusory, however beguiling it appeared.

However, he was not given long to ponder these matters because the silence of the night was broken by the deep, sonorous tolling of a distant bell. It was a mournful sound, the reverberation dying away slowly before being renewed. It rang in a slow rhythm, and its vibrations seemed to make the very air resonate, the moon-silvered leaves shiver. Luke could not imagine where the sound was coming from – it seemed to be all around him – and the note was too low for any church bell. Nor could he understand why it should be ringing now, in the middle of the night. He listened transfixed, as the entire woodland scene trembled in expectation. If Luke had been of a fanciful nature he would have said that there was a chilling kind of magic in the air, but his mind worked on more pragmatic levels. Even so, when he heard the sound of the funeral drums and the slow shuffling of feet, he could no longer deny his sense of wonder – and dread. He tried to stand up but his legs seemed to have gone to sleep. Nor could he move his arms. His fear intensified.

The cortège appeared round a bend in the track. Luke could not see the bearers clearly, but they were carrying a wooden pallet on their shoulders, on which lay a body. In the half-light there were no colours to be seen, only shades of grey and silver, pinpoints of light and liquid shadows. There was no one else, no mourners following, no drummers – and yet the muffled beat went on as the solemn procession drew closer.

Then a great voice boomed out, seeming to come from the sky itself.

'Thamous.'

Twice more the heavens echoed to those two indecipherable syllables and then, as if from an impossible distance, far out at sea, there came an almost inaudible answering cry. The titanic voice spoke again, in a tone of unmistakable sorrow, conveying a message Luke could not understand. Then all was quiet again, apart from the steady hollow sound of the invisible drums and the footsteps of the pallbearers.

By now Luke was frozen with an unholy terror, and could not have moved even if his limbs had been functioning. He could only sit and watch as the ghost-like figures drew near. He still could not see the bearers properly, except to note that they were barefoot and dressed in flimsy rags. Their faces were hidden by tattered hoods. By comparison, the dead man could be seen clearly – though Luke fought against accepting the evidence of his own eyes. The body being carried was not a man but a satyr, half-man, half-goat. The unmoving face was ugly, surrounded by coils of the unruly hair which also carpeted the thick arms and barrel chest. The lower half of the torso and the legs were even more hirsute, and ended in large cloven hoofs. The overall effect should have been ridiculous, comical, but there was a sad dignity about this creature, now travelling on its last journey and, despite his fear, Luke found a lump in his throat and tears welling up in his eyes.

They passed by, paying him no attention, and he turned his head to watch them as they trudged on, heading downhill, towards the sea. Soon they passed out of sight and the sound of the drums began to fade. Unnoticed, the bell had stopped ringing.

'That was the end of it, of course,' a cultured voice said beside him.

Luke's head snapped round to look up at a man who looked hardly less spectral himself. He seemed to glow in the moonlight, but his face was hidden in shadow beneath a large hat.

'The end of the Olympian gods, the end of the age of myth.' He sounded regretful.

'Who *are* you?' Luke whispered, aware that he was still unable to move.

The man ignored him.

'The voice you heard was sending a message that announced the death of Pan. Strange that even a lesser god should choose to die here, rather than in his homeland of Arcadia, don't you think? And stranger still to choose an Egyptian sea captain to spread the news. But the very stones of the island remember it, as if it were yesterday. All you need is the wit and imagination to see it – or someone like me to make it visible even to dullards like you.'

Luke was still struggling to come to terms with the fantastical events he had witnessed, wondering without any real conviction if he had dreamt it all – and was dreaming still. He found it impossible to think clearly.

'I can do that now, you see,' the man went on casually. 'My transformation is almost complete.'

'Allessandro?' Luke guessed, disbelieving.

'At your service.' The man doffed his hat and bowed, revealing the aquiline features that Luke had only seen before on the postcard.

'What do you want? Why show me this pantomime?' Luke was angry as well as scared now.

'Pantomime?' Allessandro exclaimed with disgust. 'Is there not an *ounce* of poetry in your dreary soul?' Then his expression changed dramatically from disdain to fury and he leant down so that his face was only inches from his prisoner's. 'What I want is this,' he spat venomously. 'Stay away from Constanza. She is mine. We will soon complete our business here – and if you remain, the consequences will be extremely unpleasant. Do you understand?'

'Who's Constanza?' Luke breathed, though he already knew the answer.

'Don't pretend to be more stupid than you are!' the sorcerer

242

screamed into Luke's face. 'Call her Anya if you wish. Call her anything. Just leave her to me.'

'Where is she?' Luke hissed defiantly, although he was shaking inside.

Allessandro's demeanour changed again. He seemed amused now, and a cruel smile danced in his eyes.

'That would be telling,' he replied coolly. He straightened up and became almost affable. 'You're loyal, like a dog, I'll grant you that much. Who would've thought you'd have the intelligence to follow us so far?'

Us? Luke thought, jolted by the choice of pronoun. From all appearances, Anya had been travelling alone, and had booked single occupancy on Tresco and Corfu. But there had been the disturbance at the Island Hotel. How could this man have been with her? Was he responsible for the fire on St Mary's? Luke felt an impotent fury rise within him and longed to strike out, to strangle his tormentor, to drag the truth from him. But he still could not move.

'It's time for you to give up now,' Allessandro went on. 'The trail ends here. Go home. She has no further use for you.'

He turned away before his prisoner had a chance to respond, and Luke noticed two small things that shook him to the core, but gave him momentary solace. The first was that Allessandro was not solid, not whole. Until then Luke had taken him to be a real person, but the moonlit branches of a tree could be faintly seen through him. His transformation was indeed incomplete. The second was that a film of sweat had appeared on Allessandro's translucent skin and there was a look of exhaustion in his dark, rabid eyes. Even if it were all an illusion, this exhibition was costing him a great deal of effort.

Luke struggled to rise, found that there was now slight movement in his limbs and pushed with all his might. Allessandro gave a last strangled grunt of disgust – and vanished.

It was an ordinary night again. Luke got up slowly, stretching cramped muscles and trying to understand what had happened. Behind him a door creaked open.

'Luke?' said a sleepy voice. 'Is that you?'

'It's me.'

'I've just had a very odd dream,' Meredith said.

Luke found that easy to believe.

36

Neither Luke nor Meredith slept much more that night. Luke was understandably alarmed and restless. Each rustle of wind, each flicker of moonlight conjured up false images and the twisted shapes of old olive trees became even more sinister. But the supernatural exhibition was over and when it was clear that there was nothing more to be seen, he and Meredith retired to what they perceived as the relatively safe surroundings of the small house. She made some herb tea while Luke sat on the bed and shivered, despite the blanket draped round his shoulders. Nothing in his life had even vaguely prepared him for such an experience, and he was having the greatest difficulty in accepting that it *had* happened, let alone coming to terms with it. He discovered, to his relief, that there was no need to describe what he had seen and heard. As soon as he began, Meredith confirmed that she had witnessed it all in her dream.

'I've heard the story of Pan's death, but I've never *seen* it,' she observed, sounding almost envious. 'And dreams don't count.'

'I still don't understand what . . .' Luke broke off, laughing without humour and shaking his head. 'I'm so out of my depth here it's ridiculous. How could I have seen . . . that?'

'Things remember,' she told him gently. 'Not in the way we do, but they remember. It could be exactly as Allessandro said; deep down, hidden from all but the most adept readers, the stones of Paxos contain the story you saw. It would take a far greater talent than mine to draw it out, but I know from personal experience that objects can retain memory traces. Not necessarily what actually happened, but what people *believe* happened, the emotions and impressions involved. And if enough people believe, and it lasts long enough, then the stories become myths and live on.'

'Even if that's true, and Allessandro has the necessary talent, why show it to me?' Luke wondered.

'Because he can?' Meredith hazarded. 'He doesn't seem the type to hide his light under a bushel.'

'He was just showing off?'

'Or making a point. Trying to convince you that his sorcery is something to be reckoned with. To frighten you.'

Luke was silent for a while. He sipped his tea and thought ruefully that Allessandro had certainly succeeded in doing that. But fear had been only one of several emotions, and Luke wondered dully if those feelings were now recorded for posterity in the stones of the wall he had leant against.

'All of which supposes that Allessandro is real,' he said eventually. 'But what if it was all inside my head? That it was a delusion and there was nothing there at all?'

'Do you believe that?'

'I don't know what I believe,' he replied truthfully, as another theory occurred to him. 'What if it was just a projection of your dream? You already think our minds are linked somehow.'

'Last time it was my waking experience that translated to your dream, not the other way round,' Meredith pointed out. 'And we had the earrings as a physical connection. I'm not sure I'm capable of anything like that, anyway. It's more likely to have come from Anya than me. Allessandro's her bogey man, after all – and we both have a natural link to her.'

'Anya?' Luke was bewildered again. 'Why would she . . . ?'

'Who's to say it was deliberate?' she went on. 'And even if it was, you said yourself that Anya didn't want to be found. Perhaps some part of her mind is trying to send you away.'

'No, I don't believe that. It doesn't make sense. She's terrified of Allessandro. And she's not psychic like you.'

'So what does that leave us with?' Meredith asked calmly.

When he did not answer, she prompted further. 'Trust your instincts, Luke. What did it *feel* like?'

There was a long pause.

'It felt real,' he admitted finally. 'He talked to me, responded to things I said. If it *wasn't* real, then I was part of the illusion.'

'You seem solid enough to me,' Meredith commented, punching him lightly on the arm.

'At first I thought Allessandro was a normal, solid human being,' Luke went on. 'Not a ghost or spirit or illusion. Here was the man who had been stalking Anya, making her life a misery. I was so angry I wanted to reach out and hit him, kill him if I could, but I couldn't move.'

'I doubt that physical violence would be effective against a creature like him.'

Luke glanced at her. She clearly accepted Allessandro's existence as a separate entity. Could Anya really have been telling him the truth all along? The idea made him feel even more chilled, and he shuddered as he saw once more the knife clattering to their kitchen floor. He was being forced to reevaluate everything that had happened, as well as his own personal beliefs – and the process was not a comfortable one. The worst of it was that he now felt guilty about letting Anya down, about not accepting her story. But how could he have known?

'Later, when I could see through him,' he said quietly, returning to the night's events, 'it was a shock – more than I can tell you – but I felt something else too.'

'Hope?' Meredith guessed.

'Yes. It was as though he wasn't complete yet, just like Anya said. Perhaps he could show me his mirages and stop me moving, but he couldn't actually harm me physically. Not yet, anyway, otherwise he would surely have done so. I was helpless, at his mercy. So he hasn't won yet.'

'And therefore, perhaps, he's still unable to harm Anya?' Meredith suggested.

'God, I hope so,' Luke said fervently.

247

'Have you been listening to yourself?' she asked. 'Everything you've said implied that when you were speaking to Allessandro, even when you could see through him, you instinctively thought of him as real.'

'Yes,' he replied, finally recognizing that fact himself. 'I know. And if he's real, if *I* saw him – whatever he is – then he's here, close by, and so is Anya.'

'Probably,' Meredith agreed cautiously. 'But a being like that may not be bound by the normal rules of space and time. His vanishing proved that.'

'Yes, but he wants me to go away,' Luke said, eager now, 'and I'm in normal space and time.'

'I see what you mean.'

'If he wants me to leave, I guess the best thing I can do is stick around,' Luke went on. 'He said I'd been following them, but that the trail ended here. *Here*. Which ties in with what your guide said. "Stay where you are." Anya *must* be here somewhere.' He paused, haunted by other words the guide had used; renegade, corruption . . . 'I want to find her more than ever now – and soon. I don't understand what's going on but it's obviously a battle of some kind, and it's not over yet. I'm damned if I'm going to let her fight it alone any more. We can still help her. The fact that Allessandro tried to frighten me away proves that.'

'You're a brave knight,' Meredith said approvingly. 'Don't his threats worry you?'

'Of course they do,' he admitted. 'Part of me is scared silly. But if it's like that for me, think what it must be like for Anya. I can't leave her to suffer that. I love her, Meredith. I need her. I could never live with myself if anything happened to her.'

The first bus of the day was due in Loggos before seven, so Meredith and Luke set off down to the village in the early morning. Meredith knew Loggos would already be bustling, with returning fishing boats landing their catches, lorries making deliveries to shops and tavernas and the locals preparing for the day, but on this occasion, even before they reached the bottom of the path, they could see more than the

248

usual amount of activity around the harbour. They glanced at each other then hurried on, without the need for words. However, when they reached the sharp bend near the base of the hill, they halted abruptly. The stones beneath their feet vibrated as though a huge lorry had rumbled by, but the sound that accompanied it came from a far more alarming source. The ground itself was shaking.

The sensation only lasted a few seconds, but was one of the most unnerving experiences either of them had encountered. When the ground on which they stood became unstable, what else was there to rely on? Instinctively, they reached out and took each other's hand to steady themselves, and both looked up apprehensively at the old brick chimney of the disused factory. It towered above them, already cracked and possibly dangerous. The tremor could easily have been enough to bring it crashing down – and they were too close to have much time to react. As it was, the apparently rickety construction creaked and shuddered but stood firm. Nevertheless, they separated quickly and hurried on, legs feeling suddenly weak.

As they crossed the open space on the other side of the abandoned factory, they found a mopping-up operation in progress. During the night the sea had evidently flooded part of the village, and although it did not look at all serious, it had obviously caused a great deal of consternation among the residents. The placid Mediterranean, calm and virtually tideless in this sheltered spot, had betrayed them, spilling over the road and lapping briefly at the feet of tables and chairs, and around the doorways of the nearest houses and tavernas. The water level in the harbour now seemed back to normal, but the latest tremor had done nothing to reassure anyone that it would remain so. Everywhere people were talking animatedly, gesticulating wildly, wielding brooms and mops as though they were weapons, dark faces betraying concern. It was obvious that with such momentous events to deal with no one was going to be too concerned with a missing tourist – let alone any bizarre events connected with her disappearance. No one would be interested in ghosts and mythical reenactments,

249

even if Luke or Meredith had any intention of describing them.

Close to the water, Luke thought, looking around. As far as he could see there had been no structural or even superficial damage to any of the buildings, but the latest tremor had surely been the strongest yet. If there had been any others while he'd been there – and what else could have caused the temporary flooding? – he had been quite unaware of them.

'It seems Poseidon might've been angry at Pan's death,' Meredith remarked.

'What?'

'Poseidon didn't just rule the sea, you know,' she told him. 'He controlled earthquakes as well – and something happened overnight to cause all this.'

'I think I've had quite enough Greek gods for now, thank you.' Luke was torn between amusement and anger at her flippancy.

'Sorry. My brain works in odd ways sometimes,' she said with an apologetic grin. 'Let's get down to business.'

An hour later, any remaining seaborne debris had been cleared away and the sun had dried the last of the water so that Loggos looked as though nothing strange had happened. Meredith had enlisted one of the holiday reps as an interpreter but, in spite of her efforts, the bus driver had no recollection of taking Anya anywhere. Nor had the two taxi owners they were able to meet later, or the driver of the morning's second bus. In the meantime, they had also confirmed that there was no news of Anya in the other resorts and Luke had made several phone calls, but without success.

All around them, the main topic of conversation was the tremors and the strange seas they were producing. Many of the older residents recalled the earthquakes of 1953, when the damage had been minimal on Paxos but devastating on the more southerly Ionian islands. There was also much speculation about what the new series of tremors portended but, as there was nothing anyone could do about it, this was just talk and no more. Life went on, and the Paxiots would deal with whatever it brought.

By midday, Meredith and Luke had exhausted all possible avenues of investigation. To know – or think he knew – that he was close to Anya and yet quite unable to find her was intolerable, and combined with his lack of sleep to bring Luke close to fury, especially as the day was unusually muggy as well as very hot. Over the mainland huge ramparts of cloud rose and fell and even on the island, the air was thick with the promise of thunder.

'Come on, we need a cold drink,' Meredith told him firmly. 'Let's get an early lunch and decide where to go from here.'

Luke saw the sense of her suggestion, and began to calm down. They sat at an outside table at the same taverna as the previous day. Meredith asked for retsina and water and told the waiter that they would order food later. When the drinks arrived they both took a thankful gulp of water and then Meredith poured small glasses of wine. However, instead of drinking her own, she slowly and deliberately tipped the contents on to the road beside the table, much to the surprise of a pair of cats who had approached in the hope of a titbit.

'What are you doing?' Luke enquired curiously.

'Pouring a libation to the gods,' she replied. 'I know you've had enough of them, but if there are any still hanging around, we can use all the help we can get.'

Luke stared at her in open disbelief, then – unsmiling – took his own glass and poured his wine away too. He felt foolish and self-conscious, but apart from Meredith no one seemed to notice and, once it was done, he sensed a small lightening of his spirit.

'Do you do it on purpose?' he asked.

'Do what?' she responded innocently.

'Act in a crazy manner to make me feel as if I'm the sane one.'

'I don't act at all. This is me, like it or not.' They smiled at each other. 'Besides, now we've mollified the gods we can drink the stuff ourselves and put our thinking caps on,' she added, pouring second measures.

251

'Maybe we'll get some divine inspiration. We could certainly use it,' Luke said, with a return to his grim mood. 'We're getting nowhere by ourselves.'

'Perhaps we're not meant to get anywhere. "Stay where you are, Luke. She will come to you",' Meredith quoted.

'Well, I wish she'd bloody well hurry up,' he said helplessly. 'I can't just sit here and wait. I have to do *something*.'

'We could widen the search a bit,' she suggested. 'Ask at more houses and the villas on the outskirts of the village and in the hills.'

'That'd be better than nothing. If Anya's here, someone must know of it. But that's hardly staying close to the water, is it?'

'True,' Meredith agreed, 'but we've done all we can here, unless you can think of something we've missed.'

Luke shook his head wearily.

'Then we'll start again straight after lunch,' she concluded, and began organizing their meal.

Some time later, as the last of the plates were being cleared away, Luke checked his wallet and found that he was running low on cash.

'Is there anywhere here to change a traveller's cheque?' he asked, wanting to at least make a contribution to the cost of the meal.

'The office round the corner,' she replied, pointing.

'I'll be back in a minute.'

Luke changed another £300, so that he would be ready to cover any eventualities, and browsed along the shelves of paperback books – which constituted an informal library for holiday-makers – while the calculations were being done. Several of the titles looked like the sort of thing that Anya would enjoy, and he wished he shared Meredith's supposed talent for psychometry. Perhaps the books would have more than one story to tell.

'I'm the man to be with,' Luke claimed, brandishing his wad of notes as he rejoined Meredith. When she did not respond but sat perfectly still, her face hidden by her hands, he added, 'Meredith? Are you OK?'

'No, no, no. Stop it!' she whispered, still without looking up. 'Why are you showing me this?'

'What?'

'What are you trying to prove?' she hissed, her voice anguished.

Luke was on his feet again, coming round to her side, thoroughly alarmed now. He had no idea whom she was speaking to, nor what her questions meant. But before he could put an arm around her shoulders, Meredith's head jerked up and she stared fixedly out to sea, her eyes wide with horror. Luke turned to follow her gaze, just in time to witness what she had obviously foreseen.

A large yacht was anchored in the centre of the small bay while her crew enjoyed a meal in the village. The explosion ripped away most of the upper part of the deck, shattered the entire superstructure and sent the mast shooting up into the sky like a misfiring rocket. A plume of fierce orange flame blossomed then shrank, leaving a pall of dark smoke and a steady blaze as pieces of debris, shrapnel from the detonation, rained down into the water all around the ruined craft.

As the sound of the explosion rolled on, echoing round the harbour and the surrounding hills, the onlookers were all silent for a few long, awestruck moments. Then everyone seemed to be moving and yelling at once. The yacht's crew could only stare in horrified stupefaction as several local boatmen leapt into their own craft and set outboard motors running. There were a few screams, numerous expressions of astonishment and fear, and somewhere several children began to cry. From the hurried conversations around him Luke gathered, with some relief, that there had been no one on board, which made the devastating accident an even greater mystery. However, Luke had the feeling that there was one person who might be more knowledgeable than she appeared. Meredith had closed her eyes and was holding her head in her hands again.

'What happened?' he asked quietly, squatting down beside her.

Before she could answer, a gasp went up from others around

them and Luke glanced up in time to see what was left of the yacht's hull tip up and sink so quickly that none of the rescue boats had had time to get close. There was a hiss of doused flame and a few bubbles, then there were only a few fragments left, bobbing on the surface of the stained water.

'What happened, Meredith?' he whispered again.

'It was Allessandro,' she mumbled, sounding as though she were in pain. 'He told me that's what'll happen to you if you don't do as he says and leave Paxos.'

37

Luke glanced out over the water again. The smoke had all but gone by now, blown by the unpredictable winds of the inlet. All that was left of the yacht was flotsam. Allessandro may not be able to harm him directly but, if what Meredith was saying was true, there were endless possibilities for an indirect assault. It was a terrifying thought but, paradoxically, the harder Allessandro strove to prove his point, the more determined Luke became not to be intimidated. He would stay now, come what may.

Looking around, he half expected to spot the sorcerer among the small crowd, most of whom were still lining the harbour, watching the scene of the explosion. But there was no sign of him. *Anya may not be coming to us*, Luke thought bitterly, *but Allessandro certainly is*. He was convinced now that his mysterious foe was there, even if he could not be seen.

Luke moved his chair next to Meredith and put an arm round her shoulders. She was still hiding her face in her hands.

'How did he do it?' he asked, leaning close. 'Did you see him?'

'No,' she replied softly. 'At first it was just a voice in my head.'

'Like one of your guides?'

'No! This was horrible – like being raped instead of making love. He told me he was going to put on a demonstration and that I should let you know about it. Then he showed me

255

pictures; gas valves, switches . . . I didn't understand. But I knew what it meant.'

'That's when you looked at the boat?'

Meredith nodded.

'Can we get out of here, please?' she whispered.

Luke stood up and helped her to her feet. He looked round again, but Allessandro was still nowhere to be seen. Leaving more than enough money to pay their bill, they set off. Meredith's face was deathly pale, and she moved so unsteadily that Luke automatically took her arm.

'My head hurts,' she groaned as they stumbled onwards. 'I have to lie down.'

'Can you make it back to the house?'

'Yes. But don't let go of my arm.'

'I won't,' Luke promised. He could see the pain in her eyes and wondered if it was another of Allessandro's tricks or whether the shock had triggered a migraine attack. Either way, Meredith was obviously ill, and he felt responsible. After all, he was the cause of the sorcerer's unwelcome attentions.

By the time they reached the cottage Meredith was on the point of collapse. Her face was white and sweating and her breathing was irregular. Luke lowered her on to the bed and pulled a blanket over her.

'There are some tablets, in the cupboard over there,' she whispered, pointing.

He found what she wanted and poured out a glass of water, then held her head up as she took the pill and sipped. She seemed to have difficulty swallowing, gulping several times, but eventually she succeeded and he let her sink back on to the pillow. Her eyes were closed and she lay very still. After a few moments the pain and nausea seemed to ease a little.

'That'll teach me to drink at lunchtime,' she said, with a feeble smile.

'Shhh. Is there anything else I can get you?'

'No. I'll sleep now. You go find Anya.'

Luke did not like the idea of leaving Meredith alone, but he desperately wanted to continue the search. She sensed his indecision.

'Go on. I'll be OK. I've been through this before. And time may be running out for her.' Meredith's voice was fading now as the tablet began to take effect.

'If you're sure . . .' Luke still felt wretched at the thought of abandoning her. What if Allessandro paid her another visit? And yet it was Anya he had come to find, who was in most need of his help – and for whom time might well be running out. Luke's final thought before he left was that by going he would at least be allowing Meredith time to recover in peace. He was the sorcerer's main target, after all.

He spent the first part of the afternoon calling on other houses in the straggling hill-top village, then moved on to the more prosperous villas that overlooked the bay. His explanation was met with blank looks and, in some cases, with understandable suspicion. His ignorance of Greek made it an almost hopeless task with many of the residents, and even those expatriates with whom he could converse easily were unable to help him. Some houses were clearly unoccupied and he felt like a criminal, trespassing in gardens and peering through windows. The only thing that kept him going was the hope that somewhere he would find the clue to Anya's whereabouts, the clue he needed so desperately.

He made several detours back to the cottage to check on Meredith but, on each occasion, she was sleeping soundly and apparently peacefully and he left again, partly reassured. Later in the afternoon, Luke returned to Loggos, which seemed to have recovered from the earlier excitements, and made yet another tour of the harbour area. Then he explored the coastal paths to the south, passing the beach where he and Meredith had bathed, and continued his investigations at various houses along the way. Under different circumstances it could have been a very pleasant few hours, as he discovered beautiful, olive-fringed coves and climbed headlands to survey the coast and the hills to the west, but he was galled by his continued lack of progress. The day was still hot and oppressive, and he went for a short swim from one of the rocky beaches. It refreshed him temporarily, but he was hot

257

and sticky again just a few minutes after he was dressed and on his way.

By the time he returned to Loggos he was footsore and thirsty as well as frustrated. Even so, he wanted to get back to check on Meredith, and was striding past the harbour when he changed his mind and sat at the end table outside their taverna, intending to have a quick drink. The afternoon bus from Gaios rumbled into the village and stopped in the central square while passengers piled on and off. Luke had just realized that he was too early for any service at the taverna, and was about to get up and return to the café when the bus set off on its way to Lakka. Luke stayed where he was as it made its slow way along the water's edge. Then, as the bus passed the far end of the building, the engine suddenly roared and it lurched forward, the nearside wing sweeping dangerously close to the unoccupied tables and chairs. Luke caught a brief glimpse of the driver wrestling with the controls, then realized that he was directly in the vehicle's path. Throwing himself sideways, he dived past the corner of the taverna, almost colliding with a telegraph pole and falling heavily to the ground. Moments later the bus hit his table, crushing it against the wall, and the chair he had been sitting on was smashed beneath its tyres. The vehicle came to rest a few yards further on with a tortured squeal of brakes.

Within moments both Luke and the bus were the centre of voluble groups of people. Luke had come to no physical harm, except for a few bruises and a grazed hand, but the narrow escape had left him shocked and shaken. While he reassured those around him that he was all right, he was wondering whether it had been an accident, or another of Allessandro's 'demonstrations'. Meanwhile, Vassili, the taverna's owner, and the bus driver were arguing wildly, shouting and gesticulating, while the unlucky passengers filed off and several volunteers examined the stricken vehicle. Loggos had never witnessed such a day before; floods, earthquakes, the violent destruction of the yacht – and now this.

Someone found Luke a chair and Vassili's wife brought him a glass of water which he drank gratefully. Someone else offered him a brandy, but he refused. From the multilingual conversations around him, he gathered that the bus's controls had gone suddenly haywire, the engine racing for no reason, steering and brakes momentarily inoperative. According to one witness, the driver had said it was as though someone had pushed him aside and attempted to take control of the wheel and pedals. Others assumed, naturally enough, that a mechanical problem was to blame. Luke was not so sure. He got to his feet again, thanked everyone for their help and added further reassurances, then set off for Meredith's house. He completed the first half of the journey without further mishap, although he glanced over his shoulder often and treated each step with suspicion. *This is how Anya was acting.* The realization coincided with a loud clap of thunder, and moments later the long threatened rain finally arrived, squalling down in shimmering bursts that whirled in from the sea. Drops clattered on to leaves, drummed on tiled rooftops and formed instant rivulets on the steep path, miniature cascades spilling over the stone steps. The storm lasted no more than five minutes, but by then Luke was soaked to the skin and thoroughly chilled. He was glad when the clouds rolled away, as if drawn back like heavenly curtains, and the wind dropped as suddenly as it had arisen. The sun returned, making everything steam gently and the scent of wet earth filled his nostrils. Olive trees glittered with watery jewels.

When he reached the house he let himself in as quietly as he could. With the shutters closed it was dark inside, and he could not see a thing until his eyes began to adjust. He heard a sigh from the direction of the bed.

'That you, Luke?'

'It's me.' He reached out to turn on the light.

'Don't touch the switch,' Meredith said sharply, and he drew back in surprise. 'The circuit's a bit unreliable and I get nervous when it's wet,' she explained in a softer tone. 'I just have the feeling that it could be dangerous. And it's the sort of thing Allessandro might use to try and harm you.'

Luke's instinctive reaction was that she was being paranoid, but then he thought of the bus – and the boat – and revised his opinion.

'Can I open the shutters?'

'Go ahead.'

'How are you feeling?' he asked as he fumbled with the catch at the first window.

'Much better. The tablets make me woozy, but the pain's almost gone. Did you have any luck?'

'None at all,' Luke replied dejectedly.

With the shutters open and the late afternoon sunlight slanting across the room, he turned to look at Meredith. She was sitting up, propped on pillows, and there was definitely more colour in her cheeks.

'Come and tell me about your day, dear,' she said with a smile, and patted the bed. 'What have you been doing while I've been lazing about in here?'

Luke sat beside her and described his futile efforts. He said nothing about the runaway bus. He would not be able to keep it from her for long, but saw no point in worrying her unduly now. When he had finished he could see the signs of renewed pain in her face and fetched more water so that she could take another tablet. They decided that there was enough food in the cottage for a scratch meal, so he had no need to return to the village.

'Are you still going back to Corfu tomorrow?'

'I hadn't even thought about it.' He was almost sure now that Anya would not be on the flight back to England, but unless he was there to check, how could he know for certain? 'I'll decide in the morning. Do you think I should?'

'Anya's on Paxos,' Meredith replied. 'I'm sure of it. With everything that's happened . . .'

'She might be going back to Corfu herself tomorrow.'

'We can check the ferries this end, then,' she said logically. 'And you can ring the hotel.' Although she was trying to help, Meredith was clearly on the point of falling asleep again.

'I'll do that,' Luke agreed. It seemed a sensible compromise. 'You rest now.'

While she slept, he prepared a simple meal, then went to

examine the light switch with the help of a torch. He saw immediately that some rain had blown under the eaves and trickled down inside the wall. The damp mark of its path was still clearly visible, running crookedly on the uneven surface but heading unerringly for the switch. Was that another coincidence, another potential accident? Luke had no wish to find out, and was glad that Meredith had warned him in time. As the evening drew in, he found some candles and lit them, then sat in a chair just outside the open door and waited. It was not an occupation that came easily to him, but he did not know what else to do. Curiously, the near certainty that he was in personal danger figured very little in his thoughts. He was preoccupied solely with Anya; where she was; what was happening to her; and how, if he ever succeeded in catching up with her, he would never let her travel alone again. This last was wishful thinking on two counts, and he knew it. He still had no idea how he was going to find her. And even if he did, she would not be the Anya he loved if she did not insist on a considerable degree of independence. He only wished he could be given the opportunity to argue with her about it.

When Meredith woke again, later in the evening, they ate some of the food he had prepared, although neither of them had much appetite. Luke cleared up, then announced that he was going down to the village to look around one more time.

'Do you feel up to coming? Or would you rather stay here?'

Meredith did not answer immediately and, when it came, her response was not at all what he had expected.

'Don't go,' she said in a small voice.

Her pleading tone was so out of character that Luke almost gave in, but there were greater demands being made upon him.

'I have to,' he told her quietly.

Meredith nodded, accepting his decision meekly, her dark eyes unreadable in the candlelight. Luke reflected that, in similar circumstances, Anya would have grown angry and argued with him. Her sister's resigned acquiescence was almost worse.

261

'I won't be long. Is there anything you need?'

'No.'

Luke's determined mood as he set off was tinged with guilt, which intensified when, as expected, his latest search proved to be a waste of effort. He hurried back up the hill, thankful that the air was now much fresher in the wake of the brief storm, and found Meredith asleep in bed. She was fidgeting and mumbling to herself, and he went quickly to the bedside, took her hand and held it. Her skin was hot and her face looked flushed. She muttered something incomprehensible, then opened her eyes and stared blankly at the ceiling.

'Tick, tock,' she said clearly, and laughed. She seemed quite unaware of Luke's presence.

'Meredith, are you all right?' She appeared almost delirious, and he glanced at the bottle of pills on the bedside table, praying she had not taken more than she should. The water glass was empty but, as far as Luke could tell, the number of tablets seemed about the same.

Meredith scowled, then looked desperately miserable.

'I can't cope with this,' she whimpered. 'It hurts.'

'What hurts? Your head? Have you taken any more tablets?'

She did not respond to any of his questions, but at least she did look at him now.

'It's hot,' she remarked, sounding vaguely surprised.

'I'll get you some water.' Luke took the glass and refilled it, and soaked a handkerchief as well. Meredith drank and allowed him to cool her forehead. Her fidgeting lessened, she grew calmer and closed her eyes again.

'Kiss me goodnight,' she breathed softly.

Luke hesitated, then leant forward and kissed her lightly on the cheek. Meredith uttered a tiny murmur of satisfaction, and seconds later was fast asleep. Luke watched her for some time, glad that she seemed to be resting peacefully again, then made up his own crude bed. Snuffing out the candles, he lay down, feeling exhausted but still unnerved by the day's events, and it was some time before he fell asleep.

Luke was woken in the deepest part of the night. He was

aware that the light had been switched on, and struggled to rise up out of the dark chasm of sleep. Through half-closed lids, he saw Meredith standing over him. She was naked.

'Luke! What are you doing here?'

The astonishment in her voice made him think that she must still be delirious. But then something else registered in his fast-reviving brain. He opened his eyes and stared, suddenly alert.

'What are you doing here?' she repeated.

There was no mistaking it now. Her voice was unusually strident and demanding, caught between outrage, fear and a vulnerable hope. She was visibly nervous and her child-like brown eyes were full of questions. Now that he was properly awake, Luke could see the subtly harsh lines of her features, the angular, rigid way she held her elfin body. It took only a moment for the realization to sink in, and when it did his heart leapt. *She will come to you.*

'Anya?' he whispered, hardly daring to believe it was true.

'Of course,' she answered impatiently. 'Who did you think it was? How did you get here?'

Luke struggled out of his sleeping bag and took her in his arms. 'Thank God,' he breathed. 'I've been looking for you for weeks.'

She returned his embrace hesitantly. Her skin felt cold against his own.

'How long have you been here?' She seemed frightened, her eyes flicking from side to side as if she was disorientated. 'You're not meant to be here.'

'Don't be cross with me, sweetheart,' he said. 'I've only been on Paxos for two days. Meredith has been helping me look for you.'

'Meredith?' she intoned slowly, as if the name meant nothing to her.

'Yes. Does she know you're here?' Luke glanced over at the bed. It was dishevelled but empty.

'Everything's changing,' Anya said in a blank voice that took away some of Luke's newfound happiness. 'He kept showing me things I don't want to see. I had to run away.'

'It's all right now,' he answered, holding her tight again. 'I'm not going to let anything happen to you.' He led her to the bed, wrapped her in a blanket then sat down beside her. Anya was still glancing around nervously.

'Allessandro followed me too, didn't he?' she asked quietly.

'Yes,' Luke admitted reluctantly. 'I've seen him. But I'm not going to let him hurt you.'

'You've seen him?' she exclaimed. In her mind this information was a double-edged sword. It was the final proof that she was not mad – but the fact that the sorcerer was not a delusion made the danger he represented even greater.

'He's nearly there. This must be the last stage. I'm lost.' She turned to look at Luke properly for the first time and he was stunned by the fear and hopelessness he saw in her eyes. 'Help me, Luke,' she begged. 'Help me!'

'Of course. Anything. You'll be all right,' he said, though his confidence in his own words was ebbing fast.

Anya detached herself abruptly and stood up, leaving him feeling rejected and bewildered.

'Why did you come? It's hopeless. You were never meant to see this.'

'Don't say that!' he cried. 'I love you. I can help you.'

'And why is Meredith here? I don't want to see her.'

'Why not?' he asked. 'She's a bit eccentric, maybe, but she's a wonderful person.'

'No. We were horrible. We were both horrible, Meredith and I. It's no wonder our father left, and Mummy . . .'

She was rambling now, but the sadness mixed with anger in her voice was almost more than Luke could bear.

'Anya, please . . .'

'I can't stop the clock ticking,' Anya stated miserably. 'I have to go now.'

'Go? Go where? No.' He jumped to his feet, then froze.

For a brief moment, Anya's eyes went entirely blank, and in that instant they were windows not to her soul but to a lonely, cavernous void. A second later, they came back to life. At the same time the lines of her face softened and the tension in her limbs eased noticeably. She glanced down at her naked body, then looked back at him and smiled, while Luke stared, mesmerized, his hair standing on end.

'Do you look at all the girls that way?' she asked, obviously not at all disturbed by her nudity.

'I . . . I don't understand,' he stuttered. 'Who . . . who *are* you?'

'I'm Meredith.'

And so she was. The transformation had taken place before his eyes. The woman now facing him had the same shape, the same bone structure as Anya – but everything else had changed. Her smile, her movements, her voice, her whole bearing; all these now belonged unmistakably to Meredith, just as, only a few seconds ago, they had been Anya's.

The twins were one and the same person.

38

Luke's mind reeled, refusing to believe the evidence of his own eyes and ears. He had always scoffed at the idea that people had auras, but now he knew it was true. Anya and Meredith each indefinably marked the space around them with an extension of their diverse personalities. And, equally mysteriously, he was able to distinguish between these invisible signatures. Like her physical appearance and her voice, it too had changed in the last few moments.

'Stop playing with me,' he protested, although in his heart he knew this was no game. 'Who *are* you?'

Meredith merely smiled resignedly and shrugged.

'Tell me!' he yelled, fear and ignorance driving him to anger as he felt the very ground crumbling beneath his feet. How much of his life with Anya had been built on deceit?

Her soft eyes registered the first signs of unease and she blinked owlishly, almost in slow motion.

And everything changed again. She whirled around, grabbed a towel from the back of a chair and wrapped it neatly around herself. Then she turned and looked at Luke calmly and confidently – and he saw, to his utter amazement, that her face had undergone yet another transformation. The complexion was softer, her features more rounded, and there was a new sparkle in her eyes. She looked younger and, when she spoke, her voice was lighter, the pronunciation precise but childlike and oddly accented.

'I think I'd better explain. My name is Verity.'

'Stop it, stop it,' Luke grated, his voice rising to an ugly screech. 'Stop it!'

'Calm down,' she continued serenely, ignoring his outburst. 'Hysteria won't help anyone, least of all Anya and Meredith.'

'Anya *and* Meredith?' he exclaimed. *'You're* Anya and Meredith.' Then, wide-eyed and spluttering as he realized what he had just said, he fell silent, controlling himself with the utmost difficulty. 'Tell me,' he begged quietly. 'Explain.'

'I'm not Anya or Meredith, but I know all about them. I'm the only one who does,' she said confidentially.

'Tell me then,' Luke repeated, grasping desperately at the prospect of some small degree of understanding. 'Tell me what's going on!'

'I think you'd better cover yourself up first,' Verity said primly. 'Anya may be used to seeing you like that, but I'm not.'

'I'm sorry.' He gathered the blanket round himself, suddenly acutely self-conscious about being naked in front of a child. In doing so he recognized his acceptance of the fact that the girl he was talking to now was neither Anya nor Meredith. The change was undeniable. If there could be two of her, why not three? Luke was shaking now, stunned by the sheer impossibility of what he was witnessing. And it was only then that the significance of her name sank in.

'You're the one who sent me the postcard!'

'Yes. I don't like to interfere, but I watch and listen, and help when I can, when it's necessary.' She turned a chair round and sat down, carefully adjusting the towel and folding her hands demurely in her lap. 'That's why I came in the first place,' she went on. 'Because Anya and Meredith needed someone to cope with things they didn't like or couldn't understand. I organize things when they need it.'

'You know about Anya and Meredith, but they don't know about you?' Luke surmised, feeling his way into the labyrinth where the truth lay.

'That's right. I'm not as old as them, but I'm much cleverer,' she replied with precocious confidence.

Luke's instincts had been right. Verity was indeed a child. Her voice, her delicate, affected movements and her self-centred awareness were the hallmarks of an adolescent. That a person from a younger generation could exist within the same body as both Meredith and Anya was a cause for wonder. However, at that moment, Luke's overwhelming sensation was one of irony. He had spent the last two days desperately searching for Anya, and she – along with the others – had been with him the whole time. To relocate her now was not a matter of geography but of psychiatry, and was something he felt singularly ill equipped to do. But he knew he had to try, and if Verity really was the only one who knew the way through this incredible maze, then he must take advantage of her presence now – because he had no idea how long she would be staying, or who would replace her.

Luke was vaguely aware of the phenomenon of multiple personalities, through the one well-documented case which had caught the interest of both the medical profession and general public. The name 'Sybil' had become synonymous with the condition, but Luke could never have imagined such a rare disorder ever having any bearing on his own life, still less that he would one day have to deal with its repercussions without any professional help.

'Do Anya and Meredith know about each other?' he asked tentatively.

'Of course not,' Verity answered, as if this should be obvious. 'They're different people.'

'But you know about —'

'That's because I'm higher up than them,' she cut in, with a touch of impatience. 'I can see. They can't.'

'But —'

'Each of them knows when a change is coming,' she interrupted again, 'but they can't control it like I can. They hear a clock ticking. That's the warning. And that's why Anya had to go away so often. She didn't want you to see.'

'Why not?' he asked, even as the pieces began to fall into place. When Anya travelled she was literally not herself, and she only returned to him when she was in her own body once more. That's why she had been so secretive.

'Because she thought you wouldn't understand. She didn't understand herself, so I suppose that's not surprising,' Verity explained condescendingly. 'Anya never knew what happened when Meredith was there. All she knew was that time had passed for others but not for her. It was all blank, she had no memories at all. And it's the same for Meredith when she's Anya.'

Luke shuddered. The idea of whole sections of your life being a complete mystery, hidden from even your own memory, was too frightening for words. Anya's eccentricities now seemed extraordinarily mild when compared to the ordeals of uncertainty she must have had to endure.

'But didn't either of them ever think to investigate?' he asked, wondering how anyone could live that way. 'I mean, there must have been clues when they changed from one to the other.'

'That's where I came in,' Verity announced smugly. 'I would always take over and smooth over the bits they couldn't understand. And besides, the process is more or less instantaneous. Why would they connect waking up as themselves with being someone else?'

'But surely they must have questioned the blank times?' Luke persisted, finding himself unable to counter Verity's purposeful logic.

'Anya was too frightened,' she told him. 'She was so afraid that she was going mad, like her mother, so she hid it away, refused to admit that anything had happened. And for Meredith it all seemed quite natural. Life for her has always been that way. What reason did she have to question it? For all she knew it was the same for everyone.'

Luke stumbled into the labyrinth, trying to make some sense of what he was hearing.

'Is it like that for you?'

'I go away sometimes, but I can always remember what

I need to,' she replied, matter-of-fact. 'Mostly I just watch and listen.'

'So most of the time, as far as other people – like me – are concerned, it's either Anya or Meredith we see?'

'Yes.'

Luke took a deep breath and tried to articulate the all-important question that had slowly been forming in his mind.

'Who is . . . the main person . . . the one whose body you share?'

'You mean who was here first?'

'I suppose so.'

'Anya.'

Luke felt absurdly relieved and somehow vindicated, as if he had confirmed that his love for Anya – and hers for him – could be trusted.

'I don't know why Meredith came,' Verity went on. 'She was here when I arrived. But I think I should put you right about something. I might share her body, as you say, but I don't look like Anya.'

'What do you look like?' he asked curiously.

'Can't you see?'

'I'm not very good with descriptions,' he improvised, though he knew this sounded feeble. 'Why don't you tell me?'

'Well, I have blond hair, straight, down to my shoulders,' she began, flicking back an invisible fringe. 'My eyes are blue and I have freckles. My nose is too small and turns up, but I'm quite pretty really.'

Luke wondered if that was actually what she saw if she looked in a mirror.

'You're not like them at all, are you,' he commented.

'I don't look *anything* like them,' she stated forcibly. 'We're not triplets, you know.'

Luke could not help smiling at her childish vexation.

'They're not even my sisters,' she went on. 'I wouldn't want to be part of that family.'

'Why not?'

'Surely you know.' Verity was clearly surprised.

'Tell me.'

'Well, they don't like to talk about it much,' she said gravely, 'but I'm sure *my* father's not going to run away and *my* mother would never behave like theirs did.'

'You have your own family?'

'Of course. They live in Boston. That's in Massachusetts, you know. I'll go back there one day.'

That explained the half-formed accent, Luke thought, as he tried to hide his own incredulity. The American family was obviously a pure fantasy, and although he saw no reason to risk her umbrage by disputing their existence, it began a new train of thought.

'Where does Meredith live, the one who's part of you?'

'You know that.'

'On St Agnes?'

'Yes. Isn't it a lovely place,' she gushed. 'So quiet and wild and beautiful.'

'So where does the real Meredith live?'

'*This* Meredith is real!' she cried indignantly. 'We're people just like you.'

'Of course you are,' Luke said placatingly. 'I meant the other Meredith, Anya's original twin.'

'How am I supposed to know?' Verity answered petulantly. 'I don't know anything about her.'

So the women that Alice and others on the Scillies knew as Meredith was actually Anya in her other guise. It was little wonder that she went home so infrequently. And it was the same person who had visited their mother two years ago – the mother that Anya had sworn was dead. More pieces of the puzzle were slowly falling into place but, as they did so, the real Meredith vanished from the picture once more. Luke put that bewildering train of thought aside as something else occurred to him.

'Are there any more people . . . er, inside you?'

'No. Just the three of us.' Then Verity's face fell and she shivered. 'Until *he* came, that is.'

For a few moments Luke failed to make the obvious

271

connection. He had been so caught up by the fact that Anya's body housed split personalities that he had forgotten her other problems. When he realized what Verity meant, the conclusion was as ominous as it was self-evident.

'Allessandro?'

She nodded, looking frightened now. When she spoke her voice sounded even younger and quavered a little.

'He's not one of us. I was always happy until he came.'

'What's he done to make you unhappy?'

'He's cruel and selfish. He hurts us. I think he's trying to steal our minds.'

Although that sounded like a line from a bad science fiction B-movie, Luke knew he had to take it seriously.

'How?' he asked.

'I don't know. He's paid most attention to Anya, but she doesn't understand either. Meredith has her guides to protect her. They may not be able to save her in the end, but they certainly make it more difficult for him to attack her. And according to Allessandro I'm too young, too insignificant. He said he could crush me whenever he wants. I didn't believe him at first, but he's getting stronger all the time.'

'Where is he now?'

'Inside us. Being in the outside world on his own is still hard work for him, but . . .'

'But what?'

'If he completely defeats Anya, takes her mind, then we're *all* lost,' Verity replied fearfully. 'No one will be able to stop him then.'

Luke thought of the recent dangers he had faced. He knew now that the real threat was not to him at all; those incidents had just been crude devices designed to scare him away. The real danger was to Anya. She might literally lose her mind, and thereby, possibly, her life.

'How can I help her?' he asked.

'I thought you'd never ask,' Allessandro remarked from the far corner of the room.

Luke leapt to his feet, his heart sinking, and Verity gave a half-stifled scream as the sorcerer emerged from the shadows.

'If you really want to help Anya,' he explained, smiling, 'the best thing you can do is stop meddling and go, as soon as possible. Leave the rest to me.'

39

Just as Luke's brain was registering the fact that Allessandro was still not yet solid, his body was instinctively going into action. Jumping forward, he lashed out, his right fist driving straight into the centre of his enemy's face. Although logically he knew that his attack was futile, he could not help himself; the desire to hurt, to destroy, to take revenge upon their tormentor was too great.

It was like punching a large, immovable sponge. His fist became a blur as it met soft, yet increasing resistance, then recoiled as if of its own accord. The sorcerer had made no attempt to avoid the blow, and it had absolutely no effect upon him. His brief smile at Luke's surprise was soon replaced by an expression of utter contempt. As Luke staggered, off balance, the blanket fell to the floor, leaving him naked. He felt ludicrous, helpless and afraid.

'How pathetic,' Allessandro commented scornfully. 'Is that the best you can come up with? Brute violence? Your presence is becoming immensely tedious.' He put out a spectral hand and shoved Luke in the chest.

Luke tried to brush him aside, but he might as well have tried to grab hold of a stream of water. There was nothing to grasp. The contact with his chest was not a normal touch but held sufficient force to make him step back. His leg caught the edge of the bed and buckled. He stumbled, and sat down.

'You are obviously too stupid to heed my warnings,' the sorcerer hissed. 'I shall take great pleasure in dealing with you properly once my business with Constanza is complete.'

'Leave her alone,' Luke rasped, noting that his adversary was breathing hard. The effort to push him over had clearly been considerable. 'I'll . . .'

'You'll what?' Allessandro snapped, then waved a casual hand.

Luke found himself frozen again. He could still see and hear, but this time he could not even move his lips and tongue, could not speak. He began to panic when he realized that he was not able to breathe, but soon discovered that his lungs did not seem to need air. He was not even sure if his heart was still beating. Rage and terror warred within him, to no avail. His entire world seemed to be in stasis; the only things capable of movement were Allessandro and Verity. For Luke and everything else, time was standing still.

'Now, where were we?' the sorcerer said, turning to the girl. Verity looked pale and frightened, but was evidently determined to show as much defiance as she could.

'Leave us alone,' she said.

'Don't be stupid, child. You know I can't do that.'

'You'll never win if you go on like this,' she assured him spitefully. 'While you're out there, you can't be in here.' And she tapped the side of her head.

'I've had other matters to take care of,' he replied coolly, glancing at Luke, but displaying distinct signs of irritation.

'You don't seem to be getting very far,' Verity taunted.

'He is of no real significance.'

'But while you're preoccupied with him,' she persisted, 'you can't make any real progress, can you?'

Allessandro did not answer immediately. Luke could only watch and listen, not sure what Verity was trying to do. If what she was saying was true, why help the sorcerer by pointing it out? If it wasn't, then she was playing a very dangerous game by needling him like this.

'You know more than is good for you, young lady,' Allessandro said at length. 'What's worse is that you're wasting your knowledge on this . . .' He waved a disdainful hand towards Luke. 'That in itself is hazardous. He may not share your good sense.'

'He's Anya's friend,' she protested, a little uncertainly. 'He would never do anything to harm her.'

'Wouldn't he? A little knowledge is a dangerous thing. How can you be sure he won't betray your secrets to Anya or Meredith? The very people who would be harmed by such a revelation?'

'No, no!' She seemed genuinely shocked by the idea. 'You'd never do that, would you, Luke?'

Luke did not answer, having no choice, but Verity misinterpreted his silence.

'You mustn't!' she exclaimed. 'It would be terrible. My whole life has been dedicated to keeping them separate. You *mustn't* tell them. Please.'

'You see now the extent of your folly?' Allessandro remarked. 'You have put yourself in the hands of this ignorant oaf. I hope, by the way, that you don't imagine he could ever be a match for me.'

'Promise me, Luke,' Verity begged, ignoring the sorcerer for the moment. 'Promise!'

'Save your breath,' Allessandro advised. 'I'll take care of him. But your foolishness cannot go unpunished.'

He moved faster than human sight, like a snake striking, and caught Verity's wrist. Her whole body contorted with pain, all thought of resistance gone. Luke strained uselessly, filled with frustration and anger as he watched her agony. He knew that it was Verity suffering, but she still looked like Anya, *was* Anya in one sense, and he shared her torment. Eventually Allessandro relented and she fell limply back into the chair, exhausted.

'Now go,' he commanded. 'I hope you've learnt your lesson. Let me speak with Anya.'

As Verity left obediently and Anya reclaimed her own body, the house dissolved about them so that she came to floating in a bizarre, make-believe seascape. The water moved about her body, silkily caressing her limbs, while refracted sunlight flickered over rocks and seaweed and vanished into dark crevasses. Hundreds of different fishes swam hesitantly, avoiding her shadow. But none of it was quite real.

Already horribly disorientated from her recent awakenings, Anya was now hopelessly bewildered by what she saw, and when she spotted an evil-looking octopus, lying quite still in its lair, she knew it must be a dream. The creature was trapped somehow, unable to move, but it still made her fearful. And then she saw that it had Luke's eyes.

Anya wanted to scream, to wake up from the nightmare, but knew she could not. There was another presence beside her now, another swimmer, unseen but casting his own dark shadow.

'Don't you recognize your own work?' said a familiar voice. 'You left it unfinished, but it has promise, don't you think? And we can do so much more here on the inside.'

Paxos, Anya thought. *I'm on Paxos. But this is my painting, the one I began last time.*

But she knew that Allessandro had defiled her creation, as he defiled everything he touched. She looked again at Luke, her heart full of pity and self-doubt. How had she dragged him into this mess?

'Nasty, ugly beast, isn't it?' the sorcerer remarked. 'But you can get rid of it.'

A spear-gun had materialized in her hand, its hard, deadly surfaces cold against her fingers.

'Shoot,' Allessandro urged. 'Do us all a favour and put the creature out of its misery.'

Anya felt a spasm of disgust and cast the weapon aside. It floated away, then vanished. Silence enveloped her. She had been within a moment of obeying and the possibility of such betrayal – and its consequences – appalled her.

'Of course. He's not worth the effort,' Allessandro said after a time, though he could not hide his obvious disappointment. 'We are all that matters now, Constanza. Think what we could achieve if you would only put a stop to this stubborn resistance. I shall win in the end anyway, but you have paradise within your grasp now, this moment. You know what I need, you've seen the possibilities. What is the point of delay? You owe it to me, to yourself, to posterity.' He paused, their shadows side by side fathoms below. 'What do you say?'

Anya remembered the exhilaration of riding the storm in Hell Bay, a very different sea from the one she floated in now. Were all his promises a delusion? She might see wonders she could not even imagine, have experiences that others could only dream about, create magic in the real world. Was her submission too great a price to pay for such rewards? Although she wavered, there was still a barrier she could not surmount, no matter how he tempted her.

'I don't trust you,' she said simply.

He stood before her in that instant, weightless still but a substantial presence now. Taking her hands in his own, he gazed intently into her eyes.

'Trust?' he said softly. 'I loved you once, Constanza. I can again. Is there any trust greater than that of giving one's heart?'

'Love?' she queried. 'You don't love me.'

'Perhaps not in the conventional, trivial human sense,' he replied, 'although that may come in time. But my love will be more sublime, with far more rapture than anything those weaker creatures could conjure up. We will love like gods, Constanza. Like gods!'

A burning river flooded from his hands as he spoke, engulfing Anya's body, filling every particle of her being with a pleasure so sweet that it was close to agony. She closed her eyes, her head thrown back. Her spine arched involuntarily and she gasped for air. And then it was gone, and its absence seemed like an icy dousing.

'That is but a taste,' he whispered, his eyes burning as she looked at him again. 'Can you doubt the power of such love?'

Anya's determination faltered again. She did not doubt the power; she wanted more, needed more. Her whole body cried out, already intoxicated, addicted. She stared at Allessandro, wondering, imagining life as the new Constanza. Had her earlier counterpart loved him too? Had it just been greed that drove her to betray him? And why, when Anya loved Luke so much and knew Allessandro for what he was, was she finding herself physically drawn to this madman? Why

278

did she have to stop herself reaching out and running her finger over those cruel lips? She took a deep breath.

'Kiss me,' Allessandro instructed, and his very voice was like a caress.

He leant forward, pulling her towards him, and she responded, her lips parted slightly. The dark glint of victory shone deep in his black eyes.

This is not love! It was seduction, impure and simple.

With a supreme effort of will, Anya tore herself away, turned her face and loosed his grip on her hands.

'Get away from me. You disgust me.'

For a moment Allessandro was too surprised to react. He seemed unable to comprehend what was happening. And then, as the reality of her rejection sank in, his confusion turned to an icy calm.

'You will regret this,' he stated quietly. 'The short delay will only make my revenge all the sweeter. You are a fool, Anya. You could have shared everything. Now you'll have nothing but pain.'

The fact that he was controlling his anger, speaking softly and without apparent emotion, made his words even more unnerving, but Anya summoned one last ounce of defiance.

'At least I will be Anya to the end,' she said. 'I am not your Constanza, nor will I ever be. She never loved you, and nor will I.'

His carefully constructed façade cracked then, and the malice that lay at the core of his being was revealed. Nothing could hide such malevolence for long.

'I do not need your love,' he spat, his face contorted with rage. 'Only your obedience – and I will have that and much more soon enough, whether you accept it or not. I could have lifted you so high, but I can also bury you in depths of misery and degradation so vile you will beg unheard for mercy. And you will not be alone. This pathetic creature,' and he pointed at Luke, 'will suffer as well – and all because of your stupid intransigence.'

'No!' Anya cried.

'It's too late,' he told her harshly. 'You had the chance to end his misery several times. He could have walked away, but now he will share your doom.'

Oh, Luke, she wailed inwardly as she looked down into his imprisoned eyes. *I'm sorry.*

'I shall look forward to our next meeting,' Allessandro concluded with a rapacious smile. 'For now, I have work to do.'

Reality reasserted itself around them. Anya almost fainted and Luke, released from his paralysis, leapt forward to steady her, then hold her in his arms.

'We have to fight him,' Anya whispered fiercely, even though her voice was weak and shook a little. 'Any way we can. I won't let him win – no matter what the cost.'

40

It took Luke a long time to coax Anya into telling him what had happened. Although she was comforted by his familiar physical presence and the warmth of his embrace, she was shocked by his unexpected intrusion into what had hitherto been an entirely private aspect of her life. And the threat posed by Allessandro seemed overwhelming now and made thinking difficult, let alone expressing those thoughts.

Dawn was still some hours away, and they returned to bed, finding comfort in each other's arms. Neither had any thought of sleep, and eventually Luke's gentle prompting overcame Anya's reticence.

'I don't understand what's happening to me,' she told him quietly.

'The blackouts, you mean?' Luke guessed.

'Yes. I could always tell before . . .'

'The ticking?'

'How do you know about that?' she asked, obviously alarmed.

'You talk in your sleep sometimes,' he improvised. 'I've only just made the connection.' Luke made a mental note to be more careful. It was ironic that he now knew much more about Anya than she did herself.

'This is horrible,' she whispered. 'I never wanted you to know.'

'I only want to help, sweetheart.'

'You don't think I'm mad?' she asked fearfully.

'Of course not.'

'You did before.'

'I didn't understand then. If you'd explained . . .'

'I'm sorry. I was scared.'

'I know,' he told her gently. 'But sharing problems can help. I love you, Anya. Don't ever be scared of talking to me.'

'Easier said than done,' she replied sadly. 'I've hidden it for so long.'

'What happens during the blackouts?' he asked tentatively.

'Nothing.'

'Nothing at all?'

'I'm just not there,' Anya replied simply. 'There's nothing to tell.'

'But what happens to your body?' Luke asked. 'Surely something or someone must control it while you're away.'

'No.'

'But time passes. You move from place to place . . .'

'Nothing happens!' she exclaimed, growing distraught.

'OK.' He backed down, remembering Verity's warnings. 'It's all right. I'm just trying to understand.'

'It must be Allessandro,' Anya said. She took a deep breath and tried to calm down. 'He's the reason everything's changing, the reason I can't control things any more. Oh, God. I wonder what he does when I'm not here? I thought I'd be able to get away from him like that, to escape, but maybe it helps him.' She looked horrified by this idea. 'Maybe it gives him access to . . . everything.'

Although Luke knew that Meredith took Anya's place and that, so far, she had not been so badly affected by the sorcerer's invasion, he could not tell Anya that.

'It could just as easily hinder him,' he pointed out. 'It's your mind he's using after all, and if that's . . .'

'He's inside my head right now,' she breathed with a despairing groan. 'Like a virus, eating away at my life. How can I fight that?' She began to cry softly.

'We *can*,' Luke insisted desperately, wanting this to be true. 'We have to. Nothing's certain, not even his power. In a way, he told us that himself.'

282

Anya looked at him, her eyes glistening, needing to believe him but clearly plagued with doubts.

'How?' she whispered.

'He needs your cooperation,' Luke replied. 'That's obvious. Think back to his first visit. He was pleading with you, and that would cost someone as vain as him dearly. It was against his nature but he was forced to do it.'

'And when that didn't work, he tried to seduce me,' she said, realizing where Luke's argument was leading and brightening a little.

'But you were smart enough to see through that.'

'Only just,' she confessed, shivering at the memory.

'And so in the end he had to use threats,' Luke concluded. 'All of which was designed to get you to give in, to help him.'

'So if I keep on resisting . . .'

'Who knows? Maybe he's bluffing and he can never succeed unless you surrender willingly,' Luke suggested optimistically. 'And at the very least you can buy us some more time.'

'Time for what?'

'I don't know yet,' he admitted, 'but we'll think of something.'

'I've been trying to think of something for ages,' Anya told him gloomily. 'Ever since . . .' She stopped abruptly as something else occurred to her. 'He's afraid of you being here. Why else threaten you or try to get me to send you away?'

Luke had reached the same conclusion, though he did not see how he could be of the slightest concern to the sorcerer.

'You're right,' he said. 'He's even arranged a few near accidents for me, but I don't understand why I should worry him. I've been helpless every time. I can't touch him at all.'

'So it must be something to do with your being with me,' Anya surmised. 'Perhaps because it means I'm not alone.'

'Yes – or it's something I can help *you* do,' Luke agreed eagerly. 'That must be it.'

'But *what*?'

Neither of them had the answer to that question, and for a

while they did not speak. Anya was now unutterably weary and, in spite of her nervousness, found her eyelids drooping. Luke was also afraid to sleep, knowing that some sort of crisis was fast approaching and that they had very little time to prepare for it.

'He must have a weakness,' he said eventually. 'We just need to find it. Tell me about him again. Not what he showed you, but how he appeared to you.'

'You mean how he's getting stronger?' she asked drowsily.

'Yes. Start at the beginning.'

'The first thing, after I saw the picture at the National Gallery, was that I started having dreams, seeing his face. But it was just fragments,' she said, forcing herself to remain alert, to think coherently. 'Nothing made much sense, they were just like normal dreams. I didn't think anything of it until I started having visions during the day, the ones I told you about. That was scary enough, and it made me think I must be ill, but then he started moving into the real world, *my* world. At first there were just flickering images, half-seen movements. Then he was able to move real objects.'

'Like the Scrabble pieces?'

'Yes. He'd become independent of me, although I didn't realize it until he appeared in the studio.'

'The day you tried to talk to me,' Luke said, feeling guilty, ashamed now of his own scepticism.

Anya nodded.

'The next day he was there with us in the kitchen,' she went on, 'but you couldn't see him. After he tricked you into leaving I panicked and tried to run away, and he got very angry. It was then I found out how fast his strength was growing. He made a real mess of the sitting room.'

'He did the same to the hotel room on Tresco, didn't he?'

'Yes. And he started a fire at my hotel on St Mary's, because I was still trying to get away from him. But that's not all. He had these crazy ideas about reviving old legends, raising the ancient land of Lyonesse from under the sea.'

'Are you saying that he was responsible for the earthquakes

on the Scillies?' Luke asked in disbelief – and remembering, with horror, what Meredith had told him of the tremors on Paxos.

'I don't know,' Anya shrugged. 'But he's not just growing stronger in himself, he's *learning* all the time, about how things work, about how changing little things can cause big upheavals.'

'Chain reactions.'

'That's right, and he's a sorcerer, so he has access to all sorts of old powers and forces.'

'And memories,' Luke added, seeing Pan's funeral again.

'I think he must have overstretched himself,' Anya went on, 'because after I left the Scillies, I only saw him once before tonight, on the aeroplane coming here. He said he could make it crash if he wanted to.'

Luke nodded, recalling the explosion on the yacht.

'There've been tremors here too,' he told her.

'So he's still getting stronger,' she concluded.

'Apparently.'

'Tonight he looked more solid than ever – and you were able to see him. That's the next stage.'

'And the one after that?' Luke asked. 'When he's here completely?'

'He'll have won,' she replied simply. 'He'll be real. And I'll be dead, or worse.'

'Don't say that!'

'I don't understand it all,' Anya went on resignedly, almost calm now, 'but I know this much. He's taking more and more of my mind. I still have control of it most of the time, but I don't know how much longer that will last.'

Luke reflected unhappily that her conclusion tied in exactly with what Verity had said earlier.

'I don't understand either,' he said. 'How can you function at all if he's already got a large part of your mind?'

'It doesn't work like that.' Anya paused, trying to put what she knew into words. 'The mind isn't a physical thing like the brain. It's an abstract . . . an energy, or consciousness. It's not really divisible. I can't say that Allessandro has taken half or

285

three quarters of my mind, but one day soon it'll be his, not mine. That'll be the end.'

'So how do we stop him reaching that point?'

'I've no idea. The only things that seem to slow him down so far have been his own exploits.'

'Overreaching himself?'

'Yes. Showing off. God, Luke, I hate to think what he'll be like when he returns fully. He'll be so powerful, no one will be able to stop him.'

They both thought about the consequence of such an outcome, but it was too appalling to contemplate for long.

'If we can provoke him into doing too much too soon,' Luke said slowly, 'we might make him so weak that he'd be vulnerable.'

'Perhaps,' Anya responded, 'but he may kill you in the process.'

'He's already tried. I'm prepared to take that risk. But I don't want to goad him into attacking you.'

'Oh, I'm safe enough in that sense,' she replied confidently. 'He needs me alive. If I was dead he'd lose his chance of returning altogether.'

'That's something at least,' Luke sighed with relief, not noticing how still and quiet Anya had become.

They were getting nowhere. Discussion and theory were all very well, but they still had no plan of action. How could they provoke a spirit who only appeared when he chose to? Lacking any insight, Luke returned to another fundamental question.

'Do you know why Allessandro needs your mind?'

'What?' Anya seemed not to have heard him.

Luke repeated the question.

'As far as I can tell,' she replied wearily, 'when Constanza imprisoned him in the painting it was only his spirit that was preserved. That's something different again, the part of us that survives even when we die. In order to re-enter the world he needs a whole mind to invest with that spirit – and so create an entire being in the real world, in real time.'

'A whole mind?' Luke queried, thinking that, in one sense, Anya did not possess a whole mind – because she shared it with Meredith and Verity. Then again, as Verity had informed him, once Anya's part was defeated, the others would soon follow. And together they surely made a whole. Even so, it might at least be a way to delay the sorcerer's progress.

'As I said, a mind isn't really divisible,' Anya reminded him.

Ordinarily, Luke thought. But her mind was hardly ordinary.

'Once he has spirit and mind,' he asked, 'what about a body?'

'He can create that,' she replied. 'He told me that himself. "Mere engineering", he called it.' She paused, as something Luke had said earlier finally sank in. 'Did you say Allessandro had already tried to kill you?' she asked, horrified.

'He can affect certain things in our world and make them dangerous,' Luke said. 'You already know that. I'll just have to be careful. But I don't think he can harm me directly, any more than I can hurt him.'

'You've tried?' Anya exclaimed, astonished now.

Luke nodded, remembering his futile, embarrassing assault.

'We can't fight him physically,' he said. 'We have to do it mentally. Our minds are the real battleground.'

'But *we're* not sorcerers,' she objected. 'We don't have any mental skills or weapons.'

No, but Meredith does, Luke realized. And so, perhaps, did her guides. He would ask her when he next saw her. *If* he saw her again. In the meantime, he still dared not tell Anya anything about her 'twin'. Verity's warning had been clear enough and Anya's interest in Meredith, after her initial bemused reaction to the name, had been conspicuous by its total absence. She had not mentioned her once, just as she had shied away from the subject when she and Luke had been on Tresco together.

'Perhaps we do,' he hazarded. 'We just don't know what they are or how to use them yet.' He knew it sounded feeble, and Anya was obviously not impressed.

'It's hopeless, isn't it?' she said quietly. 'He's so close to his goal, while we don't have the first idea how to fight him.'

287

'Nothing's hopeless,' Luke told her, with as much confidence as he could muster.

'I'm so tired. Perhaps if I sleep for a week, it'll all be over, one way or another.'

Luke saw the exhaustion in her drawn face, and felt doubly wretched.

'Let's sleep on it then,' he said softly. 'Not for a week, but a few hours' rest will do us both good. There's nothing we can do right now.'

Anya did not reply. She was already asleep.

41

When Luke awoke the light was still on, but its illumination seemed feeble now next to the bright lines on the shutters cast by the newly risen sun. Next to him, Meredith slept peacefully.

Meredith? The realization thrust Luke into full wakefulness. It was not merely the fact that Anya had gone and her twin had taken her place, but also that he had been able to recognize the difference instantly, even while she slept. Anya had said that 'everything was changing' and clearly she was right. These two personalities who shared her body had previously kept their lives separate, swapping over only once every few months. Now the change was taking place every few hours, making it impossible for either of them to remain aloof from the situation. Was this the final disintegration of an insane mind, or was it caused by the threat of Allessandro's infiltration?

Meredith stirred, then stretched like a cat and opened her eyes, meeting Luke's gaze. He waited apprehensively for her reaction but, after giving him a puzzled look, she just smiled.

'If this is the morning after, why can't I remember the night before?' she asked. 'We didn't have that much to drink, did we?' She sat up, modestly pulling a sheet round her.

'The fact that you don't remember has nothing to do with drink,' he told her, determined to test the boundaries of her self-knowledge.

'How embarrassing,' Meredith commented, her smile fading.

'I've never got myself into a situation like this before. I've always been careful.' There was a touch of regret in her voice.

'Nothing happened,' Luke said awkwardly. 'We've just been sleeping.'

'I know.'

'Tell me about the blackouts,' he prompted softly. 'About the times you go away.'

'There's not much to tell. I . . . wake up . . . and I'm somewhere else. Time has passed, I know, but not for me. It's always been like that. It hasn't stopped me from enjoying my life or from getting on with my work.'

Luke's admiration for Meredith grew. To be able to accept this bizarre affliction as something natural and continue to follow a vocation was courageous, to say the least.

'But what happens during those times?' he asked.

'Nothing happens,' she replied, echoing Anya's words.

'Then how did you get here, in bed with me?'

'I think the question should be, how did you get in bed with me,' she said, with a grin that did not entirely hide her unease.

'You're avoiding the question,' Luke persisted.

'And so are you!' she exclaimed, her usual calm deserting her for once. 'Get out of my bed.'

Luke did as he was told, realizing that his questioning would get him nowhere. He pulled on shorts and a T-shirt, thinking of the similarities between the responses of Anya and Meredith. Both insisted that nothing happened while they were 'away'; both grew fretful when he tried to pry into those gaps in their lives; and both displayed a complete lack of interest in being enlightened. If either of them realized that he had been there during their respective blackouts and therefore could logically let them know what happened in the lost hours, then they clearly meant to avoid the subject altogether. Their defence mechanisms were too strong for him to breach without considerable resistance and, quite possibly, a great deal of pain. He was not ready to deal with either.

Meredith had remained still and silent during his deliberations and jumped slightly when he spoke again.

'Allessandro's been back.'

'Oh . . . Are you all right?'

'Yes, I'm fine, but I think you're in danger too.'

'Why me? It's Anya he's been persecuting, and he's only threatened you. Apart from showing me the explosion on the yacht, he seems to be ignoring me.'

'I don't think he will for much longer,' Luke said earnestly. 'Besides, the only way to oppose him is with our minds, using our mental powers. And you're the one who can help with that, you and your guides. We need you.'

'We?'

'Anya and I.'

'You've found her?' Meredith exclaimed. 'Where is she?'

'She was here last night, but I don't know where she is now,' Luke said, noting the difference between the two sisters. Meredith seemed genuinely to want to meet her other half, while Anya consistently shied away from the idea.

'You let her get away?' Meredith asked disbelievingly. 'Again?'

'She'll be back,' he replied confidently. 'Will you help us?'

'What would she have thought if she'd come back and found us in bed together?' Meredith said, ignoring his question.

'Believe me, that'll never happen.' Luke was immensely frustrated, and tempted to reveal the secrets that he alone shared with Verity. But he held back, not sure what would be gained by doing so – but knowing that it would cause untold anguish.

Meredith just looked at him, considering, and said nothing.

'It's important that you help us,' Luke tried again. 'You may be our only hope. And I think your guides know more than they're telling us.'

'That wouldn't be unusual,' she admitted quietly. 'They have their own rules.'

'You remember when they talked about protecting someone?'

Meredith nodded.

'I think they're protecting you,' Luke went on. 'That's why

Allessandro hasn't bothered you much so far. They won't let him. And if they can protect you, why not Anya?'

'Even if what you say is true, they're *my* guides,' she pointed out. 'They might be able to help through me, but —'

'It's worth asking them, isn't it?' he cut in. 'Please. This is a battle neither Anya nor I are suited for. You are. We need your help.'

Meredith stared at him for a while, weighing his evident sincerity against her own doubts.

'I'll do what I can,' she promised eventually, 'but first I'm absolutely bursting for a pee.'

Luke smiled with relief, then turned away, allowing her to pull on some clothes unobserved.

'I won't be long,' she called on her way out. 'See if you can get the kettle to boil without blowing all the fuses. There's coffee in the cupboard.'

Luke opened the shutters to let in the early morning sunlight. Then he turned off the light, pushing the switch with a wooden spoon just in case there was still any danger from the electrics. He treated the kettle with similar respect and, after setting it to boil, he found the instant coffee and had just put a spoonful in each of two mugs when the sound of running footsteps outside made him hurry to the door. Two small Greek children were racing down the path past the cottage. They shouted what Luke took to be a greeting, but did not slow their pace. He watched them go, listening to their carefree laughter with a sudden wave of nostalgia.

There was no sign of Meredith, but he assumed she was still in the outside toilet. The kettle began to boil so he went back inside and made the drinks, taking his own to sit on the doorstep. When a few minutes had passed, he began to worry, willing Meredith to reappear. The air about him seemed very still, and he suddenly noticed that even the insects had fallen silent. Caught up by an irrational fear, Luke left his coffee, put on some shoes and went over to the toilet. He could hear nothing from inside, but knew that he could not just barge in.

'Meredith?' he called quietly. 'Are you OK?'

There was no answer and he rapped on the old wooden door, repeating his question more loudly. Finally, thoroughly alarmed now, he pulled the door open. There was no one inside.

Luke spun round, scanning the area around the house, wondering where she could have gone. He was about to call her name when he heard a small noise from the front of the house. Dashing back, he skidded round the corner and saw Allessandro leaning nonchalantly against the doorpost. The noise Luke had heard had been his coffee mug falling from the step. A dark stain of liquid was spreading on the stones of the pathway, tendrils of steam twisting in the bright morning air.

'Where is she?' Luke demanded breathlessly. 'What have you done to her?'

'I'm terribly sorry about your coffee,' the sorcerer said, ignoring his question. 'Most clumsy of me.'

'Where's Meredith?'

'Who would have thought that what was once an exotic Arabian concoction would become so commonplace?' Allessandro remarked, sniffing delicately.

As Luke took another pace forward, fists clenched, he realized that he was still free to move and wondered what his enemy was up to.

'Not more fisticuffs, surely?' Allessandro said in a pained voice. 'Haven't you learnt that lesson?'

'Where is she?' Luke repeated furiously.

'Am I her keeper?' The sorcerer's feigned indifference was designed to enrage. 'It is not I who wishes to imprison her. I want to set her free. Why can't you accept that I have so much more to offer her than you?'

'Why don't we let her decide that for herself?' Luke challenged.

'Perhaps she already has,' Allessandro replied smugly. 'That may be why she's left you again.'

'Left? Where's she gone?'

'Let's see, shall we?' As the sorcerer made an expansive gesture with his arms, the world about them vanished and was replaced by another scene. Luke could only watch helplessly as Meredith walked quickly down the lower part of the path into Loggos. The vision disappeared before he had the chance to call out.

'She's going to catch a bus, or take a boat perhaps,' Allessandro suggested. 'Whatever, I shall follow her. You, it seems, will be too late.'

Luke darted past his adversary into the cottage, glanced around the empty room, then ran outside again. The sorcerer made no attempt to hinder his progress and Luke fled towards the path, with Allessandro's mocking laughter ringing in his ears.

Heedless of his own safety, Luke hurled himself down the twisting trail, whirling down the series of spiral steps and risking a broken ankle at every step of the way. Luck and gravity were with him, however, and he reached the bottom turn, below the cracked chimney, safely and in a remarkably short time. Gasping for breath, he ran on into the village, looking round desperately. There was no sign of Meredith, but he could not see any boats leaving the harbour, nor hear any vehicles on the road. She had to be there somewhere.

He began the now familiar search of the tavernas, but could not find her anywhere, and no one had seen her that morning. Luke was now covered with sweat, despite the relative coolness of the air, and he felt shaky from the sudden exertion and fear. Where was she? It was unthinkable that she should slip from his grasp now, after all he had been through. And anyway, why would she want to escape? It made no sense.

Back in the main square, he looked round again, hoping in vain to catch sight of her. It was then that the truth crashed down upon him with the force of an avalanche. In the scene Allessandro had shown him, Meredith had not been wearing the clothes she had put on that morning.

Luke groaned aloud. He had been duped. What he had seen was the memory of another occasion altogether. Allessandro was right; he *was* incredibly stupid. The whole thing had been a trick to get rid of him – and how easy it had been.

First the helicopter, and now this. Meredith was probably still at the house, alone with Allessandro. Filled with rage and frustration, Luke began to run again.

However, he came to a sudden halt after only a few paces – face to face with the sorcerer, who had materialized at the water's edge. Wherever Meredith was, her enemy was not with her. It was a small relief. What was more, Allessandro looked thunderously angry and very tired.

'All I wanted was some time alone with her, to explain, without your interference,' he grated harshly. 'But she won't listen to reason. And she repays me like this! You've got to stop her.'

'What's happened? Stop her doing what?' Luke shouted, oblivious to the strange looks he and the newcomer were attracting.

'The stupid bitch is trying to kill herself!' the sorcerer hissed. 'Look.'

Luke followed the line of Allessandro's pointing finger and saw a thin, winding column of black smoke rising from the trees on the hill above.

42

When Anya came to, she found herself in the act of closing the lavatory door. The sudden knowledge that another portion of her life had disappeared made her feel depressed and, as usual, she had no idea how long she had been absent. The last thing she could remember was talking to Luke in bed. Had that been the previous night? Or had unseen days or even weeks passed? At least she knew that she was still at the cottage on Paxos.

As Anya turned and began to walk back to the house, praying that Luke was still there, two local children ran past, shouting and laughing. Their voices faded quickly into the distance, and the morning grew unusually silent. Then, in the blink of an eye, the cottage, the olive trees, all Dendiatika vanished and she stood looking across silvered water to the distant spires of a fantastical city, an enormous moon rising between two of the tallest towers.

'No!' she cried, but her voice was whisked away by the sea breeze.

She looked around, expecting to see Allessandro, but he was evidently in no hurry to make an appearance. The rocks beneath Anya's feet were dark and slippery and she stumbled, almost falling, as soon as she tried to move. It was a false world – one that she recognized from a favourite painting – but, as always, she did not know how to escape from it. Allessandro was the only one who could release her, and there was still no sign of him.

'Luke!' Anya called helplessly. 'Help me.'

'He can't hear you.' The sorcerer's voice came to her out of thin air. 'He has abandoned you.'

'I don't believe it,' she cried, still searching for Allessandro.

'Then let me show you,' his disembodied voice replied.

In that instant, Anya found herself back outside her own cottage, watching as Allessandro and Luke faced each other. Spilt coffee scented the air.

'Where is she?' Luke demanded angrily.

'Am I her keeper?' the sorcerer replied indifferently.

'I'm here, Luke! Here!' Anya called, but he did not hear and she despaired, realizing she must be invisible too. Her cry had masked part of their conversation, but she did catch Allessandro's next question.

'Why can't you accept that I have so much more to offer her than you?'

'Why don't we let her decide that for herself?' Luke responded with a brave note of challenge that made her heart swell with love and pride.

'Perhaps she already has,' the sorcerer replied smugly. 'That may be why she's left you again.'

'Left? Where's she gone?'

'I'm still here!' Anya yelled, though she knew it was pointless. 'I'm still here!'

'Let's see, shall we?' Allessandro suggested, and waved his arms. Luke seemed to go into a trance and Anya, her heart sinking, knew he was seeing something that wasn't there, false images created by their enemy.

'It's a trick, Luke!' she pleaded hopelessly. 'Don't go.'

Allessandro was speaking again, but she was too dejected to listen. She was not surprised when Luke dashed into the house, then flew out again and ran towards the path to Loggos. Unable to summon up the energy to call after him, Anya could only suffer in silence as Allessandro's laughter echoed all around.

The world flickered as Anya returned to reality. Her legs gave way beneath her and she sat down hard on the bare earth. Allessandro was still standing by the door, watching her.

'That happened two days ago,' he informed her with cruel

satisfaction. 'He's not been back. No doubt he has left Paxos by now, following your increasingly elusive trail.'

Anya did not have the strength to argue, nor to consider whether he might be lying. The depth of her misery was too great. She had been abandoned by the one person who had been willing to help her, the only person she loved. There was nothing she could do now, no point in even trying.

'Have you finally come to your senses?' Allessandro enquired disdainfully. 'Yield to me, and accept the riches I offer.'

Anya looked up at him, saw the loathsome confidence in his smile and knew that she was beaten. Acquiescence would be so easy. And even if his promises were false, at least it would mean an end to this torment.

'Come, Constanza. I can see that you're tired.' There was apparently genuine affection and concern in his voice now, as he stepped forward and offered her a faintly translucent hand.

Anya almost reached up to take it, in a forlorn gesture of surrender, but then she withdrew and remained sitting where she was. His mention of her predecessor's name had sparked a train of thought which, while it did nothing to relieve her wretched state of mind, made her realize that there might be one last, desperate avenue of escape. But first she must make sure that he could not hinder her.

'You're still obsessed with her, with Constanza, aren't you?' she asked, as he hesitated.

Allessandro's eyes blazed, then he hid his feelings behind a mask of indifference.

'Show her to me,' Anya went on. 'I know you can.'

'She is dead long since,' he replied. 'I am not concerned with her, only you.'

'You're lying. If you weren't, you wouldn't keep calling me by her name. I'm not Constanza.'

'But you can replace her,' he said stiffly. 'Then we can be as we were always meant to be.'

'I'll replace her, but only if you show her to me first.'

'It . . . it would be too . . . complicated.'

298

It was the only time Anya had ever seen him doubt his own abilities, and she felt a small measure of dark, vindictive satisfaction. Her hunch had proved correct.

'Too complicated, for one of your great talent?' she asked, mocking him with her feigned surprise. 'If such a simple task is beyond you, then how can I believe in the riches you offer me?'

'You are here with me. Constanza . . .' His voice faltered over the name. '. . . is no more. She is only a memory. You don't know what you're asking.'

'So be it.' Anya shrugged. 'Your self-confessed weakness . . .'

'I am no weakling!' he roared, and the air about them flashed and splintered as though a thousand mirrors had been shattered. Fragmentary images of monsters, scenes of battle and wizardry, visions of eclipses and the arrival of comets whirled about them in a dazzling, bewildering carousel.

Anya did her best not to look the slightest bit impressed. She noted, with cold calculation, that Allessandro's face was paler than usual and covered with a sheen of perspiration. He was already overextending himself.

'This is pointless,' she said, her voice filled with contempt. 'You cannot grant me one simple request. Constanza would say that made you a weakling – just as you were when she defeated you.'

The sorcerer's face was suffused with rage now, but Anya went on before he had the chance to respond.

'Bring her here from Florence, from the past. Do this and I will yield to you.'

She hardly dared believe that he would take her seriously, but Allessandro suppressed his anger – though he still regarded her venomously. Anya waited, trying to keep her mind a blank in case he could still read her thoughts, but knew that if he acceded to her demand it would be a measure not only of his vanity but also of his irrational desire for a quick victory in their battle of wills. If he realized just how close she had come to capitulation, she would not stand a chance.

'Very well.' His face was calm and serious now. His dark eyes were like black gemstones, glittering but unseeing, as he

299

summoned his resources and searched the world for memories of the woman he had loved four hundred years ago.

At first she was little more than a shimmering outline, an arrangement of dust motes caught by the rays of the sun. But, gradually, as Allessandro laboured, Constanza's image grew more solid, more alive. Her long dress and wide hat were flamboyant creations, ornamented with jewels and lace, but it was the ghostly face that held Anya's attention. Constanza was talking and laughing with unseen companions, though there was no sound to be heard. Her pale features were delicate, and what hair that was visible was black but the attractive, mobile face did not remind Anya of her own. She had half expected the vision to be like looking into a mirror, but no one would have mistaken Constanza for her. It was only when the gaze of those huge, brown eyes fell, by chance, upon Anya, that she made the connection. Here there *was* a mirror reflection, a linking of some ethereal aspect of their two existences. Anya trembled at the touch of those eyes upon her own soul, but Constanza was obviously not affected, and she looked away to continue her long-ago conversation. Now at least Anya had one reason for Allessandro choosing her to be his living gateway to the real world.

Glancing across at the sorcerer, Anya was taken by surprise. He stood mesmerized, staring at his own creation, tears running unheeded down his face. He looked smaller, weaker, and for a brief instant she felt a tremor of pity.

'Why, Constanza, why?' he whispered, his voice breaking. 'You should have come back for me. I would have forgiven you. Instead . . .' He choked on the unspoken words and swept a hand sideways, cutting short his torment. The image vanished as he hung his head.

Anya waited, tensing herself for what must come next. After what seemed like a very long time, Allessandro straightened up and turned to look at her. His glazed eyes and shaky movements betrayed his exhaustion, and Anya knew that she would have her chance. She would end it now, but not in the way he expected.

'Constanza is dead. Are you satisfied?' the sorcerer asked

hoarsely, holding out his hand again. 'You are my consort now. Come, Anya, I will carry all your burdens now.'

Anya had heard those words before, and they were as distasteful now as they had been above the imaginary Alpine cliff. Ignoring his help, she stood up, her heart full of both overwhelming sadness and a curiously passionless determination.

'I will carry my own burdens to the end,' she stated flatly, and strode past Allessandro and into the cottage.

'Treacherous bitch!' he hissed, turning to stumble after her. 'We had a bargain.'

Anya ignored him and slammed the door in his face. A moment later he materialized inside the room, but she was not concerned. She had his measure now.

'Come to me,' he begged, reaching out for her.

Anya evaded him easily, switched on the light and closed both the shutters and windows. Allessandro lunged at her again and as his hand grabbed her arm, she felt an agonizing rush of pain that made her catch her breath but only reinforced her resolve. He was too feeble to hold her; she slipped from his grasp and continued with her preparations, picking up a chair and setting it on top of the stove.

'What are you doing?' Allessandro whispered, aghast.

'Building a funeral pyre,' she informed him calmly, and added more flammable material – paper and canvasses – to the pile.

Allessandro made an ineffectual attempt to stop her, but the objects he touched hardly moved at all. Eventually he slumped down, only able to watch in horror.

'You can't do this,' he rasped. 'It's madness.'

Anya ignored him, not allowing herself to think beyond the next simple task. She found a bottle of headache tablets and swallowed some with a gulp of water, hoping they would make her sleep, or at least dull the pain that would precede her death. She was not sure how long it would be before they took effect, so she hurriedly completed her organization. A bizarre pyramid now rose above and around the stove. Her head was spinning, and she longed for some petrol or paraffin to make

301

the job easier. Turning on the tap from the gas cylinder, she lit the rings.

'No!'

The flames went out, and Anya turned to glare at the sorcerer.

'You can't keep it up,' she told him. 'I'll get this going sooner or later, and you're too weak to stop me. Face it, you've lost. I'm never going to give in to you, and when I die, so does your chance of getting back into the world.' She was too immersed in her own fate to take any pleasure from his evident dismay, and was not surprised by his next attempt to divert her.

For a few moments she was once again on the slippery rocks next to the sea. The silhouettes of distant spires were reflected in the moonlit water of the bay, but there was none of the sense of permanence Anya had always experienced before, the counterfeit solidity that had marked the earlier delusions. What she saw now was flimsy, thin, transparent – and she fought against the deception, wrestling with her own mind. The vision faded, so that two worlds were superimposed upon each other; her own small room and the wide seascape. And then the city was gone and she was back in the cottage, with no distractions. That had been Allessandro's last effort. He could do no more.

She struck another match and lit the gas again. This time it did not go out. Paper caught alight and, with a sharp volley of crackling, one of the canvasses burst into flame. Allessandro could only stare at the growing fire, his crumpled frame betraying his inner collapse.

Anya felt the first wave of heat and faced her ultimate terror. When she had first realized that suicide was the only way to prevent Allessandro's final conquest of her mind, she had also realized that her means of achieving this were limited. And so she had chosen her course. In returning to the spectre of the conflagration that had marked the end of her troubled but innocent childhood she was, in a sense, exorcising her own demons. It would be a fitting end to grief, as well as life.

Now that Luke was gone she had no reason to delay. The flames were rising higher, and the dreaded smoke was swirling around the rafters. The heat was intense now, but Anya felt colder than she had ever been in her life. She wanted to embrace the fire, clasp the flames to her, but could not. She knew then that she would never be warm again. Sadness and regret engulfed her, and she began to cry.

There was a voice inside her head now, a child pleading and weeping, but she pushed it away. Her eyesight was blurring and she was becoming drowsy. She turned automatically and, as she stumbled across the room, did not notice that Allessandro had disappeared. Falling face down on to the bed, the last thing she heard before she passed out was the crack and roar as a new branch of flame spread from the centre of the fire.

43

Luke had always thought of himself as reasonably fit but, as he pounded up the path to Dendiatika, it did not seem possible that he would ever reach the top. Every part of his body was protesting, but he drove it onwards and upwards by sheer, manic willpower. His head was throbbing, and sweat stung his eyes; his chest and stomach were being assaulted by cramps and his breathing consisted of one convulsive, painful gasp after another. His calves felt as if someone were beating them with invisible baseball bats, and every joint in his skeleton protested at each new jolting pace. He was not even aware of several small injuries; his bruised feet, grazed hand and a cut on his left knee, where he had fallen on the steps. He was driving himself to and beyond his own limits, and it seemed entirely possible that his heart might simply explode from the effort. And yet he forced himself on.

Finally he reached relatively level ground and flung himself into a desperate sprint, his aching limbs shaking with effort. When at last the cottage came into view, he was hugely relieved to see that it was still more or less intact. The smoke he had seen from the harbour was streaming from below the eaves at one end of the building. But even as his hopes rose, there was an ominous creaking and part of the roof collapsed inwards in a cascade of broken tiles. A sudden surge of bright orange flame leapt up through the newly created gap and the sound of the fire reached his ears for the first time, a mindless, terrifying crackling.

Luke made his tortured legs move even faster, forgetting all

304

his own minor agonies in the urgency of the moment. Skidding around the end of the dry-stone wall, he hurled himself down the garden path. Even as he ran he noted that the windows were closed and shuttered, and assumed the door would be bolted. He was right, but his shoulder hit the door with such panic-driven force that the hinges splintered instantly and it crashed inwards, with Luke half falling into the room.

The cottage was full of smoke but the inrush of air from the doorway caused another surge of flame, and in its hellish light Luke saw a small, huddled figure, face down on the bed. She was in the far end of the house – the end that, so far, had been less badly affected. Coughing and spluttering as the fumes caught at his already labouring lungs, he dived forward, keeping as low as he could to avoid the worst of the smoke. Meredith was unconscious and her body lay limp and heavy in his arms as he staggered, eyes streaming, towards the door. Falling embers and sparks carried by the eddies of smoke stung his limbs and face, but Luke hardly noticed as he reached the door and almost fell down the single step. Stumbling on to the edge of the garden, he sucked clean air into his burning lungs and looked anxiously at her face, praying that he had not come too late.

He could see now that it was Anya he held in his arms and, on the surface at least, she did not appear harmed. He set her down, as gently as his strained and trembling limbs would allow, and was overjoyed to see her eyelids flutter briefly. A moment later, she began coughing violently and then, as he tried to comfort her, she was sick, retching painfully and uncontrollably. A thin stream of foul-smelling liquid spurted from her lips and, even when there was nothing left inside, her empty stomach continued to heave, as if desperate to expel every last particle. All Luke could do was hold her and wait for the spasms to pass. She was alive; that was all that mattered.

That heartfelt, grateful thought gained in significance the very next moment as, with a long, drawn-out creak, the entire roof of the cottage fell in. It swayed sideways at first, then crashed down inside the stone walls, with only a few outer tiles being scattered around the garden. A huge billow of grey smoke belched from the open door but the collapse, which would certainly have killed anyone inside, actually stifled the fire within. No flames were visible now, and the volume of smoke had reduced drastically. The narrowness of their escape chilled Luke to the core, and he looked back at Anya who was very pale but breathing more easily now, her eyes still closed.

'It's all right, my love,' he told her. 'You're safe.'

Anya tried to speak but could only cough again, her face racked with pain.

'Shhh. Don't try to talk.'

Luke heard shouts then, and looked up to see several local residents approaching, many of them carrying buckets of water. Soon the ruined cottage was the centre of a great bustle of activity. The blaze, it seemed, had been put out by the falling roof, but was doused liberally to make sure. The main concern was to prevent the possibility of the fire spreading to nearby trees. Despite the recent rain, the place was still dry from the summer's heat and a forest fire would prove catastrophic.

Others, naturally enough, went to the aid of Luke and Anya. Some water was produced and Anya sipped while Luke wiped her grimy face with a damp cloth.

One of the first to arrive was a large man with a deeply suntanned face and the sort of handlebar moustache that Luke thought had become extinct after the Second World War. He introduced himself as Niko, Anya's landlord, and he took charge, organizing the relays of buckets, sending others for drinks and despatching one of his cousins to summon a doctor. He knelt beside them and took Anya's hand tenderly, as if it were that of a small child.

'My dear, what a terrible day! Are you in health?'

When she did not respond, Niko glanced at Luke.

'How can this have happened?'

'I don't know,' Luke replied, determined not to reveal that the fire had been a misguided but nearly successful attempt at suicide. 'I was down in the village. I only got back just in time . . . before the roof collapsed.'

'Is she burned?'

'I don't think so, but she must have inhaled a lot of smoke.'

'Much smoke,' Niko agreed, shaking his head anxiously, so that the wings of his moustache quivered. 'The doctor, he is coming.'

'Thank you.'

'Come. All is finish here. We take her to my villa.' He pointed vaguely to the west. 'Empty villa. You stay there.'

Two hours later, Anya lay sleeping in the largest bedroom of the holiday villa. The doctor had been and gone. Much to Luke's relief, he had pronounced her to be in remarkably good condition for someone who had undergone such an ordeal. Niko was delighted by this news, but his generosity had not stopped at allowing them the use of the unlet house, which was modern, spacious and luxurious compared to the cottage. He had promised that the debris of the cottage would be searched as soon as it was safe to do so, in case any of their belongings could be salvaged. Arrangements had been made to bring supplies of food and other necessities up from Loggos, and clean clothes had been provided by various members of Niko's extended family. Although Luke still had his wallet – it had been in the pocket of his shorts – Niko firmly refused to accept any payment for his help. Nothing seemed to be too much trouble for him. He had even arranged for the British Consular Office on Corfu to be notified, on the assumption that new passports would be required. Luke was left with nothing to do but tend to Anya, and he was immensely grateful to their concerned host.

By now, Luke had also had time to reconsider the traumatic events of the morning in a calmer manner, trying to work out exactly what had happened. The fact that Anya had closed both shutters and windows had meant a restricted air supply, which would have slowed the progress of the fire. It had only been when one of the wooden joists at the end of the roof had given way – just as Luke arrived – that it had begun to burn fiercely. He had found Anya face down on the bed, which by some miracle had not gone up in flames, and it was likely that her breathing had been partially filtered by the bedclothes, saving her lungs from some of the effects of the smoke. The doctor also reckoned that she had taken sleeping pills, or something similar, which would have slowed her respiration for those vital minutes. Luke thought that these would have probably been Meredith's headache tablets, but he could not remember what they were called and was worried that she might have taken a dangerous overdose. The physician did not seem concerned about this however, given her overall condition, but had taken a blood sample just to make sure. Anya herself had remained more or less conscious all the while, but she was still woozy and disinclined to talk. She had fallen asleep before the doctor left and seemed quite peaceful now, breathing easily and regularly. Luke watched her, alert for any change in her condition, but with time enough to consider what might happen next.

The fact that she had been desperate enough to contemplate suicide had come as a horrible shock, the full import of which was only now sinking in. He could only surmise that Anya felt the battle with Allessandro would inevitably be lost, and the consequences of that were more terrible than her own death. Even so, he was appalled that she had resorted to such a drastic solution, even in the midst of apparent hopelessness. Of course, he only had Allessandro's word for it that it had been a suicide attempt, but he could not think of any other explanation that would fit the facts.

The sorcerer's own role in these events was ambiguous and ironic. He had tricked Luke into leaving, and Anya must have been devastated by that apparent abandonment. That in turn must have been one of the factors in her decision to kill herself, a decision which had necessitated Allessandro's own mission to fetch Luke back. That the sorcerer had been the one to enable Luke to save Anya was proof of what she had said – namely that Allessandro needed her alive, at least for the time being. Perhaps now he would need Luke as well, in case Anya tried again; a strange alliance between enemies. Quite why the sorcerer had been unable to prevent Anya's attempt himself was something Luke could only wonder about, until

Anya was in a position to talk. There had been no sign of Allessandro since their meeting down in the harbour.

Niko finally left, following the various members of his entourage, who had been scurrying back and forth at his command. He promised to return later in the day but, for the time being, Luke was left alone with Anya. A little while later, as though she had been waiting for this opportunity, Anya awoke. Luke knelt at the bedside and kissed her gently.

'How are you feeling?'

'Awful,' she replied in a painful whisper.

'You'll be better soon. Do you want a drink or anything?' Watching her closely, he saw the memories filtering back into her consciousness.

'Why didn't you let me die?' she moaned, so quietly that Luke could barely hear. 'It's the only way we'll ever beat him.'

'Don't be stupid. I don't want to lose you.'

'You're going to lose me anyway,' she said desolately. 'And I'll lose everything.'

'No, don't say that,' Luke responded urgently. 'We'll find a way. He had to ask my help to stop you. That shows he's not invincible.'

Anya looked momentarily surprised.

'He asked for your help?'

Luke explained, hoping it would cheer her up, but it seemed to have the opposite effect.

'That just proves I was doing the right thing,' she said morosely. 'My death is obviously the only thing he's afraid of.'

'Then why didn't he stop you himself?' Luke asked.

Anya told him how she had insisted on the task which had exhausted the sorcerer.

'Producing Constanza took a lot out of him, in more ways than one. Once he was that tired there was only so much he could do. He tried, but it was beyond him. He may be able to stop time for you, but not for me. In a sense we're the same person, so we're always going to

309

be in the same space and time. And if I'm determined enough . . .' She broke off and coughed weakly, then resumed. 'He tried to take me into one of our fantasy realms, but he was so feeble I was able to stop him doing even that.'

'Which is when he turned to me,' Luke added.

Anya nodded. 'Ironic, isn't it,' she said.

'But surely then we can exhaust him again,' Luke persisted. 'He'll be vulnerable.'

'I don't think he'll fall for the same trick twice. And even if he did, what would be the point? The most we could hope to do is delay the inevitable. He'll still be inside my mind, a part of me. There's no way to beat him.'

'There has to be. It's not only your death that Allessandro is scared of, there must be something I can help you do, remember? And he won't be in such a hurry to get rid of me after what happened today.'

Anya just stared at him, waiting for him to go on, but Luke had run out of ideas. Eventually she looked away and took in her surroundings properly for the first time.

'Where are we?'

'Another of Niko's properties. We can stay as long as we like. He's been very good.'

Anya merely nodded, as if she expected no less of Greek hospitality, then noticed the white shift that she was wearing.

'These aren't my clothes!' she exclaimed with a sudden note of panic in her voice. 'What's happened?'

'Nothing. The nightdress came from —'

Luke was not given the chance to complete his explanation. Anya's eyes went disconcertingly blank for a moment, and when she returned it was as Verity, who looked tired and afraid.

'I tried to stop her, I *did*!' she said hurriedly. 'But those pills she took made me feel strange and she was more determined than I've ever seen her. I knew it was wrong, but I couldn't stop it. I'm only a child!' she wailed, and Luke put his arms around her and tried to comfort her, feeling utterly inadequate.

'It's all right. It's all right. It's over now,' he murmured as her sobbing lessened. 'Anya was just very depressed.'

'I didn't want to die,' Verity confided tearfully. Her earlier confidence had vanished entirely.

'Of course not. But Anya needs our help. You'll help her, won't you?'

'If I can,' she replied, sniffing.

'Do you know how we might beat Allessandro?'

'No. We're too weak. None of us could do enough to get rid of him entirely.'

'What about all three of you together?'

'We can't. You know that.' Verity was obviously horrified by the idea. 'It's impossible.'

'Then what can *I* do?' Luke asked doggedly. 'Why is he afraid of me?'

'I don't know,' she replied miserably. A moment later her expression changed to one of relief. 'Anya will be back soon. She just got confused, with the clothes. She thought . . .'

Verity lay back and closed her eyes. Luke watched, still unnerved by the uncanny process, as the lines of her face changed again. At least this time he did not have to look into those momentarily lost eyes.

'Sorry,' Anya said, blinking. 'I'm still drowsy, I guess.'

'It's OK,' Luke said, wondering at her powers of self-delusion.

There was a long pause as neither of them could find anything to say. Absent-mindedly, Anya wiped the remnants of Verity's tears from her cheeks.

'Did I tell you that I found out why Allessandro chose me?' she asked eventually.

'No.'

'Constanza didn't look much like me, but when I saw her eyes it was like looking into a mirror. There was a connection there, as if our souls were identical twins. Do you believe in reincarnation?'

'I've never thought about it,' Luke replied, but his mind was elsewhere. The link between Anya and Constanza might have been one reason for Allessandro's choice, but Luke was

311

now convinced that it was not the only one. And if he was right, then there was a course of action which would certainly prove to be risky and extremely painful, but which might give them a chance to fight the sorcerer on more equal terms.

44

While Luke was weighing the pros and cons of telling Anya about his theory immediately, against those of waiting until she had recovered from the morning's ordeal, he found the decision taken out of his hands. In some ways he was glad, because it gave him more time to judge how to approach the subject and to prepare for her probable reactions. He was excited by the idea, but realized that its execution would need careful planning. In the meantime, Anya was speaking again, harking back to her predecessor.

'Maybe I'm meant to be with him. If you'd seen the way he looked at her . . .'

'You're not Constanza!' Luke protested.

'But I could be,' she murmured, and promptly fell asleep again.

Luke was left alone with his own thoughts, reflecting that although Anya would be growing stronger as time passed, so too was the still absent Allessandro. And if Luke's theory was correct, the sorcerer would certainly do everything he could to hinder his adversary's efforts.

When Anya awoke, a little after midday, Luke was as ready as he would ever be. Some colour had returned to her cheeks and she seemed more alert, although still clearly tired and weak. She smiled at Luke and asked for some fruit juice, which he fetched from the kitchen. Anya winced as she swallowed and the cold liquid stung her sore throat, but then she brightened a little more.

'Feeling better?'

'Much.' But her expression clouded suddenly as she remembered what had happened.

Luke took the plunge before she could sink back into depression.

'I think I've found a way for us to beat Allessandro once and for all,' he began.

'How?'

He was encouraged by the eagerness in her voice.

'It's not going to be easy,' he warned.

'Compared to what?' she said quietly. 'Anything would be better than . . . what I . . . you know.'

'Have you always had blackouts,' he asked. 'Even as a little girl?'

'Oh, not that again,' she muttered, sounding disappointed but also faintly apprehensive.

'It's important, Anya.'

'I don't remember,' she replied sullenly.

Luke had not expected any immediate results.

'You told me that nothing happens during your blackouts,' he went on. 'Well, that's true for you but not for the rest of the world. Time goes on, and so do you – but as a different person.'

'Don't be ridiculous!' Anya was obviously both astonished and alarmed by Luke's suggestion.

'I've *seen* you, Anya,' he insisted. 'I know what happens.'

'No!' she cried, covering her ears and turning her face away. 'No, no, no!' Her eyes were shut tight.

'Just give me a chance to explain . . .' Luke began, but his words were overridden by her piercing scream and he watched in paralysed horror as her body began to twitch convulsively. He had been prepared for a strong reaction, but had not foreseen anything this violent. It shook his confidence. He still believed he was doing the right thing, but now he doubted his ability to carry it through.

And then, abruptly, the bout of hysterics stopped and she sat upright and faced him squarely.

'What are you doing?' Verity demanded furiously. 'You promised!'

314

Luke had anticipated this possibility. Verity obviously turned up at moments of crisis in order to protect her other selves. Now, as he faced the child-guardian, he could sense her fear as well as her indignant rage.

'I only want to get to the truth,' he said, trying to sound as calm and reasonable as he could.

'I told you so,' Allessandro remarked, as he materialized on the other side of the bed. 'You were a fool to confide in this bonehead. How could you expect him to understand the truth?'

While Verity looked even more bewildered, glancing between the two men, Luke ignored the sorcerer and locked his gaze on the girl.

'Don't you see?' he said earnestly. 'This is what he's afraid of.'

'I'm afraid of nothing,' Allessandro scoffed.

'He's afraid that if you and Anya and Meredith work together, then you'll be able to defeat him.'

'Nonsense.'

'That's why he chose you in the first place,' Luke went on relentlessly. 'Because your mind is split between three people. He knew he'd never have the strength to take over the entire mind of a whole person. But when he found you, he knew he didn't have to. Divide and conquer, except the dividing had already been done for him.'

'Are you going to listen to this drivel? I could silence him if you wish,' Allessandro offered. His disdainful tone could not quite conceal a slight nervousness.

'If he does that, it just proves my point,' Luke said quickly. 'He's afraid of what I have to say.'

The sorcerer grunted derisively, but did not speak.

'But we're all whole people,' Verity responded quietly, sounding very young. 'Each of us.'

'In a sense you are,' Luke agreed. 'You're personalities in your own right, but you're each only a part of one person. And it's that person who can throw him out.'

'We can't. It's impossible. I *told* you.' She was close to tears.

315

'Yes, you can,' he told her emphatically. 'You know about the other two, and it's not done you any harm. Why can't Anya and Meredith share that same knowledge?'

'You don't understand,' Verity wailed. 'That would be terrible. *I* know so they don't have to.'

'But it wasn't always like that, was it? What happened before you were there?'

'It was horrible,' she whimpered.

'And before Meredith came?'

'Stop it, stop it!'

'Have you heard enough yet?' Allessandro asked, doing his best to convince Verity that his only concern was for her welfare. 'Now you know how much pain your so-called friend would inflict on you all. I've let him speak all this time only to prove to you just how cruel and selfish he really is. When you tell Anya about this, it should make her choice much easier.'

'You can talk to Anya?' Luke asked quickly.

'Not properly, not in the sense you mean, but —'

'Don't tell him any more,' the sorcerer cut in sternly, and Verity clamped her mouth shut.

'You don't have to obey him,' Luke told her urgently, knowing that Allessandro's patience must be wearing thin. He had already been given more time than he had expected. 'I'm your friend, Verity. All I want is for you and Anya and Meredith to be free and happy.'

'He wants to kill you and Meredith so he can have Anya all to himself,' the sorcerer stated harshly.

'No!' Luke cried. The accusation was close to the truth, but a horrible distortion of it. 'If we let Anya and Meredith know about the split, then you can work together, heal your differences and get rid of Allessandro.'

'But what will happen to us?' she asked, wide-eyed.

'Once he's gone, you can decide for yourselves.'

'You don't believe that, surely?' the sorcerer said incredulously.

'It's your only chance, Verity. You *have* to believe me.'

There was a long pause, while Verity looked first at Luke, then at Allessandro, then back at Luke.

'I don't believe you,' she said eventually. 'And even if I did, I wouldn't help. It would hurt them too much.'

Allessandro smiled triumphantly, while Luke did his best to hide his dismay.

'Would it hurt more than being taken over by him?' he asked desperately.

'Enough,' his adversary decreed. 'You have your answer.' He made an elaborate, courtly gesture with both hands, and Luke's world became silent and still. He was left helpless, staring at Verity – whose huge, sad eyes held his gaze for only a few moments before turning away.

'You have shown good sense for one so young,' the sorcerer said pleasantly. 'But it has been a difficult and tiring day. Perhaps you should sleep now.'

'Do you want my happiness?' she asked unexpectedly. 'And Meredith's and Anya's too?'

'More than your happiness!' he exclaimed. 'Your glory. We will have such adventures, Constanza! If you can persuade Anya to accept my offer, then they will begin all the sooner.'

Luke listened impotently, and prayed that Verity would not be deceived by Allessandro's lies. She had always seemed to be afraid of and implacably opposed to him before, but now she was obviously having second thoughts.

Don't trust him, Luke begged, hoping that there might be some vague telepathic link between them, as there had been with Meredith. *Tell Anya about what I said, if you get the chance. Let her decide.*

Verity gave no sign of having heard his silent plea, and continued to look at Allessandro.

'It will be soon enough now, anyway,' the sorcerer went on. 'Once I have recovered my strength. Until then we should both rest.'

Verity lay back and closed her eyes. Moments later she was asleep and, with one last malicious smile at Luke, Allessandro faded from sight. Luke was released from his invisible shackles and stretched cramped limbs. He tried to wake Verity but she could not be roused and for a moment he panicked, but eventually recognized the truth. She was simply in a very deep sleep, nothing worse, no matter how it had been induced. Even so, he was thwarted once again. The only crumbs of comfort were Allessandro's admission that he still needed to regain his strength and the intriguing knowledge that Verity – if Luke could ever win her trust – might be able to communicate his ideas to Anya without sending her into a violent frenzy.

The more he thought about this, the more Luke was convinced that he was on the right track. Allessandro's self-serving decision to let him talk to Verity might have been a bluff, or may have been dictated by the sorcerer's exhaustion – but either way, Luke was more certain of his ground than ever. Their enemy was not yet strong enough to win a total victory, especially as his 'demonstrations' – many prompted by his own vanity – had obviously cost him too much energy.

The sorcerer's hand had been forced by Luke's unexpected arrival. He was afraid that Luke might reveal the secret of their split personality to Anya and Meredith, and perhaps even try to heal it, to re-create the whole person. As the only one who knew Anya well enough to attempt such a task, Luke's presence must have been immensely annoying to Allessandro, especially as he had been so close to his final triumph. If Luke had arrived much later, the sorcerer's progress would presumably have been unstoppable, but clearly that stage had not yet been reached – in part because of his own conceit. Luke knew he must make the most of whatever time was left.

For that, it looked as though Meredith might well be his best ally. Verity had declared her position, and he had little hope of any assistance there. Anya might still be persuaded, if she could overcome her terror, but that could not be guaranteed. Meredith, on the other hand, was a calmer individual and, in spite of Verity's boasting, probably wiser than either of the others. And she would possibly have access to mental abilities and resources that might be their only defence against Allessandro's sorcery. Luke cursed himself for letting her get away that morning. He had no idea when the change back to Anya had occurred, but he believed it might not have happened if he'd kept a closer eye on her. He glanced back at the peaceful face on the pillow. It was still Verity, but he wondered who it would be when she woke up.

In the event he did not have long to wait. Whatever hypnotic spell Allessandro had laid upon her wore off in less than an hour and, as she stirred, Luke was at the bedside instantly. Much to his delight, it was Meredith who opened her eyes and looked at him blearily.

'We must stop meeting like this,' she muttered. 'At least you're not actually in bed with me this time.' She looked around, taking in the unfamiliar surroundings without apparent surprise.

'How's your throat?' Luke asked.

Meredith swallowed, grimaced and then looked at him questioningly.

'It's sore, isn't it?' he went on.

'How do you know?'

'A lot's happened since you woke up this morning,' he told her. 'And I've seen most of it.'

Meredith was looking very nervous now, but then a strange look came into her eyes.

'I've been dreaming,' she said quietly. 'Anya tried to kill herself, didn't she.'

'Yes.' Luke was surprised and intrigued. 'But she's all right now.'

Meredith looked relieved.

'If she felt she had to do that rather than risk losing to Allessandro, then it's even more serious than I'd thought,' she said. 'And I've got a feeling you have some ideas about that. A little voice in my head tells me I ought to hear you out at least.'

Luke's hopes rose. Could that 'little voice' have been Verity? Had she turned to Meredith in her dreams? Was that the way she 'talked' to her other selves?

'Well?' Meredith prompted, and Luke realized that this was no time for idle speculation. He had been given the opportunity he wanted, and now he had to use it.

'It's about—' he began, but got no further.

The villa disappeared, and both he and Meredith found themselves in utter darkness. As they reached out instinctively for each other, the terrifying silence was broken by the baleful hissing of serpents.

45

'What's happening?' Meredith's voice was trembling with fear.

'Allessandro's playing tricks,' Luke tried to reassure her. 'It's not real.'

They clung to each other in the darkness, while all around them came ominous slithering sounds, punctuated by an occasional hiss.

'It feels real,' she whispered eventually. 'And I can't stand snakes.'

'They can't hurt you —'

Meredith screamed, kicking out one leg to throw off an invisible assailant. She was shaking convulsively now.

'It touched me,' she gasped. 'Horrible slimy thing. What if it bites me?'

Luke did not point out that real snakes are not slimy at all, but dry and smooth-scaled. He was more concerned about the fact that Allessandro's tactics were working. If he meant to distract them from the discussion Luke had planned, then he had succeeded. However, the fact that Luke was also experiencing Meredith's waking nightmare meant that it was not just in her mind – which in turn meant that it was costing the sorcerer some effort.

'Concentrate on me, Meredith. Nothing else is real. He's only doing this to —'

A loud hissing nearby made them both jump.

'If only it wasn't so dark,' she whispered.

'Ask your guides to help us,' Luke suggested urgently.

'I'm not sure I can.'

'You have to. We need to talk, and they can give us time. Ask them!' He held her tight, willing her to succeed, and felt her heart's rapid beating against his chest.

Agonized moments passed slowly, and then a light began to glow. It was no more than a faint glimmer at first but soon the candle flame burned strongly, illuminating a dismal scene. They were in a cavern that was wide but low roofed, made up of dark, damp rock. It had been moulded into jagged shapes by unimaginable primeval forces, and the protruding boulders looked like gigantic black teeth. There was no sign of any snakes. A fitful breeze moved the cold, moist air and the candle flickered but did not go out.

'Well done,' Luke said encouragingly. 'You see, your guides *can* help.'

Meredith glanced about uneasily, still terrified. 'Where are we?' she breathed.

'I don't know, but I think it's a scene from the island's memories, part of its history or mythology.'

'How do we get out?'

'We don't have to. Allessandro can't keep us here for ever. It's just a matter of —'

A green-eyed snake reared up from a shadowy corner and fixed its malevolent gaze on Meredith, who stifled a scream and shrank away. Luke moved in front of her instinctively.

'It's not real,' he told her, trying to convince himself of this at the same time. The exposed fangs and flickering tongue looked far too real for comfort. He wondered if it was possible to be killed by phantom poison – and decided he'd rather not find out. Behind him, Meredith was muttering to herself. As the snake drew back its head, preparing to strike, Luke's arms went up automatically, trying to protect his face – and so he did not get a clear view of what happened next.

Sound and movement came together in a wild blur. The noise was like the wail of an insane banshee, but the feral creature that attacked the snake was no mythical beast. Luke caught only fleeting glimpses; bright, burning eyes, needle-sharp teeth and bitter claws, bristling fur on a lashing tail. The ensuing battle was noisy and prolonged but, for the most part, moved too fast for human eyes, until the victorious cat picked up the limp carcass of the serpent in its pitiless jaws. It stalked off regally, carrying its trophy.

'Did your guides do that too?' Luke asked in awe.

'Allessandro's not the only one who can use the island's memories.' Meredith's voice was steadier now, with a slight air of complacency as well as amazement. 'When cats were first brought to Paxos they cleared the island of rats and snakes, though some people gave the credit to St Haralambis.'

'You're a genius!' Luke exclaimed delightedly, and kissed her.

Meredith's surprise made her hesitate for a moment, but then she responded and kissed him back. When they drew apart it was Luke's turn to look surprised.

'Sorry. I can't resist anyone who calls me a genius.' Her expression was anything but apologetic, and Luke found himself temporarily struck dumb. In another part of the cave there was a second noisy confrontation as another cat attacked its prey, and the sound brought Luke back from the brink of stupefaction.

'You see, we *can* fight him! Your guides are protecting you from Allessandro.'

'But if he can reach out from Anya's mind and trap both of us, then he must be getting stronger,' Meredith said thoughtfully.

'That's what I want to talk to you about,' Luke replied, returning to his original concern. 'He's inside your mind too.'

'What? That's not possible!' she exclaimed.

'Yes, it is. Because you and Anya share the same mind.'

Meredith was looking doubtful now, not sure how to respond to this preposterous suggestion, but seemed determined to hear him out.

'That's absurd,' she said without much conviction. 'I know we're twins, but —'

'Don't you want me to tell you why your throat's sore?' Luke interrupted. When she did not answer, he went on,

'What's the last thing you remember before you woke up in bed at Niko's villa?'

'Going to the loo,' she replied hesitantly. 'At the cottage.'

'So what happened in between?'

'Nothing. Nothing at all.'

'For you, maybe. But this body went on,' he said, pointing at her. 'As another person.'

'No!' Although the denial was instinctive, there was doubt and fear in her eyes now, and she was obviously close to panic.

This was the crux of the matter, and Luke had to force himself to remain calm. He did not want a repeat of what had happened with Anya.

'Don't go, Meredith. Don't leave,' he implored. 'I can explain.'

'Go?' she mumbled uncertainly. 'Go where?'

'Away. You know, when the clock starts ticking. Whenever you get too close to the truth, Verity protects you.'

'Verity?' She was utterly bemused now.

'I'll explain,' Luke repeated desperately, aware that he was not making a very good job of it. But as he grew flustered, Meredith seemed to become calmer. Even the sounds of another cat fight did not disturb her.

'Is it still the same day?' she asked.

'Yes.' Luke was relieved that the first crisis seemed to have passed. 'You were only away for a few hours.'

'Tell me what happened.'

'There was a fire at the cottage. You inhaled quite a lot of smoke. That's why your throat hurts.'

'But —'

'You don't remember,' he completed for her. 'That's because you were someone else.'

Meredith shook her head repeatedly, her blank expression masking emotional turmoil.

'Impossible,' she breathed.

'It happened,' he told her. 'I saw it.'

'Who? Who do I become?' she asked quietly.

Before Luke could answer, there was a bloodcurdling

scream from a distant part of the cave and a black shape swooped out, flying towards them. It was the size of a man but had the appearance of a deformed bird, its wings spread out like dark sails. Moving at terrifying speed, its baleful presence seemed to blot out the candle's feeble glow, but there was enough light for both Luke and Meredith to make out a white, half-human face, red, staring eyes and two pointed teeth.

The vampire ghost was almost upon them when yet another outlandish creature made its appearance. As the two humans cowered, a large white goat rose up out of the rock of the cave floor and confronted the spectre. The goat's fur was so bright that it seemed almost to burn, and a single horn stood out from its forehead like a scimitar of light.

'Begone, Yorgakis!' the goat commanded in a voice that matched its majestic appearance. 'Liokorni bids you leave. You have no business here.'

The vampire's flight had come to an abrupt halt in mid air but now, with a grotesque snarl, he flung himself forward again, only to be impaled upon the fiery horn. As his dying shriek echoed round the cavern, both he and the goat faded slowly from sight.

Luke and Meredith stared at the spot where the creatures had been, too astounded even to think. Eventually she spoke, breaking the spell of silence – and making Luke realize that he could love her as well as Anya.

'I think my guides must be getting the hang of this.'

'Let's hope so,' he laughed.

'I didn't even have to ask that time,' Meredith added, then grew solemn again. 'You were about to tell me who I became.'

There was a long pause before Luke spoke.

'Anya.'

The silence stretched. The cave was so quiet now that Luke could hear his own pulse.

'My sister and I are the same person?' Meredith asked eventually.

'Same body, shared mind, different personalities,' he replied succinctly, and waited with bated breath for her response.

She shook her head, but he could see the calculations taking place behind those soft brown eyes.

'Anya tried to commit suicide by burning down the cottage,' Luke added.

'Like Mummy,' she whispered.

'I got her out in time, but she – you – took in a lot of smoke,' he went on, but Meredith did not seem to be listening any more. She was far away now, reevaluating her entire life.

'All the time,' she murmured. 'Two lives?'

'Three, actually,' Luke said, hoping he was not going too fast. 'There's another person.'

'Verity.'

'Yes. She was the go-between. She made all the changeovers easy to accept, helped you and Anya cope.'

'Dear God. So my dreams . . .'

'Were about your other self,' Luke said. 'And I *did* follow you here from England, only you were Anya at the time.'

'So my life is . . . always has been . . . a lie.'

'No it isn't. You're just as real as I am. Your work is real. You said yourself that the blank times didn't mean you couldn't enjoy your life.'

'But I'm not *me*,' she said tearfully.

'Yes, you are,' he insisted. 'But you're only part – a very wonderful part – of a whole person.'

There was another extended silence.

'Why are you telling me this?' she asked quietly.

'Because the only way we can —'

But the cave vanished in that instant, and they found themselves sprawled on the ground in the middle of a wretched village. The daylight was almost blinding after the underground gloom, and they blinked as they looked around, rising slowly to their feet. The ramshackle huts were built of rough wood and thatch, and most appeared to be on the point of collapse. Several thin, sallow-skinned people were standing about listlessly, but they paid no attention to the newcomers. All eyes were fixed upon an ancient blind woman who was making her way laboriously through the settlement. She was dressed entirely in black and her face

326

was hideously ugly, covered in sores and dark swellings. As she tottered along, she paused in front of each person, then either passed by or reached out a dirty, long-nailed hand and touched their forehead. Those she marked out in this way immediately fell to the ground and writhed in agony, their bodies decaying visibly as the plague destroyed them from within.

Luke and Meredith watched helplessly, revolted and appalled, until the vile crone reached the spot where they stood and turned her milky, sightless eyes upon Meredith. After a few moments' consideration she turned to Luke and, almost immediately, stretched out a crooked hand. He wanted to back away, but could not move. The cracked nail was only inches from his forehead when there was a sudden rustling of the silver-green olive leaves and a light breeze wafted about them, spinning miniature dust eddies from the ground. The old woman hesitated, listening to the sounds of childlike voices and delicate footsteps.

'The lady of the wind,' someone whispered.

The air sparkled and flashed as if it were full of half-seen wings. Meredith burst out laughing, and her strange merriment was like the first warmth of spring. Luke glanced at her in wonder.

'Can't you see them?' she asked delightedly.

'Who?'

'Never mind. You wouldn't believe it.' Meredith turned to the old woman. 'I think you should go now,' she stated firmly. 'The time of plague is over.'

The crone obeyed, fading away to nothing – and taking the entire scene with her. Luke's final impression was of joyous, ill-defined movement, glittering in the sunlight. As the vision disappeared, a soft voice relayed one last greeting.

'Be strong as the mountains and rich as the sea.'

And then they were back in the real world, in Niko's villa. The bedclothes were twisted round Meredith and her pillows were on the floor beside Luke.

'Is it over?' she asked, freeing her legs from the sheets.

'I think the battle might be,' he replied, though he was not entirely convinced. 'But the war has only just begun. We've proved one thing, though.'

'What?'

'Whatever Allessandro tries, he can't stop us talking.'

'That is a matter of opinion.' The sorcerer appeared at the foot of the bed. He seemed almost solid, and was apparently quite rested – which Luke found immensely disappointing. After all the visions he had conjured up, Allessandro should have been exhausted.

'Your guides can't match wits with me here,' the sorcerer told Meredith. 'And I think it's time to inject a little realism into your view of the future.'

'You—' Luke began, but got no further. His enemy's casual flick of the wrist rendered him motionless, incapable of speech. Meredith, of course, was unaffected.

'Now that we are rid of his incessant prating,' Allessandro remarked, 'we can enjoy a civilized conversation. I have made a grave error in underestimating you, my dear. Your skills are interesting. Power, even at second hand, is always attractive. Let me show you a little of what we could achieve together.'

Meredith's eyes closed and her body shook, but Luke could not tell whether it was from pain or pleasure.

Don't listen to him, Meredith, he implored silently.

Don't worry. I have no intention of being overawed by him.

The answer came directly into his head, words without sound.

Can he hear us? Luke asked, once he had got over the shock.

No. He's too wrapped up in his own self-aggrandizement.

Then he really can't stop us talking!

That's right, she agreed with some satisfaction. *Now, where were we?*

46

Once he got used to their new form of conversing, Luke was able to tell Meredith about his theory concerning the need of the three personalities to work together, to integrate fully, combine their talents and stand against their common foe. She made few comments but remained calm, even though she was still having to cope with Allessandro as well.

The first step is acceptance, Luke concluded. *Of the nature of your existence and of the others. If you can do it, the chances are that Anya and Verity will too, eventually.*

Perhaps, she replied doubtfully. *But it will be very hard, especially for Anya. This is stranger than you can imagine.*

Luke, who had been forced to imagine some very strange things recently, was not so sure, but did not argue the point.

I'm not saying it won't be hard, he conceded, *but once you achieve that, you can come together.*

How?

I don't know exactly, he had to confess, *but it seems to me that the starting point is obvious. You all need to find out why the split happened in the first place.*

That could be even more difficult, Meredith prophesied. *It goes back a long way.*

To your childhood? It didn't take much of a detective to work that out.

Yes.

Can you tell me? Luke asked, without much hope.

No. Anya's the only one who can do that.

329

Luke had guessed as much. And there was something in Meredith's tone that worried him.

Are you all right?

Not really. How would you feel if someone had just told you that you didn't exist?

I never said that! he protested, though he could see what she meant. He struggled to put a positive slant on their speculation. *You exist. You'll still exist if you all join together.*

But only as part of someone else.

No – as part of yourself. You'll be whole again.

I wish I could believe that.

Even if I'm wrong, the alternative is even worse, Luke added desperately. *Anya tried to kill herself, to kill you all, rather than face life under Allessandro's tyranny. And if you don't all join together so that you can fight him, you'll die anyway!*

Meredith did not reply for some time, and Luke wondered whether the sorcerer had somehow discovered their link. He remained alert but said no more, watching the continuing interchange between the other two. At last, Allessandro came out of his self-imposed trance, and Meredith relaxed a little.

'Now do you understand?' the sorcerer enquired smugly.

'Perhaps.'

'Then you accept my offer?'

'Not yet.' *Don't worry, Luke. I never will.*

Allessandro scowled, glancing suspiciously at his static prisoner.

'Then at least rid yourself of this moronic distraction,' he muttered. 'If he will not leave willingly, then use other means. He is dangerous, preaching nonsense that could cause you untold pain. You know you will never join the other two. Even if you could, it would be suicide for you and would gain them nothing but unnecessary agony. I will triumph in the end. My strength is too great.'

He's bluffing, Luke put in.

Is he? she responded doubtfully.

Yes. Don't listen to him. You must keep fighting.

To the end, she added, with uncharacteristic bitterness.

'I shall give you another chance,' Allessandro said magnanimously. He held out his hand and a dagger with a long, thin blade materialized on his palm. 'Take it. It will do the job. One thrust and you are rid of him for ever.'

Meredith reached out and took the knife, weighing it in her hand. Luke stared helplessly, trying to tell himself that it was not real, that even if she turned against him, he would not be harmed.

'What are you waiting for?' the sorcerer asked.

'I'm no murderer,' she replied, and tossed the dagger aside.

Allessandro waved a hand and the blade vanished.

'You disappoint me.'

Once again he moved quicker than was possible for a mortal man, and one hand caught Meredith round the throat. She tried to struggle, but gasped as pain scorched through her entire body.

'You will find me more agreeable as a friend than as an enemy,' he told her in a low, dangerous voice. 'Consider your options carefully, Meredith.' He flung her away so that she sprawled backwards on the bed, half choking. The sorcerer disappeared.

Luke, released from his captivity, found himself gasping for breath and unable to go to her aid.

'Are you OK?' he asked.

'I hate this. I hate this. I hate this.'

Luke glanced at her, recognizing the young voice, and saw the small, telltale differences in her face.

'It's all right,' he said soothingly. 'He's gone. He'll have to rest for some time now.'

Verity said nothing.

'Thank you for talking to Meredith,' Luke added, feeling more in control of himself.

'I don't talk to them like you mean,' she replied. 'I just let them know things.'

'It was a big help. Will you do the same with Anya?'

'I don't know. She doesn't want to listen to anything at the moment.'

'Please try,' he persisted. 'Did you hear what Meredith and I talked about?'

'Yes.' Her reluctant tone implied that she hadn't really wanted to.

'It's only Anya now,' Luke went on. 'If we can convince her, we can beat Allessandro. Will you help me? At least try to make her listen to me?'

'All right,' she said in a small voice.

'Good girl.'

'You love Anya, don't you?'

The question came out of the blue and caught him unawares.

'Yes, I do,' he replied automatically.

'Meredith too?'

'I love all of you.'

'Even me?'

Luke nodded and, for the first time since she had appeared, Verity's expression changed from one of apprehensive misery to an uncertain smile.

'I need to sleep now,' she announced softly, and was unconscious before Luke had the chance to say anything more.

At first he was frustrated by the loss of valuable time – time when Allessandro would not be around to hinder his progress – but he soon came to accept her need for rest. After all, it was in dreams that Verity sometimes allowed Meredith to 'know' things. Perhaps she was doing the same for Anya now. He watched her sleeping face carefully, and saw the change after a few minutes. His hopes rose but Anya slept on for almost an hour before opening her eyes and staring at Luke.

'Hi. Welcome back.'

Although he greeted her with a smile, fear had returned to her eyes.

'What do you mean?' she asked nervously.

'You had another blackout.'

Anya said nothing, her eyes darting around the room so that she would not have to meet his steady gaze.

'It's afternoon now,' Luke said, indicating the sunlight slanting in from the west facing window.

'I've just been asleep,' she claimed, but her misgivings were clear in her worried expression.

For a few brief moments Luke wanted to allow her to keep her illusions, to spare her from the uncomfortable truth, but knew he could not. Allessandro's efforts to distract Meredith at crucial moments had just made Luke even more certain that his theory was correct, and that it was the only chance to save Anya. Even so, he decided not to charge in like a knight in shining armour, brandishing his sword. For the time being, at least, a little diplomacy was called for.

'What did you dream about?' he asked mildly.

'What?'

'While you were asleep, what did you dream about?'

'I . . . I don't remember.'

'Didn't you decide that you ought to listen to what I have to say?'

'How did . . . ?' she began, her eyes widening, then controlled herself. She sat up, pulled her legs towards her and hugged her knees as if she were trying to curl herself into a defensive ball, making herself as small as possible. 'I always listen to you,' she said quietly, without looking at him.

'You didn't want to earlier.'

'That's because you were talking such nonsense.'

'I was telling the truth. You know that now, don't you?'

Anya did not reply but her entire body became rigid, coiled tighter than a watch spring. The air on the far side of the bed quivered and Luke swore silently. He had hoped to be able to talk to Anya without Allessandro's interference, but the sorcerer obviously knew when critical moments arrived, and so re-entered the fray. His image formed slowly, and this time he was showing clear signs of anger and stress – perhaps indicating that he had not expected to return so soon or in such a hurry. That gave Luke some small comfort, but Anya did not even look up, apparently unaware of the newcomer's spectral presence. Allessandro said nothing and made no move to hinder Luke, merely watching him with narrowed eyes.

He's not going to do anything unless he has to, Luke realized. The fact that his opponent was conserving energy was another reason for hope, but Luke had the horrible feeling that the sorcerer was building up his resources for one final, overwhelming assault. In any case, he had no option but to press ahead. There might never be another opportunity.

'Why are you so scared of the truth?' he asked gently, sitting down beside her on the bed, deliberately turning his back on Allessandro and doing his best to ignore his ominous presence. 'Wouldn't it explain so much, make sense of your life?'

'Another person?' she whispered. 'Inside me? That's crazy.'

'They're really other parts of *you*. They come from you.'

'No.'

'You need them, Anya. Accept them. Welcome them back.'

'I can't.'

'You've got to. It's the only way to beat Allessandro.'

Anya remained silent, her eyes unfocused, staring into space. And still the watching sorcerer made no move.

'I've met them, Anya,' Luke went on. 'They're wonderful.'

She looked at him then, her gaze snapping back to the present.

'Them?' she breathed. 'There's more than one?'

'Two,' he told her. 'Do you want to know their names?'

Anya's quiet stillness vanished in an instant.

'No!' she shouted. 'You're lying! Trying to hurt me.' She struck out at him with both arms.

'I would never hurt you on purpose,' he protested, fending off the flurry of blows as best he could. But Anya did not seem to hear him.

'I should have listened to Allessandro!' she shrieked hysterically. 'Even *he* doesn't want to torture me like this.' She was crying now, her voice raw and wild. 'I . . . don't . . . want . . .'

'Anya, please, don't . . . I love you.'

She screamed then, a long screech of anger and torment. Her face was a livid white, and she was shaking uncontrollably. And then, in a single moment, all emotion, all movement was gone. Anya fainted, slumping lifelessly onto the bed, and in the horrible silence that followed her outburst, Luke was too shocked to do more than take her wrist and check fearfully for a pulse. Her heart was still beating, but otherwise she was dead to the world.

Unwillingly, Luke turned to glance at Allessandro. The sorcerer said not a word but favoured Luke with a sweet smile before he faded away, leaving Luke to survey the wreckage of his plans.

47

For more than an hour Luke sat in the chair next to the bed and tried not to give in to despair. Anya remained unconscious, and he made no attempt to revive her. Her second violent rejection of his efforts to save her had severely dented his already battered confidence. Time no longer seemed to matter so much. If Anya simply refused to accept his theory, then there was no way forward, no solution. And now that he had been able to consider the events of the last few hours, Luke himself was beginning to have second thoughts.

The misgivings expressed by Meredith and Verity and the accusations made by Allessandro had all taken their toll. The truth was that Luke had no idea what would happen to Meredith and Verity if Anya did what he wanted and reclaimed those parts of her personality that had split away. Would they cease to exist? Or would they still be there as part of her, as he had optimistically claimed? For that matter, would Anya still be Anya? The split had occurred for a reason, after all. What if that reason was to prevent madness? What if accepting her other selves meant that she became a schizophrenic, like her mother, unable to lead any sort of normal life? Wasn't it possible that his 'solution' would bring even greater problems, an inability to experience happiness or love?

And even if she were whole, there was no guarantee that she would be able to defeat Allessandro's gradual invasion of her mind. Luke still trusted his instinctive feeling that this was indeed the only way to beat their enemy, regardless of all the risks, but he had no proof other than the sorcerer's own reactions, his attempts to distract them from making any progress. But they had been witnessed by Meredith and Verity, not Anya, and so counted for little.

Luke was not even completely sure that the two alternative personalities could be counted on as allies. Verity had always known about the split, but had vigorously tried to prevent that knowledge being passed on to the others. Although she had eventually persuaded first Meredith, and then Anya, to at least listen to Luke's ideas, he was not sure that Verity herself accepted the need to heal the divisions between the trio. Meredith, on the other hand, probably saw the necessity of an alliance to oppose Allessandro, but was understandably terrified of the consequences for herself. She had already proved her willingness to fight, with the aid of her guides. And having been convinced – albeit reluctantly – about the nature of her existence, she had realized that Anya was the only one who held the key to understanding, the key to the past. Luke believed that Meredith was the one most likely to help him continue, but Verity was the only one who could communicate with Anya personally, even if it was in a subtle and indirect way. Either of them might be next to appear in the comatose body beside him, and he had to be ready to talk to them as well as to Anya if he ever hoped to make further progress. Assuming he *wanted* to make further progress.

Luke got up and wandered over to the window, looking out over the tree-covered hills of Paxos. It was a beautiful scene, but he hardly noticed. The sun was quite low in the sky now, and he wondered what the night would bring. It barely seemed possible that it could be any more dramatic than the last twenty-four hours – and yet, if Allessandro managed to claim his final victory, Luke was not even sure if any of the three women who were so precious to him would be alive when the next day dawned. In fact, if the worst happened, he might never see another morning himself.

He let out a long, slow breath and pushed such morbid speculation aside. In truth, his decision had never been in any real doubt. He could no more abandon Anya now than he could have stood idly by and let her commit suicide. He would fight on, using whatever means presented themselves, and at whatever cost to himself.

Luke's stomach rumbled violently, reminding him that he had not eaten a thing all day. With a glance at Anya to confirm that she was still asleep, he went to the kitchen and looked through the supplies left by Niko. He made himself a large cheese sandwich and poured out a glass of fruit juice, then found he could swallow no more than a small part of it, and set off back to the bedroom. A sound made him hurry and, as he arrived, he found Meredith climbing out of bed. There was a haunted look in her eyes, but she held herself determinedly.

'Are you all right?'

'Yes,' she replied, her voice hoarse, 'but I don't have much time.'

'Why not?' he asked anxiously.

'Allessandro has changed tactics.' She gave an involuntary shudder. 'He's decided to take me first, then Verity. When Anya knows she's the only one left, he's certain she'll give in without a fight.'

Luke took a moment to absorb this alarming information.

'Your guides . . .'

'Are doing what they can,' she said, wincing, 'but only Anya can save us now.'

'I've tried — ' Luke began.

'I know. We need something to convince her, some proof that will break down the barriers. Then perhaps . . .'

'Something from you.'

Meredith nodded.

'Get me pen and paper,' she said decisively.

Luke hurried to obey, heading for the desk he had noticed in the sitting room. He placed a fountain pen and a sheet of writing paper in front of her, then sat down opposite.

'What are you going to do?'

'Write her a letter.' She picked up the pen and began. Her script was neat and elegant, a far cry from Anya's untidy scrawl, but Luke could not see what she was writing.

'Of course, Anya will probably think this is a fake,' Meredith observed, without stopping work. 'It's your job to convince her that it's from me. At the very least give her something to think about.'

'It would be even better if she woke up with the pen still in her hand,' Luke suggested.

'Yes. But how could you arrange that?' she asked without looking up.

'Verity can do it,' he replied, hoping that his confidence was not misplaced.

'And how do we let *her* know?' Meredith asked, still sceptical.

'Just think it, as if you were trying to talk to me telepathically,' he said eagerly. 'She'll hear. Tell her what we want.'

Meredith did look up at him then, unable to hide her fear. 'I've never deliberately made myself disappear,' she said quietly, then seemed to make an effort to pull herself together. 'I hope you're right. I'll wait until I've finished and have signed my name.'

'Good. Can I see?'

'I don't think . . .' she began, then shrugged and pushed it over.

Luke took the sheet, turned it round and scanned the precisely written lines. At first he thought it must be some horrible joke, then that his eyes were playing tricks on him. The truth sank in slowly. The only word he could read was Anya's name at the top; all the rest was meaningless gibberish.

'What's this?' he said, aghast.

'Our secret language. Anya and I used it all the time when we were little. She'll remember and understand. No one else could have written it, which might make it easier to convince her.'

'You *are* a genius!' he exclaimed in admiration.

'The real work will be up to you and Anya,' Meredith replied soberly. 'This is just a letter.' She took it back and stared at the page. 'My death warrant,' she added quietly.

Luke started to protest, but she silenced him with a look and a small shake of her head.

339

'I'll talk to Verity now, then add my signature. Just make sure you're ready.'

Luke nodded, wanting to say so many things but knowing he could not. One way or another, it was quite possible that he would never see Meredith again.

She sat quite still for a few moments, her eyes closed, then opened them and wrote her name with a final flourish.

Now, Verity. Now!

Luke could not be sure whether the urgent thought came from Meredith or himself, or from both of them.

'Goodbye, Luke,' she said softly, looking up at him.

He almost broke down then, unable to bear the dread that he saw in her face. But he was given no time for regret. As her eyes went blank, he knew the only way to repay her bravery was to make their plan work. It was up to him now.

Anya awoke to find a pen in her hand, the ink of the last word still wet on the paper. She remained motionless, staring at Luke, who did his best to appear calm.

'I would never try to hurt you,' he said quietly, harking back to their previous encounter. 'You believe that, don't you?'

After a few moment's hesitation, Anya nodded tentatively.

'What's this?' she asked, picking up the sheet of paper without looking at it.

'A letter. You just wrote it. While you were away.'

'While I was someone else?'

'Yes.'

Luke waited, determined to let her take her time. She was understandably disorientated and afraid, but at least she seemed able to consider his ideas without going into hysterics. Apart from an initial glance, she had not looked directly at the letter, and her reluctance was another indication that she was taking what he said seriously.

'Who's it from?'

'Read it,' he replied gently.

With an air of giving in to the inevitable, Anya dropped her gaze and began to read. At first she seemed to be as puzzled as Luke had been, but then the shock of recognition showed in her eyes and she looked down to the signature at the bottom.

'Meredith,' she whispered, then returned to the beginning and read the entire letter without pausing. By the time she finished, tears were running down her cheeks.

'What does it say?' Luke asked, going round the table to put his arm round her shoulders.

'That she's a part of me,' Anya replied in an unsteady voice. 'That we're two sides of the same coin.' She looked up, and he wiped away her tears.

'Do you believe her?'

'No one else knew our language. How can we both be in one person?'

'I don't know. That's what we have to find out. What else did she say?'

'That it's time we overcame whatever split us up in the first place, and joined together again. Twins are never meant to be separated. She said there was someone else too, someone who can help us.'

'That's Verity,' Luke told her. 'She's been the go-between for you and Meredith, so that you could each make sense of your lives.'

'You've met them both?'

'Yes. They've been here several times today. They want to work with you to beat Allessandro.'

Anya started at the mention of the sorcerer's name, as though she had forgotten him in the midst of her personal revelations. She looked very frightened again, and Luke acted quickly to reassure her as best he could.

'It's all right,' he said, holding her tight. 'We can do this together.'

'It's impossible,' she whimpered.

'They're waiting,' Luke insisted. 'All you have to do is let them come to you.'

'How? I don't know how!' she wailed.

'It's all in your memory, Anya. Everything. Even if it's buried deep down, all we have to do is find the right trigger and release it. If we can find out what drove you and Meredith apart, then we can heal the wound, bring you together again.'

341

'I'll never be able to remember,' she protested shrilly.

'Yes, you will. When did you first start having the blackouts?'

'I don't know.'

'Think, Anya. *Think*. You've got to remember.'

'I can't.' She was crying again now.

'This may be your last chance,' he pointed out harshly, then took her by the shoulders and stared at her with such intensity that she had to look away. 'You've been living two lives for far too long. This is your chance to be whole again.' He shook her gently, his own muscles knotting with tension. 'Anya, if you don't, Allessandro will win. Is that what you want? You could die. All of you.'

His impassioned words only made her weep even harder, but there could be no going back now.

'It must have been something in your childhood,' he persisted. 'Even from the little I know, there must have been many things that could have been too much for a little girl to bear. What was it, Anya? What did you try to run away from?'

'Nothing,' she sniffed. 'I never ran away.'

'But something caused the blackouts. It couldn't hurt you then, could it. Someone else had to deal with it.'

Anya could only shake her head, sobbing convulsively.

'What was it, Anya?' Luke asked relentlessly, hating himself for being so cruel, but determined to finish what he had started. 'Was it your father? Did he do something to you before he left? Was it the fire, when your mother tried to kill herself?'

'She did kill herself,' Anya mumbled weakly.

'No, she didn't. She's still alive. I've been to see her.'

'No, no, no! She's *dead*!' It was a half-scream.

'Was it her?' Luke demanded. 'Was she the one who abused you? Or was it because she went mad and you and Meredith had to be taken away?'

'I don't know!' Anya shouted. 'Leave me alone!'

Luke had gone too far now even to consider stopping.

'Or was it later, when you and the real Meredith went your

342

separate ways?' he went on. 'Is that it? You kept your twin with you even when she went away?'

Anya's face was as white as a sheet now and, worried that she would faint again and be lost to him, Luke tried to control his own fervour.

'I'm sorry, sweetheart,' he said softly. 'I know this is hard, and it's all come too fast, but you have to try. The key to this is in your memory somewhere. You have to find it. Unlock the past, and we have the chance of a future.' He leant forward to kiss her, but she shied away like a frightened animal, and he pulled back. Her rejection of that simple intimacy made him realize just how badly she had been hurt, but he did not know how to heal her pain. His efforts so far had consisted of highlighting the most obvious traumatic events from her childhood – at least the ones he knew about – but he had to be more specific, to get her to take the lead.

'Think back, Anya,' he said slowly, trying again. 'Can you remember anything, anything at all, about when you were little?'

She remained silent.

'You and Meredith were very close, weren't you?'

'Of course,' she whispered.

'What about your secret language?' he prompted. 'What did the two of you talk about?'

'Nothing much. Just silly things.'

'What, for instance?' Luke asked, relieved that she at last seemed ready to talk a little.

'The clothes our mother used to make us wear. All frills and bows and pretty colours.'

'Did you talk about your parents?'

'We never saw much of our father. There was nothing to talk about. He wasn't a real person to us.'

'But your mother was?'

'Oh yes. She was always there, always. That's why we had to invent our secret language.' The touch of anger in her voice made Luke hope that they were getting close to the truth.

'Did she hurt you?' he asked gently, dreading the answer.

'I thought that all mothers were like that,' Anya replied simply, tears falling again. 'I'm glad she's dead.'

Luke chose not to contradict her.

'What did she do, Anya? Why did you hate her?'

'I didn't hate her. I tried to love her. She was my mother. You're *supposed* to love your mother.' She was crying uncontrollably now, and did not resist when Luke took her in his arms and hugged her. He was beginning to wish that Mary really was dead, but he needed to know the truth, whatever it was – and, more importantly, so did Anya.

'What happened?' he asked quietly, imagining a catalogue of atrocities which had culminated in the burning down of their family home. Only then did he grasp the significance of recent events.

'That's it, isn't it?' he exclaimed. 'The fire. That's what you were trying to re-create this morning.'

Anya stared at him with the eyes of a trapped animal.

'What happened that day?'

'I don't remember,' she whispered, trembling.

'I think you do,' he said calmly. 'Deep down, the memories are still there. You have to find them.'

'I don't want to.'

'You must.'

'She set the house on fire,' Anya snapped angrily. 'The firemen got me and Meredith out in time but not her. She burnt up.'

'That's not true,' Luke stated. 'What really happened?'

Anya's expression was fiercely defiant, but she never got the chance to reply. A shaft of sunlight rippled and took on an almost solid, almost human form. Allessandro had made his long-expected appearance.

'Well, this is a cosy domestic scene,' he remarked, eyeing Anya's tear-stained cheeks. 'Has he made you suffer enough, my dear? Will you come to your senses now?'

Luke said nothing, afraid of being paralysed at any moment, but he stood up and turned to face the sorcerer.

'Luke loves me,' Anya responded quietly. 'You don't.'

'Ah, I see. Luke here tortures you with painful and quite

344

unnecessary nonsense – and thus proves his love. I, on the other hand, offer you a glorious life beyond your imaginings and am thus condemned. How logical.'

'I have no reason to trust you,' she said. 'How do I know that you are offering me life and not death – or worse?'

'Allow me to demonstrate,' Allessandro replied smoothly. 'But first, just so that you are fully aware of your true situation, I should like you to meet some friends of mine.' He spread his hands wide, like a showman, and two more figures appeared beside him.

Anya and Luke both stared in horrified disbelief. Meredith was instantly recognizable, a mirror image of her twin. She was dressed in an ornate gown, similar to the one Constanza had worn, although her head was bare and her short black hair looked very odd amid such finery. The other girl was about fourteen years of age, with straight, shoulder-length blond hair, blue eyes and a sprinkling of freckles either side of a small turned-up nose. She too was dressed in historical costume. Luke recognized her instantly from her own description, but Anya had never seen her before.

'I don't think you've been formally introduced,' Allessandro commented jovially. 'This is Verity. And Meredith you already know.'

Both newcomers curtseyed, smiling broadly, but did not speak. There was something false about those smiles that made Luke feel cold and sick inside, but he still dared not speak. Anya too was dumbfounded.

'These two charming young ladies have joined me now,' the sorcerer explained. 'They are mine entirely. Whatever you do, my dear, you can never get them back. No one can help you now, Anya. You are quite alone.'

48

Allessandro's words had struck a chill in the warm air. Neither Anya nor Luke responded in any way.

'Now that you are aware of the facts,' their tormentor went on, 'I trust your judgement will improve. You have only to say the word and you may join us. And then the sky is the limit.' He laughed and clicked his fingers. 'The sky and beyond.'

Luke found himself alone in a room full of people. He could still see the others, but somehow they were absent, each in their different ways. Anya sat frozen in her chair, her eyes unseeing. She did not react when he spoke to her or touched her arm. Whatever was happening to her had made her physical body unnecessary, and what was left was just an empty shell. But at least she was showing no outward signs of distress. Luke turned his attention to the others. Both Meredith and Verity were like static holograms; they were illusions, creatures of light, and when he tried to touch them his hand passed through unopposed. Allessandro's image was also perfectly still, but he had somewhat more substance to him. He was still translucent, but only just. When Luke tried to touch him his hand met resistance but, with a little effort, passed through the sorcerer, leaving him unchanged. Partly to see what would happen and partly to satisfy a primeval urge to try and hurt his enemy, Luke took a heavy wooden walking stick from the corner of the room and attacked Allessandro with it. Each time, his blows slid through the sorcerer's head or chest but did no damage at all. After a few more swipes – made in a futile attempt to relieve his pent-up anger – Luke gave up and threw the stick aside, feeling stupid and more frustrated than ever. He moved a chair next to Anya's and sat down to guard her. All he could do now was wait.

Minutes crawled by, and the sun sank towards the distant horizon. An hour passed and Luke was still alone, still had no idea what was happening. He was made to feel doubly humiliated by the knowledge that he had been left free to do anything he chose. Allessandro obviously now regarded him as irrelevant, not even worth the effort of silencing. Luke hated to admit it, but it was possible the sorcerer was right when he said that Anya was quite alone. He looked at her now, and saw that although she was as beautiful as ever, it was the beauty of a perfect photograph, devoid of life or movement. He longed for her to come back, even if that also meant the return of their enemy. Seeing her in this state was close to unbearable. An uneasy premonition made him wonder if she would be like this for ever when Allessandro won, when her mind was gone. That idea was altogether too appalling to contemplate so he tried to shut it away, to think of something – anything – else.

A few minutes later, as the sun was setting behind the western hills, he was presented with a distraction that drove everything else from his mind. A subterranean rumbling, almost too deep for human hearing, began far away, then grew louder, more violent and rushed closer. The floor, walls, furniture and windows all began to vibrate as the noise rose to a frightening crescendo. Luke stood up on shaking legs and bent over Anya, hoping to protect her from any falling debris. The sound of disturbed crockery smashing on the floor came from the kitchen, and several ornaments toppled over – but, as the tremor died away, there did not appear to be any more serious damage. Luke made a quick inspection of ceiling and walls but, when silence returned, all was as it had been before. Anya, Allessandro and the others had not reacted to the earthquake in any way, and Luke could not help but wonder if they might know more about its origins than was apparent.

* * *

They were so high that Anya could see the curvature of the earth. There had been no sensation of movement; as soon as Allessandro had uttered the words 'the sky and beyond' they had been there, bodiless and omniscient. The planet was a gigantic blue-green jewel, etched with swirls of white and divided by a curving line of darkness that marked the edge of night.

Beautiful, isn't it?

Yes. She was lost in awe and amazement, her disembodied self adrift in space. The torment of Luke's interrogation and even the shock of seeing her other selves seemed long ago now, temporarily forgotten in the wonder of the moment.

What would you like to see? Where shall we go?

Allessandro was the only one with her, an invisible presence, and Anya felt a vague sense of loss. There were others, she knew, who should be sharing this experience, but she could not name them. Nor could she answer the sorcerer's question; the possibilities seemed endless.

Of course! he exclaimed, as if she had replied anyway.

On their subsequent journey there *was* a sense of movement, so fast it was beyond mere speed, beyond thought. Clouds evaporated as they passed by, and Anya recognized the shapes of Europe as they descended. She saw the outline of southern England, so familiar from maps, but oddly distorted now. As they drew closer, she sensed that this was not the England she knew; the Southwest peninsula extended much further into the Atlantic, so that what she thought of as Cornwall had been greatly enlarged.

Behold Lyonesse, Allessandro announced grandly. *Arthur is already dead. His knights flee in disarray, pursued by the traitorous Mordred. But Merlin still lives.*

Anya's aerial view disintegrated. She saw several visions simultaneously, as if she had many pairs of eyes; a huge earthquake, toppling castles, towns and villages, changing the shape of the land itself; the sea rising up in partnership with the shifting earth, inundating huge tracts of the countryside, swallowing valleys and plains, indifferent to the human cost of the devastation as whole communities were swept into oblivion. From a closer perspective, she saw a ragged group of exhausted men in armour, astride fevered horses, who escaped the catastrophe by dragging themselves on to the mountaintops – which became islands in the new kingdom of the sea. Others were not so fortunate, or lacked the prescience to seek out high ground. Among these was a proud young general, encased in shining golden armour – which became his watery coffin when the raging waters carried his army into darkness. And behind it all stood one old man, whose remorseless pursuit of good had been thwarted, so that his revenge was more terrible than anything his enemies had wrought. Merlin had succeeded; Arthur's remaining knights were safe on the Isles of the Dead, while Mordred had perished in the drowning of Lyonesse. Behind him, unseen, stood the woman who would betray him, take advantage of his weakness to usurp his wizardry and leave him embalmed in crystal for an eternity.

She was his Constanza, Allessandro commented. *But for her we would be colleagues now, Merlin and I.*

Anya did not know what to say. She was still bewildered by her multifaceted glimpse into the mythical past, and was staggered by Allessandro's condescending reference to Merlin. Did he really mean to compare himself to that legendary character? Before she could even begin to put any of these thoughts into words, her vision shifted again.

Now they floated far above the brilliant blue of the Ionian Sea, and Anya made out the familiar crescent shape of the island of Corfu. She looked automatically for Paxos, but it was nowhere to be seen.

What's happened to —

Watch, he told her gleefully.

Anya did as she was told. From their great height, the first sign was a growing patch of white, bubbling up in the placid sea. Soon it had grown so that it covered a massive area, almost as wide as Corfu was long. The centre was now a violent series of explosions, spouts of water and steam being flung tens of miles into the air.

His emergence was like the birth of a new star; massive

349

strands of bright, wild hair, volcanic eyes and a formless bulk of unimaginable power and strength. The ocean trembled about him, vast white wave-horses fleeing in all directions, while the land shook and thundered at his every movement. The trident that rose from the sea, grasped in a colossal fist of light, was so massive that Anya could not even put a scale to its dimensions, but he handled it as if it were no more than a three-pronged toasting fork. It rose and fell, once only, but its impact made all that had gone before seem like a mere prelude. The shock waves travelled half way round the earth, relieving many men of their lives, many more of homes and property.

The severed tip of Corfu was propelled southwards, taking up its new, isolated position. The tumult died away slowly as Poseidon surveyed his handiwork and took possession of his new and private paradise.

And all for the love of a Nereid, Allessandro remarked. *At least she did not betray him.*

Amphitrite.

Of course, the sorcerer agreed, sounding pleased. *You are among the gods now, Anya!*

She was too thunderstruck to respond. She could barely think at all.

You can't escape your destiny, he went on. *I am Poseidon and Merlin, and all the rest. My plans will proceed regardless, no matter what you do. The old kingdoms will rise, and it is I who will sit upon their thrones. I would like you beside me, to share my glory, but I will crush you beneath my heel if I have to.* He paused, letting the significance of his words sink in. *Your apprenticeship is over, Anya. Will you join me?*

Anya waited a long time before answering.

If I join you, she said eventually, *will you let Luke go unharmed?*

He is an irrelevance, the sorcerer replied impatiently.

Not to me.

Very well. Now will you yield your power to me?

Not yet. I have one last favour to ask.

Name it.

Show me my own past. I need to see the fire that nearly killed me when I was four.

What for? he asked suspiciously.

I need to know the truth, she told him. *Then all my debts will be settled. I will be free to come with you.*

There was a long pause.

No, he decided at last. *That will not be possible.*

Then show me something else, something real. Let me see my mother.

Your mother?

Yes. I want to see her.

Very well. He sounded amused.

With a speed that defied both logic and imagination, they found themselves in a dingy room where a grey-haired woman, grown old before her time, sat motionless in a wheelchair, staring at nothing. Another visitor arrived, snapped on the light and looked at her patient.

'Hello, Mary.'

There was no response, and the newcomer moved closer.

'Mary, it's me, Elizabeth.'

Abruptly, Anya's mother seemed to come alive – staring not at the doctor but at the spot from which her other visitors were observing the scene.

'Anya's here,' she announced. 'With her angel from the picture. There are flames all around them.'

The doctor glanced round.

'There's no one there,' she observed gently.

'You can't see,' Mary said scornfully. 'Doctors never can.'

Can she see us? Anya whispered.

Of course. Madness has its advantages, her companion replied.

'What's that you say?' the old woman asked tetchily, cupping one hand to her ear.

Goodbye, Mother.

'What? Oh, goodbye.' Mary gave her daughter a sad, lopsided smile.

I've seen enough, Anya said.

As they left, she heard her mother say something to the doctor, but could not make out the words.

I need to say goodbye to Luke as well.

Allessandro sighed but made no comment and, in an instant, Anya found herself back in her own body, sitting next to Luke in Niko's villa. The sorcerer's image became mobile again, though Meredith and Verity remained frozen.

Luke knew immediately that Anya was back, and was delighted when she turned and flung her arms around him.

'Hold me tight, Luke,' she whispered urgently.

'Say goodbye, then get rid of him,' Allessandro said disgustedly.

'You were right, Luke,' Anya breathed, ignoring the sorcerer. 'It was the fire. I'm sure of that now. And I know how it started. We can go back and see!'

49

Meredith and Anya Caplan, aged four years and three months, lay in their beds and listened to the whispers from below. It was dark outside, but their room was illuminated by the soft orange glow of a night light. It was impossible to tell that the walls had been painted a delicate shade of pink but, if she looked very hard, Anya could still see the darker places where Meredith had drawn pictures with her crayons. Anya suffered agonies of guilt every time she saw these patches. Their mother had scrubbed for hours in a vain attempt to remove the marks, but had succeeded only in creating larger, dirty stains. Anya had been too scared to join Meredith in her artistic vandalism, even though she knew she was much better at drawing than her sister, but she had not been able to escape Mary's wrath. As usual, however, Meredith had borne the brunt of her vindictiveness, receiving several sharp blows to her arms and the backs of her legs, before their mother had dragged her to the kitchen, lifted her up and held one small hand dangerously close to a lit gas burner. Meredith had screamed and struggled while she was told what happened to bad little girls, and Anya watched wretchedly from the doorway. When their mother's tirade had run its course, she had locked Meredith in the cold, dark broom-cupboard and left her there, among the dust and the spiders, for a whole afternoon. In the meantime it was Anya's turn to face the music. After a terrifying lecture on how she should have stopped her sister from being so wicked, she was forced to sit perfectly still for hours while Mary read endless incomprehensible passages from the Bible, frequently emphasizing certain sentences as if Anya ought to find them especially significant. The words meant nothing to the little girl but she dared not move or speak, even when she desperately needed to go to the lavatory and her insides felt as though they would burst.

Their father had been gone for a very long time, for more days than either of the twins could count, and even Anya was beginning to doubt that he would ever be coming back. Their mother talked to the Angel Gabriel now, and he decided on their punishments when they were naughty, which was almost every day. Meredith especially kept getting into terrible trouble, but this only seemed to make her even more determined to do whatever she liked, even if it was rude or disobedient or noisy – while Anya looked on, feeling guilty, frightened and just a little envious. She wanted things to go back to the way they had been and began to dream about their father's return, bringing with him laughter and presents, and making Mummy like them again. She conveniently forgot that their father had been a cold, remote and solitary individual and began to fantasize about an idealized figure who loved his children and who would make them a proper family again.

Downstairs, their mother was moving about purposefully, singing softly to herself in a dreamy, tuneless way. She had been unusually nice to the twins as she put them to bed that evening, with a rapturous smile on her face that Anya always thought made her look very beautiful. But for some reason, the girls had not been able to go to sleep.

'What's Mummy doing?' Meredith asked quietly, in their own secret language.

'Dusting?' Anya suggested.

'She doesn't do the cleaning at night.'

They were quiet for a while, listening for more clues.

'What's that smell?' Meredith asked.

'Paint brushes,' Anya replied, after a moment's consideration.

'The stuff in jars to clean them,' her sister agreed.

The smell grew stronger.

'Mummy threw some on the bonfire when she burnt Daddy's clothes,' Meredith said thoughtfully. 'It made the flames go whoosh.' She demonstrated with her hands.

The girls thought about this for a few moments, and then Meredith got out of bed.

'Where are you going?' Anya asked fretfully.

'To see what Mummy's doing.'

'You mustn't! She told us to go to sleep.'

Meredith ignored her and padded across to the door, which had been left ajar. Pulling it open quietly, she tiptoed onto the landing. Anya heard her go down the stairs and, as the top few steps creaked, she waited for the sound of her mother's angry voice. But nothing happened. Unable to bear remaining in ignorance any longer, she scrambled quickly from under the sheets and followed her sister. The smell was much stronger on the stairs, and it stung her eyes and nose. Looking down, she saw Meredith just entering the sitting room, and she hurried to join her. As she reached the open doorway, their mother's singing stopped abruptly.

'What are you doing down here?' She was standing with two large empty plastic bottles in her hands. The reek of white spirit was almost overwhelming. 'Get back to bed this instant, both of you.'

Anya turned automatically to obey, recognizing the ominous tone of her mother's voice, but hesitated when she realized that her twin was standing her ground.

'What are you doing?' Meredith asked in a small but defiant voice.

'That, young lady, is none of your business.'

'Yes it is. You're making everything wet. And it smells horrid.'

'Go upstairs! Now!' their mother shouted, her face mottled with fury. 'And stay there.'

Anya turned and fled, clambering up the stairs as fast as she could. She knew that their mother was doing something wrong, but did not have her sister's courage. As she went she heard more angry words, followed by Meredith's cry of 'I won't! I won't!' Their mother's reply was lost as

Anya threw herself into the bedroom and sat on her bed, trembling.

There were more strange noises from below, then the dreaded sound of their mother slowly climbing the stairs. Anya shut her eyes and tried to make herself very small, as if she could hide from the imminent punishment, but all that happened was that the bedroom door was pulled closed. Something heavy was placed on the landing, and then her mother went downstairs once more. She was singing again now. A few minutes later she climbed the stairs for a second time and came in to join Anya, a beatific smile on her face. As she closed the door, Anya noticed a strange wavery light outside.

'Where's Meredith?' she asked timidly.

'Disobedient children have to be punished,' her mother replied, still smiling. 'She will have to stay outside on the landing. You were always a good girl, Anya. We'll go to heaven together.'

Anya was not sure what that meant, but her mother's evident contentment made her feel less afraid.

'What was that funny light?' she asked.

'That's the Angel Gabriel. He told me what to do and now he's coming to take us all away.'

'Where to?'

'I told you,' her mother replied indulgently. 'Heaven.'

Anya noticed that the paint brush smell had gone, replaced by something thicker and nastier that made her want to cough. Then she saw a small grey tendril slide into the room from the cracks around the door.

'Look!' she cried innocently. 'What's that?'

'Nothing. Let's have a hymn now, shall we?' Her mother sat on the bed, clamped a restraining arm around her daughter and began to sing loudly. Even so, the sound of her voice could not cover a new noise, a fierce crackling that terrified Anya.

'It's smoke!' she exclaimed. 'There's a fire. Mummy, there's a fire!'

Her mother paid no attention, still singing at the top of her voice. Anya struggled, but was not strong enough to escape, and eventually gave up. The smoke got thicker, pouring in continuously now, and she began to cough. Her mother coughed too, cleared her throat, then launched into the hymn again. The smile only left her face when the smoke made it impossible to sing, and she got to her feet, muttering that there should be flames.

'You stay where you are,' she ordered, pointing an imperious finger at her petrified daughter.

Indeed, Anya was so frightened now that she would have found it hard to move. She could not breathe or see properly. There was noise all around and everything hurt. She wanted to know where Meredith was.

Her mother staggered round the room, without any apparent purpose, then suddenly fell in a heap on the floor. Anya stared at her, waiting for her to get up again, but nothing happened.

'Mummy?' she cried, almost choking. 'Wake up!'

There was no response, but the memory of Mary's final command held Anya where she was for a little longer. The spell was only broken when she heard a silent voice speaking inside her head.

Please come to me. I need your help. The flames are making me cold.

Plucking up her failing courage, Anya got off the bed, glanced cautiously at her mother, then ran to the door. Meredith's call had been one she could not ignore.

The sight that greeted her when she pulled the door open made her think of the place bad people went when they died. There was smoke everywhere, it was terribly hot, and the lower half of the staircase was covered with a mass of orange flames. Anya drew back instinctively, afraid of the noise and heat, but could see no sign of Meredith. Then, as the thick smoke swirled and shifted, she saw her, at the far end of the landing – and cried out in horror.

Meredith had been tied to an adult-sized dining chair with thick black tape round her legs, arms and small chest. Another piece of tape covered her mouth so that she could not cry out. In fact the only part of her that did not appear to be masked

357

was the rest of her face, which was stark white by comparison, her eyes wide with terror.

Anya started forward, coughing helplessly, her eyes streaming, intent only on freeing her twin. She had gone no more than two steps when, with a deafening roar, a wall of flame burst up from below, creating an impassable, fiery barrier between the two girls. Anya screamed and jumped back into her bedroom, falling over in the process. Moments later, the house gave a great sigh and the entire landing folded in on itself and crashed down to the floor below. Sprawled on the smouldering carpet, Anya could only watch helplessly as Meredith, still tied to her chair, plunged into the heart of the roaring inferno and was swallowed up.

She experienced what happened next only as a series of disconnected, fragmentary images; the wail of a siren; the sound of splintering wood and glass as the firemen broke in through the bedroom window; strange arms about her; the swaying ladder; people running, shouting and pointing; her mother's face covered in some sort of plastic mask; more sirens; and then darkness. She had tried to tell them about Meredith, but no one had listened.

When she woke up in the hospital, Anya realized that she was the only person in the whole world who knew that Meredith was still alive.

50

Luke came crashing back to the present to find Anya in his arms and Allessandro still glaring at them from across the room. He did not know how he had shared Anya's memories, her terrible journey back into the past, but knew that what he had witnessed through her young eyes had been the truth. There were tears running down his cheeks, his heart full of pity, not only for Meredith, who had died in such an appalling way, but also for her bereaved twin – so plagued by guilt at not being able to rescue Meredith that she had kept her alive in her mind. Those dark and tragic events, twenty-four years earlier, had undoubtedly been the cause of Anya's split personality, of the dual life she had led ever since. They had their answer; the only question now was, had it come too late?

Allessandro's suspicions had finally been aroused and he stepped forward, about to act – but Anya acted faster. She thumped a fist on the table and yelled something that Luke could not make out. In that instant the villa disappeared again, and she and Luke found themselves floating in a jewelled sea. Before them was a screen of dark flame that separated them from the sorcerer, who could only gesture ineffectually in response. Far above, oily black smoke stained a false sky.

Luke expected Anya to be distraught, having just discovered the horrifying truth behind her strange affliction, but she was dry eyed, and there was an expression of almost evangelical fervour on her face. He had never seen her look more determined, nor more sure of herself.

359

'What are you doing?' Allessandro cried, trying to sound disdainful but failing miserably for once.

'This is *my* mind,' she told him firmly. 'And I'm taking it back. I can choose where we stand now.'

Luke gazed at the scene in awe. These flames, the abstract sea, were of Anya's making!

'Are you insane?' the sorcerer exploded. 'You're no match for me. In a little time —'

'You *have* no time,' she retorted. 'You told me yourself to recognize the signs of power within me, to tap my own potential. Well, now I am. My apprenticeship *is* over, but I am the master now.'

'Don't be absurd,' he exclaimed.

'You taught me too well,' Anya said, and actually laughed.

Allessandro reacted furiously, hurling his will against the barrier she had erected between them. The fire spluttered, surging and flickering, but the wall was never breached.

'What's happening?' Luke whispered in Anya's ear, but she hardly seemed to hear him.

'Stay with me, Luke. Don't let go,' was all she said, without taking her eyes off the sorcerer.

He did as he was told, holding her and hoping she knew what she was doing. Allessandro's tantrum seemed to be over. It was difficult to tell, because of the intervening flame, but he looked tired and flushed by his exertions. That, Luke supposed, was what Anya wanted. But their enemy was calm again now, gathering his strength. The war was far from over.

'This is a clever trick,' the sorcerer admitted with a grudging smile of admiration, 'but you know it is no more than that. You will weaken eventually, and your disloyalty is not something I will be able to overlook. You will pay Constanza's debt in full now.'

'I am not Constanza, and never will be,' she retorted. 'She has paid her own debts.'

Allessandro laughed.

'Brave words,' he jeered. 'We'll see how courageous you are when we meet again.'

'Who's to say we will? This world is of my making, not yours. You cannot touch me here.'

'Aren't you forgetting something?' he said, a malevolent glint in his dark eyes. 'I already have part of you.' He spread his arms and the images of Meredith and Verity stepped forward, dancing to his diabolical tune. 'Release this spell or it will be the worse for them.'

'No.'

'So you abandon them to me.'

'I'm not going to abandon Meredith again!' Anya shouted, stung into anger. 'Not ever!'

'Then join us,' Allessandro suggested. 'Or accept the consequences.' He reached out and took Meredith's pliant hand. Immediately she shook with pain, her legs almost giving way as the agony increased.

'Stop it!' Anya cried, but he did not relent, merely watching her with cold, calculating eyes.

'Hold my hand,' she whispered to Luke, and he did so, surprised to find her icy cold. His own palms were sweating.

'What are you going to do?' he asked softly.

'I don't know. But I'm not going to abandon Meredith, or Verity for that matter. That monster will have nothing of me or mine. I'll die first.'

Her words did little to reassure Luke, but he was already way out of his depth and could only look on as the battle progressed. Anya moved closer to the wall of fire, with Luke just behind her. He did not know how they moved, nor what was happening to their physical bodies back in Niko's villa, but he felt the intense heat and was daunted by it. Anya did not appear to notice it, however; her eyes were fixed on the sufferings of her twin self.

'Is that your answer to everything, inflicting pain on the defenceless? Why punish Meredith? She is part of you now.'

'It is you I'm punishing,' he crowed. 'But you're right about one thing. She is mine now, for ever.' He flung Meredith aside and she collapsed in a bundle of dishevelled finery.

Anya was only a foot or so away from the constantly moving edge of the flame. She turned sideways, her left hand stretched back and linked to Luke's. Experimentally, she pushed out her right arm until the fingers were lapped by the fire. Luke watched apprehensively and sensed her distress immediately. After a few moments, she withdrew, her entire body rigid with pain. Allessandro, Meredith and Verity were all looking at her, but she seemed unaware of their regard. She stared at her hand, which appeared unharmed, and frowned.

'I told you before,' the sorcerer taunted her. 'You never will be able to reach across the flame. Give it up now. You have lost.'

Anya said nothing, her eyes still downcast, then glanced around at Luke.

'Whatever you do, don't let go of my hand. I need you to anchor me here.'

Luke nodded, even as his heart filled with dread. To his surprise, Anya turned back to face Verity, who was looking on blankly, until now a mere bystander.

'Verity!' Anya called. 'You've always been the voice of truth, the bridge between Meredith and me. Tell me, is there no way out of this impasse?'

'None. Allessandro will win,' the girl replied promptly.

'Do you speak of your own free will or as his mouthpiece?'

Receiving no answer, she glanced questioningly at the sorcerer. 'She is your creature. The word of a puppet counts for nothing.'

'Then I release her,' he replied confidently. 'Ask again.'

Verity suddenly looked around and saw the fire for the first time, the blankness in her eyes now replaced by fear.

'Come closer,' Anya told her, 'so that we can talk.'

The girl glanced nervously at Allessandro, who nodded his assent. She moved forward slowly, gliding closer to the far edge of the flame. When she was almost touching it, Anya cried out suddenly.

'Not too close! Back away. You'll—' She clamped her mouth shut.

The startled Verity leapt back and Allessandro looked puzzled for a moment, while Anya tried to hide her mistake.

362

The flames closest to Verity pulsed and wavered, changing colour.

'The bridge between you,' the sorcerer said thoughtfully, then smiled. 'A bridge even through fire, perhaps? Or would such a bridge destroy your precious screen?'

Anya's fatal hesitation before she answered made his smile broaden.

'Of course not.'

'Too late.' He moved forward swiftly and shoved Verity from behind. She tripped, and screamed as she stumbled into the fire. The wall of flame stuttered and flashed as she came out the other side, but then it resumed its former infernal but constant appearance. Verity lay huddled next to Anya, unharmed.

Allessandro roared with fury, realizing that he had been tricked but still grimly certain of his ultimate victory.

'A woman's treachery,' he snarled. 'You have just condemned yourself to greater torment that you could ever imagine. The girl was of no consequence. I still have the one that matters.' He made a grab for Meredith, but she surprised him by moving out of reach. There was a strange light flickering around her, a faint but unmistakable presence.

'She is not entirely yours,' Anya observed.

'These feeble spirits that she calls guides,' he spat. 'They are nothing. They are not even of our realm.'

'Meredith. Take my hand.' Anya stretched out her arm so that first the hand, then the forearm slid into the flame. Luke held her other hand tightly, once again aware of her self-inflicted pain. On the other side of the barrier, Meredith stirred, tried to move. The odd white flickering around her intensified as she was caught between opposing forces. She fell back and Allessandro smiled, even though his face betrayed the strain he was under.

'Fools!' he grated. 'I will destroy you both.'

'Don't listen to him, Meredith,' Anya implored fervently. 'I'm not going to lose you again.' Aside, she whispered, 'Help me, Verity. This is your battle too.' A moment later she felt a small hand wrap itself round hers and Luke's.

363

'Meredith. You can do this. I won't let you down. You know the truth now. *Come home.*' Anya was pleading, her voice shaking with effort as she forced herself to ignore the shafts of burning agony that were piercing her hand and arm.

Meredith moved again and this time she managed to get close to the fire, with Allessandro powerless to stop her. She rested there for a moment before putting out a tentative hand. Her fingers turned black and charred instantly, leaving only scorched bone and she screamed in shock, pulling back only to find that her hand was still whole.

'It's an illusion,' Anya told her, through gritted teeth. 'He's trying to stop you, but he can't. Try again. If you can reach my hand, I'll never let go, I swear.'

'You'll be dead by then,' Allessandro warned, but there was desperation in his tone now.

Meredith hesitated. The white aura around her was dimming.

'Your guides can't protect you for much longer!' Anya cried. 'Reach for my hand *now*!'

Meredith's eyes were full of doubt and terror but she lunged forward, howling as, in her eyes, her entire arm turned to blackened bone. Anya could see it as normal flesh, having discarded the sorcerous deception, but her sister's hand was still out of reach.

'Hold me, Luke,' Anya whispered and moved further into the inferno, until her shoulder was engulfed. The pain was now a living being in its own right, consuming her, shredding her nerves and whispering of death. And yet still their finger-tips did not touch, no matter how hard they strained.

Identical eyes met across that border of flame, and understood.

Now. Two voices in one mind.

Meredith almost fell forward while Anya ducked into the wall, immuring her head and chest. She was instantly blind, deaf and witless, in such breathless agony that it went beyond mere pain – but their fingers touched. Touched, grasped and held firm.

With Luke and Verity helping her, Anya drew her twin

slowly towards her, through the fire, across the flame. They emerged, exhausted but triumphant and fell into each other's arms, while a howl of rage echoed from the other side of a lost eternity.

And then Verity joined them and the three women stood, hand in hand, without the need of words. There was an aura about them, a glow that spoke of love, of longing, of anguished remembrance – and finally of resolution, as Anya at last forgave the helpless child she had been all those many years ago. Luke stood by, excluded from their reunion, but immeasurably moved. In the blinking of an eye the wall of flame and the false sea vanished, and they were back in Niko's villa. Meredith and Verity had vanished too but as Anya took Luke's hand again and smiled at him, her eyes bright with joy, he knew that they were still there, would be with her always. The two lovers faced their adversary squarely, without fear.

'I am whole again,' Anya stated. 'And I am rid of you.'

Allessandro watched her narrowly. He was a spectral figure now, thin and insubstantial, a mere ghost. He had lost, and yet he found the strength to smile weakly.

'You have indeed proved to be a worthy pupil.' He bowed ceremoniously, and this time it was a mark of genuine respect rather than the mockery of earlier occasions. 'There is more of Constanza in you than you realize, but at least I have my freedom now. Somewhere I will find another host, who will be less resilient than you. If I have to wander this earth as a homeless spirit for a decade or two, it will be as nothing compared to my long centuries of captivity.' His voice was quiet, almost humble, as he spoke, but he regained a little of his natural arrogance when he added, 'The world has not seen the last of Allessandro Massimiliano.'

Anya's victory suddenly seemed very hollow. By throwing him out of her mind and saving herself she had set him loose, and made him even more dangerous in some ways. In due course, another victim would suffer as she had done and, ultimately, the sorcerer would return to wreak havoc on the world. It was an uncomfortable thought, but she could not regret her actions. What else could she have done? And her mind was too full now to worry about matters that were beyond her control. Memories, both new and rediscovered, were there for her, the result of a life no longer torn apart. She had held her emotions in check for some time now, out of necessity, but soon they too would be beyond her control.

'Farewell, Anya. Don't waste your life on the mundane,' Allessandro said, glancing at Luke. 'And do not rule out the possibility that we two shall meet again.'

As he turned his back and began to drift away, neither Anya nor Luke was able to respond. And it was then that the final player made her appearance on the stage.

Mary's image was as shadowy and sparse as the sorcerer's, but she had a kind of determination about her that made her seem more real. Anya watched her mother in amazement, unable to fathom how or why she was there, and prey to a new mass of conflicting emotions. She held on to Luke's hand as if it were the last solid thing in the world. Mary paid no attention to her daughter, however; her bright, mad eyes were fixed upon the sorcerer.

'Well, young man,' she said, in a voice that seemed to come from very far away. 'You appear to be lost. You'd better come with me.'

'No!' For the first time ever, there was real terror in Allessandro's voice. 'Get away from me.'

'You're dead, dear,' Mary told him implacably. 'Hasn't anyone told you? The angels usually do a better job than this, but I suppose even they can make mistakes. Never mind, I know the way. We'll go together.'

'No,' he repeated, but his tone was despairing now. 'Please, no.'

'Don't be silly,' she scolded. 'There are flames all around you, just like mine. You see?' She held out a withered hand and ghostly fire sprang up. Allessandro stared at the flame, mesmerized.

'We should be going now,' Mary said.

And both their images slowly faded away, until only a tiny spark of the fire remained. Then that too was gone, leaving

366

Anya and Luke as the room's only occupants. The last sound they had heard had been a long, thin scream that had taken an age to die away into silence, but which still echoed in their stunned minds.

51

Luke was the first to recover the use of his voice.

'How —?'

Anya collapsed then, both physically and emotionally. She dissolved into an uncontrollable flood of tears as the internal barriers finally gave way and set loose a deluge. She wept as though her heart would break, sobbing violently and gulping for air, while Luke held her shaking body in his arms and murmured soft words that were meant as much for himself as for her.

'It's over, my love. It's over. Everything's all right now.'

Anya could not speak, could not think. She could hardly breathe, and her limbs no longer seemed to obey her. Her disintegration was almost complete and, by the time she had quietened a little, by painful, slow degrees, she was as weak as a baby and soaking wet from perspiration mixed with endless tears. She had had enough, both in body and in mind.

Luke carried her back to the bedroom, removed her damp nightdress and gently soothed her fevered skin with a moistened flannel before covering her with a sheet and blanket. He went to the kitchen for a glass of water and by the time he returned she was fast asleep. He sat and watched her, desperately tired himself but determined to stand guard. After what she had been through, it was the least he could do. There was no telling what state she would be in when she woke up or what she might need.

For his own part, Luke's head was full of questions. Some he was able to deal with himself, deducing answers from the facts he already knew. There were others, however, that only Anya could answer, but they would have to wait until she was ready. He had already worked out that the Meredith he had known could have had no memory of her 'own' death. That Meredith had never been born, had never died; she had been an independent fragment of Anya's personality, created spontaneously to maintain the illusion that the real Meredith was still alive. The illusion had been so successful that it had taken sorcery to break Anya's belief in it. The only problems faced by these two separate people had been connected with the fact that they could never meet, and the contradictions inherent in their respective blackouts. All these had been solved, internally at least, with the help of another fragmentary personality, Verity, who was given special knowledge and privileges but who was strictly limited in what she could actually do.

It was an extraordinary story, made all the more remarkable by the fact that they had been able to maintain their triple life for so long. It was only when an outside party – Luke himself – had become unwittingly involved with all the characters in Anya's head that the elaborate web they had woven began to unravel. And that would never have happened if Allessandro had not introduced himself, a second spider on the web.

Now all the fragments had been brought together again to make a whole. In doing so they had repelled Allessandro's threat and, wherever the sorcerer's spirit now resided, he was no longer a danger to the world. His final exit was one of the things Luke did not fully understand, and he had no great expectation that he ever would. He was far more concerned about the effect of the reunion on Anya. An emotional upheaval of such a magnitude was bound to have serious repercussions; her collapse could only mark the beginning of a period of readjustment. Luke was prepared to do anything necessary, for as long as necessary, but he still could not be certain that Anya, or his relationship with her, would ever be the same again.

His ruminations were interrupted by a knock at the front door and the voice of Niko asking if anyone was at home.

Luke realized that he had been sitting in partial darkness for some time. He went out to the sitting room to greet their host and tried to turn on the light. Nothing happened.

'The electric, it is dead,' Niko explained, appearing with an oil lamp in each hand. 'The earthquake, you know. So I bring you these.'

'Thank you. You've been very kind.'

'No problem. How is my little Anya?'

'She's fine,' Luke told him, hoping it was the truth. 'She's sleeping.'

Niko nodded his approval.

'After this morning,' he said gravely, 'she should have quiet times. It is good that she sleeps. She has had enough difficulties already, and the earthquake would have frightened her.'

Two hours later, long after Niko had departed, having satisfied himself that the villa had sustained only superficial damage, Luke sat watching Anya. She was still asleep, her face serene. If any dreams were being played out behind her eyelids they did not trouble her. The lamp was burning low and, in spite of his concern and the fact that his brain was still feverishly reliving all the bizarre events of the last few days, Luke was growing drowsy. He wondered whether he dared go to sleep himself, then decided to lie down anyway. In his present state he would probably not fall asleep for a while and, even if he did, he was certain that the slightest movement from Anya would wake him instantly. As quietly as he could, he pushed the second single bed up beside Anya's, wanting to stay as close to her as possible, then undressed and lay down.

The next thing he knew it was morning. Guilt stricken, he glanced quickly at Anya but she was still asleep, her face as lovely and untroubled as before. Luke breathed a sigh of relief, and as he did so Anya stirred and opened her eyes. She looked at him and smiled, and Luke found himself held fast by her gaze. They were undoubtedly Anya's eyes, but there were hidden depths to them now, reflections of other lives. It was an uncanny but not unpleasant experience. He was about to ask if she was all right when she spoke first.

'I love you.'

'I love you too.' In that moment, most of his worries dissolved and were washed away.

Anya threw off her sheets and joined him, snuggling close in the narrow bed. For some time they just lay there, enjoying the stillness and peace, and revelling in the warm touch of each other's bodies.

'It all happened, didn't it?' Anya asked eventually. 'It wasn't just a dream?'

'It happened,' Luke confirmed, and they were silent again for a while.

'It was amazing, wasn't it?' she whispered, unable to keep her thoughts to herself any longer.

'*You* were amazing.'

'I couldn't have done it without you.'

'What happened . . . to make you sure . . . about what to do?' he asked awkwardly, then added quickly, 'you don't have to talk about it if you'd rather not.'

'It's OK,' Anya told him, knowing that she must come to terms with what had taken place. She described her mythical flights, including Poseidon's efforts, echoes of which had been felt in the present day. 'Then Allessandro made two mistakes. The first was that he refused to take me back to see the fire. I knew he could, I could sense it, but he refused. That's when I realized it was the answer to everything.' She fell silent, remembering.

'The second mistake?' Luke asked quickly.

'He took me to see my mother.'

'Mary?'

'That proved you'd been telling the truth, that I'd been deluding myself, about a lot of things.'

'Your mother was alive?'

'When I saw her, yes.'

'But . . .'

'I know. Perhaps it wasn't really her ghost. Maybe it was

371

just a projection or something.' Anya shrugged. 'Or maybe she really is dead now.'

The prospect did not seem to bother her, and Luke was not surprised. Some things were literally unforgivable.

'How . . . how was I able to share your journey back to the fire?' he asked, returning to another of the riddles he had been unable to solve.

'Our minds aren't limited in time and space,' she replied. 'Allessandro showed me that. He even showed me the path back. He didn't think I'd seen, but it was my mind he was using, after all! Once I knew that, it was easy. And then, when I was back with you, it was a simple matter to include you in the process, like Allessandro had done before.'

'A sort of telepathic link?' Luke guessed, still all at sea.

'Sort of,' she replied doubtfully. 'All I know is I needed you to be there with me, to experience it. Reliving it on my own would've been too hard. As it was . . .' She broke off, crying softly.

'Enough,' Luke decided. 'Quiet now.'

They both knew that there was still much to be done before Anya could have any chance of peace. She needed time to mourn for her sister, and for her own lost life. Reintegrating all the hidden memories would take time and patience and heartache.

Before long, Anya had fallen asleep again and Luke gently extricated himself from her embrace and got dressed. He went out to the kitchen and prepared breakfast for them both, knowing that she would need to eat sooner or later to keep her strength up. When he returned to the bedroom, she was still sleeping and he had no intention of waking her. Luke put down the tray, sat in the chair he had used the evening before and fell to thinking.

Anya was not the only one to have been changed by this experience. Never again would he have such a pragmatic view of the world, of all the possibilities within it. Even now, just looking at her face, he was aware of so much more than he would have dreamt possible only a few weeks ago. All the women that she had been were there, and all the women she could be. His Anya was there, with her artistry, her strength and her stubborn, defiant nature that was quite capable of taking on the whole world; Meredith was there, contributing her gentle spirituality, her self-deprecating humour and her mental agility; Verity was there too, the young guardian of truth and memory, whose intervention had rescued them all and whose happy and confident nature was now part of the whole. In a sense, Luke thought, that was the most significant aspect of the entire sequence of events.

In regaining those parts of her that had been lost, Anya had recovered her lost childhood; not only the pain, but the joyful innocence as well.

Epilogue

Anya and Luke arrived back in Devon four days later. During that time Anya's physical health had improved steadily, but emotionally she was still in the middle of a wild roller-coaster ride. Times of intense happiness had been interspersed with moments of debilitating misery and grief; in between there had been long periods of confusion and uncertainty, and others where, superficially at least, she seemed calm and contented. Through it all Luke had been at her side constantly, helping, listening and trying to understand. He had protected her from as much of the outside world as he could, and had taken it upon himself to deal with all the formalities involved in their return journey. Even in the midst of her turmoil, Anya had appreciated his unstinting generosity and kindness. She had never felt more loved, nor loved anyone more.

They had stopped in London on the way back, staying overnight in the flat which both Anya and Meredith had used, each assuming that it was shared with another woman whom they never saw. It had two bedrooms, each with a wardrobe full of clothes. In one there were garments of all the colours under the sun, in the other only black.

The following morning, at Anya's insistence, they had visited the National Gallery. Luke had been very concerned, not sure whether it was a good idea for her to see the painting again. But she would not be denied and, in the event, she had remained calm, even if she had grown awfully quiet. Looking into Allessandro's eyes once more made Luke feel very uncomfortable, and he was glad when Anya announced that she was ready to leave – and even more relieved when she was able to talk about the portrait with no outward signs of distress. It was a marvellous painting, she told him, but that was all it was – a painting. The spirit that had once haunted it was gone.

Then they had caught a train from Paddington to Newton Abbot. There would still be other pilgrimages to make – to the house on St Agnes, for instance – but they could wait. Anya had even realized that Meredith must be buried somewhere and said that sometime – not yet, but sometime – she would like to visit the grave, to lay the past to rest once and for all.

Neither of them had mentioned Mary since leaving Paxos, but Luke was forcibly reminded of her when they got back to their own house. He was exhausted, and did little more than glance at most of the mail that had built up in their absence. However, there was one letter, addressed to him, that he could not ignore. It was from Elizabeth Burrows, and informed him that Anya's mother had died of a second stroke five days earlier. Luke felt the hair on the back of his neck stand on end when he realized that the timing was exactly right. Mary had died shortly after the spectral visit by Anya and Allessandro, and just before her image had appeared in the villa in Greece. Elizabeth added that her delusions had probably been a factor even at the end because, in a curious incident that the doctor was at a loss to explain, Mary had claimed to see her daughter with an angel. She had then declared that it had been a sign, that it was time for her to go, and the attack that had killed her had come only minutes later. The doctor ended her letter by telling him that she had also written to Meredith, as well as leaving a message on her answering machine, and she signed off with the hope that he had been able to locate Anya.

Luke decided not to show the letter to Anya for the time being – she already had enough to cope with – but he hoped that, at some time in the future, he would be able to persuade her to meet the doctor. Elizabeth would be able to tell her about her mother, and it would be good for her to have some professional help in dealing with everything that had happened. Right now, however, Luke was just happy to be back.

For her part, Anya was also overjoyed to have returned to familiar surroundings. She was infinitely grateful to Luke for carrying all her burdens, and knew that it was time now to let him rest for a while. She had to start taking responsibility for her own life – all of it – and to begin to look at their future together again. Although she knew that, in so many ways, they were going to have to start again, at least this time they had all the advantages.

As Anya sat watching Luke doze in his chair that evening, she realized that, for the first time in twenty-four years, she was truly *home*. And with someone she could trust with her whole heart.